## Shortlisted by the Crime Writers Association for the Debut Dagger Award

**Here's what the CWA judges had to say:**

'Confident writing with vivid energy coming off the page ... arresting and gritty ... the plot is surprising and gripping ... great series potential.'

**Quotes from best-selling crime writers:**

'I believed I was in Breakfield's Glasgow and felt the chill of the city wrapping around my shoulders ... or was it going to be my throat? Throughout the book I felt a sense of threat. It hung in doorways. In bars. Even in seemingly innocuous conversation.' **author of the best-selling DC Goodhew series Alison Bruce**

'Punchy and with a strong sense of place' **Best-selling Scottish crime writer and former policewoman Karen Campbell**

'...gripping debut from an exciting new author' **Sunday Times best-selling author Lee Weeks**

## ABOUT THE AUTHOR

JON BREAKFIELD is the author of three books. These include the Amazon bestseller Key West, Naked Europe; as well as the short story Liverpool, Texas ... London, Arkansas. He and his wife divide their time between Glasgow, Scotland, and Key West, FL.

# DEATH BY GLASGOW
## by
## Jon Breakfield

**Gallowgate Press**

A society would be wise to pay attention to the people who do not belong...if it wants to find out where it's failing—**Arthur Penn, director, *Bonnie and Clyde***

To Gabrielle

## ACKNOWLEDGEMENTS

I would like to thank Mike Sharkey, George Lambie, and Margaret Grue, without them there would be no book.

And the following people deserve a special mention: Ian Menzies, Andrew, Anthony, Patti Bright, Tony Quinn, Rob and Angela Mc, Alfred, Gerald Squire, Warren Rodgers, Rick Fagan, Steve Church, Alison Church, Eric TC Wilson, Paddy Bettesworth, John and Angela Bunce, Gillian Sergeant, Neil Grue, Lee Weeks, Karen Campbell, Eric Myers, and George Redmond.

And a big shout out to Alison Bruce for her support and advice, and Alex Gray for her encouragement.

**AUTHOR'S NOTE:** As the story takes place in the UK, this book has been written employing the spellings and punctuation of British English.

A glossary can be found at the end of this book for clarification of the vernacular.

# CHAPTER ONE

The teenage lad with the volcanic acne had never smelt death before.

But then he'd never cut out a man's tongue.

Pizza Face wasn't sure if his victim had died from the severed tongue or from the slit throat. Either way, he had succumbed from choking on his own blood. Not from bleeding out.

He knew he should bolt before the filth arrived. He'd done what the Sutherland crime family had instructed him to do. But he wasn't finished. He wanted to add his own historical touch. It didn't matter to Pizza Face that it was broad daylight. Or that he was in the car park of Buchanan Galleries shopping mall in the Glasgow City Centre. Or that the car park was queued out with Christmas shoppers.

Or that women were screaming bloody murder (for that's what it was).

He dragged his mark out of a brand-new red Range Rover, rolled him over, pulled the victim's Kappa trackies down, spat on the barrel of his shotgun, inserted it up the dead man's arse. And pulled the trigger.

He wanted to give the corpse what was known in the trade as a 'Glasgow send-off'.

To make a statement, you understand.

Despite having his new balaclava and prized, albeit counterfeit, Berghaus jacket splattered with someone else's blood and faeces, Pizza Face was more than happy to help the Sutherlands make a statement, as long as making a statement for the Sutherland clan meant making a name for himself. He'd do whatever he had to do to impress. Build his status within the gang. Rise through the ranks.

And fuckin' A!

Takin' a life!

Talk about a rush!

He was on top of the fuckin' world. Glasgow was the murder capital of Europe, after all, and he was proud of it. Crime was in his blood, or at least he wanted it to be. Plus, on a personal note, Pizza Face was going to do everything in his power to keep Limerick from taking back the top spot.

But all that happened this afternoon.

This evening, he was shiting himself.

Pizza Face just found out the bam he had offed was the number-one-fuckin' son of the godfather of all Glasgow drug lords, Tattoo McQueen.

# CHAPTER TWO

A light snow was falling as Fleet Sharkey and Fiona Lyon-Jones strolled past the twinkling Christmas lights decorating the Glasgow City Centre. To those not in the know, they seemed the perfect couple. Sharkey tall. Athletically built. Film-star good-looks. The type of guy you wanted on your side when trouble erupted. Lyon-Jones a siren. Emerald eyes. Full lips. Great legs behind a flirty hemline. Impressive curves under a Gucci zebra-print leather jacket.

That was on the outside.

On the inside it was a marriage made in hell: Detective Inspector Fleet Sharkey born and bred in the depressed East End of Glasgow. Rough. Nearly impenetrable accent. Street smart. Street tough. Detective Sergeant Fiona Lyon-Jones raised in the affluent Morningside area of Edinburgh. Posh accent. Educated to the gills. Cheeky to a fault.

On any day of the week, there wasn't much love lost between Glaswegians and Edinburghers. Or to employ the more colloquial: Weegies and Edinbuggers.

This was Lyon-Jones' first day in Glasgow, and Inspector Sharkey was doing his best to show his cheeky new charge around. The cheeky new charge he got unceremoniously *stuck* with. Sharkey was proud of Glasgow and wanted Lyon-Jones to see some of the city he so dearly loved. To show it off. Show that they had everything Edinburgh had from opera to galleries to fine dining.

Not just the crime.

Plus he wanted to see what she was made of out on the street. Wanted to see if her eyes took everything in as the two of them walked along, conversing. See if she would be an asset or a liability when things got rough.

This was Glasgow, after all.

Sharkey adjusted his collar against the blistering cold. 'Let me bring you up to speed: Two families control the majority of drug trafficking in Glasgow, the Sutherland family on the south side of the river and the McQueen family on the north side...'

Lyon-Jones listened intently as her eyes scanned her environment. Scanned the shadows. Acutely in tune to her physical surroundings. She saw a heavily pregnant teenager, no more than fifteen, light up a fag. A young mum texting, not looking both ways, as she pushed her pram across a busy street. A father having a heated argument with his son—in sign language. A lone male, arm wrapped around a five-foot-tall Christmas tree, waiting for a bus.

Then she sneaked a closer look at Sharkey.

This is not how she had envisaged her new boss. Kinda cute. And a long scar running down the right side of his face from just below the ear to the jaw. And the accent, not just rough Glaswegian, there was something more in there. She listened. Then she had it: His rough Glaswegian was peppered with a curious abundance of American slang and colloquialisms. It had the same annoying effect as fingernails on the blackboard.

'...the murder of Tattoo McQueen's number one son this afternoon has Sutherland family written all over it—'

Lyon-Jones interrupted. 'Why would you think that?'

Sharkey gave Lyon-Jones a look. Had she just rudely interrupted or was she just keen? 'The Sutherlands are encroaching on the north side of the river. Just last week a Sutherland enforcer killed the barman at the Kingston pub because he wouldn't let drug dealers operate on the premises—'

Lyon-Jones interrupted again. 'Let me guess. The Kingston pub is on the north side of the river. This encroachment by the Sutherland family on to McQueen turf has kicked off a gang war...'

Sharkey regarded Lyon-Jones. Astute. Intelligent. But already a right pain in the backside. He noticed her nose had gone pink from the cold. Noticed the fetching freckles around that nose.

'High marks, Jones. And your timing is impeccable. Welcome to Glasgow.'

*Welcome to Glasgow, indeed!* Lyon-Jones was freezing her you-know-whats off. She had tried to dress smartly to meet the

Inspector. Hadn't dressed for polar exploration. Christ, she hadn't even brought a scarf.

Sharkey's icy foray into the world of the tour guide was suddenly breached as a hearse turned a corner and motored slowly past. He watched it move off, then twigged and blurted out: 'Holy shit!' and took off running, bulling his way through early evening Christmas shoppers. Confused, Lyon-Jones took off after him.

'I know where the killer's headed!' Sharkey yelled back.

'Which killer?'

'The wee shite who killed the barman at the Kingston! Can you not run faster!'

Lyon-Jones picked up the pace. Matched Sharkey stride for stride. 'Where the hell's the Kingston?' Pant. Pant. Pant. 'I'm new here, remember?'

'Down by the river!' Sharkey grabbed his Airwave radio, depressed the emergency button and barked into it: 'Request back-up at Kingston pub in Holm Street!'

'How do you know...' Pant. Pant. Pant. '...the killer's headed to the Kingston?'

'Because the barman's family is planning to testify! He'll try to intimidate witnesses!'

'But how do you *know* this?'

'It's a hunch.'

Under her breath: 'A hunch? For fuck's sake.'

Sharkey was a former long-distance runner. Lyon-Jones was in Giuseppe Zanotti heels.

But she kept up. Had to.

Didn't want to show her superior that she couldn't cut it. Didn't want a Weegie to think she was inferior.

Sprinting through the Glasgow City Centre in non-sensible shoes was not how Fiona Lyon-Jones had expected her secondment with Strathclyde Police to start. Christ, she wasn't even supposed to actually start until tomorrow. Is this what it was going to be like working with this cowboy? Relying on hunches? She'd have to set him straight. There were rules to follow. There was protocol. A hunch? Give me a freaking break!

'Hurry up, Jones!'

'It's Lyon-Jones!'

CHAPTER THREE

Laughter seeped out of the Kingston pub. The Kingston was not one of Glasgow's finer watering holes and would never be featured in any of the tourist brochures. It was one of those pubs you wouldn't go into if your life depended on it. Because it just might.

The pub had large leaded windows, but they were always curtained day and night. Whoever was in there didn't want anyone else to know.

Above the windows, The Saltire, tattered and fading, flapped proudly in an icy wind that had the bite of an inbred pit bull. Below the windows, a single bulb illuminated three signs: 'A Real Glesga Pub!', 'Football Tonight!' and 'Free Beer... Tomorrow!'

Only one sign was accurate 24/7.

Inside, the pub was poorly lit and tired, yet warm and oddly inviting. A Christmas tree with red, blue and green lights stood in the corner. A lurcher snoozed in front of a roaring fire, its feet moving, dreaming, chasing a rabbit, perhaps. A fruit machine winked from the area of the bar.

Curiously, all the patrons were dressed in black.

It may have been against the law to smoke in an establishment such as this, but this was a drinkery that didn't live by the rules of others. Half the punters were puffing away like the stacks on the QEII when she was first launched just a few miles downriver in Clydebank.

Holding sway in the middle of the floor was a shaven-headed, ear-ringed steroid abuser of fifty years. Clearly, this was someone you didn't want to piss off.

Steroid Abuser raised his pint in the air. Coughed out in a cigarette-hoarse voice, 'Weren't goin' tae mention this, but then thought ma son would've wanted it this way...' He looked as if he would either laugh hysterically or break down bawling like a wee babe. It was a toss-up. Could go either way. 'Some of youse may have heard laughter at the crematorium. Not appropriate, God knows, but I can now let youse in on what happened.

'When me and the Mrs arrived at the crematorium, I noticed that the hearse driver had forgot his TomTom. Left it sittin' on the dash. I knew it wouldn't be there when we came back, so I unhooked it and put it in ma pocket...'

Laughter.

'I know what youse thinkin', but I planned on returnin' it...'

More laughter.

'Anywho, as the casket bearing our Mikey wis carried in by the lads and placed on the rollers upfront, the TomTom went off and chirped: YOU HAVE REACHED YOUR FINAL DESTINATION.'

The pub exploded with that spontaneous laughter that comes from a combination of quirky circumstance and thank-fucking-Christ, much-needed relief.

Then Steroid Abuser spoke again, 'Those of us who loved Mikey know he would've wanted me tae tell this wee story. Tae Mikey!'

Everyone toasted the fallen Mikey and were wondering if they should carry on with the laughter or go back to the crying, when the front door swung open.

Standing there was Decoy Brody. Chiseled. Eerily handsome. Piercing blue eyes. And he, too, was dressed in all black.

The room went cryogenically silent as everyone sized up Decoy. But Decoy did nothing. Said nothing. Just stared back with those piercing blue eyes as Steroid Abuser silently placed his pint on the table next to him and slipped a hand inside his suit jacket. Another patron pulled a knife under a table. Yet another cocked a handgun under a different table. And those eyes didn't miss the older woman at the bar, the one with the spiked white hair, as she pointed at the interloper as if she knew him.

One thing was very clear: These locals dressed in mourning black were not to be fucked with and they weren't intimidated, until Decoy opened his hand, revealed a grenade and let it roll out of his hand and across the sticky, beer-stained carpet.

# CHAPTER FOUR

Out on the street, in front of the Kingston pub, DI Sharkey and DS Lyon-Jones were just running up. Out of breath. Puffed.

And the establishment looked peaceful and serene in the falling snow.

'Place is a morgue, sir. Your hunches stink. Didn't you know 97-percent of hunches prove to be false?'

On that, Decoy Brody burst out the front door of the pub.

Decoy froze. Looked at Sharkey. Looked at Lyon-Jones. Knew right off that they were police. Gave them a catch-me-if-you-can smirk. Took off.

Just as a ball of fire blew out the leaded front windows, blasting Sharkey and Lyon-Jones all the way out into the road.

## CHAPTER FIVE

Sharkey and Lyon-Jones lay on the slushy glass-covered tarmac. Stunned.

Sharkey shook his head to clear it. Lyon-Jones shook her head. Sharkey glanced over at Lyon-Jones. 'Your statistics suck.'

They heard a screech of tyres. Two patrol cars skidded to a stop. Officers jumped out and attempted to access the burning pub.

Another screech of tyres. Sharkey looked up to see the suspect on a bright-red motorcycle zoom away in the direction of the West End.

Sharkey and Lyon-Jones struggled to their feet. Sharkey spotted the world's oldest VW Golf parked illegally just down the road. Motor running. Driver's window open. He rushed the rust-bucket. Flashed his warrant card at a teenage hoodie with fat cheeks and gelled spikes.

Fat Cheeks shot back attitude: 'Am I supposed to be impressed, like?'

Sharkey yanked open the door. Grabbed Fat Cheeks by the scruff of the neck. Threw him the hell out.

Threw Lyon-Jones the hell in.

Sharkey flipped on the wipers against the snow. They didn't work. He raked through the gears and sped after the darting bright-red motorcycle. Lyon-Jones held on for dear life and fought to strap herself in.

Sharkey slalomed through rush-hour traffic, leaning forward, trying to peer through a streaked windscreen. 'What you just saw at the Kingston is a by-product of the turf war—'

'You should buckle up, sir. It's the law.'

'What! What! I'm outlining Glasgow's gangland activity and you're telling me to buckle up!'

'Watch out!'

11

Sharkey swerved wildly and narrowly missed an impressive contingency of the Glasgow fire brigade heading to the Kingston.

'It's the law, sir.'

'Fuck the law, Jones!'

Lyon-Jones peered at the lower left-hand corner of the windscreen. 'Tax disc looks to be expired, sir...'

'FUCK IT!'

Lyon-Jones glanced up at a heavy metal CD swaying from the rearview mirror. Looked down at a marijuana roach in the ashtray.

Noticed her nude ultra-sheer Chantal Thomass had laddered. Shredded, actually.

Sharkey slammed on the brakes to avoid a wobbly pisshead crossing the street. Downshifted. Jammed the accelerator to the floor. Blew through a red light. Lyon-Jones' ears were still ringing and she had a small cut on her forehead. This is not how police work had been at her previous secondment—the Shetland Islands. The Shetland Islands dotted with verdant green fields and white woolly sheep.

Lyon-Jones turned her head and looked back at the Kingston pub.

Jesus, God.

The entire structure was engulfed in flames.

They would need body bags.

Lots of them.

# CHAPTER SIX

Katie Sharkey self-consciously tugged at her low-cut top to prevent her boobs from decamping and cased the student bar. Her father would give her major grief if he knew she went out dressed like this, but that's what teenaged girls did.

Perhaps he was harder on her because he was a cop.

The bar was called 'The Stud'. Originally a stable, now it was a meat market. The popular University of Glasgow haunt had large windows, brick walls and stone floors. It was located down a wee lane, near the university and around the corner from where Katie lived in Great George Street. She liked this fact. She could come out of an evening with the wind chill disputing global warming and still not have to wear a coat.

Katie was sitting with two short-skirted, immoral classmates from Moral Philosophy, but she wasn't listening as they rabbited on. All those two ever talked about were five-inch heels and six-inch dicks. Katie had had enough of the talk. What she wanted was romance. Her perfect man. A spoony cliché, she knew, but that's what she had her heart set on. Something more than the uni lads could offer. She didn't want a boy. She wanted a red-blooded man. Someone virile. Someone exciting.

Three more Red Bull and vodkas arrived and Katie watched as her two classmates immediately threw theirs back. Gawd! Now what were they talking about? Ewww, their idea of the perfect man: Kelvinside, a fat portfolio and a cottage on Loch Lomond.

Katie's idea of the perfect man: Gorgeous, a stab of excitement and mystery behind bedroom eyes.

The evening was going downhill. Now her classmates were talking about where to buy pole-dancing shoes and if they should exfoliate before applying their fake tans.

Movement over by the front door breached Katie's attention, and she glanced up. Standing there was a stranger with an air of sophistication and piercing blue eyes. He was older than all the students in the bar, well-built and a killer in the looks department.

Katie's two mates watched, gobsmacked, as this hunk scanned the room, made a beeline for their table, then cosied up next to Katie rather than the two of them who had just hiked their skirts halfway up to Hadrian's wall. It was clear to them that this handsome creature wasn't acquainted with Katie. And it was clear he was gagging for it. He couldn't keep his eyes off Katie's heaving breasts. How'd she make them heave like that on cue? Guess one had to have the big knockers to begin with.

Decoy Brody whispered something in Katie's ear, then rose and held out his hand. How gallant! Less gallant was Katie not saying goodbye to her mates as she stepped out into the cold night air with her perfect man.

A perfect stranger.

Parked on the cobblestones out in front of The Stud was a bright-red Kawasaki. A motorcycle! Excitement, indeed. Decoy climbed on and motioned for Katie to slip on behind him. She did just that, putting her arms around his tapered waist.

And then, for some inexplicable reason, she experienced a deep chill. And she wished she had brought a coat.

Decoy fired up the motorcycle. Looked back to see Sharkey and Lyon-Jones round a corner. Now on foot. Now too late.

Decoy gave Sharkey and Lyon-Jones a sinister salute and rocketed off into the night.

# CHAPTER SEVEN

In Katie's candle-lit bedroom, desperately parched love making had spawned something that had never happened before: She was cumming for the *third* time—even though Decoy hadn't shot his wad yet. Sly little sod, well, he was anything but little, but sly sod, indeed. She hadn't done cocaine before, but she didn't think it was supposed to have this effect. He must have spiked it with something. She was absolutely aflame.

Decoy placed a hand alongside her hip, rolled her over on to her stomach, spat on his fingers and caressed her anus. He wasn't going to try that, was he?

Wicked!

Here came number four.

## CHAPTER EIGHT

Two hours after the explosion and ensuing firestorm at the Kingston pub, a hastily arranged meeting was under way at Strathclyde Police in the Glasgow City Centre.

Inside, sullen-faced Detective Chief Inspector Maggie Squires briefed a group of plain-clothed and uniformed male and female officers. '…we're not sure if there's any connection to the Buchanan Galleries hit of this afternoon, but just before seven this evening an unknown individual walked into a post-funeral gathering at the Kingston pub in Holm street and threw a hand grenade…

'The perp took off on a motorbike, but was pursued by DI Sharkey and DS Lyon-Jones to a bar called The Stud—aye, that's the actual name—in the West End. Sharkey and Lyon-Jones spotted the perp leaving with a female student, but lost him…

'We've now learnt the perp accompanied the young woman to her apartment. Later, the student's flatmate came home just as the guy was leaving. Said he seemed very polite, charming even. Then she went into the bedroom and found her flatmate with her throat slashed.'

Squires stopped.

Threw daggers with her eyes at Sharkey.

More daggers at Lyon-Jones.

A theatrical pause.

'DS Lyon-Jones, I don't know what was going through your head, you're not even on duty yet—'

Lyon-Jones interrupted. 'If I may make something clear, ma'am, it wasn't my—'

Squires exploded. 'Don't you ever interrupt me again. Is that clear Lyon-Jones?'

'Yes, ma'am.'

'Go get that cut on your forehead seen to…'

Lyon-Jones shrank. Tried to become part of the woodwork. Subconsciously hid the runs in her nylons.

16

Squires stared at Lyon-Jones. 'NOW!'

Lyon-Jones scarpered from the room. Everyone watched her go.

Squires consulted her notes and stalled. She waited for the room to settle back down, then she turned her wrath on Sharkey. 'I dare say if Inspector Sharkey had not tried to go it on his own, the young girl might still be alive—'

Before CI Squires could spew venom any further, the briefing was disrupted by yelling and shouting and a horrific commotion out by reception. Everyone turned towards the door as it flew open and a distraught, albeit attractive woman in her late thirties forced her way in and rushed Inspector Sharkey.

'Katie's dead!' the woman shrieked, with a distinct American accent. 'DEAD! You said America was too dangerous and you wanted to come back to Scotland! You wanted her to go to university in Glasgow instead of Edinburgh. You said Glasgow was better than Edinburgh and that the West End would be safe. Now she's dead! AND IT'S ALL YOUR FAULT!!!'

And on that, the American woman slapped Sharkey viciously across the face.

# CHAPTER NINE

No parent should ever have to endure visiting a child in the mortuary.

The Glasgow City Mortuary in Saltmarket, not far from Glasgow Cross and the Tollbooth (where hangings once were viewed as a social outing with as many as 100,000 present),was obligatorily cold, and the lighting subdued, at least at this ungodly middle-of-the-night hour. And it was eerily quiet.

Sharkey was accompanied by two Family Liaison Officers. They were met at the front door by a young, blond Anatomical Pathology Technician, dressed in light-blue scrubs, and respectfully guided to an empty waiting area where they took a seat. Sharkey put his fist to his mouth. Realised his hands were shaking. Tried to keep from losing it. Looked around. The walls were painted a pinkish mauve. The trim was a mellow fuscia, if fuscia can be mellow. He knew the colours were meant to calm and soothe, but there was no calming or soothing in this tomb. When he was a detective constable, Sharkey had had duty as a Family Liaison Officer, but he never expected to be one of the shattered souls sitting here in the middle of the night like this with an officer on either side.

One of the liaison officers leaned close. 'Two-doc PM, sir. Shouldn't be long now.'

Sharkey knew the drill. Two forensic pathologists working together, knocking off as many as eight post mortems a day. It took a special breed to work in a mortuary and toil all day long or all through the night with the deceased who were often brought in, in a grisly state, and Sharkey had great respect for them.

'Sir?'

No response. Lost in a time gone by. Perhaps lost forever.

'Sir?'

18

Sharkey looked up. Both liaison officers were standing over him.

It was time to go.

The APT led them to a viewing room that was only about the size of a doctor's examining office. Since Sharkey was with the Force, the post mortem had been pushed up. Not normal procedure, but there you go. And here he was, standing in a mortuary waiting to identify and say goodbye to his wee Katie.

Up above Sharkey, to the right, was a small TV monitor. Next of kin identified gruesome murder or accident victims from the safe distance afforded by close-circuit TV. In front of him was a viewing window with vertical blinds. These would be pulled back and the corpse or remains could be viewed openly if the family wished to forgo the TV monitor. Despite all his times in this room, Sharkey had never noticed the details before.

A noise on the other side of the viewing window signalled the arrival of the corpse. The blond APT looked to Sharkey. He hesitated. Finally nodded. The blinds were drawn back and Sharkey looked on in horror. Standing on the other side of the window was a male pathology tech eating a Subway sandwich. Caught in the act, mortified, the tech scurried from the room, and a pathologist returned pushing a steel trolley bearing a lump under a white sheet.

The APT looked at Sharkey. 'Who's identifying with you?'

No response.

'Sir? You know we need a second person close to the family for the ID.'

As if on cue, the door to the viewing room opened and in stepped Detective Sergeant McDade of Govan CID, on the south side of the river. McDade was known around Glasgow as 'Kojak' on account of his bald dome and predilection for candy. Kojak was Sharkey's old mate when Sharkey been stationed down in Govan. Kojak was hideously overweight, out of shape and sported the distinctive blue-veined flush on his face of the excessive drinker.

'Jaysus, Fleet...sorry I'm late.'

Kojak was sweating like a pig. He took out a handkerchief. Wiped his glasses. Wiped his forehead. Then his bald dome. Pulled out a small tube of Tiger Balm, squeezed a small dollop of

19

the opaque substance on a finger and swiped his upper lip just below the nostrils. He handed the tube to Sharkey. Sharkey declined.

He wanted nothing masked.

Sharkey turned to the young blond APT. 'Please, I need to go to her.'

'Best not to, sir,' one of the liaison officers cautioned.

Sharkey was well aware that family weren't allowed in the chamber with the body, but he was a detective inspector and the young blond APT could feel his pain. She looked to the pathologist. He nodded his assent.

The APT led the way. The pathologist pulled away the sheet and unzipped the body bag, alas, a bit too far exposing the fatal laceration. Sharkey gasped. The pathologist quickly adjusted the sheet and masked the wound.

Katie's head rested on a pillow. She seemed at peace. Sharkey looked down the length of the body. The outline of Katie's feet, clearly visible. He choked. Just that afternoon he had finally figured out what he was going to buy her for Christmas: shoes. He was going to take her to L.K.Bennett in Royal Exchange Square and let her pick out whatever her heart desired. When he had been showing Lyon-Jones around the city centre, he had proudly talked about his daughter Katie. Said he didn't know what to get a teenaged girl for Christmas. Lyon-Jones had suggested shoes. Said he couldn't go wrong. Shoes and girls. A horse and carriage. Said he should go to L.K.Bennett if he wanted to splash out. Being from a posh part of Edinburgh, Sharkey had figured that Lyon-Jones must know all about fashion. So he decided that was what he was going to do. And why not? Why worry about the big bucks? It was Christmas after all and Katie was his only daughter.

He had planned to take her for a curry afterwards. At a proper restaurant. The Dhabba in Merchant City, perhaps. Indian at Christmas, daft, but it's what the two of them always did ever since Katie got him hooked on curry.

Sharkey heard a strange wheezing sound. Raspy and guttural. It was his own breath leaving his body. He felt as if he were going to pass out. He closed his eyes and tears spewed out and streamed down his face. His legs started to go and he could no longer bear the terrible pain stabbing at his heart. It was all he could do to identify his daughter in a whisper and flee as fast as he could.

Outside, it was nearly first light. The sky was smeared like a bad bruise. The snow had turned to sleet and Saltmarket was wet and shiny and deathly cold. Sharkey stood there and looked back at the classical Greek façade of the neighbouring building: the High Court.

Where was there justice?

A noise behind Sharkey brought him back round. He stood face to face with his mate, Kojak, unable to speak, then big tough guy, he broke down on his dear friend's shoulder.

And sobbed.

# CHAPTER TEN

Sharkey had been at St Anne's Catholic Church in the East End since he'd left the mortuary. Sharkey didn't attend church, but he felt the need to go and it was the only church he could access. When he worked out of the Shettleston Police Station, Sharkey had become friends with the altar server. The altar server was a man who didn't like to miss meals and he always had a full fry-up breakfast at the same greasy spoon, the Station Diner, by the Carntyne Rail Station. Sharkey found him mid-bite and was let into the church. It was the first time Sharkey had been in a church since his wedding.

And Sharkey had prayed, wept, reminisced, and he had wondered where it had all gone wrong.

Where *he* had gone wrong.

At the age of 17, he was the leader of the Shettleston Aggro, a once staunchly sectarian gang known for avenging any affront swiftly—and brutally. After an Old Firm football match at Ibrox, with Celtic having clutched victory from the jaws of defeat, Sharkey was jumped near the Woodville Street subway entrance by a rival gang, beaten with a crowbar, had a razor taken to his face and then was kicked in the face to split open the wound and make it much more difficult to heal. So it would leave a scar. A reminder.

After emergency surgery and two weeks intensive care at Southern General, Sharkey was transferred to Glasgow Royal Infirmary where he convalesced for another month and then was rolled out in a wheelchair and conveyed home by ambulance. The very next night, in front of a pub called the Goalkeeper, and not far from the stadium in Ibrox, the rival gang leader was found lying in the gutter, dead, his face 'scalped' and stitched to a football.

Word of the artistic deed spread like the plague through the

22

city. No one could implicate Sharkey, as he was at home in Shettleston, on the other side of the river, recuperating under the watchful and unimpeachable eye of his single father, a detective sergeant in Glasgow's East End.

That night, the tenement where Sharkey lived with his father was firebombed and they only just managed to escape out a window in the loo. After the fire brigade and police left, Sharkey caught all kinds of hell from his father. 'T'is the last time I compromise my integrity for ye!'

Late the next morning, Sharkey's father, deeply conflicted, spoke to his beloved son.

'Word on the street is that you'll be dead within a week.' And he handed Fleet a one-way ticket to America. His only chance at survival was to emigrate to the States, to Charlotte, North Carolina, and live with his paternal grandmother. Sharkey packed, his father drove him to the airport, then his father went home and cried. The first time he'd cried since Fleet's mother went 'doon tae offy' and never returned.

Sharkey spent the first year working as a 'gofer' at the Terminal Velocity Gun Range, off Billy Graham Parkway, not far from the Charlotte-Douglas International Airport, and not far from his gran's double-wide mobile home. The owner of the gun range, a first generation American of Scottish parents, lived next door to Sharkey's gran and took a liking to the hard-working, brash young Scot, drove him to work every morning and taught him all there was to know about pulling a trigger. 'This is the South, boy, the home of Robert E Lee and the Confederate Army. You need to learn your Second Amendment rights to keep and bear arms!'

Sharkey adjusted quickly and even learned to speak with a North Carolina drawl so he could fit in. But he missed Glasgow desperately. Then his neighbour told him about the high incidence of first generation, second generation and ex-pat Scots in the nearby Blue Ridge Mountains, and about an event which took place every July, not far from the ski town of Boone, at nearby Grandfather Mountain. These were the North Carolina Highland Games and 'gathering o' Scottish clans'.

With homesickness burning a hole in his heart, Sharkey wasn't about to miss this, but he didn't have transportation. It was a tortuous hundred mile drive high up into the mountains. When his neighbour realised Sharkey was desperate to go, he told him, 'Got me an old car in the shed out back of the gun club. If you can get it runnin', you can have it.' The neighbour handed Sharkey two keys: one for the shed, the other for the car. Sharkey ran out the back door of the gun club and unlocked the shed. It was dark and the car was covered in dust and bat guano, but he knew right off he had struck gold in America.

The car was a red, 1988, Ford Mustang GT.

Sharkey would later learn his neighbour had purchased the second-hand Mustang for his only son, as a surprise for his 16<sup>th</sup> birthday. The lad never lived to see the day, having been knocked down and killed by a hit-and-run drunk driver after a Carolina Panthers away football game down in Tampa Bay.

Sharkey had always been good with his hands, and his father had taught him a bit about cars, so he replaced the sparkplugs, the wires, did an oil change, installed a new oil filter, a new air filter, and pumped a nickel's worth of air in the tyres. Then five hours to get it running and three days polishing, waxing, hoovering and spraying on all the ArmorAll he could get his hands on, and Sharkey had one of the most coveted cars in the foothills of the Blue Ridge Mountains.

Then he filled it with petrol costing $1.16 a gallon, and he was over the moon.

On the first day of the Highland Games, Sharkey rose in the wee hours after restless sleep and certifiable dreams and drove up to the college town of Boone, then swung left on Highway #105 and climbed up to Banner Elk and finally majestic Grandfather Mountain.

And it was here at these Highland Games, in the mountains that so resembled the Highlands above Perth, that Sharkey met 18-year-old, blond, blue-eyed Brooke Walsh who was drawn to his startling good looks—and of course the kilt and accompanying *sgian-dubh*.

Shortly thereafter, Brooke found out she was pregnant. Pregnant with a little girl who they ended up naming 'Katie'.

And now Katie was dead.

'Eternal rest grant unto her, O Lord, and let perpetual light shine upon her. May the souls of the faithful departed, through the mercy of God, rest in peace. Amen.'

For reasons unknown, Sharkey crossed himself. Rose. Thanked the alter server for letting him in. Exited St Anne's. Turned to look back at the red-brick façade.

Wished he were dead, not Katie.

CHAPTER ELEVEN

In Govan, down at the docks, Decoy Brody awoke, yawned and stretched.

He hadn't slept so well in months. He hadn't done coke, mind you, only the girl. He didn't do drugs. Felt it took away his edge. An edge he couldn't afford to lose. Having said that, he knew the ins and outs of pharmaceuticals, what effects they had and how he could use them for his own devices.

Decoy did chin-ups, press-ups and sit-ups, then made a cuppa in the galley and walked out on to the afterdeck of his illegally moored fishing boat, the *What A Catch*. He sipped his Tetley's and watched as another fishing boat chugged upstream, followed by a flock of gulls. When he had been a young lad, the Clyde was one of the world's most polluted waterways, with bloated dead fish a common sight in the filthy, oxygen-starved water. More than a century of shipbuilding and heavy industry had seen to that. From the city centre all the way to the Tail O' The Bank at Greenock and the Irish Sea, over twenty miles downstream, oxygen levels were so low the Clyde was unable to sustain marine life.

Like many, including his docker father, Decoy had anguished over the shipbuilding decline, but it had done wonders for the river. Salmon had returned to the Clyde in 1983—after a 120 year absence—and the water was now teeming with other fish and even seals, otters and cormorants.

Glasgow was a city that was on its way up and Decoy loved the 'second city of the Empire' as it had once been known. He finished his tea. Cut some bait from a large mackerel he had on ice. Chummed with the remains of the mackerel and some maggots he kept in a tin on the afterdeck. Put out a fishing line. Then washed his hands and pulled on a skin-tight T-shirt, which showed off his build.

The T-shirt read: YOUR MUM WOULD LOVE ME.

CHAPTER TWELVE

Over at City Centre Division, Sharkey sat at his desk, behind a closed door, head in hands, shaking uncontrollably with rage and grief. He was dressed in the same clothes from the night before. He had shaggers hair. Was unshaven. Hiding from the world. And he hadn't eaten. Couldn't eat. Couldn't keep anything down.

A jolting knock. Sharkey jumped. The door swung open without being granted and banged loudly against the wall. A rude intrusion. Standing there was Detective Chief Inspector Maggie Squires.

'The door was closed for a reason, Maggie.'

'Listen, I know this may not be the best time, but I need to address what went on yesterday.'

Sharkey stared back, appalled that the chief bitch would dare to breach the previous day's events at this time.

'What were you thinking, Sharkey?'

'For Christ sakes, Maggie. You're grilling me now?' Sharkey gripped the top of his desk. 'I knew there was a post-funeral gathering at the Kingston. It suddenly dawned on me—'

'One of your hunches, Inspector?'

Sharkey ignored the jab. 'It suddenly dawned on me that the killer of the Kingston's barman might return. So I just took off running...'

'With your new DS...'

No response. Staring off into space. 'If I had only known...'

'Don't have time for a poor-little-me act, Sharkey. If you're unfit to carry on your duties, I'm happy to arrange alternatives.' And she turned and closed the door.

Sharkey sat there. Numb. Breathing heavily. Fucking cold-hearted bitch. He looked out the window, the sky was the colour of dirty dishwater. He noticed a dead wasp burial ground at the bottom of the window he hadn't seen before. He reached into his lower desk drawer and extracted a bottle of whisky. Hands shaking, he held it, coveted it. Desperately tried to control the runaway train his life had suddenly become.

A deferential knock at his door. He quickly hid the whisky and looked up to see a suit stick his head of silver short-cropped hair in. Detective Chief Superintendent Danus Ferguson was ex-Scotland rugby. When he smiled, which was not a common occurrence, it was difficult to determine where the scars left off and the wrinkles began.

'Ye get any sleep?'

'What are you doing over here?'

'You have better coffee here than the HQ, five-star leaded. Go on home, Fleet. Go home. You're due compassionate.'

'No, I need to work. Need to be here.'

DCS Ferguson regarded his detective and realised he was being ripped limb from limb emotionally. He understood that Sharkey needed to hold on to work to keep from falling off the end of the earth. 'We'll, get the bastard, Fleet.'

Sharkey stared out the window. Nodded. Flashed to his wee Katie lying on a steel gurney. Gnawed on his lower lip.

'Heard your new DS starts today.'

'Pardon?'

'Heard your new DS starts today.'

'Oh, right. Double-barrelled, no less. What a crock of shit.' Sharkey looked at his feet.

'Beggin' your pardon, sir.'

DCS Ferguson was an old school, hard-nosed cop and he liked Sharkey for his abrasive 'take-no-shit-from-nobody attitude'. Of course he would never tell Sharkey that.

Ferguson added: 'Double-barrelled *and* a PhD in psychology from the University of Edinburgh.'

'A PhD as a cop. *That* has to be a first. I'm not going to have to address her as Dr?'

'No, that's to be kept on the QT. And also that DS Lyon-Jones' father is Fergus Lyon-Jones.'

'And that would make daddy...?'

'Lord Lyon-Jones, the Edinburgh millionaire. DS Lyon-Jones was fast-tracked through the college, the Force. Privilege can

28

move mountains...'

Sharkey, under his breath, 'Fast-tracked, fucking bullshit.'

Before Sharkey could protest further, there was another knock at the door and a uniform entered.

'Morning, sir.' Just a whisper. Said respectfully. Said knowingly.

The uniform plopped a folder in Sharkey's in-tray. Spotted the DCS in there. Got the deer-in-the-headlamps' look. Backed out, bowing Japanese.

Both watched the uniform flee. It would have been a light moment any other day.

Sharkey rubbed his eyes with the heels of his hands.

Another knock at the door. Loud and obtrusive this time. Obnoxious even, if that could be said about a knock. Sharkey gave his Chief Super a look of *Now, what the fuck?*

The door opened a crack and Fiona Lyon-Jones leaned in and flashed an awkward smile, a smile nevertheless that would make any dentist proud.

'Sir?'

Struck dumb, Ferguson gave Sharkey a look of 'This is your new DS?'

Without being invited, Lyon-Jones pushed open the door and entered. Sharkey wasn't in a proper mental state to notice that Lyon-Jones was dressed as if she had just stepped out of a fashion mag, but Ferguson did.

No one spoke. Just stared. Sharkey because he was lost in another universe. Ferguson because this was not how cops looked when he entered the Force.

The silence continued.

Trying to break the silence, what with her being of shrink ilk and *au courant* with all things manipulative, DS Lyon-Jones ventured, 'Guess we'll be spending an inordinate amount of time arguing about which one is better...'

'Better?'

'Glasgow or Edinburgh.'

Feeling as if he'd just been hit in the stomach with an axe, Sharkey rose and fled for the door. 'Excuse me, Jones.'

'That's *Lyon*-Jones...' Fiona said to a closing door. It was her first day at work, a PhD was hanging on the wall of her new two-bedroomed, ensuite, upmarket apartment in Giffnock, with the two off-road dedicated parking spaces (one a garage), and she had read the moment wrong and gone over like a bucket of cold sick.

Shit.

She had wanted desperately to make a great first impression, that's why she'd dressed down—yes, dressed *down*—and dyed her natural blond hair, black. She was fed up being hit on and treated as a lesser intellect. If only she could escape back to her other apartment, the one on Princes Street in Edinburgh, and crawl in a hole.

A two-thousand-square-foot hole with an open-plan and a killer view of the castle.

DCS Ferguson read her confusion. 'Listen, don't take it too personally. That university student was his daughter.'

Lyon-Jones let this sink in, then: 'Seventy-four percent of those grieving, feel uncontrollable rage, sir.'

Ferguson just started dumbly back. 'If you say so...'

Lyon-Jones looked out the window at the restive sky. Moved close. Checked the view. Saw that the window was grimy. Spotted the wasp graveyard. Crossed to the wall closest to the door. Nosey as hell, she studied a framed, glass-enclosed Carolina Panthers American football jersey hanging there. The glass was clean. She turned back to DCS Ferguson. 'Heard a lot about him. Raised in the East End of Glasgow. Lived in America. A Marine sniper. SWAT team in North Carolina. Married to an American woman—'

'Divorced. Give Fleet, I mean DI Sharkey, some time.'

'*Fleet?*'

'Sorry. *Inspector Sharkey.* I misspoke.'

'But you said "Fleet"?'

'It's nothing.'

'Of course it's something.'

Silence again.

'A nickname?'

'You're pushing it, Lyon-Jones...'

Pushing it was Lyon-Jones' forte. 'A nickname?'

'Aye, a nickname, his Christian name is "Ferris", but you didn't hear it from me.'

30

'Let me guess, with a nickname like "Fleet" he used to be in a gang?'

'Didn't we all, Lyon-Jones. Didn't we all. No, it comes from "fleet" as in "fleet of foot". In the late eighties he was British junior 1500 metres champion.'

Fiona looked out the window again, then turned to Ferguson.

'And may I ask who *you* are?'

'I'm your Chief Superintendent.'

CHAPTER THIRTEEN

Sharkey needed to find a witness.

He needed to find where the survivors of the Kingston pub inferno were being treated.

He put in a call to the detective who was leading the investigation over at the Kingston only to be told that information was not available. This was highly unusual. Sharkey went above the detective's head and hit another brick wall. Then he called a crime-reporter pal at the *Herald*, but he knew nothing. He rang each hospital in the greater Glasgow area, identified himself and was told that no victims from the Kingston were being treated at their respective facility.

What was going on? This information was always readily available by going through proper channels. Then he figured it out: The survivors of the Kingston bombing were still in jeopardy. Their identities and whereabouts were not being announced to the world. To anyone who may want to do them harm. To the likes of the Sutherland family henchmen.

When Sharkey was the leader of his gang, there was a young gang member who had been fascinated by blood. He wasn't the violent type and he certainly had never wanted any of his own blood spilt, but he was oddly fascinated by gore. Of which there is no shortage in Glasgow's East End.

Fittingly, Sharkey's old mate now worked for Emergency Services and he knew precisely where the victims had been taken.

The snow had turned to rain as Sharkey pulled his white V-reg Rover 600 up in front of the Glasgow Royal Infirmary. He turned the key and killed the engine, but the engine kept juddering along for at least another minute. Sharkey sat there. Collecting his thoughts. Formulating his game plan. He hadn't been to this particular hospital since his days recuperating from the beating at the hands of the rival gang.

He climbed out carrying his gym bag and walked toward the hospital's entrance. Then he stopped, turned and aimed his Rover key fob at the vehicle. He zapped it. Nothing. He zapped it again. Still nothing. He swore a blue streak under his breath, approached the Rover and jammed the key in the lock. He regarded the old white motor for a moment and almost broke down right there in the car park. Katie had nicknamed the big lumbering Rover the 'Polar Bear' when she had been little, and the name had stuck. Sharkey had taken her to the Glasgow Zoo in Calderbury Park. That trip had been the first time that Sharkey had done something with just Katie. It had been Katie's idea. 'Let's go to the zoo, Daddy, just you and me.'

She had always been a daddy's girl.

The Polar Bear: Besides the zoo, so many day trips up to Loch Lomond with the entire family or to the beach at Largs to look for crabs or to the Highlands to ski. So many memories.

So much pain now.

Sharkey hurried through the hospital's main entrance and aimed for Reception. A young lass with big green eyes and a fake tan looked up from her illicit game of Spider Solitaire and did a double take when she saw Sharkey, pleased by what she saw. She gave him the once over, head to foot, back up to head.

Noticed the long scar which ran down his right cheek from the ear to the mouth.

'Can I help?' Big smile. Facial scars are not that uncommon or off-putting in Glasgow.

Sharkey showed his warrant card. 'The survivors from the Kingston bombing, where would I find them?'

'Afraid they're not at this hospital, Inspector.'

Sharkey leaned close. 'I know it's all hush-hush and everything, luv, but it's important. Please. It...ah...has to do with family.'

The lass looked around to make sure no one was within earshot. She hooked a wisp of hair behind an ear and leaned close, followed by a draught of toxic perfume.

'There's just the one, Inspector.' Said conspiratorially.

'Just one? Where are all the others? Different hospital?'

'There are no other survivors. A real tragedy, that.' Then the lassie pointed a finger in the sky. 'Burns Unit. Top floor.'

Sharkey started to move off. The lass stopped him with: 'If there's anything else you would like to know, I'll be here till five. Then I'm off.' The batting of green eyes against a tan background. Posture suddenly erect and uplifting.

'I'll make a calendar event in my mobile.' Sharkey smiled back. All charm. He turned, lost the charm, his face now resolute. The *top* floor of the Burns Unit. That's where they kept patients who were under police protection.

Sharkey took the lift to the top floor. Some prat had pushed all the buttons and it stopped on each floor. It took a bleeding eternity, but it gave him plenty of time to think: Would Katie still be alive if he had followed procedure? If he had not tried to go it on his own? Had he fucked up royally?

The lift pinged and the doors hissed open. Sharkey looked right, left. Clocked a uniform with a choir boy's face sitting in a chair down at the end of the corridor, guarding one of the rooms.

Sharkey approached with authority. The uniform recognised him right off and jumped to attention. He smoothed the front of his uniform and subconsciously checked his fly.

'Inspector!'

'Constable. Alright?'

'Yes, sir.'

'How long have you been on duty?'

'All day, sir.'

'All day?'

'Cut backs, sir.'

'Have you eaten?'

'Ah...not so very hungry the now.'

'Go get yourself something to eat, lad. Go down to the cafeteria. Get some food in you. Come back in a half an hour.'

'But, I'm not to leave my post, sir.'

'Go ahead, son. Go on. I'll be here till you get back.'

'Ta, sir.'

Sharkey watched the uniform until he entered the lift and the doors closed. Waited a moment. Pushed the door to the patient's room open. Heard the lift ping. Stopped. Looked back. Couldn't

34

believe his eyes.

Walking toward him was DS Fiona Lyon-Jones.

Sharkey was not happy with the turn of events and curious about the flipping timing.

'What are you doing here?'

'Followed you.'

'You followed me?'

'Aye, sir.'

'Why?'

'DCI Squires said I should keep an eye on you.'

This didn't sit well with Sharkey. 'Why?'

'Don't know. Just do what I'm told, Boss.'

'Please don't call me that.'

'Sorry, sir. What's in the gym bag?'

'Listen, Jones, there's no need for you to be here. The shit is hitting the fan.'

'Prefer to stay, sir.'

'And I prefer you don't.'

On that, Sharkey pushed open the door and slipped inside.

Lying on the bed was the woman with the spiked white hair. She was connected to monitors and had oxygen tubes in her nostrils. Her arms were dressed with salve and she was sleeping peacefully. Sharkey pulled up a chair and sat at her side. He watched her sleep, then put his head in his hands and stayed that way for an eternity. When he looked back at the woman, she was looking at him. There was an effort of a smile, but eyes were welling with saltwater.

'Inspector Sharkey?'

'Aye.'

'Seen ye on the telly.' Sigh. 'I wis at the fucking Kingston.'

'I know, darling, I know.'

Spiked-Hair put two fingers to her lips and mimed smoking. Sharkey opened his gym bag and took out a pack of cigarettes. He shook one out, stuck it in his mouth and sparked it up. Then he removed Spiked-Hair's oxygen and placed the fag between her lips as soldiers do for a wounded mate.

'No smoking in here! Health and safety!'

Sharkey looked back at the door and expected to see the tyrannical Nurse Ratched from *One Flew Over the Cuckoo's Nest*.

35

Instead, he saw Lyon-Jones' head sticking in, infinitely worse than Nurse Ratched and becoming a major pain in the arse.

'Fuck health and safety, Jones!' Sharkey spewed. He turned back to Spiked-Hair.

'You can smoke, darling.' And Sharkey lit one up for himself.

Lyon-Jones stepped in, leaned close to Sharkey and hissed in his ear, 'Rules, sir!'

'You sure that's the tone you want to take with me?'

'With all due respect, sir…one must abide by the rules.'

Sharkey fixed Lyon-Jones with a look that could wither a charging rhino. 'Fuck the rules, Jones. Fuck 'em! Didn't you get it when I said it the first time?'

Sharkey reached back into his gym bag and extracted a bottle of Low Flyer whisky. He took Spike-Hair's plastic water glass, removed the straw and dumped the water in a vase of mixed flowers on the windowsill. Then he poured a generous three fingers in the plastic glass, put the straw back in and handed it to Spiked-Hair.

Spiked-Hair in the hospital: ciggie in one bandaged hand, whisky in the other.

Lyon-Jones about to have a cow.

Spiked-Hair sucked greedily on the straw, then blurted out, 'It's the Sutherlands! They're comin' tae our hooses an' bustin' up our cars. They're puttin' petrol bombs in through our letter boxes. They want us all oot, so they can surround themselves with clan. They're gobblin' up turf, Inspector. There are children doon there what need jabs, but the parents are too afraid tae go tae the health centre because it's become a no-go area. We cannae go tae Mass in the local church anymore. Cannae go down tae the shops anymore…'

Sharkey looked into Spiked-Hair's eyes and he saw a level of fear he had only seen once before.

'You know who rolled the grenade, don't you, darling?'

'No! I didnae see nothing.'

'It's okay.'

'Nowt to tell, Inspector.'

'You can tell me, darling. I'll stop him.'

Spiked-Hair sucked on the straw some more and made it gurgle. She emptied the glass. Her eyes were wide eyes. She was deathly afraid. 'The scum who rolled the grenade...it wis Decoy Brody.' Shaking uncontrollably now.

Sharkey stunned, poured more whisky into Spiked-Hair's glass. He took the stub when she was finished smoking and extinguished it with his bare fingers. He replaced the oxygen tubes and gave Spiked-Hair a gentle kiss on the forehead.

'I'll make it stop, darling. I'll make it stop.'

Sharkey rose, grabbed Lyon-Jones roughly by the arm, escorted her out the room and into the corridor.

Lyon-Jones was fuming. 'Did that woman say "Deacon Brodie"? How dare someone from Glasgow—'

'Don't throw a shit-fit, Jones, and lose the high-and-mighty Edinburgh crap. It's *Decoy*. Just a *nom de guerre*. He thinks he's being sinister, but he's just being a prick.'

'You've heard of this suspect?'

Sharkey looked down at his hands and they were shaking just like Spiked-Hair's, but not out of fear.

He knew Decoy Brody.

He now knew the name of the man who'd killed his wee Katie.

# CHAPTER FOURTEEN

Back at City Centre, Sharkey was in his office, pacing back and forth. A caged animal. His mind was racing. The fuse burning.

Detective Chief Inspector Maggie Squires banged open the door again and walked in without knocking.

'What was that cowboy stunt you pulled at the hospital?'

'You feel the need to send a sodding spy after me, Maggie?'

'You're warned off any involvement in your daughter's case. Do you understand?'

'That's bullshit!'

'That means Decoy Brody is off limits, as well. Do you read me, Inspector?'

'Wait just a goddamn minute, Maggie, you and I went through the College together. We came up through the ranks together.'

'Decoy Brody is off limits. Take some time off. I don't want you becoming a liability.' DCI Maggie Squires spun on her heels and exited, purposely leaving the door open.

*Fucking cow!* Sharkey ready to blow a gasket. Ready to strangle Squires. Ready to throttle the next person he came in contact with.

Lyon-Jones stuck her head in.

Sharkey's landline rang. He shot daggers at Lyon-Jones. Picked up the phone receiver. It was Kojak from Govan CID returning his call.

'Kojak, thanks for getting back. Got a witness up here says it was Decoy Brody.'

On the other end, Kojak was incredulous. 'Decoy Brody? You certain, laddie?'

'Witness is from Govan. She was at the Kingston.'

'Thought there weren't any survivors.'

'Just the one.'

'Decoy Brody, jaysus, he hasn't been around since Jimmy the Pouch Sutherland pissed off to the continent. All our spies said he was down in Spain. I'll pass the info on and start turning over rocks.'

'Do whatever it takes, Kojak. Get some douche bag to vomit him up.'

'I'm on it.'

Sharkey rang off.

Lyon-Jones was staring at him as if he were from Mars. 'Kojak? Douche bag?'

'Aye, Jones, "Kojak" and "douche bag". It's all a part of the way we speak around here. Got a problem with that?'

No response from Lyon-Jones. Believe it or not, she did know when to keep her trap shut. Sometimes.

Fighting inner demons, Sharkey took a pack of Regals out of his top desk drawer, sat down, lit up, then turned to Lyon-Jones who was now flabbergasted that he was smoking in the building.

'Listen up, Jones. Decoy Brody is an enforcer in the Sutherland gang...'

Fiona held up a hand. 'Let me stop you right there, sir. Weren't you just warned off?'

'How do you know that?'

Lyon-Jones pointed to the door. 'I was listening.'

'Well, fuck that, Jones, you'll be involved so you need to know. Understood? You can be my goddamn eyes and ears.'

'Yes, sir.'

'You do as I tell you. You learn something, you come right to me first. Understood?'

'Yes, sir.'

'You don't go to DCI Squires. Understood? AND NO FUCKING FOLLOWING ME.'

Lyon-Jones irritated now. 'I get it...sir.'

'Pull up a chair. Take a load off.'

Lyon-Jones did just that. Sat down. Crossed her legs. Double wrapped them.

'Two years ago I arrested Decoy, but the case collapsed—'

Lyon-Jones sat upright and interrupted. In spite of the friction with Sharkey, she was eager to assert. Trap back open. 'On account of witness statements withdrawn in the face of relentless intimidation. I know all about the case.'

'Sorry? How do you know about the case?'

'I've done my homework.' Pleased with herself. 'Would you've done anything different, sir? In hindsight, I mean.'

'Aye. Should've put a bullet in his head when I had the chance.'

'A bullet, sir? A bullet?' Lyon-Jones studied Sharkey. He was a father wrestling with deep pain. He was frustrated. And he was different, not at all what she'd expected from a new boss. From someone in Glasgow. And then there was that scar. There was something about him she couldn't put her finger on—and that had never happened to her before. She prided herself on being able to read people. She ran Sharkey through the myriad of psychological profiles she had committed to memory. Sharkey didn't fit any of them. Didn't come close.

'Have to play by the book, sir.'

Sharkey fixed Lyon-Jones with a weary look. He couldn't believe it. Her first day at the station and she was cheeky as a fucking Gibraltar monkey. 'Listen, Jones, lose the attitude. I don't need anyone—especially you— telling me what I need or don't need. Now or ever. DO YOU GET IT?'

'Loud and clear, sir.'

Sharkey pinched the bridge of his nose. Rubbed at his eyes. He was exhausted. He was climbing the walls. He knew the name of his daughter's killer and he was powerless, and powerless was not something he handled well. Engaging in a tug of war with a frisky Gibraltar monkey was not what he needed right now.

Sharkey took a desperate drag of his cig.

'Is that really necessary, sir?'

'Aye, it is. Very necessary. And it's getting more and more necessary by the minute. May I continue?'

'Yes, of course, carry on whenever you're ready. I'm all ears.'

'Jimmy the Pouch Sutherland is the patriarch of the Sutherland family. He calls the shots from Benidorm—'

'Benidorm? I was under the impression that he was right here in Glasgow?'

'Not since the Criminal Assets Bureau took away his Bentley and drove his arse out of town. Anyway, where was I?'

'The Pouch.'

'Right, his nickname is the Pouch—'

'Oh, I know that too, sir. He's known as the Pouch because he carries a small calibre handgun right below his stomach. Left-handed. He never has his left hand out of that pouch.'

'Would you like to finish, Jones?'

'It's *Lyon*-Jones, sir. And, no, you carry on, it helps me to adjust to your accent. It's diabolical. I'm really struggling here.'

Sharkey sighed. 'I'll buy you a *Parliamo Glasgow* CD and you can play it every morning on the way to the station. Look, Jones…'

Colour rose in Lyon-Jones' cheeks.

'…Jimmy the Pouch Sutherland's son, Denny the Screwdriver, oversees the Glasgow operation ever since his older brother was murdered—'

Sharkey's phone rang. He went for it, but Lyon-Jones grabbed it first.

'DS Lyon-Jones speaking.' Sharkey couldn't believe her nerve! 'Someone at the bar for you…sir.'

'Tell them I'll be right out—'

'He's busy right now. Try again later.' Rang off. 'Where were we, sir?'

'You answered my phone. *My* fucking phone.'

'Yes, sir, it was ringing.'

'You told them I was busy!'

'Correct, sir.'

'You told them to try again later!'

'Of course, sir. It might've been important.'

'Am I missing something, Jones? Is the air different over in Edinburgh? Were you raised by wolves? What am I missing?'

'Nothing, sir.'

'You grew up less than forty five miles away from where I did, yet for all practical purposes, it could have been different planets. Mars and Pluto, I'm thinking. What do you have to say to that?'

'I would have to agree with that assumption, sir. Edinburgh and Glasgow are light years apart.'

Sharkey regarded Lyon-Jones. She just eyed him right back. Two pit bulls wrestling with the same piece of meat. He looked out the window. Looked at his Carolina Panthers American football jersey hanging on the wall. Took a deep breath. Crushed out his cigarette. Lit up another. Carried on, 'The son is a loose cannon. Once mooned a judge while yelling "This is what the Sutherland family thinks of the court"...'

'Mooned a judge, sir? They *moon* judges in Glasgow?'

Sharkey ignored her. '...flamboyant. Sent out a threat to the McQueen family on YouTube. Brazenly flaunts his wealth in public. Fancies himself a celebrity criminal. Drives an armour-plated BMW. Two years ago, both he and his older brother were abducted by the McQueen gang and taken out to the reservoirs near Barrhead...older bro was shot twice in the chest and twice in the back of the head—'

'Execution style, sir?'

'Aye, Jones, execution style. Execution bloody style. Tried same on Denny the Screwdriver, but the gun jammed. Stabbed 17 times. Had his throat slashed—'

Lyon-Jones interrupted again, 'Let me guess: lived to see another day and testified against McQueen family members.'

'Correct.' Sharkey wanted to wrap his hands around Lyon-Jones' throat. Keep them there for about an hour. Perhaps longer. 'Tattoo McQueen calls the shots from inside Bar-L...'

'Bar-L?'

Sharkey erupted. 'For the love of God, Jones, there's actually something you don't know? You see, you don't know what "Bar-L" is because you learnt about crime from a book. I learnt about crime from the street. You were just down the road, not stuck in a bog somewhere. There *is* life west of Edinburgh, you know? Haven't you ever heard of Bar-L? Y'know, the Big Hoose? The Riddrie Hilton? HM Prison *Barlinnie*?'

Sharkey made fists with both hands. Released. Made fists. Released. 'You're here on secondment, correct?'

'Correct, sir.' Cheeks on fire now.

'Where did you come from?'

'Northern Constabulary, sir.'

'Can you be more specific? That area's as big as Belgium.'

'Shetland Islands, sir.' Said proudly.

'Shetland Islands? Doing what? Do they even have crime up there? Some drunken bam try to nick the ferry? Some poor sheep got knocked down and you strung police tape around it? Wore forensic suits? Measured the skid marks?'

Lyon-Jones was annoyed, but not intimidated, and she saw where this was going, down the toilet—and fast. She had two choices or her dream career with the Strathclyde Police was going to be over before it began: She could bite back, or she could try to defuse the situation. The diploma hanging on her wall at home told her to defuse and disarm…and her gut instinct told her to try something bold and daring. This Detective Inspector Sharkey had been around, and he had seen it all. It better be good. Without being asked, Lyon-Jones rose, screeched her chair over to his computer, squeaked the screen round to face her, sat down and scooched her chair up close.

'Now what the hell are you doing?'

'Pulling up Decoy Brody's file.' Lyon-Jones was a psychologist. And this was all about 'transference'. Get Sharkey off her back, and back on to Brody…even though Sharkey wasn't allowed anywhere near that arena.

'This is not the time! Plus, you don't know my password—'

Lyon-Jones looked over at the Carolina Panthers football jersey on the wall.

'CAROLINA?'

'No!'

'CHARLOTTE?'

'No, Jones! Now get the fuck away from my computer or this will be the last day you set foot in this building—'

'AL PACINO...'

'What?'

'Your password is AL PACINO. Statistically, sir, 40 percent of passwords can be hacked within five minutes because the choice is simple-minded.' Fiona clicked the mouse. 'I'm in.'

Sharkey was beyond annoyed, but oddly mesmerized by Lyon-Jones. She was not at all like any other officers in his stable. 'Aren't you worried about Professional Standards?'

'Not my computer, sir.'

Lyon-Jones stared at the screen for a moment. Adjusted the brightness. 'You have a lot of unanswered emails here, Boss.'

'Please don't call me that.'

Lyon-Jones ignored Sharkey. Her fingers flew over the

keyboard. She made a few entries, perused the text on the screen, scrolled down, scrolled back up, perused some more then turned to Sharkey and recited what she'd read, verbatim. 'Okay, listen up...sir.'

Sharkey blew out his cheeks.

'At the age of 17, Decoy Brody entered the Royal Marines. Based at RM Condo, Arbroath. Deployed to South Armagh in December, 1990. Brody was credited with the kill of a Sinn Féin member near a checkpoint in Cullyhanna...'

Lyon-Jones stopped and looked up at Sharkey. She was pleased he was finally paying attention. 'Shortly thereafter, a young female student from Saint Catherine's college was found raped and left for dead in nearby Armagh. Brody was questioned and released.

'In 1991, Brody was deployed to Kuwait—'

'Kuwait?'

'Yes, sir, Kuwait. While on duty he was credited with the longest kill at the time, with a shot of nearly 1500 metres. Later that night a young Kuwaiti girl was found sodomised and had her throat cut—'

Sharkey's turn to interrupt. 'Jones?'

'Yes, sir?'

'You're not looking at the screen...'

'That's correct, sir.' Lyon-Jones was eidetic and carried on looking directly at her boss. 'Brody was tried, but acquitted. Back home, his name and likeness were splashed all over the papers and an Islamist group in the UK threatened his family. Upon his completion of military duty, he returned to Glasgow—'

Sharkey interrupted again. 'When was that?'

'Doesn't say.'

Sharkey made a note on his desk.

'Threats were made on Brody's life and his family's. During this time, his father was killed and Decoy was accused of the revenge murders of three Islamist terrorists, lads who had come up from Bradford. Charges never stuck—'

'Let me guess: There was no forensic evidence, or witnesses alive to file charges?'

'Correct, sir.'

Sharkey pulled out his mobile and hit speed dial. It was

picked up on the other end. 'Anything yet?' Sharkey rang off, then turned to Lyon-Jones. 'Is that it?'

'Just his two passions…'

'Let's have 'em.'

'Nothing out of the ordinary.'

'C'mon. C'mon. Let's have 'em.'

'Fishing and football.'

'Enough for today, Jones. Enough. You review the witness reports. You learn anything, you hear anything, you give me a bell.'

Lyon-Jones rose and exited, worried about her career.

More worried about her boss.

Sharkey picked up his landline and dialled. 'Hello, ma'am, it's me, Sharkey. I'd like to take your advice and take the rest of the day off…sort out some of Katie's things…Thank you, ma'am.'

Sharkey went to his computer. On the screen, a photo of Decoy Brody stared back at him. He reduced it 50 per cent and hit 'PRINT'.

# CHAPTER FIFTEEN

Sharkey was cold.

How long had he been sitting in the Polar Bear in the car park of the police station? His toes were numb, that's how long. The conundrum: If he could get an arrest. Get Decoy Brody behind bars. Get Spiked-Hair to testify. Then justice would prevail.

But it would not be the kind of justice he wanted.

Not the kind of justice he needed. Or could live with.

He cranked up the car, switched the wipers on and punched the heater, but the heater was thinking of taking the winter off and didn't comply. He swore under his breath. Swore out loud. Jammed the car in first. Raked through the gears. Fishtailed out on to Maitland Street and headed for the motorway.

A few minutes later, Sharkey exited at Junction 11 in Glasgow's East End, drove into the heart of Shettleston and parked in front of the Trinity Methodist Church at 1104 Shettleston Road. Like it or not, the timing being all wrong or not, there was one thing he had to do first. He had to do something for Katie. It's what she would have wanted.

He killed the engine, jumped out, opened the blue metal gate fronting the church and entered the hall at the back just as a meeting was beginning.

The assembled introduced themselves one-by-one, and then it was Sharkey's turn.

'My name is Ferris...I'm an alcoholic.'

# CHAPTER SIXTEEN

After the AA meeting, Sharkey motored past two businesses in the East End that reminded him of Katie: one called The Glasgow Smile was where she had had her braces fitted, and the other, the Ubiquitous Chib, was where he had purchased cutlery for her student flat. Is this what his life was now going to be like? Thinking of Katie every waking moment, whereas when she was alive he had barely given her any thought at all?

Sharkey drove up to Sharma's Takeaway at 1207 Shettleston Road. Sharma's was famous. People came from all over Glasgow to get their carry outs here. Katie had turned him on to Sharma's years ago. Up till then, he had probably been the only cop in Glasgow who didn't live on curry. Cops and curry. It was obligatory.

Sharkey wasn't hungry, but he wanted to be around someone he knew. Someone who had known Katie. He double parked and hurried inside. Standing behind the transom was an elderly gentleman with sad eyes. He was from Sylhet, in Bangladesh. No one working in an Indian restaurant in Glasgow ever hailed from India.

'Evening, Shahid.'

'Good evening to you, Mr Sharkey.' Unusually subdued.

*He knew.*

Sharkey didn't want to get into it. Couldn't get in to it without having his heart ripped out all over again.

Sharkey ordered and watched as Shahid quietly, respectfully, loaded three Styrofoam containers and carefully placed them in a plastic carrier bag. Then he added some extra chapattis and popadoms, trying to do his part without bringing the subject up. Shahid slid the takeaway across the counter like a screw slides a meal into a prisoner's cell.

Sharkey paid with exact change and watched as the elderly man placed the money in an old-fashioned till that snapped at him like that till in OPEN ALL HOURS.

Sharkey, keeping up the charade: 'Still on your game, Shahid.'

'It is being thirty-five years and it has only been catching me the once,' Shahid said, playing the desperate game.

Sharkey thanked his friend, stepped back outside and abruptly stopped. Hovering over the Polar Bear was a female traffic warden. She knew this car. Knew the owner. Smiled a sad smile when she saw Sharkey step out of the takeaway. 'Better get home before your carry out gets cold.' Staring at her feet now.

*She knew, too.*

Sharkey unlocked the Polar Bear, being careful not to disturb the spider web that magically appeared everyday on his wing mirror, then jumped in and turned the ignition. The Polar Bear backfired. It sounded like gunfire. Loud gunfire. Sharkey grimaced. The hole in the exhaust was getting bigger. He shot a wee shooftie into his rearview mirror and the few pedestrians who felt it necessary to be out in this crap weather had stopped walking and were huddled together like meerkats. Mortified, Sharkey shifted into first and slowly sputtered and polluted his way down to Wellshot Road. At Wellshot, he hung a left, braked as he passed the now derelict Cartyne Old Church of Scotland, then crossed over in front of a charging Eddie Stobart lorry and parked on the right side of the street between a skip and a Bingo Bus. Sharkey shut down the engine and stepped out, cradling his takeaway with both hands to keep warm.

He looked around: The East End of Glasgow. Where he had grown up. It would never be thought of as one of the garden spots of Scotland, but he loved it here. *Had loved it here.* He knew his neighbours. Knew everybody on his street. And he loved the colourful pubs, Parkhead, the funky Barras, the People's Palace in Glasgow Green, the Wellpark Brewery home of Tennent's Lager (perhaps that should have been closer to the top of his list), even the Barrowland Ballroom where he had taken Katie to see Ozzy Osbourne, Oasis, and Ned's Atomic Dustbin. Sure, the East End was a bit removed and owing to chronic medical and social problems had the lowest life expectancy for males in the UK at just 53.9 years.

Crazy, that thought coming into his mind right then, he would have to live almost another 14 years to hit 53.9.

At the moment, he didn't know how he was going to make it till tomorrow.

He balanced his takeaway and tried to beep the driver's door locked, having forgot that the key fob was broken. But now it worked just fine. He glanced up at his down-at-heel, rented, one-bedroom flat just above the haberdashery. Then he turned his attention to the flat above his: a curtain twitched. *His neighbour knew. Deaf old lady Gladstone knew.*

Sharkey darted across the street, dodged a speeding white van with WALES HAS THE BEST FAGGOTS painted on its side, made it to the safety of the kerb and froze: The communal entrance door to the flats above was slightly ajar. This NEVER happened. The residents were vigilant. Had to be in this neighbourhood.

Sharkey set his vindaloo on the pavement. Nudged the entrance door with his foot and slipped into a darkened close that smelt of sour urine. The lights were on a timer. Sharkey felt along the wall. Flipped the switch. Nothing.

He took a baby step forward. Then another. He could hear laboured breathing coming from down on the floor, just in front of him. Even though he couldn't see, Sharkey aimed his mobile at the source. Punched a button with his thumb and used the light from the screen to illuminate the floor. He saw the soles of a pair of badly worn shoes. A pair of legs in ratty trousers. A thorax wearing a heavy ski jacket. Finally the face. A bearded face. A jolt of electricity shot through his body and he gasped.

He knew this man.

# CHAPTER SEVENTEEN

Sharkey leaned closer to the bearded man lying on the floor.

'Evenin' tae ye, Mr Sharkey!'

'For the love of God, Donny!'

'Heard yer motor comin' doon Shotwell. It'll nae pass its MoT.'

'You cannae be in here, Donny'

'Jist tryin' tae keep warm.'

'And you know I'll look the other way…'

'Aye. Ye always been good tae me.'

'You had a hit-or-a-miss in here, Donny, it reeks of pish?'

'Never, Mr Sharkey, ye know I respect yer hoose.'

Sharkey closed the communal entrance door. Then he remembered his carry out and opened it back up. The carry out was gone. Nicked by some lowlife bottom-feeder who was keen on vindaloo. For fuck's sake.

He aimed for the stairs, taking two at a time.

'G'night, Mr Sharkey.'

'Still using, by the way?'

'Squeaky clean, Mr Sharkey. Almost three months now.'

'Night tae ye, then, Donny.'

'Night.'

Sharkey reached his landing and stopped.

*Donny didn't know.*

Sharkey used his mobile again for light and inserted the key into the mortice lock to his flat. Then he took another key and opened a Yale lock high on the door. Then yet another key and opened another Yale lock down near the floor. Before entering, he pushed the door open a crack and flipped on the lights. Something he had picked up in America: Unlock, open door, turn on lights, all before stepping a foot inside. This was his daily routine. He had learnt it the hard way.

He closed the door, locked all the locks, then crossed to an old CD player and, out of habit, jabbed the POWER button. The CD skipped. Skipped again. Country & Western music seeped out. 'Achy Breaky Heart'. Quickly he hit the button and killed the music.

Sharkey did fifty angry press-ups. A hundred incensed sit-ups. Thirty pissed-off chin-ups. He took a shower, let the hot water nearly scald his skin and tried to wash away a lifetime that wouldn't wash away. Then the water went cold. Ice cold. It always did. Usually he bolted, but this time he stayed in until his teeth were chattering. He felt exhausted after the shower. He towelled off, and pulled on jeans, a T-shirt, a fleece and a pair of black-cherry cowboy boots. He moved into the kitchen, opened his fridge and peered in. The only item in there was an opened box of bicarbonate of soda. What happened to that last ping-ping meal? He closed the door to the fridge and opened the door to the cupboard. There were three tubes of salt & vinegar Pringles, a Snickers and an opened bag of tangy cheese Doritos. Big decision. He grabbed the Doritos. Moved a week's dirty dishes around in the sink. Exhumed a tumbler. Swilled some cold water into it. Opened the cupboard above the sink and peered at two bottles of Scotland's finest whisky: one was Grouse, the other Dalwhinnie. Sharkey lovingly fingered the expensive bottle of Dalwhinnie, but pulled down the bottle of Low Flyer instead. He glugged in a few fingers into the tumbler. He stared at the tumbler in his hand and his hand was shaking so badly he could only just keep from spilling the whisky. Sharkey sniffed the fiery aroma, inhaled the fumes and licked his lips. *Daddy, why do you always need to drink so much?* He removed a small funnel from a kitchen drawer and, with fumbling hands, poured the Grouse back into the bottle and repaired to a sad, wee living room and a radiator with issues.

The living room was Spartan, by design, minimalist by 'being a lazy fucking sod' (as his ex-wife had so oft reminded him): no curtains on the bay window, no pictures on the walls and no telly. Just books. Books everywhere, stacked high like a city's high-rise skyline. And boxes that he had never unpacked containing a life he no longer had. Boxes labeled: photos, kitchen, bathroom and sock drawer.

Sharkey needed to escape right then and there, so he did what he always did in time of need: He fired up his laptop and Googled radio station WXKW 104.9 in Key West, Florida. Came up with www.keywestshow.com

The station was pirate radio at its best, and the on-air host this time of night was a madman named Gary Ek, known affectionately down there at the end of the world as the Soundman From Hell.

A destination, Sharkey would be visiting sooner rather than later, and he wasn't thinking about Key West.

Sharkey listened to Key West Chris sing one of the Trop-Rock songs he's famous for, then switched on a two-bar electric fire and took a seat in his dentist's chair. The flat had once been used by the dental surgery downstairs, next to the haberdashery. The dentist's chair had been left behind when the dentist was imprisoned for filling female patients' mouths with his organ instead of the amalgam after they had been administered 'conscious sedation'. When Sharkey had moved in, his landlord had promised to have the chair removed, but never did. Sharkey had tried to shift it himself, but the dentist's chair was bolted to the floor. He had tried to unbolt it, but the bolts were stripped. After an hour of struggling with no victory in sight, Sharkey had thrown his hands in the air.

The chair had won.

Then he sat in it.

*And crikey it was comfortable.*

Without the spectre of the drill. And needle. And spittoon. And conscious sedation.

By the time he'd bought proper furniture, he had bonded with the chair and decided he couldn't part with it.

Men who lack female supervision.

Men who no longer live with their family.

*Family.*

Sharkey popped a Dorito in to his mouth. It was stale. Bugger it, he had another one. He liked the salt. And that tangy chemical shit. Out the bay window and down on the street, he could see a red handicapped scooter parked in front of the Cottage Bar across the road. A few rough lads stood in the doorway sheltering under the orange sodium glow of a streetlight, stomping their feet and smoking. He'd kill for a fag right now, but he was trying desperately to quit. Yeah, right, like that was ever going to happen. Like he even wanted it to happen.

Sharkey went to his wardrobe and pulled out the football strip that Katie would wear when they went to the games. He smelt it and held it close. He went back into the living room and picked up the cardboard box labelled 'photos'. Took a few out. Sat back in the dentist's chair. Looked at the photos.

And cried his eyes out.

# CHAPTER EIGHTEEN

Across from the red, Dumfriesshire-sandstone façade of the King's Theatre on Bath Street in the Glasgow City Centre, was Massimo, an Italian restaurant where many theatre goers dined pre-curtain, or as in the case tonight, pre-*panto* curtain.

In the back, along the wall that separates the kitchen from the dining area, two tables had been pushed together. Seated here was Denny the Screwdriver Sutherland, his overly tanned, electric-pink-lippy wife Jade, and their two weans.

Jade and the kids were there to enjoy the panto, the Screwdriver was there to meet Decoy Brody and pay him with a kilo of coke secreted in a Cadbury Roses tin.

There was no better cover than a wife and the wee ones.

The children were hyper and excited to be going to the panto. Or perhaps that was from the chocolates removed from the tin to make room for the blow. To make a lasting impression on the primogenital son, the Screwdriver took a roll of hundred pound notes out of a pocket and slapped one on the table in front of nine-year-old Denny, Jr. 'That C-note is yers if ye can make it tae sixteen without getting nicked!'

'What about wee Drew?' Jade whined.

The Screwdriver slapped another hundred in front of eight-year-old Drew. 'And that, ma pet, is all yers if ye can make it tae fourteen without getting up the spout!'

Both children reached for what they presumed was rightfully theirs, then the Screwdriver snatched both C-notes back. Motivation.

The Screwdriver consulted his watch.

*Where the fuck was Decoy?*

His mobile jangled. The Screwdriver looked at the caller ID, murmured 'Shit!' loud enough for both children to hear. Then an aside to his wife: 'It's the Pouch.' Answered. 'Hiya, Da…'

On the other end, Jimmy the Pouch was livid. 'What the fuck kind of an operation are you running up there, laddie? Killing an inspector's kid! Have ye gone mental?'

'Sorry, Da, it's just that—'

'DON'T FUCKIN' INTERRUPT ME!'

'Yes, sir.'

'Have I not taught ye tae keep below the radar? Do I have tae come up there and wipe yer arse for ye?'

'No, sir.'

'What did Decoy have tae say for himself?'

'He's late—'

'What!'

'I'll kick his arse when he gets here. I promise ye, Da.'

'Ye fuckin' better! Ye fuckin' better get yer heid out of yer arse!' The Pouch slammed his phone shut. Mumbled to himself, 'Never should've had the vasectomy reversed!'

The Screwdriver slowly closed his mobile. At forty, he was still afraid of his father. He shot a glance over at his wife. She was smiling back at him.

'I love it when ye stand up to yer father like that.' Jade blinked her spider lashes and regarded her husband's good looks with the glow that only comes from true love, devotion and being filthy rich. Filthy rich in this case meant dirty money. Not bad for a wee shite who never finished school. But then neither had she. Who needed an education when you had a body like Pamela fucking Anderson?

Plus there was more: Her husband was popping for a third round of cosmetic surgery. And if that wasn't romantic, Jade didn't know what was. Besides the bum-lift, he was paying for her to have a prosthetic hymen fitted so they could celebrate her virginity all over again. This thrilled Jade to no end because she had been so fucked up on jellies and diet pills, she couldn't remember how she lost it the first time around.

The Screwdriver suddenly scraped his chair back and hissed under his breath, 'There he is. About fucking time!'

Decoy Brody stood just inside the front door. But he wasn't paying any notice to the Screwdriver and his family in the back of the restaurant, he was undressing three young lasses with his eyes who were seated up by the front window.

The Screwdriver grabbed a WH Smith bag with the Cadbury Roses tin off the floor and stepped outside with Decoy. He planned to chew Decoy a new arsehole for his freelance shenanigans.

Jade waited until her husband and Decoy were out the front door, then she snapped her fingers at a waiter from Poland and quickly ordered another large *rioja*.

Her second large *rioja* in a ten-minute span arrived and Jade gulped at it like a camel that was running on empty. The buzz kicking in, she regarded her children. Drew was texting a friend. Denny, Jr. was playing *Grand Theft Auto* on his iPhone (as a thug-in-waiting should). This indulgence brought a warm and tingly feeling to Jade because she could concentrate on the second *rioja* and not have to deal with the wee bastards. Some days she wished she could just give them back. Trade them in for anything, really, anything that wasn't so clingy and demanding of her time.

Outside, Decoy and the Screwdriver were smoking ciggies.

The Screwdriver was not a happy-camper. 'Are ye up to yer old tricks, Decoy? If ye haven't figured it out all on yer own by now, let me be the one tae tell ye: That was Detective Inspector Sharkey's daughter ye nearly decapitated. He's one mean son-of-a-fucking-bitch, that Sharkey, and if he starts sniffing around, the pigs will be on us like flies on a pile of pig shit. That, I donnae need. And what about the Kingston? There was one survivor. Ye fucked up, Decoy. Weren't supposed to be any survivors, they all needed to be silenced. So, what are ye goin' tae do about it?'

Decoy, not alarmed, not defensive, frightfully submissive. 'Gee, Boss, I used an accelerant and everything. That should have done the trick. I don't want any agro from anybody, least of all you. I'll make it right. I promise. Ye got my coke?'

'Ye get the blow when ye deal with the survivor...'

'Yes, sir. Yes, sir. Completely understand. Yer always right. Yer the captain of the ship. Ye hold on to the coke...'

The Screwdriver gave pause. Christ, how was he going to enjoy the panto with a kilo of Class A drugs resting on his sodding lap? He was hoping for a cheeky hand job when the Widow Twankey strutted out and the weans were glued to all the action down on the stage.

'Here, ye take it Decoy...but *take care of it*, and I'm not talking about the Charlie.' The Screwdriver handed over the WH Smith bag.

Decoy Brody wet his lips, intoned sincerely. 'For another tin of Roses, I'll make the detective inspector go away.'

The Screwdriver looked at Decoy Brody long and hard. 'For a dim-shite ye come up with some fucking good ideas. Let me chew on that one, amigo.'

Decoy gave the Screwdriver a big school-boy grin.

The Screwdriver grinned back. Christ, Decoy was a sick, twisted motherfucker. Docile like a puppy one moment, vicious like a rabid Rottweiler the next. And he was happy as fucking Larry to have Decoy under his control.

Decoy slipped off into the night.

The Screwdriver watched him go, for some reason got the shivers and not from the cold, then he peeped in through the front window of the restaurant. He watched Jade and the kids for a moment. Bless their innocent little hearts. They were really enjoying the 'family together' night. The kids were playing with their gadgets. Jade had a wistful smile on her face.

The Screwdriver wondered what his wife was thinking...

His wife sucked greedily on her *rioja* and thought about how lucky she was to have a family. She truly loved them to death and in a few days she would be able to show her affection even more when they moved into the big new house and got the nanny so she could get away from the wee brats and really learn to appreciate them. They did get on her nerves. Christ, nonstop noise, wanting attention every goddamn minute of the day and night, asking questions all the time about every goddamn thing, and every five minutes was another crisis. *Children have to understand it's not all about them!* Aye, soon life would be good in the new house overlooking Whitecraigs Golf Club and they could move out of the shit terraced house they now occupied in Govan. Would they miss Govan? Sure. They'd purchased the terraced houses on either side of their own home with hard-earned drug money and knocked out the walls, essentially creating a fortress. And then they'd purchased the terraced houses on each end of those to use for storage. So that was a plus. And the Sutherland lieutenants had driven other families out of the housing scheme who were a bit too righteous and felt it was their duty to summon the police for normal activities like loud music or the occasional all-night, alcohol-and-drug-fuelled party. After the culling of the neighbours, the remaining residents were now mostly lads and their partners who worked in one capacity or another for her husband, so the Screwdriver now owned the street. So that was a plus. It wasn't Shangri-fucking-La, but it had become downright dangerous for any unwanted outsiders to go in there. And, of course, the polis weren't so very keen to venture in. So that was a plus, as well.

Oh, they would keep their base in the low-rent section of Govan for business purposes, mind, but it was time to reside in a more upmarket postal code.

After all, they had earned it.

Overlooking one of Glasgow's finer golf courses was not the draw for Jade, and she wasn't about to take up the game of golf and have to chitty chat with all those snobby old biddies who would just talk down to her and scoff at the way she dressed (like a tart). She just wanted to impress all her mates and prance about a bit and show off her tits (even though they weren't real), the tattoo of a gun on her right breast and her new 60's fringe cut (which in reality looked more fringe festival), and if one of them righteous bitches dared to look her way, she'd hit 'em with, 'Whit the fuck ye looking act!' and that would shut the rich old crow up.

It was just a small price she would have to pay to move up the property ladder.

Perhaps she would get Denny, Jr. in the Scouts at the Giffnock Scout Hall. The historical fact that Nazi Rudolf Hess was locked up in there during World War II after parachuting from his plane would, of course, be lost on Jade, what with her not finishing school and being only as clever as a rug beater.

The Screwdriver continued to watch through the window.

Now, he *knew* what Jade was thinking: She was hoping to get laid after they got the weans in bed.

Close, but no cigar.

Jade was thinking: Just up the Ayr Road from their new home was Parklands Country Club. She used to go there before she was married and sit in Michael's Bar when a Rangers football match was on the telly. She got laid nearly every time she went, but never found her dream man, until she found the Screwdriver who was working as a bouncer at his dad's club on Sauchiehall Street. She'd go back to Parklands, mind you, to strut about, the new queen of Whitecraigs, and she wouldn't feel at all like the slut she used to when she bleached her bum-hole and went there to pick up the sons of rich Newton Mearns businessmen, who thought she had an upper-crust body, but a less than common accent and the intellect of an aubergine.

At least her husband didn't feel like he had married down.

Perhaps they could build an enclosed pool at their new spread, so she could keep out of the wind when it was warm enough to lie out. Okay, okay, *if* it was warm enough to lie out. Then she could stop visiting the tanning salons her husband owned where no one ever wiped down the bed between sessions...or after having sex.

She looked up and saw her beloved Screwdriver smiling at her through the front window.

She looked at spunky Denny, Jr. and puckish Drew.

The family was having a meal out and going to the panto.

And life was soon going to be idyllic.

Oh, yes it was.

Oh, no it wasn't.

# CHAPTER NINETEEN

A tear dripped down on to one of Sharkey's family photos. He wiped it away with a thumb.

He went to a deep stack of books next to the front window, extracted the Bible and opened it to Matthew 5:38...an 'Eye for an Eye'. Here, the pages had been cut out of the middle of the great book. He pulled out the .38 calibre Smith & Wesson snub-nose he had brought back from America illegally. It had been frightfully simple to smuggle a gun into the UK. He had hidden it in a hairdryer.

The Bible, how appropriate, Sharkey thought: verse 38...Smith & Wesson .38...

Sharkey checked the chamber. Jammed the gun in the back of his jeans, snatched his airwave radio off the kitchen table and set about unlocking locks.

Within minutes, he was on the M77, climbing out of the Clyde basin, leaving Glasgow behind in a sodium-glow mist. He turned down the volume on his Airwave radio. Flipped on the car radio: Searched for a News station. Heard nothing but talk of depression, recession, meltdown and collapse. Changed stations and heard woeful moans of cash, credit crisis and crunch. Changed again. Talk of the upcoming game: Rangers hosting lowly St Mirren. Hit another station: Christmas music. Christmas music was a no-go genre. He tried a few CDs, but the music just conjured up images that he didn't want conjured up at this particular moment. Perhaps never again.

Twenty minutes later, he had climbed up to the Fenwick Moor and the rain had turned to snow. And the snow was beginning to stick. The perfect scenario for black ice. Not a night to be out, but what the fuck was he supposed to do now? Stay back in his shit flat that was a B-movie trailer of his shit life? His life where he had failed as a husband—and as a father.

Black ice?

Fuck it.

Sharkey mashed the accelerator to the floor.

Close to the village of Fenwick, Sharkey jerked the Polar Bear off the motorway, skidded at the roundabout, fishtailed back under the M77 and headed in the direction of Stewarton. The road was void of traffic and there were no tracks in the pristine snow as he steered the Rover under the Stewarton railway bridge and carried on up the hill to the hamlet of Dunlop.

At the far end of Dunlop were new council flats, which disconcertingly looked like old council flats. A few had Christmas lights in the windows. One had blue and white lights for Hanukka. Here, Sharkey turned right down a deeply rutted, snow-covered dirt road and felt as if he were in a rodeo for nearly a mile. The Polar Bear hit a deep pothole and this somehow goosed the heater but killed the lights. The heater now pumped out so much heat, Sharkey had to turn it down.

And then the lights came back on.

He slowed. In front of him was a two-storey, stone farmhouse with a crumbling barn out back. A beckoning light flickered within the farmhouse on the ground floor and smoke rose from a single chimney.

The snow was coming down heavily as Sharkey turned off the ignition, waited for the engine to stop juddering and climbed out. He looked about at the silent, idyllic-at-any-other-time winter landscape, then hurried up to the front door of the farmhouse. Before he could knock, the door swung open, revealing a wizened man in a wheelchair with a tartan travel rug across his lap. The man wore a stoma filter and didn't speak, just spun around in his wheelchair and moved deeper into the house. Sharkey closed the front door and followed him into the kitchen where the old man flipped on a light, went to the refrigerator and pulled out an opened box of bicarbonate of soda. He handed the box to Sharkey. Sharkey stuck a finger in the box, probed around and pulled out a single key. He gave the box back to the older gentleman who replaced it in the fridge. The old man wheeled to a cupboard next to the sink, opened it, extracted a dusty unopened bottle of Dalwhinnie, handed it to Sharkey, then wheeled into the living room and pulled up in front of the fireplace.

Sharkey watched the old man as he sat in front of the fire, staring into the flames. Without taking his eyes off the fire, the old man removed the tartan travel rug from his lap and placed a pistol on a side table.

Sharkey went to a back door off the kitchen, opened it and stepped outside.

He trudged through a few inches of snow to the barn, unlocked it with the key he had exhumed from the bicarbonate of soda and flipped on an overhead light. As the overhead light flickered to life, a wave of mixed emotions flooded over Sharkey.

Resting in front of him was a bright-red Mustang GT, with left-hand steering.

Sharkey approached his beloved motor. Ran a finger along the side. Took his sleeve and buffed the nearside bonnet. Actually kicked a tyre.

He crossed to a nearby cupboard, coaxed a ripped, dog-eared cardboard box out from under a stack of crushed boxes and rested it on top of the work surface. Next to the box, he lined up a series of photos. The first photo was of when life was good: Sharkey, his wife and two smiley kids at the Highland Games up in the mountains of North Carolina. The second photo was of Katie in pigtails proudly holding up a fish that she had just caught. The third photo depicted him wearing the dark blue of the Charlotte-Mecklenburg Police Department in North Carolina. The fourth was a United States Marine Corps photo of him in full camouflage and painted face. The final photo was the printout of Decoy Brody.

Sharkey left the photos on the workbench and moved to a sliding door at the back of the barn, behind the Mustang. He removed a Hide-a-Key from the wheel-well of the Mustang, then unlocked the sliding door and shoved it off to the left. He flipped on another light, illuminating a room that resembled a safe room or panic room: Kevlar fortified walls, deadbolt with lock-plate screws, no windows, secure ventilation, monitor for external cameras, dumbbells, a portable commode, a single bed and provisions for a fortnight.

Displayed along the walls of the room was an impressive arsenal of weapons, weapons the untrained eye wouldn't be able to identify: a Marine Corps M-4OA3 sniper rifle, a CheyTac Intervention M-200 sniper rifle (like the one Mark Wahlberg used in the movie *Shooter*), a Micro-Uzi, a SCAR-LIGHT, an XM-25 (with microchip-embedded explosive rounds that can be detonated at precise ranges), a CORNER SHOT LAUNCHER (a video screen allowed users to shoot *around* corners) and a HAND-HELD ROCKET LAUNCHER. A veritable assassin's gallery of state-of-the-art weaponry. But Sharkey didn't take any of the high-tech killing machines, just a pair of miniature earphones, a device which looked to be a SAT-NAV, a small square of clear plastic film with five sticky dots the size of pencil erasers and a serrated fish filleting knife. Then he threw on a Carolina Panthers sweatshirt and a Carolina Panthers ski jacket, and packed his toys into a black leather satchel with the letters USMC embossed in gold.

Wait! He forgot something! He crossed to an old deep freezer purring away in a far corner. Opened the lid. Extracted two good-sized T-bone steaks. Closed the lid. Now he was ready to rumble.

Sharkey jumped back in the Polar Bear. Opened the bottle of whisky. Took a hellacious slug. Then another. He switched on the heater to defrost the T-bones. Prayed the heater would hold. And headed down the potholed road he had come in on and back toward Glasgow.

He had decided how he was going to kill Decoy Brody.

He would rip out his throat with the filleting knife as Decoy had ripped his wee Katie's throat out.

But he needed to find him before the police did.

## CHAPTER TWENTY

Pizza Face wiped his nose on the sleeve of his Nike Aero Full-Zip hoodie, fingered his sovvy ring and peered down Argyle Street. No movement other than a prossie entering the Alexander Thompson hotel. Fuck-a-duck, he couldn't believe the Screwdriver expected him to be back out on the street dealing drugs the day after his first hit. And why had they moved him from the Saltmarket over to here? Hadn't he done a killing selling to the recovering addicts over at Hope House?

Pizza Face had hoped for an all-expenses-paid hol down on the Costa del Crime where the Pouch lived. He'd never been to Benidorm, mind you, but he had once eye-balled some colour pictures in a brochure at a First Choice branch over near the Buckfast Triangle.

He raked his sinuses. Spat. Lit a fag with trembling hands. For fuck's sake, he was still trembling like a fucking toy poodle. He'd have to munch a couple jellies to stop the jitters. Sure, he may have banjoed and bottled his fair share, and given enough malkies to make an impression, but he had never wasted anyone before.

And he had never used a shotgun before.

He was shiting himself.

Shiting himself, big time.

Pizza Face nervously tugged the tunnel earring on his left ear. If he could just tell someone that he had killed a man. That would make him feel better. Brag to his mates. Boast to the ladies. But he had taken an oath of silence when he had joined the Sutherland gang, and he was all about loyalty. He knew what happened to those with a rubbery gub.

No, he could never tell anyone.

Not a soul in Glesga would have ever looked at Pizza Face and thought of him as someone to fear—and that's why he got the gig. He was a pure-dead skinny ned with an Adam's apple like a love-sick testicle. A rival gang member had made fun of him once and ended up with a Glasgow smile. Pizza Face could be quite the surgeon with a Stanley knife.

He checked his position on the street, being sure to stay within the pitch his handlers had chalked off, so he wouldn't be captured by the CCTV camera down on the corner of Wellington. Then he looked up and down Argyle Street. Where the fuck was Fat Cheeks? Fucking mucker was late. Fat Cheeks was supposed to be towing the line with him tonight. How was he supposed to provide professional customer service without a lookout?

A spitting wind swirled a blizzard of litter his way. Pizza Face adjusted his hoodie against the blast and observed the detritus as it floated by: McDonald's, KFC, The Body Shop, Garage Shoes, Millie's Cookies, and something called Ferrero Rocher. Wind must be out of the St Enoch Shopping Centre.

Pizza Face wished he had a long scar on his face, but he didn't want to endure the pain or terror in order to get one. He was happy to inflict pain, but wanted nothing to do with being on the receiving end.

Perhaps he could look into cosmetic surgery.

He bent over and tucked his bright-white trackies into his bright-white socks, as dictated by *gansta fashion*. Then he stood up straight and yanked the trackies up over his arse. They were always hanging off his bahookie. He thought the statement cool, but decided to forgo it tonight, what with the Baltic wind.

And nobody around to be offended.

Nature called. Pizza Face pulled out his boabie. Had a slash in the recessed doorway behind him. Careful not to splash the bottle of Buckie he had secreted there. With hygiene always a concern, he was conscientious about not getting any pish on his new Nikes either. They had cost over a hundred fucking quid. Not that money would matter anymore once the Sutherland family greased his palm for this afternoon's extra-fucking-curricular activities. They *would* pay him, wouldn't they? Shite, now he was getting paranoid. Fuck that, not only would they pay him, they would probably give him a bonus. Want to keep him happy.

Bring him into the fold.

Groom him for bigger and better deeds.

Epic!

After he was paid, he would go see that heavy stunner from Possil. The hot senga with the cheap foundation, the hoop earrings and the shag-me shoes he'd met under the clock at Central Station. She lived with her maw, but fuck that, she said her maw didn't give a flaming rat's arse if he spent the night as long as they kept down the fucking noise and didn't get into her Stellas or JD.

Damn, what was the lass's name? Emma? Gemma? Jenna? Morag? Fuck knows, he'd figure it out when he got there. He'd flash a wad of boudo in her face. Prove he wasn't glaikit like all the other lasses said. And straightaway she'd start with a sooky and then open the skid racks for him. Fucking A, he'd go in without a Johnny. Hated Johnnys. Took away the feel. If there was a problem, he'd know how to deal with it. He knew 'bout things.

Shite, he was king now.

Invincible.

Plus, if there was a problem, he could always just walk away.

Genius!

He spat on the pavement. Rubbed a hand under his nose. Took up the obligatory menacing posture with the Robert DeNiro snarl. For Pizza Face life couldn't get any better. Or could it?

Tomorrow was his birthday.

He was going to be sixteen.

If he lived that long.

* * *

A red BMW motored slowly down Argyle Street, coming Pizza Face's way.

And he didn't like the look of it. He stepped back into the shadows, wishing he hadn't worn the fucking beacon in the form of his blinding-white trackies and watched the Beemer carefully as it cruised by. Then he almost shit himself. Inside the ride were five blokes, all ballied up. Fucking hell, why were they masked up? Pizza Face didn't know what to do. What if they were looking for him? What if they knew he had offed the McQueen lad and were coming to slice him up? He crouched down low in the shadows and hit Fat Cheeks' number on his mobile. Fat Cheeks was supposed to be here by now, being his edgy. Ensuring he didn't get fucking bumped. Shite, he'd take bumped to dead, right now. Where the fuck was Fat Cheeks?

Pizza Face's mobile buzzed at the other end and was finally picked up with, 'Wass-up?'

'Fat Cheeks! Where the fuck are ye?'

'Chill, mate, I'm on the bus. I'll get there when I get there.' And then he rang off.

Fucking cunt! He didn't need the agro. If Fat Cheeks only knew what he had done, then he would show him some respect.

Pizza Face looked down the street and couldn't believe his fucking eyes. The red BMW was back, moving even slower this time, the way a motor moves when the occupants are looking for something and can't find it. He thought about making a run for the Alexander Thompson, but the management took to locking the doors of late to exclude 'certain elements' (probably tourists) and he couldn't risk it. He slipped into the deeply recessed store front of the old Victor Morris shop and got down flat on the ground, soiling his new trackies in cat shite. The red BMW crawled closer and closer. And stopped. A ballied lad in a dark Adi-bok shellsuit climbed out the back and took a step towards Pizza Face, then turned and went to a neighbouring store front and had a nice long pish, unfortunately splashing all over Pizza Face's secreted bottle of Buckie.

Shellsuit Lad shook off his dick, then calmly turned, and on that, as if it were some sort of a signal, the four other lads in the BMW threw open the doors and jumped out. One carried a baseball bat, another a machete, the third a meat hook, the fourth a Samurai sword.

Pizza Face watched in horror as the five ballied men rushed him.

He would have pissed his trackies if he hadn't emptied his bladder half-an-hour earlier. His life flashed before him and it wasn't a long trailer. Or very impressive. He was about to die. Die at the hands of these five, as Tattoo McQueen's number-one son had died at his hands. Life was all about death. Would they cut out his tongue? Would there be retribution in the form of a Glasgow send-off? It was done with a knife sometimes. Would they do it with the meat hook? *While he was still alive!* He wasn't king. He was just a piece of insignificant shite, the next fucking Weegie statistic and he wouldn't even make page five in the *Daily Record*.

He couldn't run. And he couldn't fight. There was only one thing left to do. He stood up, put his hands in the air and vomited.

And this somehow froze the murderous five. And do you know why? They burst into laughter. Fall-down, in-your-face, slap-the-ground laughter. And then the heaviest thug of the five whipped off his balaclava, exposing a round face crowned with multiple gelled-fringe spikes.

And Pizza Face stared into his eyes. 'Fat Cheeks? Whit the fuck?'

'Yer stinking o' cat poo and ye boaked! We scared the living shite oot of ye, and ye boaked all over yer new Nikes. Yer so gay!'

# CHAPTER TWENTY-ONE

Halfway between Ibrox Stadium and where an old Singer Sewing Machine factory had once been located was a rundown four-storey brick warehouse with large double doors on the ground floor. The warehouse was derelict, excluding the section with the double doors. This was now used as a garage. This was where you might take your motor to have its MoT.

But only if you were a Blue Nose.

Above the double doors a poorly illuminated blue-and-white sign read: SUTHERLAND MOTORS. Other than the garage, the entire area was dark and desolate, located in a godforsaken no-man's land of crumbling abandoned tenements and boarded up factories.

Across the street, Sharkey sat in the Polar Bear. Drinking straight from the bottle of whisky. Observing. Thinking. Still trying to get his head around what had happened, and then realising he would never get his head around what had happened.

His initial game plan had been to dispatch Decoy Brody, rebuild his life, stick with the Force, try to do good. But for what?

Sharkey was intelligent enough to know he was losing it emotionally. Knew he had to find Decoy before the sand ran out in his hourglass.

He looked back over at Sutherland Motors.

Wind and sleet. A filthy night. He grabbed the two T-bone steaks and stepped from the car.

Sharkey moved quietly, cautiously, like the best Indian scout. He spied the CCTV cameras on the corners of the building and hugged the wall. He moved toward the large garage doors. Ears straining. Sleet turning to rain. Rain stoating the ground now. Pant legs sticking to his shins and uncomfortable as hell, but the sound of the downpour masking his steps. Or so he thought until he heard the low rumbling growl. Sharkey unwrapped the now defrosted T-bones. Chucked them over a chain-link fence to two slabbering pit bulls. Guard dogs from hell. That would keep the wee bastards quiet, just as it had kept two guard dogs quiet at a liquor warehouse in the East End he had broken into back when he was in a gang.

Sharkey scaled the fence and shimmied down the other side into the unwelcoming domain of the pit bulls. The area reeked of doggy poo and wet killer-doggy fur. Neither pit bull even looked up, lest the lapse in concentration at the matter in hand resulted in having its precious and unattended T-bone set upon by about a thousand pointy teeth.

He tried the first window. A window which led to the garage. It was unlocked. No need to secure it what with the brothers very grim out here to prevent access and create teethy bother. Or not. Sharkey slid the window open. Slipped inside. Dark as your Auntie Dot's larder in here. He waited until his eyes adjusted to the dark. When they didn't, he pulled his mobile out of the pocket. Illuminated it. Had a nose around. The usual garage detritus: oily rags, old tyres, rusted exhausts. Then a surprise.

Hidden nearly out of sight in a far corner was a bright-red motorcycle.

Sharkey aimed his mobile at the back end of the bike and took a photo of the license plate. He jammed the mobile back in his pocket and moved slowly back toward the open window he had come in.

He scarpered back out the window. Stepped in a steaming pile of dog shit. Moved past the muscle-bound pit bulls who were now licking their chops and regarding Sharkey.

Sharkey hissed, just audible above the rain: 'Don't you dare even think about wagging your tails at me.' And then he was up and over the fence. All those chin-ups were paying off.

Sharkey scraped his shoe on the tarmac and jumped in the Polar Bear. Shook himself out of his drenched windbreaker. Started up the Rover. Turned up the blower and aimed for the West End. He called in the license plate number to a friend of his who used to be in his gang. The bloke now worked at the

70

DVLA. He got the job on account of knowing so much about cars—stealing cars—although that bit of background info had gone unmentioned at the interview.

Sharkey held on the line. The friend came back on. The motorcycle was registered to Denny Sutherland. Denny-the-fucking-Screwdriver Sutherland.

Shit!

Sharkey drove down Paisley Road West, crossed the river on the Squinty Bridge and cruised the university district. He parked the Polar Bear just off Byres Road, not far from where Katie had lived, and walked over to Ashton Lane and The Stud. As he moved through the lane, he looked up at the fairy lights which were strung overhead. Why hadn't he ever noticed these when he'd met Katie here for a meal? He looked up and down the lane. Why hadn't he ever noticed how romantic and continental this wee cobbled lane was until right now? Where had his head been at when he'd spent 'quality time' with Katie? On work? On women? On booze? On anything, but Katie. *Katie.* He knew she liked to hang out here at all times of the day and night. But he had never worried for her safety. Not here in Ashton Lane. Not here in the West End. By the university...

He stepped inside The Stud. It was filled with the usual mix of young students, just like Katie. Young people doing what young people do: laughing, teasing, drinking, flirting, kissing, planning. Their whole lives ahead of them.

Why did Decoy Brody commit murder and then go pick up a young girl? What twisted motivation existed? Who could kill in cold blood and then make heated love? Ugly images kept rearing their ugly heads. But Sharkey was beyond being a grieving father. He was bent on revenge and he would not rest until he had tasted Decoy's blood.

He walked up to a young hostess and identified himself by showing his warrant card.

She looked him up and down. 'Police were already here.' Not attitude, just stating a fact.

Sharkey showed her the picture of Decoy Brody. 'Have you ever seen this man?'

'Yes, sir, last night. I saw him in here last night.'

'Sure?'

71

'Oh, aye, don't get many blokes like him in here.'

'How so?'

'A bit older.'

'Anything else?'

'A cut above the rest. Seriously good-looking.'

'Did he come in here regularly?'

'First time I saw him.'

Sharkey thanked the hostess and turned to go.

'Sir?'

'Yes?'

'She looked really happy.'

Sharkey repeated it, unsure what the hostess meant. 'She looked really happy?'

'The girl he left with.'

Sharkey exited The Stud. Walked back along the cobbled lane. Under the fairy lights. Turned down a darkened alleyway—and vomited up his whisky.

# CHAPTER TWENTY-TWO

From Central Station over to Anderston in the Glasgow City Centre is an area known as 'the drag'—the red-light district. Or what's left of it. This is where you can find the massage parlours and the saunas and the kinky clubs: dwarfs, dominatrix, bondage...and the last taboo, animals. Ask anyone about the animals and you will be told that that particular twisted sin is urban myth. But it's there. Not like in the past, mind, but there nevertheless, behind locked doors, blacked-out windows, bricked-in warehouses. *Leviticus 18* has not been followed. Most assuredly not even read.

The drag is the domain of the ladies of the night. Vice girls from the Far East. North Africa. And the former Eastern Bloc. Some are even British, up from Liverpool, Manchester, Newcastle and Blackpool. At the bottom of the food chain are the streetwalkers. Ninety-five percent are drug users. Many have now been pushed out of the city centre by increased CCTV, crackdown by police, and pissed-off residents. They've taken their trade over to Gallowgate (not far from the city mortuary) and to Glasgow Green. They charge twenty to thirty pounds for whatever a john may fancy. The top of the food chain sell their souls for seven-hundred and fifty pounds and up. 'Up' can mean fifteen-hundred pounds and for that they'll stay the night.

These top acts don't look like painted, hollow-eyed prossies, they look like successful businesswomen (for that's what they are) or students. They don't use cars or back alleys or doorways or fleabag hotels, they use the city's top luxury hotels. The top establishments have security, CCTV and the vice girls feel safe there. Seven prostitutes have been murdered in Glasgow in recent years. Most have been killed by misogynous sickos. There have been no convictions. And nobody really gives a you know what.

Sharkey worked the red-light district when he was in uniform. Knew the girls on the game by first name.

Both ends of the food chain.

He entered a venue called 'Strictly Cum Dancing' that featured pole dancing, lap dancing and face dancing. Oddly it was decorated with Christmas lights. Pop music seeped out of a distant room. Sharkey was into Country & Western, so he wasn't so sure who was singing. Perhaps that outrageous blonde girl who dressed in all the weird costumes and fell off her piano while performing live. 'Lady Gag-me', some folk in Glasgow call her when she goes OTT.

Sharkey was greeted by a saftig woman wearing not much more than a jewel in her navel. She was straddling a pole which ran all the way to the ceiling. Sharkey looked up. Saw the monitor above her head. She had seen him coming and had taken her position -- pole position. Along the back wall, young, bored, painted lassies sat on a long bench as if they were waiting for the bus to Maryhill.

They all perked up when they saw Sharkey.

'Long time, good-looking,' Miss Pole Dancer said, in a Geordie accent so thick it would make Cheryl Cole appear to be speaking the Queen's. Then: 'I heard. I'm so sorry, Fleet. Who are you looking for?'

'Someone who likes young girls, Ruby.'

'That would be 99 percent of my trade.'

'Someone who likes educated girls?'

'That would be a zero percent.'

Sharkey showed the photo of Decoy Brody.

Miss Pole Dancer studied the photo. 'Is this the bastard?'

Sharkey choked.

Miss Pole Dancer put a hand on Sharkey's arm. 'You're shaking, luv.'

Sharkey didn't respond.

But Miss Pole Dancer did. 'I'll keep my eyes open. I see anything. Hear anything. I'll give you a bell straight away.'

Sharkey thanked her. Clocked a young lass at the end of the bench about Katie's age. She met Sharkey's eyes. Smiled. Put two fingers in her mouth. Lubricated them.

Sharkey fled.

Miss Pole Dancer watched the CCTV monitor over her head. She saw Sharkey hurry off down the street, then spied someone else come into view and enter the establishment. It was a young, frightfully attractive woman. Killer body. Dressed to the nines.

'I'm not hiring, luv, but in your case I just might make an exception.'

'Thanks for the offer,' Lyon-Jones said. 'But it's about the man who was just here...'

'What's it to you?' Protective of Sharkey.

'He's my boyfriend. I'm worried he's cheating on me.'

'Not to worry, luv, he's just doing his job. Asked me if I knew someone.'

Lyon-Jones held up an A4 sheet of paper. 'Was it this man?'

'What are you talking about? That's a sheet of Sudoku.'

'Oh, sorry.' Lyon-Jones held up the photo this time. 'Him?'

'That's the one.'

Lyon-Jones thanked Miss Pole Dancer and turned to go.

'Wait!' Miss Pole Dancer barked.

Lyon-Jones turned back around.

'Where ye frae? Ye donnae sound like a Weegie...'

'Edinburgh.'

'An Edinbugger, then.'

Lyon-Jones ignored the remark, slipped out of the club and moved off down the street.

Didn't notice Sharkey watching from the mouth of a nearby alley.

# CHAPTER TWENTY-THREE

Sharkey sat in the Polar Bear, across from what was left of the gutted Kingston pub. The Saltire had somehow survived the inferno and was still flying indomitably above the burnt-out carcass. A small wreath and a load of cellophane-covered bouquets of flowers were propped up against the blackened stone façade. Nearby a 'Police Appeal for Witnesses' board gave a number witnesses could contact. Not that anyone would now have the guts to come forward.

Sharkey powered down his window. The stench of burnt flesh was still overpowering. Once you've smelt it, you will not soon forget it. He shuddered. What terror those poor souls must have experienced.

He powered the window back up. Snow was still falling, but flurries only, and nothing was sticking down here near the Clyde. That sign on the front of the pub which had stated 'Free Beer…Tomorrow!', had melted and now just proclaimed 'Tomorrow!'.

*Tomorrow.* Sharkey didn't know how he was going to get through *today*. He had become a ticking time bomb and this had only happened to him once before: When he was the leader of the Shettleston Aggro, lying hooked up to tubes in Glasgow Royal Infirmary.

Sharkey looked down at the seat next to him. Resting there was that bottle of Dalwhinnie. He patted the bottle of coveted elixir as one would pat man's best friend.

Tick. Tick. Tick. Tick.

When he had been with the police in America, he didn't always agree with the aggressive, often cowboy tactics employed. If there was a manhunt on, they would just go and kick in doors until they found the perp and screw your civil rights, motherfucker. If yours was a crime family and you didn't like the heat, then get out of the fucking kitchen, bubba, and take your syndicate off to Atlanta or over to Charleston or even down to Savannah.

No, the American way didn't work over here—but that's exactly what he wanted to do right now: Kick down doors and stick his size-eleven cowboy boots up the arse of every scumbag until someone spewed up Decoy Brody.

Sharkey unscrewed the top of the bottle of Dalwhinnie. Took a long pull on the whisky. Wiped his mouth with the back of his hand. Then he took another long pull. Felt the burn on the way down. Loved the burn on the way down. Then the glorious euphoria. But the euphoria didn't last, pushed aside by the scorching reality of it all: Did he really think he could just cruise around the largest city in Scotland and find a serial killer?

Another pull of whisky.

Out the corner of his eye, movement behind him. Sharkey turned. Watched a family with three small children hurry down the street. Everyone was dragging large overly stuffed suitcases, even the weans. Where were they going this time of night? Then he had it, a moonlight flit.

Family.

Sharkey turned the ignition and the Polar Bear sprang to life. He turned on the headlamps, slipped into first, let out the clutch and motored up to W. Campbell. He was about to turn right, when he spotted something way down off to his left: two hoodies, standing down on the corner of Argyle Street.

W. Campbell was a one-way system, but that was the least of Sharkey's concerns. He took a righteous swig of the whisky, swung round and his lights cut a swath through the snow flurries as he slowly motored the wrong way down towards Argyle.

As the Polar Bear crawled up to the two Buckfast Commandos, Sharkey clocked that they were smoking like chimneys and spitting like cobras—posturing. The roly-poly mental-midget of the two approached. Sharkey's keen street-eye studied the punk: *fat cheeks…gelled spikes…*

Sharkey powered down his window. A shot in the dark. A *long* shot in the dark.

Fat Cheeks had a long, hard look at Sharkey. Bellowed in his face. 'Yer the fucking pig what nicked my motor, yeah?'

Bingo!

Sharkey held up the photo of Decoy Brody. Fat Cheeks looked at the photo. Took a Stanley knife out of his right pocket, slowly placed it in his left. Theatrics.

Sharkey pushed the photo closer to Fat Cheeks' fat face. 'You know him?'

'Donnae know the fuck.'

'You were at the Kingston pub. You were his lookout.'

'Said, donnae know the fuck—'

Pizza Face pushed Fat Cheeks out of the way. 'I'll handle this.' He got right in Sharkey's face. 'On yer beat, pig shit. I call the shots in this toon—'

Sharkey didn't budge, just smiled.

'Yer drunk, copper. Piss off while yer safe. The trade sees me talkin' tae ye they get nervous like.'

Movement in Sharkey's wing mirror. Fat Cheeks was urinating on the nearside back tyre.

Pizza Face spat. Postured. 'Don't even think about it. Ma boss'll have us out within twenty-four hours. Now, piss off, wankstain, or I'll pay a late-night visit tae yer family...'

And these two ill-breds didn't get to Sharkey, but the word 'family' did. He powered the window back up and pulled away from the kerb. As he motored off,
Sharkey could see the two hoodies having a good laugh.

Fat Cheeks gave him the finger.

Pizza Face gave him an air jerk.

# CHAPTER TWENTY-FOUR

Bellahouston Park was already closed for the night, so Sharkey parked the Polar Bear on the perimeter in Paisley Road West, snagged his bottle of Dalwhinnie and sneaked in to the park the same way he had when a girlfriend had dragged him to see Pope John Paul II, in 1982.

He hiked over to the dry ski slopes. All the skiers had gone home, but the lights were still on. The flurries had turned to a proper snowfall and it should have been a magical sight. Sharkey cast his mind back to a night like this when he had come with just Katie. Just the two of them. It was snowing then too, and it was the first time Katie had seen snow in Scotland. Oh, aye, she'd often seen snow in the Blue Ridge Mountains of North Carolina, but never in a big city. And she was enchanted.

Sharkey left those thoughts and the flood-lit ski slope behind and trudged into the darkness, through skeleton trees and up to the top of Ibrox Hill where there is a commanding view of the city.

Some say it's a view to die for.

The twinkling lights of the city brought to mind something he had read recently: Nearly all the lonely souls who jumped off the Golden Gate Bridge in San Francisco faced the warm beckoning lights of the city before taking their own life. Few turned to face the blackness of the open sea. Why did they face the city before they jumped?

Sharkey eyed the warm beckoning lights of Glasgow.

Then he looked down at the bottle of whisky in one hand. And the Smith & Wesson in the other hand, the snub-nose that he had purchased at a flea market in America without having to show ID.

Just as the hourglass ran out off sand.

* * *

At the Methodist Church in the East End, in Shettleston, an AA meeting was just about to get underway.

As the wayward took seats, scraped chairs, settled in and greeted their fellow recovering alcoholics, the moderator looked over the modest gathering. He was deeply troubled.

One of the regulars hadn't shown for two nights running.

\* \* \*

Off to the northeast of Bellahouston Park, bright lights licked the bottom of the snow clouds.

The lights emanated from an outdoor event.

Sharkey took a long draw from the nearly empty bottle of Dalwhinnie and peered through bleary eyes in the direction of the outdoor event.

The outdoor event was at Ibrox Stadium.

And like a bolt of lightning, Lyon-Jones' words thundered into Sharkey's brain, '*Just his two passions...fishing and...*'

Shit! Decoy was from the south side of the river. From Govan. Rangers would be his team.

Sharkey dumped the bottle of whisky in a nearby bin. Jammed the S&W into the back of his jeans. Took off running. Running down Ibrox Hill, but not jogging like he had done so many times before.

This time, he ran like a man with no time left.

## CHAPTER TWENTY-FIVE

The snow was dusting the streets as Sharkey mashed the gears on the Polar Bear and belted along in the direction of Ibrox. He jammed the accelerator to the floor. Blared his horn. Blew through red lights. Red-lined. Drove on the wrong side of the road. Hit a pothole. And then, greatly impaired by the whisky and before he could react, a heavily pregnant young mum pushing a pram loaded with her kid and Christmas shopping was in front of him. And Sharkey's life became a movie in slow motion. In HD quality. The young mum was texting. She didn't hear the Polar Bear. And she didn't see it.

The Polar Bear's headlamps had failed again.

Still in slow motion the young mum turned towards the now skidding motor and Sharkey saw the terror in her eyes that only a protective mother can have for her offspring. And just at the moment of impact, when the young mum's life would be over...and that of her child...and that of her unborn child...and that of Sharkey, even though he hadn't pulled the trigger on his Smith & Wesson just moments earlier, the young mum pushed the pram out of harm's way to save one life just as the careening Rover hit a patch of black ice, spun as if in a *pas de deux* with the rolling pram and slipped harmlessly by, stalling in front of a chippy called 'The Fish Friar and the Chip Monk'.

Shaken sober, Sharkey watched as the young mum gave him the finger and moved off to safer environs where she could text without having to watch where she and her brood were going, and Sharkey was never so happy to have been flipped off in his life.

And it was only at that very moment, as he sat there in the Polar Bear watching the snow come down, did he realise how unhinged he had become. Decoy Brody wouldn't be foolish enough to attend a football match, fanatic or not. He would've gone underground. Never to surface again. Or would he? He didn't know that he had been fingered. But even if he did go to the game, how was Sharkey going to find him? Ibrox Stadium held 51,000 fans and there would be hundreds of others milling about selling drugs, pickpocketing, stealing hubcaps and generally causing bother all around the stadium.

The vibrating of Sharkey's mobile snapped him out of his descent into hell. He peered through the windscreen. The Polar Bear rested at a wonky angle in the middle of the street, facing the wrong way.

'Sharkey.'

'It's me, sir. Lyon-Jones.'

Wrong person. Wrong time. 'Can't talk now…'

'I have something you might be interested—'

'Not now, Jones!' Sharkey snapped his mobile shut.

Almost immediately the mobile vibrated again.

'I said, "Not now!"'

'He was in that gang, sir.'

'Who was in what gang?'

'Decoy Brody was in the gang…'

'What are you talking about?'

'Decoy Brody was in that gang that gave you that scar.'

'How did you find this out?'

'I Googled you.'

# CHAPTER TWENTY-SIX

Think outside the box. That's what he'd always done. Where he'd always excelled.

Sharkey was parked just down the street from the Goalkeeper pub, where the rival gang leader's faceless corpse had been found all those years ago, only now the pub's name had evolved. More fitting for the environs, perhaps. Someone had switched around the 'O' and 'A'.

And the sign now read 'Gaolkeeper'.

A sea of blue swept down the street as Ibrox Stadium disgorged its fans. Sharkey switched on the radio to catch the results: Rangers had had their arse kicked 0:3 by perennial bottom-feeder St Mirren. St Mirren who were just a ball's hair from being relegated. Rangers supporters would be drunk, agitated, aggressive and looking for trouble.

Same as after a win.

The own goal hadn't helped.

As if by Darwinian selection of the survival of the sociopathically unfittest, only the arse-end of fan-dom entered the Gaolkeeper.

When Sharkey was with the police department in Charlotte, he had been repeatedly reprimanded for hunches and thinking outside the box—until he found that wee 13-year-old girl in the mobile home down by the river just west of Charlotte, still alive. Greatly traumatized. Sexually assaulted. Repeatedly. And every which way. But *physically* alive. It had been a hunch that paid off. Sharkey had taken a bullet for his efforts, but the step-dad had taken all the bullets in Sharkey's service revolver. The Charlotte police had concentrated their efforts up in the Appalachian Mountains, knowing the step-dad was a keen hunter. But Sharkey had thought outside the box and had told his superiors, 'He won't take her where *he* likes, he'll take her where *she* likes.

She's a tomboy. She likes fishing for crawdads. He wants to get in her good favour. She'll be near the river.'

And near the river she was.

Sharkey turned his attention back towards the growing mass of blue sweeping his way and realised that being here was not about a desperate man clutching at straws. Being here was simply a hunch. He was thinking outside the box.

Sharkey waited. Eye-balled each and every passerby as a worker on the conveyor belt at the tip sorts rubbish. Didn't have to wait long. Walking right towards the Polar Bear was his validation for creative thinking: Decoy Brody…and a surprise guest, sports fans—none other than the living, breathing scum of Denny the Screwdriver Sutherland. They were both wearing Rangers colours and were jawing and gesticulating in that animated fashion that wannabe footballers do anywhere within a thousand yards of a stadium.

Or a telly.

Sharkey grabbed a New York Yankees baseball cap off the passenger seat and pulled it on, low over his eyes, just as Decoy and the Screwdriver aimed straight for the Rover. Then Sharkey heard the WHAP…WHAP…WHAP…of an approaching helicopter and he started to salivate. What the fuck? His pulse elevated. He sweated profusely. His vision blurred. And as quickly as it had come, WHAp…WHap…Whap…*Victor Mike 70*, the Strathclyde Police helicopter moved off in the direction of the stadium and, when Sharkey looked out the windscreen again, his vision had returned to normal, and there was no Decoy and there was no Screwdriver.

Sharkey slammed the dashboard with his fist. 'Fuck!' That hadn't happened for twenty years. Since Desert Storm.

Through the kaleidoscope of passing bodies, Sharkey spied commotion inside the pub: Decoy and the Screwdriver, carrying pints, were ejecting two lumpy drinkers seated in one of the large front windows, right under a massive Rangers flag.

How fucking rude! *And how fucking brazen!*

Sharkey reached into his glovebox and withdrew a Leupold Mark 4 scope that he had requisitioned from the Marine Corps. He raised it to his left eye and Decoy Brody filled the eye piece.

If Sharkey had had his sniper rifle with him, Decoy would already be dead.

Sharkey dug into his black leather Marine Corps satchel, pulled out that clear plastic film with the five small dots stuck to it and threw the door of the Polar Bear open. He climbed out, then suddenly dived back in. He looked down at his ski jacket. The colours of the Carolina Panthers American football team were nearly identical to the St Mirren away colours. In this emotionally charged atmosphere, if he exited the Polar Bear, he might never make it to the front door of the pub. If he did make it and entered the pub, he would be eaten alive, spat out and stomped on.

Sharkey watched as the devout littered the street with empty cans of Tennents, spent bottles of White Lightning, Lanlic and El Dorado, and a bottle of Irn-Bru (which most likely had been sacrilegiously spiked with vodka).

Bang!

Loud noise. Laughter.

A plastic bottle of Strongbow was tossed by a lower cretin and bounced out of bounds, then was corner-kicked (with a fairly impressive cross, considering the condition of the player) and headed at the Polar Bear. It rattled up against a rear tyre.

And this gave Sharkey an idea.

He opened his door just wide enough to be able to snag the bottle and haul it in, then he shrugged out of his ski jacket. Stripped off his sweatshirt. Stripped off his T-shirt. And bolted out.

And not one Rangers fan even batted an eye at this piss artist with the bare chest as he yelled: 'Fuck the buddies! Fuck St Mirren!' and staggered towards the entrance to the pub and discreetly pressed a sticky dot to the front window, just on the other side of where Decoy Brody and The Screwdriver sucked on their bevvies.

Sharkey staggered back across the street to the Polar Bear, climbed in, shivering, threw on his sweatshirt and ski jacket, rubbed his arms and took the device that resembled a SAT NAV and placed it on the dashboard. Then he extracted that pair of ear plugs, plugged them into the device, inserted them in his ears and wasn't fucking technology great? Sharkey had audio and, through the raucous expletive-laced ambience of the pub, he could clearly hear Decoy and the Screwdriver prattle on.

Sharkey hit speed dial on his mobile. Got voicemail. 'Kojak? Fleet. I've found Brody! He's at the Gaolkeeper!' He snapped the mobile shut again.

Then Sharkey heard these words explode in his earpiece: 'If you don't kill him, Decoy, then I'm going to do the job myself...'

Sharkey couldn't believe it. 'C'mon, incriminate yourselves!'

Sharkey listened. And Decoy Brody said it as clear as was audibly possible: 'I'm going to cut the baws off that English goalie, I am.'

The Screwdriver and Decoy were only talking football.

Suddenly, the quality of the audio took a dive as two pierced harpies waddled out of the pub to have a wee ciggie and the corpulent one, the one with the backside wide enough to project a motion picture on it, stuck her prodigious rump up against the window smothering the sticky dot and killing technology.

Sharkey couldn't hear shit, so he picked up his mobile and speed dialled again. 'Jones? Thank Christ you're a sodding workaholic! Listen, I'm down in Govan and I've spotted Decoy Brody. Get CI Squires to pull some strings and get the goddamn ARU down here ASA-fucking-P to seal off the area around the Gaolkeeper pub. Now!'

'She's gone out, Boss. Said she's not to be bothered.'

'Shit!' Sharkey snapped his phone shut. He'd fucked up. What the hell was he doing, thinking he could possibly go through proper channels? Why had he brought the fish fillet knife, if he was going to rely on others? On red tape? Get a grip, Sharkey! Get your ass in gear!

Suddenly he was a bull at a rodeo, in its pen, snorting out fire, ready to explode out into the arena, but right about then, the harpies went back inside, the audio came in gangbusters again and all Sharkey could hear was a mobile ringing. He watched as the Screwdriver slid his mobile open, listened for a moment, then said: 'Aye, he's with me.' He handed the mobile to Decoy. 'Someone's been tryin' to reach ye...'

Decoy listened, casually stood up, shook the Screwdriver's hand and made for the back door like his life depended on it.

Sharkey burst out of the Polar Bear and blew inside the Gaolkeeper. Instantaneously a rough, raucous pub became silent as a morgue: All the half-shot wastrels stared licking their chops at this fucking eejit who dared enter the sanctity of their precious domain wearing the colours of St Mirren. St Mirren who had just vanquished their heroes in the most humiliating manner and on their turf!

One patron took a swing at Sharkey, another threw a bottle which bounced off his shoulder, and just when the entire bar set on Sharkey as a pack of hyenas might set on a helpless dic-dic to savage it, Sharkey pulled the Smith & Wesson out of the back of his jeans and the scum-section of Ibrox jumped back and made enough room to drive a beer lorry through.

Sharkey burst out the back door in pursuit of Decoy Brody.

But the back door of the pub led to an adjacent street. And this street, too, was a river of menacing Rangers supporters and Sharkey didn't have a clue where Decoy Brody had gone. Sharkey looked right, left, then was grabbed from behind by someone in all blue, and quick as a viper, ex-Marine Sharkey spun and poked the muzzle of his S&W in the prick's face, but it wasn't Decoy, and it wasn't some whacked-out Rangers supporter, it was Detective Sergeant Kojak, and Kojak was so hideously unfit, he was panting like a pig in heat.

'Jaysus fuck, Fleet, a gun!'

'I had him and I lost him...'

'Got yer message. Was at the fitba. Came as soon as I could. Jaysus, Fleet, Ye look like yer gonny explode.'

'Decoy Brody was fucking tipped off and I know who did it!' Sharkey took off running back in the direction of his car, waving his gun in the air like the madman he'd become.

And blubbery Kojak could do no more than watch him go...so he broke out a Twix and took a bite.

CHAPTER TWENTY-SEVEN

In the Glasgow City Centre, the snow had ceased but conditions had deteriorated to a less than appealing ball-shrivelling cold.

And only one hoodie remained on the corner of W Campbell and Argyle Street. It was none other than Pizza Face himself. Having chased a couple jellies with that pish-riddled bottle of Buckie, Pizza Face didn't know if he was coming or going. Going uptown or downtown. One thing he did know was that he was King again. And that he goddamn rocked! Fuck it, when Fat Cheeks returned from the Paki chippy with the takeaway, he'd tell him all about his nefarious deeds. He couldn't keep it in any longer. Plus Fat Cheeks was showing him no respect and he'd had enough of that fucking shite.

Fuelled by abuse and unencumbered by fear, Pizza Face watched with great interest as a man wearing a football strip came his way. As the fan approached, Pizza Face peered through dilated pupils and surmised that this bloke somehow looked familiar.

What Pizza Face didn't know was that Fat Cheeks was observing from a darkened store front where he was polishing off a kebab with one hand and having a slash with the other (short of meat in both hands). Fat Cheeks watched with great interest as the stranger walked right up to Pizza Face and said something so fucking funny, Pizza Face's head snapped back. The stranger split. Pizza Face spotted Fat Cheeks and walked in his direction, holding his stomach, bent over, laughing hysterically.

'Yer laughin' like a fuckin' eejit, Pizza Face. Whit the fuck's so fuckin' funny?'

One would've expected Pizza Face to respond with a ned-esque quip, but he didn't—couldn't—only gurgles of blood came out, nothing clever and biting. And then Pizza Face crashed to the ground at Fat Cheeks' feet as dark highly oxygenated blood spewed out from where his stomach used to be and wended its way in the direction of his discarded bottle of Buckie now resting in the gutter with all the other city centre debris.

Fat Cheeks stood over the pale, twitching corpse and saw that Pizza Face's intestines had spilled out on to the pavement and were lying there as if someone had dumped a carry out of large Szechuan-style liangpi noodles.

And then it was Fat Cheeks' turn to boak.

## CHAPTER TWENTY-EIGHT

Ping!

The lift doors hissed open at the Glasgow Royal Infirmary, Burns Unit, top floor, and a uniformed constable down at the end of the corridor looked in the direction of the lifts. This constable was different from the other day. This constable was female. Short. Fit. Pretty. She quickly jumped up and hid the Lee Weeks crime-thriller she was reading behind her back. Didn't want the approaching detective to give her any grief.

'Evening, sir,' the constable said. She saw that the detective was carrying a brolly and dripping wet. 'Still filthy out there, sir?'

'Pissing like a racehorse.'

The constable laughed. She liked this detective. He seemed so easy going. So in command. That, plus he was amusing and drop-dead gorgeous.

'How long have you been on duty, constable?'

'All day.'

'You've eaten?'

'Not as yet, sir, no.'

'Go on then. Take a half hour. I need to ask her some more questions.'

The constable was about to say she wasn't supposed to leave her post, but then she remembered the book behind her back and was more than happy to scarper.

Decoy Brody watched her until she entered the lift, nose already in the book, then he pushed down on the handle to Spike-Hair's room.

Entered.

And locked the door.

# CHAPTER TWENTY-NINE

Up a wee lane in the Glasgow City Centre was a pub called the Horse Shoe Bar.

The façade was red with two large windows framed by entry doors. To complement the décor, red rubbish bins lived permanently out front guarding the main entrance. Glasgow's answer to the Yeoman Warders. Having said that, the only Beefeaters in this city would be found behind the transom of a pub.

The Horse Shoe Bar, oh aye, spelt that way, was an old-fashioned boozer that had it all: cheap drinks, eclectic music and stinky toilets. And the Gents was where Sharkey was standing when his mobile vibrated in his pocket. He hated it when he had to answer his mobile in a public lavvy. Voices echoed. Everyone was privy to your conversation. It was embarrassing as hell. So he didn't answer.

Sharkey wasn't in there for reasons you might think. His right contact lens was giving him major-league grief, and he was standing there balancing a soft contact lens on the end of his right index finger.

Behind him, two drunks at the urinals:

'Should've taken a slash two pints ago.'

'Ah cannae disagree wit ye.'

Sharkey's mobile went off again. Annoyed, he picked up.

'What?'

'It's me, sir. DS Lyon-Jones.'

'Bad timing, Jones? I'm pretty busy.'

A toilet flushed.

'What's that noise in the background?'

'Not important.'

'There's been a murder.'

'Where?'

'On Argyle.'

'Where on Argyle?'

'Just down from the Alexander Thompson on the corner of W Campbell.'

Lyon-Jones waited for a response, but none was forthcoming. 'Sir?'

'I've taken the evening off.'

'You're needed now, sir.'

'Says who?'

'Chief Inspector Squires.'

'Thought she went out?'

'She's resurfaced.'

'Bugger.'

'Sir?'

'I'll be there in fifteen,' Sharkey said, knowing he was just a few streets away.

Sharkey closed his mobile and endeavoured to replace the contact lens. His hand was shaking. Deed done, he exited the Gents and returned to his stool at the bar.

The bar in the Horse Shoe was, as one would rightly surmise, shaped like a horseshoe. The interior was Edwardian décor with etched glass and decorative timber. It was a popular watering hole with a colourful clientele. It was where you went to meet people. It was where you went if you just wanted a warm room on a shit wintry night. It was where you went when you didn't want to go home. It's where you went if you wanted the bartender to just pour whisky and not ask questions.

Not ask you if you needed a hug.

The bartender looked at Sharkey. He'd been serving drinks to him off and on for ten years. And he could read people. Read Sharkey. Knew what to say. Knew what not to say.

'Somethin' tells me yer no' stoppin'.'

Sharkey regarded the bartender. He had red hair and looked to be the type of guy that you wanted for your best friend. After the booze, that is. 'Was it written all over my face, then, Quinn?'

'Yer face an' yer posture comin' oot the cludgie.'

'Another large, please.'

Quinn poured a double Grouse. Slid the glass to Sharkey. 'This one's on me. Two for the road.'

'Yer a good man, Quinn. Cheers.' Sharkey sipped the whisky. Looked around. The usual crowd in tonight: woman in the corner talking to herself, couple sitting over at a table, not talking at all, an alcoholic doctor endeavouring to anesthetize himself, an up-and-coming crime writer tapping away on his laptop and forgetting to 'save' frequently enough.

Sharkey threw down the remainder of his whisky, rose from his bar stool and looked over at the fledgling crime writer. The crime writer was watching him. Seemed to suddenly gain inspiration. Went back to the lonely slog.

Sharkey stepped outside.

Not so very steady on the Scotch eggs.

# CHAPTER THIRTY

The crime scene was only five-minutes away, but it was a perishingly cold five minutes' hike into a pesky headwind. Sharkey had changed out of his Carolina Panthers gear and was now wearing just runners, jeans and a navy-blue fleece from a store long extinct. And he was freezing his arse off.

When he arrived, two uniformed constables were securing the scene with police tape. Two other uniforms were setting up a blue windbreak so passersby couldn't view the body. Another officer was blocking off Argyle Street so there would be no more passersby. The entire area would have to be treated as a crime scene. It would wreak havoc with the morning rush hour, but eventually boost business at the neighbouring hotel.

CI Squires and Lyon-Jones were standing outside the scene of the crime, watching Sharkey approach. Squires didn't look so very happy. But then she never looked happy. Always looked as if she had just received really bad news.

Sharkey stopped in front of Chief Inspector Maggie Squires and Lyon-Jones, but didn't offer a greeting. Sharkey and his chief inspector shared a mutual disrespect for one another. They had both been up for promotion at the same time and Squires had won out. Officially, she won the position on account of her level of education, but everyone knew she didn't win, Sharkey lost it on account of his cowboy ways. Not the type of guy that the Force wanted the younger detectives to look up to—although they all did.

'You'll be leading this investigation, Sharkey,' CI Squires said, not caring to take into consideration where his head was.

'Look, Maggie…'

CI Squires bristled at the lack of formality and respect in front of the new kid on the block.

'You gave me the evening off, remember, compassionate—'

CI Squires spun on Sharkey. 'You reek of whisky, Inspector. I gave you the evening off to take care of your daughter's effects, not to sit on your arse in a pub—'

'Don't get your knickers in a twist...'

'Whisky making you aggressive, Sharkey? Am I reading you wrong? You just go right ahead and speak up if you feel I'm impugning your character...'

'You got a wild hair up your arse tonight, Maggie?'

'Enough! One more word from you and I will arrange it that you have more than just the evening off. Understood?'

No response.

'UNDERSTOOD, INSPECTOR!'

Belligerently. 'Aye.'

'Good. Now that I have your attention: You'll be leading the investigation. You're a policeman. Do your job. Is there a connection between this murder and the Kingston? Is there a connection between this murder and the Buchanan Galleries hit? And before you open your mouth, I've already spoken to Detective Chief Superintendent Ferguson and he agrees we need all hands on deck. The sky is falling, Sharkey. When the city wakes up tomorrow, there's going to be even more frightened citizens. DS Lyon-Jones is going to neighbour you. I want both of you in my office first thing tomorrow morning. I want answers.'

Sharkey glared at Squires. Squires glared back. The woman had ice in her veins and a cold stone for a heart.

CI Squires started to leave. Stopped. Turned. 'With all due respect to your loss, sort your head out, Inspector.'

Squires crossed Argyle Street, beeped open the door on an unmarked CID pool car parked up on the kerb. Opened the door. Climbed in. Turned the ignition. Drove off.

Sharkey looked around to see if any of the other officers had witnessed this dressing down. If they had, they weren't showing it. Only Lyon-Jones.

Lyon-Jones studied Sharkey. Tick. Tick. Tick. Tick. Ready to blow sky high. As a psychologist, this is what she did best, study people. But she had never encountered someone struggling to keep his head above water on so many levels. Sharkey had been a right jerk and condescending to her at best, but he was a deeply wounded and troubled man.

'Are you alright, sir?'

'No, Jones, I'm not alright. Not alright at all.'

It wasn't some sense of duty lying dormant that propelled Sharkey forward, it was his daughter Katie. He would do whatever he had to do to avenge her death and deep down, he felt even here, even now, there was some inexplicable link.

Off to the side of the *locus* were two other uniformed officers. One was lying prostrate on the floor, the other was down on all fours.

'What's with those two, Jones?'

'One fainted, the other is vomiting, sir.'

'Is it that bad?'

'For some.'

'Talk me through what you know so far.'

'Teenage lad. Nothing to identify him. Over two hundred in cash, a pocket full of temazepam and a few strips of ecstasy, so we can rule out a mugging.'

'Any witnesses?'

Lyon-Jones jerked a thumb toward the hotel just down the street. 'Front desk girl from the Alexander Thompson called it in. Came out to have a cigarette and saw the corpse lying there. Said she'd seen the same guy out here for the past couple of days selling drugs…'

'And she didn't feel the need to report the drug pushing?'

'I asked her that. She's Polish. English wasn't so good. She broke down crying.'

A noise to their right interrupted them. The PC on all fours retching again.

'Any other witnesses?'

'None.'

Sharkey looked up and down the wide sweep that is Argyle Street. It was now void of traffic. Suddenly quiet. Eerily quiet. The litter more apparent. Then something close by caught his eye.

'Vic wasn't alone.'

'How do you know that, sir?'

'Look over here, Jones. Another vomit slick. Someone with a taste for kebab by the looks of it.'

'You know your takeaways, sir...'

Sharkey gave Lyon-Jones a wry smile. 'There were two here...two big fish in a wee puddle of pish. We have to find the other guy.'

'I've been onto Traffic, sir, to get a look at the CCTV footage for our time slot.' Lyon-Jones pointed up at the CCTV camera on the corner of Wellington.

Sharkey regarded the distant camera. He hadn't been aware that camera existed. 'I'll deal with Traffic on this. Why isn't the pathologist here?'

'She's on the way.'

'And SOCO?'

'Same.'

'Well, let's have a squizzy, shall we?'

'Where are you going?'

'In there...'

'You'll contaminate the crime scene, sir.'

Sharkey pulled two pairs of blue nitrile gloves out of a pocket. Handed one to Lyon-Jones.

'Sir! Rules!'

'You know my take on rules, Jones. Are you neighbouring me or not?'

Conflicted, Lyon-Jones snapped on her powder-free, latex-free gloves, followed as Sharkey approached the cordoned off area and showed his ID to a female constable standing just in front of the police tape.

'No need for that, sir. I know who you are.'

It was a grisly crime scene for all involved, yet just the hint of deep admiration for DI Sharkey from the female constable didn't go unnoticed by Lyon-Jones.

The female constable looked at Lyon-Jones. No admiration here. 'Sorry, ma'am, I need to see your ID. Never seen you before.'

Lyon-Jones knew that Sharkey would say that she was with him, that hauling out the warrant card wouldn't be necessary. But Sharkey was thumbing his mobile and didn't pick up her body-language cry for respect.

Lyon-Jones reluctantly dragged out her warrant card for the constable to see. Held it in her face like the ref holds a red card.

Short duel of eyes between the two women. Could probably have heard the dueling banjoes plinking away if you'd listened closely.

Sharkey closed his mobile. Held the tape up for a tentative Lyon-Jones. Motioned for her to go first. They both entered and approached the two officers setting up the windbreak. The officers had their backs to the corpse and were fighting the cold and the horrific stench of bodily fluids. Sharkey took a torch out of his coat pocket and bent down to examine the body. Lyon-Jones had breached protocol, but it would be Sharkey's head that rolled, not hers. She was holding the Get Out of Jail Card. She bent down right next to the corpse, pulled out her torch and mimicked her boss. The light from their torches illuminated the corpse. Breath from the two of them entered the beams. Dissipated. Entered the scene. Dissipated.

Pizza Face was lying on his side. Body contorted. Eyes still open. Black holes leading to a long lost soul. A white, foamy froth had pushed its way out of his mouth. Had pooled on his chin. Had dripped on to the pavement. Suddenly the corpse burped. More foamy froth pushed its way out of the mouth and dripped on to the floor. Lyon-Jones ignored the eruption. 'He's been disemboweled.'

The upper and lower intestines were curled in front of the body like a twisted mass of thick pink snakes. And Pizza Face had evacuated his bowels. Excrement expelled by a body no longer able to maintain its integrity stained the pavement. The smell alone was enough to make most heave. Sharkey had been here before. Often. But he was sure this was Lyon-Jones' first. He shot a quick glance her way. She didn't seem to be fazed in the least by the ghoulish nature of the scene. Clinically interested, if anything.

Lyon-Jones gestured toward the wound with her torch. 'I think they went for him with a fillet knife—'

'They?'

'Sorry, sir, just a turn of phrase.'

'And why the fillet knife?'

'Because it's designed to cut flesh. This was no bread knife you take to the football. It was, well, surgical. Meant to create the result that it did. Meant to make some sort of statement.

98

This was more than just taking a life. Footprint here, sir.'

'Where?'

'Here.'

Sharkey studied the footprint. A partial footprint in the edge of the congealed blood. The freezing temperatures had helped preserve it.

Sharkey pointed. 'Look at the blood trail, Jones. He was eviscerated over there. Both hands are covered in blood. He held his guts in and tried to walk in this direction. He tried to go for help.'

Lyon-Jones jumped in: 'Then for some reason, sir, whoever killed him, watched him stagger away, followed him and accidentally stepped in the blood as he lay dying...'

No response from Sharkey.

'Want me to get on the council and suspend refuse collection in the area, sir? Search all dustbins and grates in the vicinity?'

'For?'

'The murder weapon, sir?'

'There'll be no need, Jones, there'll be no murder weapon. This was done by someone who is—'

Lyon-Jones interrupted, 'A professional, sir?'

'Ayes, Jones, aye. A professional.'

'Reprisal for the Buchanan Galleries hit?'

'Don't think so. More like a silencing. More like Decoy Brody.'

# CHAPTER THIRTY-ONE

What if?

What if he hadn't tried to go it alone?

What if he had driven faster?

What if he had realised that the young lass sitting on the back of the red motorcycle had been Katie?

It had been a long time since Sharkey spent the entire night just driving around Glasgow, but going home was out of the question. Could you go home if that had been your daughter? Go home and pick out a good crime novel? Curl up with a wee glass of your favourite brandy? Switch on the telly and watch *Dancing on Ice*? *The Royal Variety Performance*? Perhaps pull out the Christmas DVDs and screen *It's A Wonderful Life*?

Or just sit there with a gun in your hands.

Decoy Brody couldn't be that far away, so Sharkey cruised each and every street of Govan and would do so until first light.

He started by driving over to the Gaolkeeper. He parked around the corner. Went in. Did a turn. The place was nearly empty. Just a few alkies pissing away their pay cheques. Or, more likely, their benefit cheques. No Decoy, and none of the assembled even remembered Sharkey from the other night. Then he did the same thing at the Grapes Bar and the District Bar. There was one person making love to a pint and a whisky in the Grapes, three old guys in the District playing darts. He cruised Govan's lesser schemes and entered the fortified estate where the Sutherlands called home. He parked out in front of darkened Sutherland Motors again.

And one thing was clear, Govan was under lockdown and curtains were drawn and blinds pulled. The middle of the night in Glasgow was usually the play time of its feral creatures and there was almost as much movement in the middle of the night as during the day. But not tonight.

# CHAPTER THIRTY-TWO

In Orkney Street, in Govan, an alarm went off awakening Willie Wallace.

Willie hit the alarm, then sat up and swung his feet off the edge of the bed in his modest, albeit tidy, basement bedsit. Willie wore striped flannel pyjamas and striped woolly socks. He reached over and picked up his glasses which were on the bedside table, put them on, double checked the time on the alarm clock and took a full glass of water he kept by his bedside and drank it down. He always had a glass of water before he went to bed and another just when he woke up.

Supposed to be healthy for you.

He had read that somewhere.

Willie switched on a nearby radio set to Clyde 2 and Christmas music seeped out: '...THE SAVIOR IS BORN...CHRIST THE SAVIOUR IS BORN...'

As the yuletide music played, Willie rose, went to his window and pulled back heavy woolen curtains that could have functioned as black-out curtains during the Second World War. The sun wasn't up yet, but Willie could just see by the glow to the east that there wasn't a cloud in the sky. He frowned. He didn't like the sun. Preferred it when it was overcast. Heavily overcast. The darker, the better.

Willie padded to the toilet. Sat down. Urinated. He never stood while urinating. Didn't like the unsanitary condition the splashing created.

Urine was acidic.

He had read that somewhere.

Willie flushed the toilet by using just his palm, no fingers, then he washed his hands for ten seconds. Brushed his teeth for two minutes with his Braun Oral-B electric toothbrush. Ran water over the toothbrush when he was finished. Whacked the brush bit twice on the sink to get the excess water off. The walls in his bedsit were paper-thin, so he only allotted himself the two whacks to avoid upsetting the neighbours. Neighbours he had lived next door to for seven years, but had rarely seen. Had never spoken to.

He padded to his galley kitchen. Ran cold water into the kettle. Didn't use the hot, supposed to have too much *something or another* in the hot. He put the kettle on. When the water had boiled, he religiously poured the boiling water into his favourite Rangers mug to heat it, brought the water back to boil, then poured out the first cup of water into a spotless sink. He placed a PG Tips tea bag into the mug, poured the water over the tea bag, gave it a good stir with a teaspoon and covered it with a saucer. Then he opened a half fridge, took out a pint of skimmed milk and poured it on top of a bowl of Spar's whole-wheat muesli he had set out the night before. He sat on the edge of the bed, had his breakfast and sipped his tea, listening to the Christmas music, keeping an eye on the shimmering pinks and magentas of the soon-to-be rising sun as a sliver encroached through his window.

When he was finished with breakfast, he washed his bowl out, washed the tea cup, washed the saucer, teaspoon and the spoon he had used for the cereal, dried them and placed them back in their respective homes.

Then he went into the bathroom and brushed his teeth again. When he'd finished, he washed his toothbrush off. Gave it the two whacks on the sink.

Willie flossed. Then washed the used floss and placed it on a shelf. He would use the same strand again tomorrow.

Willie enjoyed shaving in the shower, but he was careful not to stay in too long on account of the electric bill. When he had finished, he towelled off, wiped down the shower, put his glasses on, meticulously combed his hair, applied underarm deodorant and placed a small swatch of loo paper on a bleeding razor cut on his chin to stem an annoying flow of blood.

Willie repaired to his living room/bedroom, opened a narrow cupboard and took out a pair of boxer underwear and a pair of navy-blue socks. He stepped into the boxers, sat on the bed and pulled on each sock, always the left one first. He went back to the cupboard and removed an ironing board. He set it up, then went to his bedside table, opened a polished wood door and removed an iron, filled it with distilled water, plugged it into the power point and flipped the wee switch. In a wardrobe to the right of his one window, were seven shirts, all the same colour, white. Willie retrieved one, removed it from the hanger and carefully ironed it, using spray starch heavily, ensuring that it was perfectly pressed. He put on the shirt, pulled a pair of navy-blue trousers out of the wardrobe and put them on, retrieved his black thick-soled shoes that he had polished the night before and put them on, always the left one first. He returned to the mirror, tied a blue-and-green tartan tie in a Windsor and had a good look at the figure staring back at him in the mirror. Something was wrong. Ach! Willie removed the swatch of toilet paper with dried blood on it.

Willie slipped into his navy-blue jacket, gripped the edge of his right sleeve with his right hand and buffed the breast badge he had received for five years' service.

He looked over at a photo of Jimmy Reid he had hanging over his bed. Crossed to it. Adjusted the right side up a fraction.

Finally he was ready.

Ready to go to work, back in the subterranean domain that was known in Glasgow as the Clockwork Orange.

# CHAPTER THIRTY-THREE

Over in Ibrox, the day was just beginning at Sutherland Motors. It was bitterly cold, but the sun was gracing Glasgow with an appearance for the first time in over a fortnight. A private-hire taxi was already lined up for its MoT. It was inside the open double doors, up on the rack. The owner of the vehicle was smoking in the forecourt, eyes closed, hands-free headset stuffed in one ear, face raised to the sun.

Sharkey pulled the Polar Bear in behind the occupied bay. Killed the engine. Jumped out. The two well-fed pit bulls went ballistic, slabbering from behind the chain-linked fence. Sharkey eyed them. Eyed the taxi driver. A face like a pit bull after a bad fight. A fight he'd lost. The cabbie responded with mute ill will. Sharkey ignored the mutt and entered the open garage door. Looked for the bright-red motorcycle.

It was gone.

A wiry mechanic stood under the hoisted vehicle, fitting a new exhaust.

'Oi, ye cannae come in here!'

'Looking for the Screwdriver.'

'Still no' allowed in here.'

Sharkey held up his warrant card.

'Were ye born stupid or did the polis make ye that way? YER...NOT... ALLOWED ...IN...HERE!'

The cabbie laughed like a hyena on drugs.

'I detect a certain hostility.' Sharkey, intimidating in his lightheartedness.

It didn't sit well with the mechanic. He was used to being the bully. He moved in Sharkey's direction. Wiped his hands on an oil-blackened rag. Horrid tattoos up both arms. Bad breath. Challenging now. 'It can get worse. A lot worse.'

Sharkey held his ground. 'For who? You, Mr Goodwrench?

Where the fuck's the Screwdriver?'

'Fuck if ah know. Now, piss off, porker, ah have work tae do...'

'Thanks for the offer, but I think I'll stay.'

About now, the Screwdriver stepped out from an inner office followed by a cloud of aftershave. The Screwdriver sported a gold earring. Expensive suit. Authentic Rolex. Unauthentic tan.

'Morning, Inspector. My apologies. He's allergic tae mornings. C'mon into my office where it's warm. Besides, out here ye could catch yer death...and we wouldnae want that tae happen, would we?'

Sharkey followed the Screwdriver into the office. A Christmas tree decorated with lights and chocolates stood in the corner. Prezzies underneath. Asleep underneath the tree, snoring, another pit bull.

'Coffee?'

'Where's Decoy?'

'Y'know, I used tae drink my coffee with four spoonfuls of sugar, then I cut down tae three, then two, then one, then none. Cut out the cream, as well.' The Screwdriver sipped and savoured his coffee the way we do when we have that first cup in the morning.

'Cut the shit! Where the fuck's Decoy?'

'Cannae I even enjoy my first cup of coffee in the morning, Inspector?'

'WHERE IS HE!'

The Screwdriver leisurely sipped his coffee. Looked Sharkey straight in the eyes. 'Havnae seen Decoy in years. We had a falling out. Didnae subscribe tae his violence. He's a sick fuck. And I donnae have no time for sick fucks.'

'Ye were at the fuckin' Gaolkeeper with him last night.'

'True and false. True, I wis at the Gaolkeeper last night. False, I wisnae with Decoy Brody.'

'I saw youse.'

'Inspector, please donnae take this the wrong way, but ye look as if ye haven't slept so very well in the last couple of days. Yer unshaven and ye got dark circles under yer eyes. Those eyes must be playin' tricks. If ye donnae believe me, go tae the

Gaolkeeper. Ask anybody ye want if they saw Decoy Brody in there last night. Go ahead. Ask 'em.'

The Screwdriver took another scoof of his coffee. 'I'm a respectable businessman, Inspector. Donnae want no agro from no one.'

'Listen, ye wee piece of shite, ye don't want to fuck with me—'

'NO! YE LISTEN! Yer a bunch of total clowns and ye cannae touch me. Ye come after me, I got friends. Ye come after my business interests, I got lawyers.'

'It just takes one bullet. Yer lawyers cannae shield ye from that?'

'Are ye threatenin' me, Inspector?'

'Aye, don't ye fucking know it. That's exactly what I'm doing. I'm threatening ye.'

Sharkey turned to go. Stopped. The taxi driver and the mechanic were blocking the doorway. Sharkey knew the cabbie, a real piece of work known as Taxi Boy.

'Shouldn't ye be away catching crims, Inspector?'

'Step aside, Taxi Boy, or I'll rip yer cock off and stuff it up yer arse.'

Taxi Boy came at Sharkey, fast. But Sharkey was faster. Had a forearm against Taxi Boy's throat. S&W at his temple. Quickly, the gun swung to the mechanic. Then to the Screwdriver. Then back, pressed against the temple of Taxi Boy.

And that froze them.

But what shook them was the look on Sharkey's face. A look the three of them had never seen in all their days of bullying and intimidating.

Sharkey was smiling.

# CHAPTER THIRTY-FOUR

Sharkey needed sleep.

He closed his eyes and prayed that sleep would come—without the demons. Without the image of Katie lying on the trolley at the city mortuary. Without the face of Decoy Brody or the Screwdriver or Taxi Boy.

But it was not to be.

The demons came again, and this time it was in the form of DCI Maggie Squires. She was waving a fist at him and yelling, but he couldn't make out what she was saying. He fought to rid her from his dream, but couldn't. His only means of salvation would be to thrust himself out of this nightmare. Force himself to wake up and extinguish the horror of her gnarled face.

Finally he did. He was awake. The nightmare was gone. Or was it? CI Maggie Squires was still right there in his face. Sharkey had fallen asleep in the Polar Bear in the Strathclyde Police car park.

'My office. Now!'

It was a quarter of an hour later when Sharkey approached his office door, eating a bacon roll, a pig buttie as he liked to call them, and carrying his preliminary report of the previous night's deeds. Lyon-Jones intercepted him.

'Squires is on the warpath.'

Sharkey ignored her.

'Said she wants to see you, *now*.'

Sharkey's blood boiled. He didn't care for Lyon-Jones' righteous, do-it-by-the-book attitude. It was getting old real quick. He gave her a good hard look and headed towards what he knew would turn into a shoot-out at the not-so-OK Corral.

Chief Inspector Squires had had her office redecorated the second she was promoted. Her predecessor had been a closet smoker and she despised the smell of smoke, rancid or otherwise. So she had it repainted in institutional tones and accented in bad taste. Hanging on a side wall was a miasma of photos and diplomas: a photo of her graduating class at the University of Edinburgh … a photo of her graduating class at the Scottish Police College in Fife … diploma in Applied Criminology from Cambridge University.

'Have a seat, Inspector.'

'Prefer to stand.'

'Sit down for Christ's sake!'

Sharkey remained standing and regarded CI Squires. She reminded him of Meryl Streep in *The Devil Wears Prada*: Close cropped, prematurely grey hair, strikingly good-looking, frightfully cultured, educated at private schools. A barracuda. A bitch of the highest order. And what was worse, much worse, she was from Edinburgh.

At one time they had worked well together and Sharkey was impressed with her will and energy and strength, the strength it took to climb the ladder despite the Force's inbuilt, blatant sexism.

And then, two years ago, just before Christmas, an alcohol-fuelled night changed everything between them. No, it wasn't sex. Might've been heading that way, but it turned into a battle of the two egos extraordinaire. And then into a shoving match and it got rough. And CI Squires saw what whisky did to Sharkey. The power of alcohol had a frightening ability to alter behaviour—on all fronts.

'What the hell were you thinking?'

'I just closed my eyes for a moment.'

'And I won't have that.'

'You're rattling my cage because I fell asleep in the Polar Bear? Jesus, Maggie, I'm not stealing drugs or taking graft or beating minorities to within an inch of their life. You go lose a child and see how well you sleep!'

Squires didn't know how to respond to this, so she pointed to the report in Sharkey's hand. 'Let's have it.'

Fleet handed it over and watched as she read it quickly and without emotion.

'Eviscerated. Time of death between eleven and midnight. I assume that's preliminary?' she asked, with a glance at Fleet.

108

He nodded.

'Thoughts?'

'That pitch is a new Sutherland pitch. Lad had money and drugs on him. This was premeditated. DS Jones—'

'*Lyon*-Jones.'

'Right. She reckons he was taken out as a reprisal for the McQueen boy. I disagree…'

'Let's hear it, then.'

'Why eliminate the lowest scum on the totem pole to avenge the number-one son of Tattoo McQueen?'

'Sounds like it's just the beginning.'

'I don't see it that way. The kid was fifteen or sixteen. He'd been dining out on the Sutherland name. Had a real mouth on him—'

'And you know this, how?'

'Had dealings with him in the past…'

CI Squires squirmed in her seat.

'I think he knew something the Sutherlands didn't want spread around town. I think the Sutherlands felt he was going to get diarrhoea of the mouth.'

'What are you saying?'

'I'm saying, I don't think the McQueen family killed him. I think he was taken out by the Sutherlands. I think Decoy Brody wasted his ass to keep him quiet.'

'Look, Sharkey, that's idle speculation. I think you're fishing for ways to get involved in your daughter's case and you are not to. Do you understand? Not in any shape, in any form, in any way. Decoy Brody's off-limits. DS Lyon-Jones was here this morning, *early*. I've seen her report. I think DS Lyon-Jones has made a good point and I have every confidence in her. That's the direction we'll go.'

'For fuck's sake, Maggie, he murdered my daughter—'

'It's "ma'am" to you, Sharkey. You'll do as you're told and you won't use that language in this office! Do you understand?'

No response.

'DO YOU UNDERSTAND?'

'Is that all?'

'Is that all, *ma'am*,' Squires chided. 'Start throwing some respect my way.'

Sharkey ignored her. Headed towards the door. Stepped out. 'And no smoking allowed in this building at any time!'

# CHAPTER THIRTY-FIVE

Sharkey grabbed Lyon-Jones roughly by the arm. Whisked her into his office. Slammed the door. 'What the fuck're ye playin' at, Jones?'

'Get your hands off me!' She ripped her elbow out of his grasp.

'Ye grass me up to Squires?'

'Certainly not, sir.'

'I get my chops busted over a couple ciggies!'

'Wasn't me, sir, I swear.'

'Like fuck it wasn't! You two Edinbuggers get together and have a wee chat? Tip a few Bacardi Breezers together. Show off your diplomas?'

Fiona ignored the aggression. She was above it. Could handle it. But she knew something Sharkey didn't and this outburst was only a mild tremor, the whole goddamn volcano was going to erupt. And it was going to erupt right this very second.

'Sir, I took a call while you were upstairs with the CI—'

'Not now, Jones!'

'Aye, now, sir! Now! Another murder last night.'

'I DON'T GIVE A FUCK!'

'Glasgow Royal Infirmary...'

'What?'

'Glasgow Royal Infirmary, sir.'

'Who was it?'

'The woman you visited. The lady with the white spiked hair. She was sexually assaulted and had a umbrella jammed down her throat.'

'Jesus.'

'This was done by someone who is a bespoke assassin, sir. Creative. Someone who takes pride in finding new ways to kill.'

'Fuck!' Sharkey slammed his desk so hard the whole office shook. 'That's Decoy Brody's work. He's hiding in a rat hole in Govan, then comes out at night to hunt.'

'Sir…'

'I want Govan cordoned off. I want a Circulation sent out on Brody. I want a facsimile of his likeness at every airport, train station, subway station, bus station, car hire agency, harbour, marina—'

Sharkey stopped in mid-sentence. The blood had drained from Lyon-Jones' face. Sharkey turned to see what she was staring at. Froze. Standing in the open doorway was Chief Inspector Squires.

'You don't have the authority to do that. Have you completely lost it? And what part of "not involved in your daughter's case" don't you understand, Sharkey?'

'For the love of God, Brody's killed our only witness!'

'Can you prove that?'

'I know it's him!'

'One of those hunches you're famous for, Sharkey? I will tell you this for the last time: I call the shots. You want something done, you go through me! Do you understand?'

'Ach, don't blow a bowel, Maggie.'

'DO YOU UNDERSTAND!'

Sharkey just stared back. Defiant. Lyon-Jones had never witnessed such insubordination.

'He took my Katie away from me! He took all I had left! You have to back me up on this, Maggie!' Sharkey slammed a fist into the wall so hard, the framed, glass-enclosed Carolina Panthers American football jersey crashed to the floor, shattering the glass. Sharkey bent down. Moved a shard of glass out of the way. Picked up the jersey. Shook the glass splinters off. Held on to it.

He had precious little left.

# CHAPTER THIRTY-SIX

'Do ye have a passport?'

It was midday. Fat Cheeks sat in the back seat of a dented Ford Mondeo that was parked illegally on a double-yellow along Elder Park in Govan. He was shaking like a leaf and not from the cold. A shaven-headed goon sat on either side of him. Stickmen. Henchmen. Bottom of the barrel bookends. Fat Cheeks looked as if he had been up all night crying. Which he had. He was scared shiteless and getting hypoglycaemic. To calm his nerves, he lit up a fag and waited for the nicotine hit.

Denny the Screwdriver Sutherland sat behind the wheel. The Christmas tree pit bull sat on the passenger side. Facing back. Slabbering. Eyeing Fat Cheeks' ... fat cheeks.

'I'll ask ye for the last time, Fat Cheeks. Do ye own a passport?'

'A passport, aye, Mr Sutherland. Went tae Tunisia with me maw an' her partner last summer. Wisnae very British. Couldnae even get a poke of chips.'

The Screwdriver studied Fat Cheeks. The Screwdriver was not the sharpest knife in the drawer, couldn't even hold his own with a butter knife, but even he was amazed that Fat Cheeks was such a dim shite.

'We think the McQueen family killed Pizza Face and ye could be unfinished business.'

'I wis only doin' ma edgy!' Beads of sweat popped on Fat Cheeks' forehead. Two degrees Celsius out and sweating like a frigging guffy.

'We're goin' tae send ye doon tae Spain. So ye can lay low. Keep below the radar for a while—'

'Pizza Face said he might be goin' tae Spain.'

'Did he now? Did he say anythin' else tae ye?'

'Nowt.'

'Ye sure?'

'Aye, sir.'

'Donnae be tellin' porkies, Fat Cheeks…'

'Ah, swear, Mr S…nowt.'

No one spoke. Fat Cheeks thought his bowels were about to let loose. He clamped down on his sphincter. The Christmas tree pit bull growled.

'Why ye so jumpy, Fat Cheeks?'

'Hungry, Mr Sutherland. Starvin'. Huvnae eaten for almost two hours.'

'Well, where ye goin' they'll have all the chips ye can munch. The lads, here, will take ye home now.'

Fat Cheeks looked over at the first goon. He was the size of a door, a door with a Bluetooth hanging off one ear. Fat Cheeks shot a glance at the other goon. He was the size of the whole bungalow. Both men worked as bouncers ('Front door managers,' they had said, thank you very much) for a security firm controlled by the Sutherland family. Looking for trouble by night. Making trouble by day.

'Ye grab yer passport, Fat Cheeks, and ye donnae open yer fucking mouth tae yer maw, eh? She asks, ye tell her yer going bowling.'

'Do ah need tae pack a bag, sir?'

'Why would ye pack a bag if yer going bowling, Fat Cheeks?'

Denny the Screwdriver threw open the driver's door and climbed out. He lit up a Marlboro. Sucked the freaking hell out of it. He stomped around to the other side of the Mondeo and let his pit bull out, so it could squat in the park grass. The park grass where children would be playing football tomorrow. The goon with the Blue Tooth climbed into the driver's seat. The other goon assumed the passenger seat. The Screwdriver leaned in and pointed the burning tip of his ciggie at Fat Cheeks' eye. Stuck it right on up there.

'Remember, ye'll not be mentioning Spain.'

Sitting in the Polar Bear, Sharkey and Lyon-Jones observed from a discreet distance. The last person Lyon-Jones wanted to be around right now was Sharkey, but Chief Inspector Maggie Squires had told her to stay with Sharkey like a bad cold. Report back any misadventure. Lyon-Jones wished that she had feigned a bad cold and gone home early.

'Listen up, Jones,' Sharkey said, pointing with his head. 'You know who the thug with the fake tan is?'

'No.'

'That's Denny the Screwdriver Sutherland, but who's the cubby punk?'

'The source of the other emesis?'

'The what?'

'The other vomit slick?'

'Could well be. But if it is, why has the Screwdriver lowered himself to slug level to deal with him? Why not use one of the many Sutherland slugs?'

'Arrogance?'

'Coupled with stupidity.'

* * *

The Ford Mondeo pulled into a litter-riddled estate not far from the disused docks and stopped in front of a squalid apartment block that looked as if it should be at the top of the list of next homes to be condemned. In front of the neighbouring block, a still smouldering, burnt-out VW Golf rested, fused to the tarmac. Nearby, old bed-springs and trashed furniture partially blocked the path. There was so much broken glass it would be dangerous for young children to play outdoors.

And adults to walk home from the pub.

The goon with the Bluetooth yanked on the emergency brake and kept the engine running. A curtain in a neighbouring ground-floor flat pulled back. Another, upstairs, twitched. Bluetooth turned around to Fat Cheeks alone in the back seat. 'Ye go in. Ye snag the passport. Ye come back out. No jerking off.' Long beat. 'And no gabbing of Spain!'

Fat Cheeks opened the car door and jumped out. Inexplicably he had a spring in his step. He swung open the front door of his apartment and a cat in the throes of mange screeched out. Fat Cheeks stepped over a pile of unopened post and into the middle of a burnt-orange shag carpet which brought great gloom and tackiness to a gloomy, tacky living room. Bringing even more gloom was the dingy, grey sheet pinned across the living room window. Someone hadn't been using the new, improved Oxi Action Crystal White.

Fat Cheek's maw was splayed on the couch. Already blootered. Her partner had his arm lobster-clawed around her shoulder. Maw was rolling a joint. Her partner drinking a can of Tesco lager. Empty beer cans, crisp wrappers and other munchie flotsam covered the coffee table, along with over-filled ashtrays purloined from various pubs, pre-2006. A sad, fake Christmas tree leaned at a perilous angle over in the corner. The leaning tower of kitch. A burst binbag guarded the entry to the kitchen. An absurdly large flat-screen TV blared out *THE FILTH FILES*. There was a distinct possibility Fat Cheeks' flat would be featured in an upcoming episode.

From the other side of the wall, the neighbour's telly could be heard blaring out a different programme. For the first time in his life, Fat Cheeks realised what a shit-hole he lived in. And that it stank. But he didn't mention it, rather, 'Ah'm goin' tae Spain, Maw!'

Through glazed eyes, Fat Cheeks' maw regarded her son for a moment, trying to input this data, then gave up and said, 'Pass me the zapper, will ye?'

High on self-esteem, Fat Cheeks bellowed. 'Get it yersel!' Then he grabbed a packet of Walker crisps off the coffee table and aimed for the back of the flat where he shared his single bedroom with the washing machine and the cat box.

Moments later, Fat Cheeks returned brandishing his passport and sporting a knock-off Burberry baseball cap, visor pointed to the heavens. Important to sport fashionable kit when travelling abroad.

'Goin' tae Spain!' Fat Cheeks announced again as he grabbed another pack of crisps off the coffee table and scampered out the front door, leaving it ajar.

'Shut the fucking door or there'll be no tea for ye tonight!'

Fat Cheeks' mum got her useless doley arse off the couch. Slammed the door shut. Picked up a full ashtray. Went to the front window. Slid the dingy, grey curtain/sheet over. Opened the window. Emptied the ashtray out the window. Watched Fat Cheeks go. Failed to close the window fast enough and half the ash blew back inside.

From their vantage point just down the road, Sharkey and Lyon-Jones observed as Fat Cheeks exited the apartment block, climbed in the Mondeo and was whisked away.

'Okay, I'm sure of it. He was Pizza Face's edgy…'

Lyon-Jones looked over at Sharkey. 'Edgy?'

'Struggling with the Glaswegian patois, Jones? It means 'someone's lookout'.

'Edinburgh and Glasgow, two cities separated by a common language, sir.'

'Don't I fucking know it.'

'Why do Glaswegians feel the need to punctuate each sentence with "fuck"?'

'We don't want anyone to confuse us with Edinbuggers.'

Sharkey turned the key in the ignition.

'What are you doing, sir?'

'Going to follow them.'

'You can't do that.'

'Why the hell not?'

'We need his name, sir.'

'And how do you plan to get it? Just going to walk up to the front door and politely ask? The people in these schemes won't even open the door for you.'

'Leave it to me.'

'Forget it! We're going to lose them!' But Sharkey was talking to an empty car. Lyon-Jones had already jumped out.

Sharkey pulled out his monocular and observed as she crunched her way through the minefield of broken glass, accompanied by an overture of twitching curtains. A rat ran out in front of Lyon-Jones. She ignored it. Kept going. Rang the bell at Fat Cheeks'. No answer. Rang it again. Then knocked. Still no go, so she climbed through a privet hedge gagging for a drop of water. Stopped. Stared down at a mound of cigarette stubs nearly as high as the dying hedge. Shook her head in disbelief. Rapped on the front window.

*They won't open the door, Jones*, Sharkey thought to himself.

Lyon-Jones climbed back through the hedge. Waited.

The front door opened.

Sharkey could see a skanky woman eating crisps from the packet, jawing at Lyon-Jones in an animated get-the-fuck-out-out-of-my-face fashion. Lyon-Jones presented some sort of an ID. The woman's face metamorphosed. Became absolutely angelic. She beckoned Lyon-Jones in. Lyon-Jones gestured 'Next time, perhaps.' The two shook hands.

Lyon-Jones returned to the car.

Same curtains twitching.

She opened the passenger door and slid in. 'Fat Cheeks.'

'That's his name?'

'His street name. The name everyone knows him by.'

'Did you show your warrant card?'

'Sir, that would have been fruitless. Only set her off.'

'What did you show her?'

'My library card. Figured she wouldn't know what one looked like.'

'What did you say?'

'Said I was from the lottery.'

'And that worked?'

'That and psychology, Boss. I used psychology. Techniques you can't learn on the street.'

Sharkey gave Lyon-Jones a big-house stare, then something breached his attention. 'Hold on a sec...' He had the car radio on low. The news was about a gathering of Rangers players and fans for that evening. It was to be held at a trendy club called 'Heaven' in the Glasgow City Centre. Sharkey punched the radio off. 'Yeah, well, tonight I'll show you what you *can* learn on the street.'

'There will be no *tonight*, Boss, I've got plans.'

'Not anymore.'

'What are you saying?'

'I'm saying, you and I, Jones, are going clubbing.'

'Hold on, Boss, you know Squires won't grant us the overtime.'

'Squires doesn't need to know.'

# CHAPTER THIRTY-SEVEN

Glasgow to Alicante is three hours. Four if you factor in the delay caused by Fat Cheeks smoking in the lavatory, setting off the alarm and being bodily removed by the Garda Civil upon landing. The only thing that saved Fat Cheeks' fat arse was that he was met at the airport by someone who spoke Spanish, albeit with a Glaswegian accent, Jimmy the Pouch Sutherland. The Pouch had silver hair and tanned skin as tough as alligator hide. And he was accompanied by an arms-akimbo, busty, bleached-blonde, forty years his junior.

In frightfully fluent Spanish, the Pouch explained to a bored Immigration Inspector that as a wean, Fat Cheeks had been in a pram that had rolled off the platform in Pollokshields East when his mother had had a lapse in attentiveness while adjusting her thong, and baby Fat Cheeks had been run over by the approaching 15:24 out of Nielston.

Fat Cheeks had never really developed like others his age.

Perhaps it was the Pouch's eminent presence of being both courteous and menacing, or his quirky command of the Spanish language that had impressed the Garda Civil or, then again, it may have been the hundred euro note pressed into the hand of the senior officer that had sealed the deal.

'We go now?' Bleached-Blonde asked, in heavily accented Eastern European English. 'You give me drink now?'

'Ach, aye, ah'm goin' tae gie ye more than jist a bevvy when we get home!' Jimmy the Pouch Sutherland said, as he put his leathery hand on her prodigious, yet tight, rump and guided her toward the car park.

Fat Cheeks trailed behind. 'Any chance to get something to eat, like? The stewardesses ran out of food before they got to my row. I'm starving Marvin.'

But his request fell on randy ears.

# CHAPTER THIRTY-EIGHT

DCI Maggie Squires had requested a private sit-down with Detective Chief Superintendent Danus Ferguson in his office over at HQ in Pitt Street.

'He's fighting demons, sir, that I understand, but he's become a loose cannon and he's doing more harm than good...I don't want him reprimanded, one more cock-up and I want him suspended...'

DCS Ferguson regarded DCI Squires. This is not what he'd expected.

'There's more,' DCI Squires said. 'I've instructed DS Lyon-Jones to report back if she sees him so much as cough without covering his mouth.'

# CHAPTER THIRTY-NINE

After the sun goes down, the Glasgow City Centre comes alive.

Even when there's a gangland war going on. And multiple murders.

It could never happen to me, that's what most think. I don't go into those parts of the city. I don't frequent that particular club. I don't associate with that sort of crowd. I don't go home alone with someone I just met. I never accept a drink from strangers. I always make sure I see my drink being poured and then it never leaves my sight. I know my limit. I know who I buy my drugs from...

Yeah, right.

\* \* \*

In Blanefield, a young Glasgow Rangers footballer was preparing to go clubbing. The first thing he needed to do was visit the gym. To pump up. For the ladies. And since he had his own private gym in the four-bedroomed detached house he owned and lived in—alone—he didn't have far to go. And he didn't have to wear proper attire.

He enjoyed working out in just his HOM string underwear, so he could admire his physique in the full-length mirrors which adorned every wall in the 500-square-foot weight room. He began with the upper body, doing bench presses, overheads, curls, pull-downs for the lats and flies for the pecs.

Tonight was not a night to work out the lower body. He had tried that once and then had a particularly long fucking session and it just wasn't symbiotic. Then again, it might have been the drugs. Who knew? He didn't, but he wasn't about to risk it. He lived for sex. It was the hunt. The pursuit. And he was not too shabby at foreplay, he had to admit.

\* \* \*

In Partick, a young lass was preparing to go clubbing. She had shaved her legs, then, for the first time ever, she had shaved down there. Tonight was the hen party, she was maid of honour and there was no telling what was going to happen even though she had a well-organised game plan: dinner at La Tasca (it was a Fajita Hen Party), buckets of margaritas and mojitos and shots of Cuervo Gold, and then around eleven they would repair to that club where the Rangers footballers purportedly hung out. The club was called Heaven, and it was just a wee bit naughty. She had arranged male strippers and the private room. A friend had recommended the club because just about anything went. And if the male strippers were tipped handsomely, they would do whatever you asked. It was the bride's last night as a free woman, after all, so why not? Just so no one was videoing. She didn't want to end up featured on the Internet on the *Girls Gone Wild* website. She didn't want to sully her reputation. Such as it was.

She had aspirations.

Lofty aspirations.

She aspired to be a WAG.

* * *

In Newton Mearns, the Procurator Fiscal and his new wife—a former legal trainee—had just finished making love and were now behind schedule. The PF had an important dinner engagement and he was eager to wax political to the assembled and show off his trophy wife. He had only recently dumped his first wife of twenty years and was in the process of ignoring the three children.

Christmas or not. His career came first.

And the new wife couldn't wait either. She was an aspiring actress and she hoped the Press would make an appearance and she would be splashed all over the tabloids the next day. If Carla Bruni could do it, why couldn't she?

* * *

In Giffnock, Fiona Lyon-Jones was preparing to go clubbing. She couldn't remember the last time she went out. Or dated. Men were intimidated by her intelligence. And her education. And her looks. And her wealth. Some were even intimidated by her accent. Then when she threw police detective into the mix, that was the end of all sincere interest from the opposite sex. She stood in front of the mirror applying lip gloss and trying to remember how much cleavage to show. She had pulled the only dress out of her closet that she felt might be appropriate. It was a silver mini-skirt in lycra stretchy fabric, with matching halter draping top and a buckle to the centre of the bust. But she hadn't worn it in years. And it did show a lot of skin. All that to worry about, plus she was a mess. She couldn't separate her emotions. She was angry as hell for having to cancel her plans for the evening (staying home and watching *CSI:Miami* on TiVo), yet she was oddly excited to be going on a 'date' with Inspector Sharkey...even though it was anything but a date. Christ, what was the matter with her? She loathed the insufferable bastard yet she was looking forward to going. She never had felt so discombobulated. Plus, Sharkey was slipping further and further from police protocol, and that scared the bejesus out of her.

* * *

In Glasgow's East End, Fleet Sharkey was preparing to go clubbing: He was loading his Smith & Wesson .38 revolver.

# CHAPTER FORTY

Glasgow's nightlife is legendary, and its clubbing scene is generally recognised as the most vibrant outside of London. When it comes to restaurants and pubs, you would be hard-pressed to find a more eclectic choice anywhere.

The Paragon restaurant on Bath Street was Glasgow's equivalent of the Ivy. Upstairs from the Paragon, was Heaven. Glasgow's equivalent of Manumission. If you wanted the fine-dining experience in a snobbish environment, you gave your custom to the Paragon. If you wanted to winch, pull, snort and shag, you toddled upstairs.

The Paragon was where you went to be seen.

Heaven was where you went to be obscene.

The entrance to the Paragon was through two stained-glass doors and the feeling was as if you were entering a cathedral.

Access to Heaven was down a dark alley and up a two-storey, wrought-iron outside staircase (the 'staircase to Heaven'), and the feeling was not unlike entering the Second Circle of Hell.

The Paragon boasted a classical pianist and Scotland's finest beef, trout, salmon and wild fowl.

Heaven boasted a whacked-out DJ and Scotland's best E, skag, glass and blow.

From Decoy Brody's position, he could clearly observe Glasgow's crème-de-la-crème as the valet parking crew dutifully opened doors and they stepped from their late-model Jags, Mercs and Beemers, rubbed fur coats and entered the Paragon. And just as easily, he was able to observe all the hoochie-mamas who conveyed by taxi and were queuing to get into Heaven.

Decoy illuminated the dial on his Royal Marines Commando watch. It read just after 11.00 pm. He yanked the hood of his ski jacket against the wind and shifted his weight. He had been lying on the roof of the Premier Inn, six streets away from the Paragon, for the past three hours and needed to reposition his nuts. He adjusted the night scope on his Russian-made Dragunov sniper rifle, then tenderly screwed on the silencer. What a doddle it was for Decoy to access a roof, most any roof in the Glasgow City Centre. Ever since the smoking ban, these rooftops had become clandestine venues for nicotine aficionados.

The night scope was military grade and it brought the distant world of the Paragon up close and personal. Decoy watched as the crème-de-la-crap of Glasgow society, having now finished their over-priced dinners, exited the posh eatery and waited for their motors to be brought around.

Decoy's mobile vibrated in his pocket. He didn't need to answer. There was no text. It came from the bouncer six streets away. Decoy peered through his night scope and watched as the Procurator Fiscal and his wife stepped out the front door of the Paragon. With one shot he could alter the pulse of Glasgow.

Then he gently swung the barrel of his sniper rifle in the direction of the queue waiting to get into Heaven and smiled: lying smack in the middle of the crosshairs was Detective Inspector Sharkey arm in arm with a hot date.

Decoy slowed his breathing.

Placed his index finger against the trigger.

In the alley next to the Paragon, a bouncer positioned at the bottom of that outside staircase listened to his Bluetooth for a moment, then moved a few bright yellow cones out of the way and made enough room for only one car to park in the alley—a red Mercedes SUV.

At almost the exact same time, a Black Hack disgorged a hen party with all the lasses sporting blonde Cleopatra wigs. The bouncer whisked them to the front of the queue and up the outside staircase. The bride was dressed in Latin attire, but still wore a frilly bridal veil and had her bra and knickers on the outside. As one should.

The bouncer watched the gaggle of Cleopatra wigs endeavour to conga line up the stairs. 'Da. Da. Da. Da. Da. Hey!'

Sharkey and Lyon-Jones stood in the lengthy queue watching the bouncer. 'I know him from somewhere...'

Lyon-Jones was freezing in her mini-skirt and annoyed. 'Why are we here, Boss?

'It's just a hunch, Jones.'

'I thought you were going to show me how it works on the street.' Said sardonically, no *worse* than that, said with exasperation.

'Patience, Jones.'

Lyon-Jones rolled her eyes. Listened to the music pumping out from the club above. Turned to Sharkey. 'Is that Cee Lo?'

'Cilla?'

'No, Cee Lo, sir. Cee Lo Green?'

'You mean "Black".'

'Huh?'

'Cilla Black?'

'No, the American.'

'Cilla Black's not American, she's a Scouser.'

'*Green*, not Black.'

'What are you talking about?'

'Were you raised by wolves, sir?'

Sharkey shot poison darts with his eyes.

Halfway up the stairs, our well-shaven hen stopped and rushed back down, having left something behind in the taxi.

Sharkey pointed over to the bottom of the stairs.

A scrum was forming as our rich footballer stepped from the red Mercedes and was ushered to the front of the queue. Being super fit, he quickly moved up the stairs. Just as he reached the top, someone must have recognised him as his name was yelled out. Our footballer turned, waved and then blew a kiss, but only a spray of blood came out. The second shot took off the top of his head. In spite of being already dead, his body didn't topple over for a nanosecond, but when it did, it just happened to collapse right into the arms of our young hen who was hurrying up the stairs from the taxi having had to retrieve her purse with the cocaine. Of course she couldn't be blamed for freaking out, screaming and then reacting really as anyone of us would, by violently pushing the corpse away from her face. Unfortunately, the deceased toppled over the railing, fell two stories and landed flat-slam-bang spread eagle in the middle of his Mercedes SUV's roof, his blood gushing in torrents down the sides. Not that anyone would know, mind you, what with the Mercedes being arterial red.

'Get down!' Sharkey yelled and threw himself on top of Lyon-Jones. She could smell whisky on his breath.

And then there was panic. Unbridled panic as all punters ran for cover. Except one, he stood there curiously regarding the corpse. He had recognised him upon arrival.

'Someone's shot the Rangers goalie!'

And our hen stopped running and looked back. She didn't know it at the time, but that was as close as she was ever going to get to becoming a WAG.

Sharkey pushed Lyon-Jones up and behind the red Mercedes as blood leaked on to the tarmac next to them.

'When I say Go! Make a run for the Polar Bear.'

'We need to call in the shooting!'

'Call it in as you're running!'

'In my stiletto ankle-boots...no worries, Boss.'

CHAPTER FORTY-ONE

Young Siobhan Wilde shuffled in place, trying to keep warm. It was cold out here in Bath Street, as she waited for the bus to take her back to her bedsit in Maryhill.

She had finished her shift at Costa Coffee in Buchanan Galleries, and then she and a colleague had changed their clothes in the unisex toilet, inserted vodka-soaked tampons for a quick, cheap high and gone to the Firewater bar in Sauchiehall Street hoping to meet any and all eligible men. At Firewater, they did Jägerbombs and 'eyeball shots of vodka' by holding a full shot glass up to the eye. She got righteously hammered and did permanent damage to her eye, but fuck it, you're only young once.

Later in the evening, her friend had someone try to get a leg up and now Siobhan was left finding her way home, alone.

Siobhan was from Belfast and she was thrilled to be in Glasgow. It had always been her dream: work in Glasgow, perhaps meet Mr Right, not go back to Belfast, ever. There was nothing for her back home. She had never known her father and her mother was in the process of becoming a teenager again, dressing like a slut, acting like a scobe.

Siobhan was tired of getting hit on by her mum's new boyfriends. The last one had crawled into her bed in the middle of the night (after her mum had passed out from farmer's strength Poteen) and she had woken up with his hand between her legs. She had enough of that shit, so she was on the next ferry to Stranraer.

'Fancy a drink?'

Siobhan looked up and saw a well-dressed businessman standing in front of her. She might have been only 18, but Siobhan knew enough not to get involved with a total stranger in a strange city. Plus she couldn't handle her liquor very well and she was already way over her limit. No, level heads had to prevail. Siobhan was no dummy, so she looked the businessman straight in the eyes and said, 'Just one drink. And I choose the bar.'

'You lead the way,' the businessman said, then, as an ambulance and two marked

patrol cars sped by, 'There's some sort of police activity down there. What's your name?'

'Siobhan.'

'From Northern Ireland?'

'Nothing gets by you, does it,' Siobhan teased. 'What's your name?'

'Decoy.'

'Decoy? That's a funny name.'

'Isn't it just.'

Siobhan led him up to Lauder's on the corner of Renfield and Sauchiehall, where they found an empty booth in a dimly lit corner. Siobhan threw caution to the prevailing westerlies and ordered a bottle of WKD Blue, Decoy a pint of Bavaria Premium Malt.

Siobhan was unaware that the beer was zero percent alcohol, but was impressed nevertheless and squealed, 'You're so continental!' then excused herself, saying she wanted to go freshen up. Decoy watched her go. She was on the plump side, but astonishingly well-proportioned and she would do nicely. The drinks arrived, Decoy had a sip of his beer, then he dropped a tiny tablet known as 'yaba' or 'Thai pill' into Siobhan's drink.

Siobhan returned, beaming. She had texted her friend: AWHFY? IM.

'Do you believe in fate?' Siobhan asked, quaffing her drink.

'Absolutely.'

'Were you working late?'

'Came from a Christmas office party. You?'

Siobhan had another swig. 'I work at Costa Coffee. Went out for a few after work.'

Siobhan's cheeks flushed and she suddenly felt warm. Warm and tingly.

'I'm from Belfast.'

'Never would've guessed…'

'Ever been?'

'Never've been west of Kilmarnock.'

'Glasgow's not as dangerous as Belfast.'

'It's a great city.'

'Anyone ever tell you that you have bedroom eyes?'

'Always.'

Siobhan laughed, then slid up close to Decoy and brushed her ample breasts against him. He put his hand between her legs. This time a stranger's hand between her legs wasn't a problem.

'My sister just had her first child. A girl. Little Maeve. I just love the name "Maeve".'

'So do I.'

'It means "intoxicating one".'

'Oooh,' Decoy cooed, and moved his hand deeper, leading with his middle finger.

'I think I'd better be going,' Siobhan said warningly.

'Where?'

'Your place.'

'Finish your drink first.'

'Where do you live?'

'I live on a boat.'

'Romantic. I don't usually do this.'

'Neither do I.'

By the time they arrived at the docks in Govan, a few snowflakes were falling from the heavens. Mother Nature could be quite quirky in Glasgow.

'Motorcycles are not that great in the snow. You may have to spend the night.'

'I think that can be arranged.'

'In fact, I may never let you leave.'

As Decoy inserted the key into the wheelhouse door, Siobhan grabbed his crotch.

'You're naughty.'

'Let me just go into the stateroom for a moment,' Decoy said.

'To freshen up?' Siobhan teased.

'Something like that.'

'Wait!'

'What?'

'Where's your Christmas lights?'

'Don't have any yet...'

'I could help?'

'I'd like nothing better. Take your shoes off. Leave them out here.'

'Hurry.'

Decoy went into his surprisingly large stateroom and removed all the sheets off the bed. He took out a plastic fitted sheet like some classless hotels use and stretched it over the mattress, then he carefully made the bed back up again. He placed a fish filleting knife on the nightstand behind a poinsettia, a jar of KY jelly next to it and lit a candle. Then he swung the door open.

'I'm ready now...'

'So am I,' Siobhan said. 'I'm on fire.'

Siobhan was standing there, stark-buck naked.

There's nothing like true love, and this was going to be nothing like true love.

Decoy led Siobhan to the bed and she slowly and erotically undressed him. Then they slipped on to the top of the covers. It was cold and damp in the boat, but heat wasn't a problem at this stage of the game. Decoy tenderly and expertly caressed and fondled Siobhan until she couldn't take it anymore.

'Enter me now! But use a Johnny.'

And he did, and it didn't take him long to make her cum. But he didn't.

'Let's do it again,' Decoy said.

The drug coursing through Siobhan's body was unrelenting and there was nothing she wished more than to fuck again. Over and over, until she bled, she didn't care, she was so out of control. What was it about this man?

Decoy gently applied a hand to Siobhan's hip. 'Roll over.'

Siobhan just wanted to please and get on with it, so she rolled over and pulled her buttocks off the bed. She drew her knees up and dropped her head on the bed. As Decoy slipped behind her, he noticed the tramp-stamp on her lower back. It read: 'This Side Up'. He reached to the bedside table and extracted a large dollop of KY jelly and massaged her anus.

'Oh, wasn't expecting that...'

131

Then Decoy grabbed a hold of her strawberry hair and pulled her head back.

'You're hurting me...but I like it...'

Decoy penetrated her anus and rhythmically began to move. With each thrust, Siobhan let out a groan of pleasure.

'Do it harder! Hurt me!'

Decoy was more than happy to oblige. He thrust deep inside her and reached for the fish filleting knife on the nightstand, and just as young Siobhan was brought to orgasm and shuddered over and over again, he severed her left carotid artery with a quick ripping motion. With his left hand, Decoy covered the gushing wound so the arterial spray would not spurt all over the walls, rather pump between his fingers, and then, right then, he climaxed as he watched the rich dark blood spread and pool beneath her naked body.

And then he did something he'd never done before.

He put his finger in the blood and tasted it. Oooh, it was rather sweet. That was a surprise. And metallic. Coppery, perhaps. He would have to do this more often.

And then Decoy had an idea. A brilliant idea. A great bloody brainstorm: He was going to save something from each victim from now on in. Wished he had done it with the Inspector's daughter as she was particularly scrumptious. But what to save? What would you save? An article of clothing? Panties? Perhaps cut off a finger? Or an ear? Shit man! Then he had it. He knew what he would save. He would build up a collection. Keep them all in a jar. Right out in the open. In the galley. Up on the shelf with all the other condiments and spices.

Decoy grabbed his fillet knife.

And circumcised Siobhan.

Decoy thought back to his time in Kuwait where he had become familiar with the practice of female genital mutilation. Actually had watched it being performed with a scissors on one occasion. Had to pay for the pleasure. Had asked if he could masturbate during the procedure if he paid more, but was refused. Said that since the nine-year-old girl wasn't sedated, and was able to look around at all the men present, it would be looked upon as barbaric.

The masturbating, not the cutting.

Decoy dismounted, put the genitalia in a jar with the pickled herring, tied a rope around Siobhan's neck, attached a 20 kilo dumbbell to her feet with duct tape and dropped her over the side and into the river. The body sank instantly and he tethered it to a cleat on the stern. He would check from time to time to see if any gases were building and how she was deteriorating. If she became a floater, he would have to reel her in and puncture the abdomen with an ice pick to release the gases.

And if the decaying corpse attracted any creatures in the frigid Clyde, he just might go fishing.

Decoy took a deep breath of the winter night air. He was pleased he was able to blow the tubes out tonight. He went back inside, to the galley. Took a bottle of Coca-Cola out of the fridge. Unscrewed the top. Drank half of it down. And then peed in the bottle, filling it nearly back to the top. He set the bottle of Coke/urine on the sink, then grabbed a heavy-duty glass 1000-ml Pyrex beaker out of a cabinet. Carefully he poured the mixture into the beaker and set it down in the sink basin. Then he reached under the sink and extracted the can of WD-40 that he kept there for all occasions and all purposes. Like a scientist in his laboratory, Decoy skillfully sprayed the oily lubricant on to the surface of the Coca-Cola/urine. Then he retrieved his fish fillet knife that he had used to kill Siobhan and submerged it in the concoction. This cleansing method he had learnt from an old mate who had been a crime-scene cleaner. Even the most sophisticated Forensic Scientist would not be able to pick up any trace of blood once the knife sat in the solution overnight.

Decoy returned the WD-40 to its home under the sink, then pulled it back out. He'd almost forgot that he would need it tomorrow. He always sprayed the WD-40 on his fishing hooks and lures. It was supposed to be an urban myth that the WD-40 actually helped to catch fish, but myth or not, it sure worked for Decoy. That, plus he had to take a couple of cans out to his mum on the farm.

If it was sprayed on cows, it kept the flies off.

Decoy chuckled. There was not much more that one needed in life besides duct tape and WD-40.

Decoy took a long shower, towelled off, climbed into bed

and was about to doze off, when he remembered Siobhan's shoes and clothing. She had left them all outside. Quickly he rose. Went to the afterdeck. Grabbed the clothes. Threw the shoes overboard. Went back inside with the clothes. Climbed into bed with them.

And nodded right off.

Tonight was a night for erotic dreams.

# CHAPTER FORTY-TWO

During the night, Glasgow was hit with three inches of snow and miraculously the dawn broke with sunny skies for the second day running.

Sharkey had spent the night in the dentist chair, having fallen asleep, exhausted, covered with only a leather jacket for a blanket. And he had had certifiable dreams. Unrequited dreams. He'd bolted awake twice to save Katie who was in peril, but couldn't. In the first dream, Katie was little again and they were skiing up in the Cairngorms. Katie kept skiing closer and closer to the edge of the mountain. Sharkey tried to warn here, but she couldn't hear him and just kept looking back, laughing and smiling. He tried to go to her, but he couldn't get his skis to turn. And she slipped over the edge. In the second dream, it was Katie's wedding day. Sharkey was escorting her down the aisle toward the altar to give her away. Katie looked beautiful in a glorious strapless wedding gown. As they approached the front, Sharkey looked over at all the guests and the hostess from The Stud was standing there, holding a Bible with the centre cut out. Nothing in it. No gun. The hostess leaned closed to Sharkey and whispered: 'She looks so happy.' And Sharkey looked on in horror as the groom turned to look back. And the groom was Decoy Brody. A priest was smiling angelically and holding a small silk pillow in his outstretched hands. On it was a fish fillet knife. Sharkey tried to charge forward, but was restrained by two of the ushers: the mechanic with the greasy arms and Taxi Boy, smoking a fag.

* * *

Sharkey drove past a pharmacy. Slowed. Pulled over. Left the motor running.

Like most pharmacies in the city, this one had a queue of addicts lined up out front, anxiously waiting for the doors to

135

open, so they could get their heroin substitute: methadone. He watched as the doors opened. The first addict rushed in. Moments later he was back out. A haunted-eyed woman stepped from the wings. The addict took money.

And spat the methadone in her mouth, the famous *Methadone spit*.

Sharkey blinked. Blinked again. Slipped the Polar Bear into first. Motored on.

The scene of the crime on the stairway to Heaven was condoned off and the area had become a winter wonderland accented with a blue-and-white tent, light-blue 'Noddy suits', masks, gloves and booties. If you didn't look too closely, you would have only seen a snowscape with blue accessories.

Sharkey swung the Polar Bear into the alley, yanked the emergency brake and climbed out. He was wearing a woolly scarf and carrying two Costa coffees. He loved winter mornings like these. Or at least he used to: Crisp, cold and just before Christmas in the greatest city in the world. But his world had changed now. Would never be the same. Could never be the same. He'd lost his eldest daughter in America and had somehow managed to carry on. He'd never lost the pain, but he had resolve. Made a promise to himself that he would never let anything happen to Katie. And he had failed.

'What are you doing here?'

Sharkey put his wallowing in self-pity on hold and looked up. DS Fiona Lyon-Jones was standing there.

'Grabbing a coffee around the corner.'

'You always get two cups?'

'One was supposed to be for the detective managing the scene of crime.'

'A bribe?'

'Something like that.'

'What are you doing here, Jones?'

'Managing the scene of crime, sir.'

'You?'

'I called it in. It's my baby.'

'Does Squires know we were here last night?'

'Just knows *I* was here last night.'

'Thanks. You been here all night?'

Lyon-Jones opened the heavy winter coat she had borrowed from one of the uniforms. She was still wearing the slinky mini-skirt of the previous evening.

'Goes well with the Doc Martens.'

Lyon-Jones gave a wry smile. 'Can I have my bribe now?'

Sharkey handed over one of the coffees. 'Americano. Cream in the left pocket, Jones. Sugar in the right.'

'One from the left, three from the right, sir.'

'Three?'

'I like anything sweet, but I'm cutting down. Getting back into jogging.'

Lyon-Jones poured the creamer and the three sugars into her coffee. Pocketed the debris. Took a sip. Hot!

'We think he was shot from that rooftop,' Lyon-Jones said, touching her tongue to the roof of her mouth. She pointed up at the neighbouring roof. 'The bouncer working the queue said he heard the shot come from up there. He's still here. Hasn't gone home yet. Quite shaken up, but been a great help.'

'I need to speak to him.'

'Why you really here, sir?'

'You know why I'm here...and you didn't see me here...'

'C'mon, then.'

Lyon-Jones led Sharkey over to the bouncer who was rolling a cigarette and leaning with his knee up, foot flat against the neighbouring building. Sharkey noted the Bluetooth hanging off one ear.

'This is Detective Inspector Sharkey,' Lyon-Jones said. 'He'd like to ask you a few questions.'

'Go on then,' Bluetooth said. 'Anything I can do tae help the polis, just let me know.' He swiped the rollup across his tongue. Placed it between his lips.

Sharkey still thought he knew this guy from somewhere. 'Any idea who may have done something like this?'

The bouncer lit up. Sucked hard. Smoke came out his mouth. Swirled up his nostrils. Life suddenly good. 'After the other night, I think half of Glesga would've liked tae blow his brains out.'

'Can you be less insensitive and more specific?' Sharkey said.

The complexity of the question was a bit much for the

bouncer and it took a few moments for him to break it down into smaller pieces and digest. 'The hit has the McQueen gang all over it.'

'And the reason you're saying that, is?'

'Donnae want tae open ma gub too much, but check with the bookies and read between the lines.' Immensely pleased with himself.

Sharkey thanked the bouncer for his incisive take on the murder and let him return to his wall. Fleet looked at Lyon-Jones and held both palms up.

'Tattoo McQueen is a known heavy gambler. Perhaps he had the goalie in his pocket and the goalie messed up.'

Sharkey drained his coffee. Looked at Lyon-Jones. Wanted her take on the motivation for the killing. 'So you think McQueen lost a bundle?'

'Yes, sir. Big bundle.'

'What were the entry wounds like, Jones?'

'Throat: entry tight, exit large.'

'And the head?'

'Cavitation at its worst…there was very little left from the eyebrows up.'

Sharkey knew what that meant. The goalie was most likely shot with a .50 calibre, or similar ilk.

'Anyway for us to get above the crime scene?'

Lyon-Jones looked up at the staircase. 'Both the Paragon and Heaven are owned by the same company. A company with a Russian sounding name. There's a service lift at the back of the kitchen in the Paragon. We can access the nightclub from there and come down from above.'

Lyon-Jones guided Sharkey through a back door and into the kitchen of the Paragon. They entered a rickety lift with no door. And no gate. The lift took an eternity to reach Heaven. They stepped out of the lift and were hit with the same stale stench you're hit with when you step on to an airplane.

Lyon-Jones and Sharkey slalomed through the previous night's detritus of tiny plastic bags, vials, bottles brought in from the outside and something that looked suspiciously like a spent condom (if horses used condoms), and aimed for the front door of the club.

Lyon-Jones grimaced. 'Sorry to have missed all this last night. You take me to only the finest places.'

Sharkey didn't respond. He was already pushing the bar on the front door open. Eyes adjusting to the light. Scanning the rooftops of the surrounding buildings.

They stepped out onto the stairway to Heaven, just above the scene of the crime. Sharkey could see the blood splatter on the steps below and part of the wall. He reached into a coat pocket and extracted the Leupold Mark 4 sniper scope he kept in the glovebox of the Polar Bear. He looked through the scope at the roof of the neighbouring building. The angle was all wrong. Sharkey went rooftop by rooftop away from the *locus*. He came to the flat roof of the distant Premier Inn.

'Listen, Jones, if you hear of anything…'

'I'll give you a discreet bell.'

'Thanks. And, remember, I wasn't here.'

'I never saw you, sir,' Lyon-Jones said.

And then wondered if she should grass up Sharkey.

## CHAPTER FORTY-THREE

Sharkey climbed into the Polar Bear and drove over to the Premier Inn, double parked and climbed out. He took a laminated piece of A4 paper which read PRESS in big black letters, slapped it under a windscreen wiper and entered the hotel.

Sharkey was well aware that employees had been scrambling for clandestine places to suck on a fag and that the roofs of Glasgow had become coveted sanctuaries.

Within seconds he was opening the door to the roof of the twelve-storey hotel. He spotted an area just outside the door where there were footprints in the fresh snow and cigarette stubs galore. He walked to the far end of the roof and around large heating vents. He held up his sniper scope and focused. He could easily make out Lyon-Jones still standing just above the scene of the crime. It was over a thousand yards. An impossible shot for most, but not for a sniper. Not many shooters could have made the shot that killed the Rangers goalie. At night. Through swirling inner-city winds.

Sharkey left the roof and stepped back in the lift and hit LOBBY. The lift doors closed, making the noise a guillotine makes.

As the lift descended, it came to him. Sharkey knew who the bouncer was. He was one of the feral goons he had seen in the car with Fat Cheeks.

# CHAPTER FORTY-FOUR

Denny the Screwdriver Sutherland entered the Ibrox subway station, bought a ticket, descended into the bowels of the system and shuddered. The subway gave him the creeps. He suffered from claustrophobia and didn't like confined spaces, but he had to do it. Felt it was the only safe place to talk business. The Screwdriver's train came, heading clockwise. At the next stop, Govan, he detrained, took the overpass to the platform of the trains going counterclockwise and entered a car with only one person in it—Decoy Brody. Decoy Brody was reading the *Daily Record*. The Screwdriver pulled out a rolled-up copy of the *Herald* even though the level of the journalism was beyond his grasp. Even the Sports.

If you had been seated opposite them, you would have heard two newspapers talking. Talking headlines.

'Jaysus, Decoy, 'I wasn't serious when I said you should kill the English goalie...'

'Golly gee, I'm sorry, Boss. But you said cut his baws off.'

'Just an expression, ye dim shite, we was just talking football.'

'My bad....I could make up for it by killing Inspector Sharkey.'

'It just may come to that. He's been sticking his nose in every fucking crack. We'd better let the English goalie fiasco die down a bit first, though.'

'Okie dokie, Boss.'

'And you'd better pray the Press don't make a big fucking deal of this.'

* * *

They came, one by one, first from Argentina and Brazil. And oddly Japan. Then Germany, Sweden, France, South Africa and Ghana. And Australia. And even Switzerland and tiny Cameroon.

The world's media—photographers, journalists, TV crews—descended on Glasgow and a circus atmosphere was born out at Ibrox and in the city centre around Heaven.

The killing of a football goalie had become a killer story.

Sales of Rangers kit, souvenirs and memorabilia went through the roof (not that there is one). Queues at Heaven had never been so long and another bouncer had to be put on.

He was the other Sutherland goon.

Decoy Brody sat in the galley of his houseboat and gloated.

He had wanted the Press to make a big deal of the killing.

And it was just the beginning.

# CHAPTER FORTY-FIVE

Lyon-Jones burst into Sharkey's office without announcing herself.

'I would appreciate the courtesy of a knock before you enter.'

'Sorry, sir.' Lyon-Jones threw a pile of morning newspapers on his desk. 'Better take a look at those, Boss.'

'Why do you keep calling me "Boss" when I've asked you not to, Jones?'

'I'll stop calling you Boss when you stop calling me Jones.'

The sodding cheek.

Sharkey picked up the first newspaper, the *Herald*. The headline read: FOOTBALLER MURDERED IN COLD BLOOD. Then he picked up the *Daily Record*. Its headline stated: GLASGOW CRIME HITS NEW LOW. Then the *Sun* quoted: THOUGHT IT ONLY HAPPENED IN THE THIRD WORLD.

Lyon-Jones went to Sharkey's computer.

'Leave it alone, Jones!'

'Hang on a minute, Boss.' Lyon-Jones was about to make an entry. Saw that Sharkey had an old email from Katie up there. Felt awful for a fleeting second. Then made an entry before Sharkey could stop her. 'Check it out.'

On the Internet, a sacrilegious blog known as the 'Blog Hog' stated rather insensitively: RANGERS GOALIE SLAIN, WAS PLANNING TO RETURN TO ENGLAND ANYWAY.

'That's cold.'

Sharkey looked at the other newspapers on his desk. 'What about those?'

'Newspapers from the south. They say much the same thing.' Lyon-Jones held up the *Daily Mail*. 'With the exception of this one.' She handed it to Sharkey. The headline read: TOP MP: 'I'M GAY AND I'M LEAVING MY WIFE'.

Sharkey turned it around so Lyon-Jones could see it.

'Sorry, sir.' Lyon-Jones ripped the newspaper from Sharkey's hands. 'Not that one, this one.'

Sharkey read the headline: GLASGOW IS BECOMING THE LONDON OF JACK THE RIPPER.

'First of all that's a bunch of crap, and second of all how does any of this help me get the killer of my daughter?'

* * *

A briefing was about to get underway.

Sharkey and Lyon-Jones were standing at the back of the Incident Room. Lyon-Jones was playing Sudoku on her iPhone as DCI Maggie Squires rifled through her notes in preparation.

Sharkey leaned close to Lyon-Jones and whispered: 'Both the Press and the public are baying for blood and Squires needed to cough up a suspect, and fast.'

Squires looked up from her notes, eyed Sharkey. 'Okay, listen up, people, we now believe Decoy Brody was also behind the two killings: at the Glasgow Royal Infirmary and that of the Rangers goalie…'

Sharkey hissed at Lyon-Jones: 'My position all along!'

Squires glowered in Sharkey's direction. 'May I carry on, Inspector?'

Everyone turned to look at Sharkey. Lyon-Jones tried to become part of the wall.

'We have been receiving numerous anonymous tips that Decoy Brody was seen brazenly moving about Govan…'

Sharkey to Lyon-Jones: 'This is all about getting the target off her back!'

Squires glowered at Sharkey again.

Lyon-Jones moved away from Sharkey.

'I've instructed that a net be thrown around Govan the likes of which Glasgow has never seen: 500 officers are being deployed, 160 armed, 20 armoured carriers, one helicopter and an RAF Tornado jet—both with thermal imaging capability.'

Squires puffed her chest out with pride, a chest that didn't need puffing out.

'An effort of this scale had not been mounted in the UK since Raoul Moat was hunted in Rothbury down in England. Glasgow will go on the map as a city of "You can run, but you cannot hide!'"

Sharkey shook his head. He had moved among killers his whole life. Lived among them. Was one, as a gang leader. And during the Gulf War. The one thing a really clever killer could do was hide. For as long as he—or she—wanted.

Squires was in for a big surprise.

# CHAPTER FORTY-SIX

As darkness fell, Decoy Brody sat in the wheelhouse of his fishing boat, a rust-bucket on the outside, a comfortable Tardis on the inside. He was enjoying the play-by-play on the Airwave PR he was 'renting for the evening' by supplying drugs to a bent copper friend of his. In Glasgow drugs were a more coveted currency than Scottish pounds.

Decoy watched the sealing off of Govan by the Strathclyde Police and their River Clyde Police Marine Unit. He watched as busloads of officers were shuttled across the Kingston Bridge. He counted the armoured carriers as they did the same. He saw the polis pilots run through their check list on *Victor Mike 70* at its heliport right across the river on Stobcross Quay next to the Armadillo, and then take to the skies. And he heard the distant rumble as the Tornado roared into Govan air space and made its first pass.

It was an impressive show of force and Decoy was over the moon.

A kid from Govan had made it big.

And when the RAF Tornado flew directly overhead, or the Strathclyde chopper hovered nearby, he would simply slip below deck. The deck was lined with a layer of Mylar and painted with a concoction made from harvested magnetic tape so no heat source would register on the thermal imaging.

Toying with the police was always something that had brought Decoy great joy, mind you, not as much joy as taking a life or the 'snuff sex' afterwards, but great joy, nevertheless. When Decoy was a gang member with the Govan Fleeto as a young lad, he was involved in a murder. Two if you count the Paki youth, which of course he didn't. And back then, the polis were always on the right track, but too often, too many steps behind. He had even been brought in and interviewed, but he had been cool as an ice pick and had those eyes which shouted out innocence.

In spite of bullying his classmates at primary, Decoy hadn't risen from the twisted beginnings of the classic sociopath: pulling the wings off flies and torching kittens, and he hadn't been sexually abused by a parent or a teacher or a man of the cloth (although he had been hosed down in the back garden by his father for wetting his bed). He had simply been involved in a killing when he was fourteen and was pleasantly surprised to find out that taking a life aroused him. The way fire arouses an arsonist. It was a powerful aphrodisiac.

One summer night, he bludgeoned a prostitute to death with a brick in Paisley Road West, just to see what it was like, then he had lain the corpse across the nearby railroad tracks and waited. A few minutes later, the train to Cardonald passed through and severed the body completely in two. Decoy had been so turned on, he'd run all the way home and masturbated. Numerous times. And he just couldn't get the image out of his mind. And he couldn't douse the flame of sexual desire. This blood lust created great anxiety for Decoy and it simmered until he turned sixteen and was able to join the Royal Marines.

And he worked hard to become a sniper.

A killing machine.

And then he made his first kill as a sniper with the Sinn Féin hit near that checkpoint in Cullyhanna.

And had his first snuff sex shortly thereafter.

When Decoy grew bored watching the polis scurry about like an ant hill that a child had mussed with his hands—and a good hunk of taxpayer's money had been wasted—he decided to ratchet up the bother. Wait till they saw what he now had in store for them. His next deed would really light a fire under their arses.

And kick the snot out of their budget.

The first thing he did was to check on Siobhan to see how she was faring. Her corpse was covered with flesh devouring crabs and some sort of a sucking cephalopod. So that was going well. He let her slip back under the inky Clyde, then he double checked the bow line and the stern line and adjusted the spring lines. Then he locked the wheelhouse, fetched his torch and stepped off the *What A Catch* and onto shore.

The polis were so predictably stupid. They would have the subways of Ibrox and Govan and Cessnock covered, and they would have checkpoints at all major intersections in Govan and all roads leading out. And the Kingston Bridge and the Squinty Bridge and Bell's Bridge and the Millennium Bridge and the Clyde Tunnel. And, aye, the police boat would be cruising up and down the river contributing absolutely fuck-all.

And that's why his next move would be so genius.

In actuality, Decoy considered himself a genius. An evil genius. Sure he loved playing the docile, imbecilic dolt. And he loved being paid in cocaine by the Sutherland family. But he was his own man. His own boss.

His long-term goal in life was to set Scotland on its ear. Kick the polis' arses back to the 19th-century. Make a name as the most evil creature who ever walked the earth north of the border. Fuck that. How about the most evil being to walk the streets of Great Britain. When the likes of Jack the Ripper, The Yorkshire Ripper, Jekyll and Hyde, the Acid Bath Vampire and Dr Harold Shipman were mentioned, he hoped to one day be at the fucking top.

Decoy wanted his name's very mention to strike such fear into the hearts of his countrymen, that children would not be allowed out of doors, women would not go out after dark and men would only venture to pubs in groups of three or more.

Unless it was Quiz Night, of course.

Wait. Hold on just a minute. He was lying to himself. Deceiving his very being. Like the scummiest syphilitic druggie, his appetite for *his* drug—sex—was getting out of control. And he needed more and more fixes to whet his voracious appetite. If that mad bastard Denny the Screwdriver didn't give him steady employment, he just might have to branch out on his own.

Decoy ambled slowly away from his fishing boat and along a darkened path which led to the perimeter fence of the old dry docks where his boat was tied up. He jumped the fence and entered Festival Park to avoid the walk along the Clyde by the Millennium Bridge and Bell's Bridge, both of which were crawling with cops. Cleverly, he had waited until the industrial estates were emptying and workers were spilling out of the BBC

Scotland and STV buildings.

Just metres from the Govan side of the Squinty Bridge, and the two marked patrol cars guarding its entrance, Decoy Brody was ready for his coup-de-fucking grace. Ready for the wee manoeuvre which would land him on tomorrow's front pages.

Above the fold.

Finally by name.

# CHAPTER FORTY-SEVEN

The Polar Bear was parked in Govan, along the River Clyde.

Sharkey and Lyon-Jones listened to the sealing off of Govan on the Airwave radio that Lyon-Jones held in her hand. She waved the handset in Sharkey's face. 'Hope like hell he doesn't have one of these.'

'Oh, but he will. He'll know exactly what the police are doing.'

'I don't buy it.'

'My dad was a cop. If he brought his Airwave home after an event, I would nick it for the night. If we heard the police were on to us, we'd scarper and change clothes or just disappear. I thought I was really cool until my dad caught me and beat me to within an inch of my life.'

'But if Decoy Brody's stolen one, then surely we could block the handset's signal.'

'*If* he's stolen one. And *if* we knew whose radio it was.'

'What about tracing it with GPS?'

'Same answer.' Sharkey pointed up in the sky as the Tornado roared into Govan air space and made its second pass. They watched the movement of police vehicles across the Kingston Bridge. 'Decoy Brody is enjoying every second of this, and the night is still—'

'Shit!'

Sharkey looked over at Lyon-Jones. 'What?'

'Do you want my take on this? My book-learnt, didn't-grow-up-on-the-streets-of-Glasgow take on this?'

'Go on then.'

'Do you agree that he's just toying with us?'

'Hundred percent.'

'If he's playing, the only way for him to win is to show himself.'

'Keep going.'

'Just getting the police to mobilize en masse is not winning. Winning is showing his face. Naa naa naa naa naa naa. The way a child teases.'

'Fuck!' Sharkey slammed the dashboard so hard, he made Lyon-Jones jump. 'When I was in the gang, we would slip over to Govan to bother our rivals then go back across the river and thumb our noses at them.'

'But there's no way out of Govan tonight?'

'Oh, but there is. Same way I slipped *into* Govan as a teenager. The old Harbour Tunnel. You'd only know about it if you grew up here. There used to be an entrance over by the Squinty Bridge!'

Sharkey fired up the Polar Bear and they passed cops on nearly every corner as they rocketed over to the now derelict rotunda-shaped brick building which marked the entrance to the old tunnel on the south side of the river.

The Govan side of the river.

Sharkey pulled the Polar Bear on to the pavement and killed the engine. He and Lyon-Jones jumped out. At the back of the building was a rusting metal door.

'This is where we used to go in as kids...'

'It's locked!'

'A locked door won't stop him.'

'I don't buy it, sir.'

'There's a lot you don't buy, Jones.'

'Look around you. The place is crawling with cops. I think your sixth sense is letting you down on this one. It's just too risky.'

'Jones, it's why we did what we did when I was in the gang. The risk. It was a natural high. The best high ever. The riskier, the better.'

'Still don't buy it.'

'Try to humour me, Jones. If you were Decoy Brody and you wanted to thumb your nose at the police, where would you go?'

'But...'

'Where does a sociopath go, Jones?'

'Somewhere where the whole world is watching.' She looked at Sharkey. Could see a superior intelligence at work.

'Some place where there's shit-loads of CCTV in order to verify his feat.'

'Sauchiehall Street?'

'No, too far from the river.'

'St Enoch Shopping Centre?'

'Close to the river, but still too far from the harbour tunnel and his rat hole.'

'Where then?'

Sharkey thought. Thought some more. And then he had it.

'Central Station!'

# CHAPTER FORTY-EIGHT

Opened in 1879, Central Station in the Glasgow City Centre is the busiest railway station in Britain, outside of London. Nearly 34-million passengers use the station per annum. Many of them pay.

The station has more CCTV then some city centres.

To some, it would feel as if the whole world were watching.

If you entered the front of the station, from Gordon Street, and walked into the middle of the main concourse you would see the large illuminated scheduling board straight in front of you with trains to destinations such as London Euston, Norwich and Penzance. Directly below the scheduling board were the obligatory Starbucks and Tie Rack. Off to the right, Costa Coffee. If you turned and looked behind you, you would see six ticket counters.

Wearing a bright-red Berghaus ski jacket, and toting a bright-red backpack, Decoy Brody stood at ticket window number 6. He chose number 6 because it was his lucky number (the number of times he brought one woman to orgasm—before he strangled her with her brassiere). Also he picked the young woman teller as she was the most likely to remember him.

Taking his time and paying with cash, Decoy booked his journey and openly flirted. After receiving his change and ticket, Decoy thanked the woman and then turned and looked up at the atrium's 48,000 panes of glass that once had been painted black to deceive World War II enemy bombers. Viewing the atrium would give the multiple CCTV cameras on the two posts facing the ticket windows the best angle to capture his best side.

Decoy chuckled, some of the lassies thought his posterior to be his best side.

Back at the ticket window, the young lass had been quite taken with Decoy's good looks, especially those eyes, but she had not as yet looked down at the colour photo of fugitive Decoy Brody taped next to her till.

Decoy crossed from the area of the ticket windows over to WH Smith. He stood patiently in a long queue, ensuring the CCTV camera to his left captured a good long loop of his profile. Then he purchased a pack of Benson & Hedges and stepped back out into the main concourse. Methodically he slapped the pack of cigarettes against the palm of his left hand and withdrew one cigarette from the pack. He wasn't going to light up, as that was against the law, plus he didn't smoke, so that could have been theoretically factored into the equation. These dedicated movements were all about smoke and mirrors. Decoy stuck the unlit cigarette into his mouth as teenage smokers do, in a smoking *verboten* environment, to get the pre-smoke psychological kick and, more importantly, to show the world that they are grownup and therefore cooler than the backside of the pillow, then he preceded to aim for the Hope Street exit.

By now, Network Rail security and British Transport Police were already following the bloke in the bright-red jacket and bright-red backpack on CCTV as he moved through the main concourse and in the direction of Hope Street. He resembled the man in the photo, stuck with blue stickum just below their bank of monitors, but they reckoned it couldn't be Decoy Brody, because they all knew Decoy was holed up in Govan. And Govan was sealed off. Nevertheless, they would keep their eyes on the backpacker. They would love to harpoon such a big fish.

\* \* \*

All cars were being stopped and searched as they tried to leave Govan and cross the Squinty Bridge into the city centre. This pissed off Sharkey to no end. Govan was so well sealed off, even the police couldn't get out.

'This is a waste of time, Boss.'

\* \* \*

As Decoy moved towards the Hope Street exit, with cigarette protruding from lips, he had one eye on the last three CCTV cameras: the one up to the left, another just before the hotel sign and the one directly in front and overhead. Just as he slipped out of range of the last camera, he stopped. He was ten metres from Hope Street and the CCTV camera up on the corner of Hope and Gordon, high above the statue of the fireman.

* * *

The Polar Bear screeched to a stop in front of the main entrance to Central Station and Sharkey piled out. Lyon-Jones followed reluctantly. They entered the main atrium and Sharkey pointed to the impressive bank of CCTV cameras.

Sharkey rushed the ticket windows. Pushed punters out of the way. Got verbal abuse for doing so. Flashed his ID and held up his photo of Decoy Brody for the tellers to see. '

Sharkey turned to Lyon-Jones who was just walking up. 'The teller at #6 says someone who looked like Brody just bought a ticket to Hull and then she watched him go into WH Smith.'

Sharkey hurried over to WH Smith. Lyon-Jones didn't bother, just watched Sharkey go, and shook her head. Now she knew she would have to report Sharkey's questionable mental health to Squires.

* * *

One-hundred feet away, and only just out of sight, Decoy moved to the right side of the exit and stopped next to the curmudgeon, sitting on a chair, selling the *Evening Times*. Barking: 'Ab'enen Tams!'

* * *

Back in WH Smith, Sharkey thrust Decoy's photo in the face of the Indian woman working the till. 'This man, did you see him?'

'*Pagal!*' The Indian woman wasn't used to this much brio, except from the under-aged neds who tried to buy ciggies. 'Sorry, I am not seeing this man,' she said, and handed Sharkey a flyer for 10% off on a future purchase.

* * *

Decoy slipped off his backpack and removed his ski jacket, exposing a reflective high-visibility yellowish-green vest. The same as construction workers wear. Then he reached into his backpack and pulled out a blue hardhat.

These uncharacteristic movements did not raise an eyebrow from the wizened bloke selling the newspapers, but it did catch the eye of the cheery lad selling copies of *The Big Issue* just to his left. Even the cheery lad's loyal pooch lying on a blanket at his feet was suddenly interested.

Decoy smiled at *Big Issue* guy. 'How many issues do you have

155

left?'

'Ten.'

'I'll take all ten and give you a twenty pound note if you put on my ski jacket and backpack and walk up to platform #15.'

'What for?'

'Playing a joke on my mate…'

*Big Issue* guy knew this was not acceptable protocol, leaving his pitch, and he certainly didn't want to jeopardise his job now that he was finally getting back on his feet, but his portion of the rent was coming up on his flat-share and he didn't want to get in arrears. *Big Issue* guy regarded Decoy for a moment. 'What'll I do with the jacket and rucksack?'

'You keep 'em both.'

Decoy helped *Big Issue* guy into the jacket. Then he helped him pull the backpack on. 'What about your dog?'

'He'll be waitin' on me till I come back. Say, could I have the ciggie if yer no' goin' tae light up?'

'What's mine is yers. Have the whole fucking pack.'

*Big Issue* guy put the single fag behind his left ear, stuffed the pack of fags into the pocket of his new ski jacket and aimed for the main concourse of the train station. Of course by the time he reached the overhead scheduling board, he had realized he was being used for nefarious means and this ate away at his sense of doing what's right. So he went looking for a police officer.

Decoy grabbed a nearby broom, pulled the hardhat down over his eyes and then stepped out on to Hope Street and mingled with 30 other workers wearing blue hardhats and high-vis vests.

Carrying the broom, Decoy ambled under scaffolding down Hope Street to Argyle, dumped the broom and stopped to look back at the section of Central Station known as Hielanman's Umbrella. He smiled, not because he wasn't being followed, he knew that wasn't about to happen, rather he smiled because for some reason he remembered coming here as a young lad to catch a glimpse of Frank Sinatra who was staying at the then Central Hotel. Decoy knew so much about Glasgow that other locals didn't. In fact he considered himself a bit of a historian. And it was because of his interest in the city he so dearly loved, he would be back onboard the *What A Catch* within the hour, while the polis chased their tails and cut deeper and deeper into their beleaguered budgets.

Decoy turned right on Argyle, bore left on James Watt Street and carried along down to Anderston Quay. Then he cut under the M8 and walked briskly along Lancefield Quay where he dumped the hi-vis jacket and the hardhat into the river. He watched the jacket and hardhat slip beneath the surface of the water. Thought about Siobhan for a moment. And toddled the short distance up to the Rotunda Restaurant.

And then Decoy did something that few were even privy to: He entered the back door of the Rotunda and slipped down into the cellar, beneath the kitchen. Here was an access door to the old Harbour Tunnel on the north side of the river. He removed a key from his jeans' pocket and inserted it into the mortice lock.

To acquire a key for the tunnel legally had been out of the question. And to pay the price the gent wanted to acquire the key was out of the question, so Decoy had struck a deal, they would do a trade: The owner of the key would relinquish a copy of the key and in return Decoy would kill whomever, whenever. The owner of the key was reluctant to enter into such a transaction, but Decoy had so scared the bejesus out of him, he reckoned he better make the deal or Decoy would simply torture him, kill him and take the key. The deal was made. They shook hands and the owner of the key handed over  copy and wished he had never met Decoy Brody.

Until the messy divorce came along.

Decoy locked the access door behind him. Pitch black. He flipped on his torch and cautiously descended a rusting cast-iron staircase. He hadn't been in the tunnel much as an adult, but had 'lived' in here as a youth. He heard a noise behind him and swung around with his torch. Rats. Sewer rats. Big and fat, with beady wee eyes. This brought another smile and a fond memory of playing down here as a youth.

Before Decoy knew it he was at the south rotunda, the other side of the river. Here he had to be marginally careful as the access door would put him nearly face-to-face with the southern end of the Squinty Bridge and those two marked patrol cars guarding the entrance.

* * *

Lyon-Jones waited in front of Starbucks while Sharkey ran around like a chicken with his head cut off, checking exits. And there were plenty. When he returned, he looked a beaten man.

'With all due respect, sir, I don't think he was ever here.'

* * *

For Decoy, it was just a short stroll back through Festival Park to his fishing boat.

And Siobhan.

Who was floating off the stern!

Gases had built up alarmingly fast and Siobhan's shiny, porcelain-white stomach was bloated grotesquely, so he went to the galley, unearthed his ice pick and punctured her abdomen. Hissss.

And that aroused him.

After a healthy wank, Decoy repaired to the wheelhouse and watched the lights shimmering on the Clyde. Perhaps in a day or two, he would untie his boat, head down the river in the direction of the estuary, troll for salmon and then cut Siobhan loose so she could swim with the fishes.

If there was anything left of her.

# CHAPTER FORTY-NINE

All lights were burning at Strathclyde Police, City Centre, and the radiators were working overtime.

Chief Inspector Maggie Squires was in the middle of another briefing. Sharkey and Lyon-Jones stood side-by-side in their usual place along the back wall. Lyon-Jones had made up her mind: Sharkey was her boss, and he was struggling with the loss of his daughter, but he needed to be reported. She would get Squires alone after the briefing.

Sharkey had never seen Squires like this. She was on the warpath and she was sensing blood. A phone was ringing off the wall on the other side of the room and nobody was answering. Tension hung thick and heavy.

'For the love of God, can someone answer that?'

Half the room went for the phone, but Detective Constable Wilson got there first. CI Squires carried on with her briefing, demanding attention from the assembled, but was interrupted by DC Wilson.

'It's for you, ma'am.'

'Are you incapable of taking a detailed message, DC Wilson?'

'No, ma'am, but it's important.'

'Of course it's important, DC Wilson. WE—ARE—THE—POLICE.'

'It's urgent, ma'am—'

'Take a message!'

DC Wilson, good-looking as hell, three years with the Force, got a late start, already in his thirties, born and raised in the tenements of Gallow Hill, Paisley, should have been fearless, but he looked beyond mortified. If he pushed it with Squires, he was dead meat. If she didn't take this call, this particular call, right then and there, he was dead meat. Squires ate her young, that was a known fact, so surely she would eat him alive, as well,

159

either now for a late-night snack, or in the morning for a decidedly high-protein breakfast.

Quaking in his Magnums, and not knowing how to deal with the situation, DC Wilson looked as if he were about to shit a brick and the only thing he could do was hold the receiver out in his outstretched, trembling hand in the direction of his CI.

DCI Maggie Squires was a religious person. She attended the Church of Scotland in Clarkston, well, religiously. Cursing was something that she just did not do. She was above it. Above it all. She never wanted to slip to the lowest common denominator of the station or the Force. It wasn't allowed in her office. Or her presence. So you can imagine the surprise of all present who could just make out the barely audible: 'Fucking goddamn it to hell. Like I need this shite!'

So many detectives gasped at the same time, Lyon-Jones wasn't sure there'd be enough oxygen to go around.

CI Squires snatched the phone from DC Wilson and shouted down the line. 'This better be good!'

And it was.

She listened. And listened. Listened some more. The colour drained from her face. And then she went ashen. If that was cosmetically possible. She replaced the receiver the way you would close a book after you've finished reading one with a confusing ending.

A bad ending.

A *seriously* bad ending.

And then she turned to face her charges.

'Decoy Brody was caught on CCTV at Central Station. He's slipped the net.'

Lyon-Jones looked up at Sharkey, gobsmacked.

CI Squires continued. 'How? No one knows. Network Rail security informs us he bought a ticket to Hull only minutes before the train departed.'

Sharkey knew that nothing rattled DCI Squires, but she seemed clearly rattled by this costly (in all terms of the word) development: As far as she was concerned, Govan had been sealed off tighter than a snake's bumhole and Decoy Brody had waltzed right on out.

Squires carried on: 'We're going to stop that train before it reaches Edinburgh.'

After the briefing, Lyon-Jones grabbed Sharkey. 'Why didn't you call it in if you were so sure he was at Central station?'

'There wouldn't have been time to muster officers.'

Lyon-Jones heard what Sharkey had just said, but that wasn't why he hadn't called it in. She'd just figured it out.

He wanted Decoy Brody all to himself.

## CHAPTER FIFTY

Lyon-Jones looked everywhere for Sharkey. The locker room. The Gents. The canteen. Finally she found him out in the carpark, sitting in the Polar Bear, on the brink of imploding. She climbed into the passenger side.

'Decoy's still playing games, Jones. He's not on that train. He's already back in his rat hole in Govan.'

For the umpteenth time, Lyon-Jones wanted to remind him that he could have nothing to do with Decoy Brody, but how do you tell a father not to be obsessed with his child's murderer.

'Get out...'

'Why?'

'For Christ sakes, Jones, you are the biggest pain in the ass.'

'True, I am a big pain in the ass. Where are you going?'

'None of your business. Get out.'

'Here's another one for you: Where are you going?'

'OUT!'

'No, I'm staying. I'm your partner. I've not been giving you credit.'

Sharkey didn't respond. Might have been happy that she didn't get out. Might be happy that she was starting to believe in him now. He turned the ignition. Exited the carpark. Headed for the south side of the river.

Mind racing.

Polar Bear racing.

## CHAPTER FIFTY-ONE

Spencer Wembley and Bruce Formby were happily married, having tied the knot in a civil ceremony the previous year in San Francisco.

Both were forty years old. And they were extremely handsome gentlemen, indeed. They'd come to Glasgow for the very first time to do the rounds: the People's Palace, the Package Store and a club called 'MEAT'.

Spence and Bruce were impressed with the People's Palace. They hadn't really known what a 'single-end' was, or much at all about Jimmy Reid and his oration skills until they saw the enormous painting of him and then read how he almost single-handedly saved shipbuilding in Glasgow. And they had never seen a clothing shop quite like the Package Store that was strictly for gays. Oh sure, there were upmarket and trendy shops back home, but they weren't true stores that understood the nuances important to gay men: jeans cut and sewn from just the right cocktail of material to attractively display the basket, the low-cut string-tops for the gym so the nipples would peep out and even the underwear with the opening in the back. And they hadn't been to a gay spa quite like MEAT, where perfect strangers could dance in the buff or lounge about naked in the subdued lighting of the baths, where exotic and fragrant oils were located on the walls in handy hand dispensers, where the attendants wore black leather chaps, nothing more, and where there were multi-functional love chairs and fist-fuck chairs.

So they had saved their money for a short break and come north, across the border, to the best shopping mecca in the UK, north of London.

And now they were on their way home. Back to Hull. And they couldn't wait to have friends over for espresso and Gü chocolate puds, and tell the tales of their adventure to Glasgay.

## CHAPTER FIFTY-TWO

Lyon-Jones held her Airwave radio up as they sped along. They were waiting for an update on the capture of Decoy Brody.

They wouldn't have long to wait.

As the train from Glasgow approached Edinburgh, it passed an area of open fields with very few trees or other shelter, and it was here the train came to a metal-against-metal screeching stop and over one-hundred police officers stormed onboard while *Victor Mike 70*, with its thermal imaging, hovered overhead to keep an eye on the countryside in case Decoy Brody bolted. Presently, the reading of the thermal imaging only saw a herd of what appeared to be exceedingly hairy highland cattle.

At first, no passengers looked up from their paperbacks and magazines. No one stopped texting or yammering away on mobiles. This was perfectly normal, wasn't it, the train finding a reason to not reach its destination on schedule?

Of course, when the armed officers burst into each car and pointed their guns, that was a different story. Even the four noisy teenagers illicitly seated in the Quiet Carriage were shocked into silence.

\* \* \*

Back in the Incident Room, Detective Chief Inspector Maggie Squires' mobile rang. She answered. Listened. And for the first time in two hours the blood started to flow back into her face. She still had a job. Still had a career. Derek 'Decoy' Brody had been nabbed after putting up a furious fight. He had been tasered, roughed up just a bit too much, handcuffed and was being transported back to Glasgow under heavy guard.

'You don't fuck with Detective Chief Inspector Maggie Squires!' is what you would have heard if you'd been standing nearby. But, of course, no one heard, as no one was foolish enough to stand anywhere near the barracuda after what had transpired.

DCI Maggie Squires met the convoy bearing Decoy Brody upon its arrival back in Glasgow at the City Centre Police Office. The Press had somehow got wind of the capture and stalked the vehicles as they arrived, running alongside, holding up cameras with flash attachments to the windows of the CID car bearing Brody as it bulled its way into the entrance of the carpark.

Squires demanded that Decoy Brody be strip-searched before she interviewed him. She didn't want any surprises. It goes without saying that the officers doing the strip-searching were in fact sincerely surprised to find the underwear with the hole in the back. Plus Decoy had somehow grown a couple of inches. Reference was to height.

This did not sit well when Maggie Squires found out. Three hundred officers, sixty armed, the police helicopter and four armoured vehicles had been deployed to capture a harmless gay caballero.

And you can imagine how confused Spence was. He had lost his red hat during the arrest, and ensuing scuffle, and his red ski jacket had been ripped. And for what? He wasn't exactly sure what he had done wrong.

Hadn't buggery been legalized in Scotland?

## CHAPTER FIFTY-THREE

The Polar Bear was just piercing the dimly lit perimeter of Govan when Sharkey and Lyon-Jones heard the news.

Sharkey was not surprised. 'Squires is a sodding imbecile!'

'Where are we going?'

'Going to try things my way now.'

'Haven't you been doing that all along, sir?'

Sharkey ignored the comment. 'I'm looking for a grass. His name is Eddie the Hat—'

'Is there no one in Glasgow with a normal name?'

'I'm sorry, Jones, but we can't all be posh double barrels like you.'

Lyon-Jones probing, 'So who's the infamous Eddie?'

'Eddie the Hat's always moved on the fringe of the law. He used to work as a Germinator.'

'A what?'

'Still struggling with the patois, Jones? A "Germinator", a crime-scene cleaner.'

The money that Eddie the Hat was paid was outrageous, sometimes as much as four hundred pounds an hour, but as good as it was, Eddie just didn't have the stomach for it. He'd been shocked to learn that just a drop of blood on a carpet could translate to a two-foot in diameter stain beneath it. Government regulations deem all bodily fluids to be biohazards, so any crime scene was considered a potential source of infection. Permits were required to transport any bio-hazardous waste and this was when life went south for Eddie the Hat. After working a particularly grisly scene of crime where a single mum had had her baby cut out, Eddie stopped at his local to have 'just one' and forgot about the container containing the bodily fluids. You can imagine how surprised the two addled neds were when they broke into his van and stole the container...and prised it open…thinking it was Cornish Scrumpy.

Lyon-Jones probing further, 'What does he do now?'

'He tried his hand at being an entrepreneur. Ran his own bouncy castle business down in Motherwell for a while, then lost a bundle when the castle got airborne in a freak wind storm and ended up on top of a Pound Store that used to be an independent bookshop.'

'So he's unemployed now?'

'No, he likes to keep busy. Likes to work. He's become a sanitary engineer.'

'You mean a *sanitation* engineer, a bin man?'

'No, *sanitary*. He has a contract with all the shopping centres in greater Glasgow. Goes into the Ladies…and you know those little bins in the stalls?'

'Too much information, Boss. Too much information.'

'He got the job because he had experience from when he was—'

'I get the picture!'

'I've used him over the years to help scrape scum off the bottom of the barrel to find out what was underneath. If anybody has any info that will lead to the whereabouts of Decoy Brody, it will be Eddie the Hat.'

'Why didn't you go to him right off?'

'If you haven't noticed, Jones, I've had quite a bit on my mind recently.'

Lyon-Jones slunk down deep in her seat. Wished that she would think sometimes before opening that big trap of hers.

Sharkey went to the venues Eddie the Hat was known to frequent. First stop was at a massage parlour, that used to be a library, just off Govan Road. This is not a place that Eddie, himself, would frequent, but his sister did. She ran the joint. After all the commotion had died down from having what was clearly two cops stroll in, Eddie's sister, Hanna the Hand, said she had not seen hide nor hair of Eddie for yonks. Then she said to Sharkey, 'If you see him, ask him if I'm getting anything for Christmas this year.'

Sharkey and Lyon-Jones took their leave and went to a warehouse near the river where there was dog fighting. Sharkey knew the bloke who ran this place from when he worked out of the Govan police station. Once again, after the chaos of having two police officers strolling in calmed down—and the owner found one of the dogs that had escaped during all the excitement (he was found down the road in a Chinese takeaway and had the owner up on the counter…pay back?), Sharkey was informed that Eddie the Hat had indeed been in earlier that evening and had won big time by betting on a riotous pit bull by the name of The Crass Desperado.

Sharkey and Lyon-Jones eventually found Eddie the Hat in a dark back corner of the Grand Ole Opry, Scotland's shrine to all things country and western. Eddie was outfitted in a Stetson cowboy hat, a denim and chambray shirt, and had a good view of the dance floor. He was watching the line dancing and drinking a pint of Bud, with a Depth Charge.

Sharkey gave him a start. 'Howdy pardner.'

'Jesus, Mary an' Joseph! Whit ar' ye doin' here?'

'Looking for my favourite buckaroo.'

Eddie the Hat was as nervous as a polecat. He looked back and forth between Sharkey and Lyon-Jones.

'Who's she?'

Lyon-Jones responded: 'I'm his edgy.'

Sharkey gave Lyon-Jones a look.

She was learning the patois. A hint of a smile from Lyon-Jones. Quickly wiped off.

Eddie the Hat's eyes darted around the bar. 'Cannae be seen talking tae ye, ye know that.'

'Things have changed, Eddie.'

'Aye, I heard. Sorry for yer loss.' Eddie pulled the cowboy hat low over his forehead, looked around. 'Are ye here why I think yer here?'

'Glasgow is becoming the Wild West.'

'I donnae want ye tae ask the question…'

No response from Sharkey, just a long hard stare.

'Donnae ask me, Fleet. This is one time I cannae help.' Eddie doodled nervously on his beer coaster.

'Ye be wanting money, then?' Sharkey said.

'It's no' about the boudo.'

'Please, Eddie…'

'No' this time, Fleet, the entire city's scared.'

'She was my daughter…'

'Sorry.'

'I'm beggin' ye, Eddie…'

Lyon-Jones could see that things were getting out of control. Sharkey was slipping further and about to lose it.

Eddie the Hat didn't know what to say. Just stared into his beer. Then he chugged the brew and got up to leave.

'Cannae be here the now, Fleet. Cannae help ye this time.' And he hurried for the front door.

Sharkey put his head in his hands…and held on for dear life.

Lyon-Jones had a degree in psychology. She knew how to deal with grief…desperate souls, but she was at a loss with Sharkey. She put a hand on his shoulder. Couldn't think what else to do.

'Will ye be staying? It's Replica Gun Fighting Night.'

Sharkey and Lyon-Jones looked up and saw one of the saloon girls, working the tables. 'No. No. We're not staying.'

The saloon girl smiled at Sharkey's good looks and turned. This somehow bothered Lyon-Jones.

Sharkey put his head back in his hands…and that's when he saw the beer coaster Eddie the Hat had been doodling on. Only he hadn't been doodling, rather scribbling: B N TOUCH.

# CHAPTER FIFTY-FOUR

Outside in the Polar Bear, Sharkey grabbed the steering wheel with both hands. Rested his head on his hands. Once again, Lyon-Jones, the shrink, felt helpless. She could recite Freud's theory of psychosexual development backwards. She understood the theories of Psychoanalytic, Behaviourism, and Humanistic and Existential, yet damn if she could do anything to help Sharkey. And it frustrated her to no end.

Sharkey sat like this for an eternity. When he raised his head, he had a look on his face she had never seen before. If she had to read and decipher the look, she would have to say he looked like a man would...just before he pulled the trigger.

'We've a Judas among us!'

'Sir?'

'We've got a fucking leak!'

'Where?'

'If I knew fucking where I'd blow the cock weasel's fucking balls off.'

Sharkey was at the end of his rope, hanging on by the finest of threads.

'How do you figure, sir?'

'It's a hunch, Jones, just a fucking hunch.'

Lyon-Jones went silent.

Sharkey had an idea. 'I need you to do something for me...'

Lyon-Jones leery as hell now.

'I need you to cross reference everyone in this division with Decoy Brody and the Sutherlands. Then do Glasgow West and Govan and the HQ. Go back as far as you need to go. Where they went to school. Where they go to church. Where they take a shit. Check for common patterns.'

'But, sir...'

That look again, the trigger about to be pulled. But the voice just a whisper, with a hint of life-ending vitriol.

'Just do it, Jones.'

# CHAPTER FIFTY-FIVE

The black limousine, which would later bear the immediate family, rocked slowly over the frozen dirt road, followed by the hearse, and pulled up in front of a 19th-century stone cottage. The cottage was located in the countryside southwest of Stirling, in between the Stirling Golf Club and Cambusbarron.

Sharkey stood outside his ex-wife's home and solemnly watched the arrival. Standing with him were only Kojak, Detective Chief Superintendent Danus Ferguson and his father. Sharkey's father wasn't in his wheelchair as the cottage's crushed gravel forecourt wasn't suitable for wheelchairs. Someone had fetched the elderly man a wooden chair from the kitchen, and he just sat there with his tartan travel rug covering his lap, an old wooden cane resting on the rug, one eye kept on a heavily laden sky.

Brooke Walsh, Sharkey's ex-wife, and her family stood a distance away. Sharkey regarded his ex-wife. Cast his mind back to when they first met in North Carolina. At the time, Brooke was a student studying 'partying' at nearby Appalachian State University in Boone. She was the only daughter of a millionaire congressman and furniture magnate from Hickory, a hick town on Highway #321, halfway between Charlotte and Boone. Brooke's daddy 'freaked out and went ballistic' (Brooke's words) when he found out she was seeing 'trailer trash' from the gun range, and that had brought Brooke great joy.

Six months' later, Sharkey had joined the United States Marine Corps and, later that same day, Brooke found out she was pregnant. A marriage was quickly arranged by Brooke's horrified, patently distraught parents who were afraid of having *their* reputation sullied. Brooke was 'banished to the tower' by being sequestered at the Pinnacle Inn Resort up on Beech Mountain at 5,500 feet, out of range of the circling, blood-thirsty vulture Press, who were always in the hunt for any scandal they could attach to her congressman daddy.

Sharkey looked at his ex-father-in-law. He was glaring at Sharkey with such hate in his eyes. Sharkey glanced at his ex-wife. She, too, was looking his way, glaring, then she coldly turned her back on him.

Katie's body lay in repose in a ground floor bedroom. Her grandmother was of Irish lineage and had stayed with the body all night, talking to her and warding off evil spirits. She had turned or covered all mirrors in the house.

The man driving the hearse and the driver of the other limo stepped from their respective vehicles and motioned to Sharkey and DCS Danus Ferguson to enter the house with them. They proceeded to the bedroom, closed and locked the casket, and then all four men lifted the casket and struggled to get it through the narrow front door and into the hearse.

The task completed, Sharkey walked across the gravel to the limo, but all seats had been taken by his ex-wife's family. Sharkey's ex-father-in-law, Congressman Walsh, powered down his window and spewed: 'This car is for family only! I've *never* considered you family!'

Sharkey faltered back. Shaken. He hitched a ride to the crematorium with Kojak and his father. Kojak drove, Sharkey rode shotgun and his father sat in the backseat of the R-reg Land Rover that Kojak used to transport his golden retrievers.

Sharkey spoke to Kojak. 'I would like you to do something for me...'

Kojak didn't speak. Didn't need to speak. He would do whatever Sharkey asked.

'Decoy Brody knows every move we make. There's a leak somewhere in the Force. I ask you to keep an ear to the ground. If you find out anyone has been a bit too cosy with Brody, let me know ASAP. As you know my hands are tied, officially, but I will find this scum and I will bring him down. This conversation did not take place.'

Kojak murmured his assent through a mouthful of Smarties, and then there was silence, right on up until they pulled into the car park of the Camelon Cemetery and Crematorium in Falkirk, nine miles away.

Inside the chapel, the family of Sharkey's ex-wife filled all the seats on the right side. The left side looked sadly bare with just Sharkey, Kojak and his dad in the front row.

And a last-minute guest on Sharkey's side: an old gang member from the Shettleston Aggro. The gang member had risen from proverbial humble beginnings and was now a highly respected Councillor for the Calton. Known around the East End as the 'Mayor'. The Mayor and Sharkey were like brothers. Blood brothers.

And then a surprise guest on Sharkey's side: Detective Sergeant Fiona Lyon-Jones. Sharkey was stunned to see Lyon-Jones there. He had been such a shit to her from day one, taking everything out on her. He was touched that she came.

The pallbearers brought the casket into the chapel. Four men, all from the ex-wife's side of the family. Sharkey didn't recognize one of them. Four strangers carrying his daughter. They placed the casket at the front, to the right of the dais, and moved to their seats.

A small mourning cardwith a picture of Katie, outdoors, beaming, happy, was passed around to all. The minister spoke of 'a life taken from us much before her time' and a few hymns were sung. The memorial was over—or so everyone on the right side of the aisle thought.

Until Fleet Sharkey stood up.

Walked to the lectern.

Looked at the gathered.

Still received icy glares.

'When Katie was born, she only weighed two pounds eight ounces. She was born eight weeks prematurely. And that was the last time she arrived early for anything.'

The assembled let go with a few nervous laughs.

'Doctors didn't think she'd make it. Her mother wouldn't let the nurses take her away. She removed her gown and put wee Katie against her breast instead of letting her be placed in an incubator. She gave Katie a cuddle and breast milk on the end of her finger. We were scared to death, but both felt very blessed. Katie fought through the first twenty-four hours, then grew up healthy, spunky and feisty, and was a bit of a tomboy. When other little girls wanted to be princesses, Katie wanted to climb things. Anything. And catch frogs. And snakes. We would go camping up in the Smoky Mountains of North Carolina along the Blue Ridge Parkway and there was this one pretty good-sized lake that Katie just loved. And she caught her first bass. I said I'd build a fire and we could cook it up for dinner, and she gave me such a Bad-dog look...'

Polite laughter.

'She had me take a photo and then she released the fish. "It doesn't deserve to die, Daddy", she had told me, "It doesn't deserve to die".' Katie was eight years old and I still have that photo...'

Sniffles.

'She and her mother had a special relationship. As only a mother and daughter can have. They were best friends. Her mum had grown up in those mountains and loved the camping and fishing just as much as Katie did. They would go off hiking together and I remember the time they came back so excited— and just a wee bit afraid. They had seen an adult black bear while they were out walking. It had crossed the trail right in front of them. It stopped and stared at them. Just curious about these two strange creatures. Her mother knew about bears and what to do. She instructed Katie to crouch down and look real small, and not to make eye contact. The bear left and what was a very scary moment was over. I didn't recognize it at the time, but her mother had saved both of their lives.

'Then, we moved back to Scotland and Katie fell in love with the foothills around Stirling and the lakes above Perth... and...Oh, dear God in heaven, I miss her so much...'

And Sharkey fell apart.

Broke down sobbing right up in front of God and everyone. The past few days had finally caught up with him and he was a broken man, shattered by the life he had led and the life he hadn't. No one budged, no one knew what to do or how to react, except his father and the Mayor. Slowly, the senior Sharkey rose, the Mayor supporting an elbow. Fleet's father took his cane and struggled his way to his son's side, put his arm around him and led him back to the front pew. And there wasn't a dry eye in the chapel. Even Sharkey's ex-wife. Even her Congressman father.

Outside, the heavens opened and sheets of slashing rain slammed into the stained-glass windows of the chapel.

And a desperately sad day became somehow worse.

# CHAPTER FIFTY-SIX

In Spain it was the start of another glorious day.

The wind was out of the south and it was already a respectable fifteen degrees Celsius.

High above Benidorm, hugging the Puig Campana Mountain, was the sleepy village of Finestrat. With its Moorish-influenced architecture and eclectic enclave of foreigners, it was an endearing combination of old Costa Blanca and the new-laundered money. Irish, Russians, Canadians, Americans, Saudis, Moroccans, Romanians, Moldavians and Scottish could be found here. Even some Spanish.

To the north of the village, secreted on the edge of a deep *barranca*, was Villa Nariz-Azul, an impressive structure even for this part of the Costa Blanca. The villa had a 15-foot electric vectorized wrought-iron security gate, 10-foot stone wall with protruding glass shards and the most sophisticated surveillance gadgets dirty money could buy. If one approached this compound, not that one could ever locate this compound, alarm bells would sound and floodlights would bleach the night white. While security guards and dogs sniffed out any interlopers, the owner of this property would move swiftly down a one-man lift from his bedroom into deep catacombs dug during the Spanish Civil War.

Nariz-Azul was more heavily armed than the White House, more impenetrable than Gaddafi's compound (had once been), and nearly as inaccessible as Castro's Sierra Maestro mountain hideaway.

This was where Jimmy the Pouch Sutherland hung his hat. Called home. Proffered the best cocaine that money could buy. Cocaine which found its way from Medellin in Columbia to the port of Guinea Bissau in West Africa and then up the coast to Morocco and over to the Spanish ports of Alicante or Porto

177

Banus or Benalmádena, or really any cove where a swift boat, Zodiac, Jet-ski, any craft with a next-to-nil radar signature, could slip close to shore in the middle of a new-moon night.

The route through Guinea Bissau was a new trade route. And it was the brainchild of none other than Jimmy The Pouch. He had heard through the cocaine grapevine that this tiny West African country of 1.5 million was one of the poorest in the world and the weak state offered the least resistance as a substitute for traditional smuggling routes in Central America and the Caribbean, which were being blocked.

Guinea Bissau was ripe for the picking. It couldn't control its own territory, couldn't administer justice and was plagued by corruption.

If you asked Jimmy, he would tell you a wee story to appreciate the malaise of tiny Guinea Bissau: 'Imagine that you are a policeman in Guinea Bissau and are tipped off about a drug shipment coming in by private plane. First, you have to find a vehicle to drive to the dirt landing strip. Second, you must procure official permission—and funds—to fill up the vehicle with petrol. You don't have to worry about calling for backup because you don't possess a two-way radio and there's no electricity to charge your mobile phone. Not that you had one in the first place. If you manage to reach the scene of the drop in time, the next challenge is to build a makeshift roadblock to stop the truck that has off-loaded the cocaine.

'Curiously, the truck's driver is wearing an army uniform and is not too concerned when you seize his cargo. You take him to the police station in the back of your vehicle—without handcuffs, because you don't have any. Oddly, a senior government official quickly intervenes, secures his release and confiscates the cocaine. The cocaine is then broken down into smaller amounts and transported up the coast to Morocco.'

Once upon a time, Guinea Bissau's chief exports were cashews and shrimp. Now, thanks to The Pouch, they were cashews, shrimp and cocaine.

Never one to be a piker, Jimmy The Pouch was working on an alternate plan to move the cocaine from Morocco to Spain. And he had already held a trial run. Which was frightfully clever. Deviously simple. And nearly successful.

He had hired a private pilot who rented a Cessna 172 from the airport in Alicante. The pilot then flew to a dirt airstrip north of Casablanca to pick up contraband. He waited until nightfall then took off and headed back towards Spain. Customs surveillance aircraft, operating in the hotbed of drug trafficking that was the Strait of Gibraltar, spotted the private plane and followed from a distance as the aircraft entered Spanish airspace. With sophisticated night vision scopes, custom agents planned to tail the smuggler until he set down on some off-the-beaten-track airstrip in the boondocks of Andalucia. And then they would arrest him, seize the contraband and decide how much of it should be declared.

But The Pouch foiled government agents: The single-engine Cessna didn't land in Andalucía, it carried on all the way past Alicante—then crashed. The pilot had simply put the aircraft on autopilot and then bailed out over the remote dessert on the other side of Puig Compana with the contraband strapped to his body. A four-wheel drive Jeep waited for the pilot while the Customs planes dutifully followed the offending (and now unmanned) aircraft for a hundred more miles before the rented aircraft ran out of fuel and simply fell out of the sky.

Only snag in the operation came when the Jeep pulled up to the designated drop-spot and found the pilot/parachutist hanging in a juniper tree. He had 50 kilos of cocaine strapped to his body—and a broken neck.

\* \* \*

Jimmy the Pouch watched a half dozen nymphets in various stages of undress (Brazilian, Moustache, Landing Strip) rub oil on each other and toot up out by the heart-shaped swimming pool, and smiled.

A Sultan adoring his harem disporting.

The Pouch fornicated until the wee hours of the morning, never touching the drug himself. Cocaine was not a friend to erections, so he stuck to his Mondariz bottled water and his beloved wee blue pill, Viagra.

A teenage girl with platinum-blond hair smiled at him. She would do just fine for tonight. He would make sure her coke was laced with yohimbine as it crept towards the bewitching hour. He was glad his lassies agreed to be blindfolded to come to the villa. But then girls would agree to just about anything if they had an appetite for cocaine. Even kill for it. He had learned that long ago as a young man.

The Pouch had always had a strong sex drive. At the age of twelve he was sleeping with his secondary school teacher, repeatedly. They were eventually found out and she was convicted of statutory rape. She lost her teaching position, lost her husband and was disowned by her family. But she hadn't been the initiator, Jimmy had been.

Jimmy had only been mildly upset when he learnt she had committed suicide at the age of 23.

Jimmy was born in Paisley Road West on Hogmanay, 1941, under a tenement roof shaken by Hitler's bombs. He attended Broomloan Primary and Govan High School with a bright kid by the name of Alex Ferguson. Jimmy's father was a single father, with his mother having died of an incurable 'wasting disease' at the age of 25.

Since Jimmy's father was never home, working first at the Govan shipyards, then the Hillington Estate as a laborer, wee Jimmy played hooky from school and ran wild. And when his dad died young, having fallen through an unfinished stairwell, Jimmy was taken in by his estranged uncle, an alcoholic doctor (who sold drugs on the side) and found brotherhood in the Govan Fleeto, coincidentally enough the same gang that Decoy Brody would be a member in 30 years later.

The Govan Fleeto was where Jimmy got the nickname the 'Pouch'. There was a struggle for leadership within the gang between Jimmy and the existing leader. The leader was the son of a longshoreman and the size of an American refrigerator. One night, the leader challenged Jimmy to chib of choice, but Jimmy balked and pulled his left hand out of his sweatshirt and displayed a broken hand. This cooled the heels of the leader. Later that night, when the leader was charred on cider-piss Jimmy had spiked with a new drug, fondly referred to by the Rolling Stones as *mother's little helper*, Jimmy clubbed the leader to death with the cast on his left hand. Then he went to his uncle (who had provided him with the Valium) and he removed the brass knuckles in the plaster on the bogus broken hand and the murder weapon was cut off and thrown in the Clyde.

The next year, Jimmy's uncle performed a vasectomy on his favourite nephew.

Jimmy was 16.

That was 50 years ago.

Traditionally, the Pouch sat around most of the day in an aroused state, but things had changed of late. He knew it wasn't his age. He couldn't put his finger on it, but then it came to him and he decided to make an executive decision: He wasn't going to pay for breast enhancement anymore. The gals looked okay with clothes on but scary in the broad daylight. Plus the lassie over by the diving board, the scrawny one who always pouted, she was starting to look like the brunette from that over-the-hill girl band.

He would have to ask the girls to disappear when his literary agent arrived. He was penning a True Crime book about his years in Barlinnie prison and had signed a two-book deal with a publisher that only had a PO Box for an address. He had desperately wanted an *über*-agent to represent him and had hoped for a contract from one of the sexy six (now the not quite as sexy five), but no *über*-agent would touch him with an extended barge pole, so he had signed with Dicky MacWick, an ambulance-chasing attorney turned literary consultant.

The Pouch took a sip of his Mondariz, then turned to the corpulent bloke next to him.

'Could you get used to this, laddie?'

'Fucking A,' Fat Cheeks said.

Fat Cheeks always had a way with words.

## CHAPTER FIFTY-SEVEN

Christmas was less than a week away.

And Decoy Brody had completely vanished into thin air.

The local Press reckoned otherwise. Had to, to sell papers. Every day they printed a fresh 'sighting' of Decoy, be it from a reliable source or not: Decoy had been spotted walking across the Squinty Bridge, the Squiggly Bridge, up on Sauchiehall Street, down on Argyle, riding the subway, using the Gents at Ibrox Stadium without washing his hands.

The public was on edge and newspapers were selling like, well, newspapers.

Over at the cop shop, Sharkey needed to clear his head.

'C'mon, Jones, let's get some fresh air. I want to show you something.'

Sharkey walked Lyon-Jones out of the police station and down to Sauchiehall Street. It was perishingly cold and there was that bite in the air that we put up with at Christmas time. Simply because it's Christmas time.

'Take a look around you, Jones. This is your first Christmas here, so you may not be aware of it, but shopping in Glasgow over the holidays is usually like the running of the bulls. Now it's just a shadow of its previous years.'

Lyon-Jones looked up and down Sauchiehall Street. Shoppers were in short supply, no question about it. Those who were out moved quickly, casting furtive glances. There was little window shopping. There was little holiday spirit. Even the guy who played the bagpipes for tips in front of Marks & Spencer and the Gypsy panhandler were knocking off early.

Sharkey and Lyon-Jones turned off of Sauchiehall Street, right in front of the Glasgow Royal Concert Hall, and viewed the glorious sight that is the pedestrianised sweep of Buchanan Street falling away from them and all the way down to the river.

'See off below you. I brought Katie here last year about this time. She said that she wanted to go Christmas shopping with just me. No one else. Do you know what that does to a father when his daughter says she wants to do something with just her dad? There is no better feeling in the world. Last year we got to see all the street entertainment, the roving comedy theatre, the light projections and all the live music. This year it's all been cancelled.'

This was more than Lyon-Jones had heard her boss say since she arrived in Glasgow. And she hoped it wouldn't stop.

Sharkey walked Lyon-Jones down to the ice rink at George Square. There were no skaters. 'Katie even managed to get me on the ice last Christmas and she let me hold her hand as we skated...' Sharkey struggled to hold it together. 'Then I took her to the Christmas Reindeer parade with Santa. She knew she was too old for that, but she wanted to go anyway.'

Lyon-Jones looked up at Sharkey. In her wildest nightmares she couldn't imagine the pain and guilt he was feeling right now. Without thinking, she put her hand on his back. Turned him around. Aimed for the station.

Left her hand there longer than she should have.

Didn't care.

Bugger what anybody thought.

Was she bucking the system?

Was Sharkey beginning to rub off on her?

\* \* \*

After lunch, in the incident room, CI Squires was in the process of bringing the assembled officers up to speed. She had already gone over petty theft, ASBO, a 999 call from someone who wanted to sue the Benefits Agency because their benefits cheque hadn't arrived. Now she was biting into the meaty bits.

'In spite of what the Press are reporting, I'm taking the position that Decoy Brody has quit Glasgow, travelled to Stranraer, taken the ferry to Belfast and is making his way down to Spain. We think he's going to hole up at Jimmy the Pouch Sutherland's Costa Blanca hideaway above Benidorm—'

This was news to DI Sharkey. 'And this new theory is based on what?'

Squires knew Sharkey would question this and was ready for

him. 'A ScotRail employee said he saw someone matching Decoy's description detrain in Stranraer and head towards the ferry terminal.'

'When?' Sharkey badgered Squires. Kept up the heat.

'Earlier today, but we've only just now learnt of it.'

'Why didn't he call it in right then and there?'

'He was on holiday. Wife pregnant. She needed the toilet. He had to watch the wee ones.'

Guffaws of laughter broke out.

Sharkey not thrilled with the answer. 'Why didn't he just use his mobile?'

Squires snippy now. 'We did think to ask that very question, Inspector. He said he was on a pay-as-you-go and didn't want to use up his minutes.'

Moans of disbelief.

A glare from Squires. 'We've notified our Spanish counterparts about Brody, but that's like trying to bail a sinking ship with a syringe. We are scaling back all efforts on Decoy Brody until further notice.'

This was yet another dagger in the heart for Sharkey. He studied Squires. Was she getting some sort of twisted enjoyment from this?

Squires flipped through her notes. 'We've learnt today that Tattoo McQueen is to be released from Her Majesty's Pleasure early—before Christmas—so I'm afraid things will get worse before they get better. Be prepared to put in longer hours.'

More moans filled the room.

CI Squires consulted her notes again.

'And lastly, that footprint that had been found at the scene of the murdered teenager who went by the name Pizza Face? Forensics reports it came from a cowboy boot.'

# CHAPTER FIFTY-EIGHT

Sharkey looked out his office window.

Darkness was falling. The clock on the wall in his office read: 3.15 in the afternoon. Winter in Glasgow: the time of the year you woke up in the dark and you went home in the dark. By four o'clock the city centre streets would be nearly devoid of Christmas shoppers. And then, when the work day was over and workers spilled from shops and banks and office buildings, they would move in packs of four or five, and they would avoid the subway, take only crowded buses on heavily travelled routes and fight for taxis.

Twenty percent of the private hire taxi firms in the Strathclyde Force area were either owned by major underworld figures or had links to them. They used this 'gangster service' as a cover for drug trafficking, human trafficking, prostitution, money laundering, to mobilise their enforcers and to keep an eye on communities where they wrestled for control with the police and government.

Decoy Brody had scared the living shite out of the public, and the crime families were profiting.

Sharkey clawed at his temples and stared at the top of his desk.

The sound of shoes with leather soles approached. Stopped at Sharkey's open door. Without looking up Sharkey queried, 'What is it, Jones?'

'How did you know it was me, sir?'

'No one else in the station wears shoes like you. High-quality leather on low-quality vinyl makes a peculiar sound.'

'You wanted to see me, sir?'

'Come in and close the door, please.' Lyon-Jones did just that. 'How have you been getting on with that task I gave you?'

'Which task was that, sir?'

'Cross referencing all staff with Decoy and the Sutherland family. Trying to find the leak, remember?'

'Yes, sir, I remember.'

'And?'

'Haven't done it.'

'And why would that be?'

'Off limits.'

'Says who?'

'CI Squires.'

'Did you mention this to her?'

'No, sir, I just thought—'

'Just do it, Jones. I'm your immediate superior. I want it, and I want it by tomorrow morning. Understood?'

'Understood, sir.'

Lyon-Jones skulked to the canteen. Poured herself a 'cup of ambition'. She sat in a corner by herself and sulked. She was caught between the proverbial (and dreaded) rock and a hard place. And she didn't know what to do.

She took a sip of her coffee. It was vile. She took another sip. Vile coffee is better than no coffee. She opened a dark-chocolate KitKat. Had a bite.

CI Squires had made it abundantly clear that DI Sharkey was not to have anything to do with Decoy Brody, yet her boss was all over her case for not following up on something which involved Decoy Brody.

If she disobeyed Sharkey, she was in deep trouble.

If she obeyed Sharkey, she was in deep trouble.

She wrapped both hands around the coffee. Come on, lassie, get a hold of yourself. You are a Doctor of Psychology and that makes you more educated than the vast majority. Having said that, at the moment, she didn't feel more intelligent than the vast majority, especially DI Sharkey. His was an intelligence born in the womb and honed on the street. University had been at the College of Kill or Be Killed in Kuwait. Graduate school in the killing fields of North Carolina. Plus he had that sixth sense. His 'hunch sense'. For all her degrees and all her classes and all her hours spent studying psychology, Fiona was downright dyslexic compared to Sharkey.

She needed to come up with something that would keep him

occupied and subsequently at bay for a while longer, and then perhaps she could avoid having her career crushed between that rock: DI Sharkey. And that hard place: DCI Squires.

* * *

Sharkey pulled out his mobile and put in a call to Kojak to ask if he had heard anything through the scum grapevine. Negatore. No one had come up with a connection to anyone on the Force. Kojak said he would continue to keep an ear to the tracks and would let him know the minute he heard a train coming.

Sharkey was greatly appreciative.

And that wasn't good enough.

Then Sharkey put in a call to his old gang member, the City Councillor known as the 'Mayor.'

'Mayor? Fleet. Are you free tonight?'

'I always got time for you.'

'I've got to ask a big favour...'

'Is it illegal?'

'Only if we're caught.'

'I'll bring some muscle.'

# CHAPTER FIFTY-NINE

Denny the Screwdriver slammed his phone down so hard it almost shattered. Christ, he could never please his father. Sometimes he wished the Pouch would just croak already.

The Screwdriver killed the lights in his office at Sutherland Motors. Stepped outside. Triple locked the door. Rattled the door handle.

He lit up a ciggie. As the match flared he could see his breath. He surveyed his darkened forecourt. Took a life-threatening drag. Blew out the smoke. Fantasised about the rack on that cocktail waitress at The Penitentiary. The Penitentiary was Glasgow's newest, 'baddest' late-night venue. It offered unsigned band night, Detroit techno night, Latin night, underground night—and *communal* urinals. Clubbers, aka prisoners, also enjoyed the pornographic photos on the walls in the more traditional Ladies and Gents and, most importantly, the Nite Zone with taxi marshals just out front to aid single women to find their way into a legitimate taxi and not into the clutches of some sicko posing as a cabbie. To the side of this buzzing establishment, a new chippy (The Cheesy Chippie) had sprung up like a mushroom overnight, its Cambodian proprietors ready and eager to suffer nightly verbal, racist abuse for the right to serve the chips 'n' cheese.

The Screwdriver provided the bouncers and the muscle for the new owner of The Penitentiary: Luciano Rubin. Luciano was a Scouser. Took Premier League shite growing up with a name like that. Got tough real quick and started giving it back. Mother: Italian, Sicily, Palermo. Father: English, Merseyside, Toxteth. Crime *was* in his blood. Luciano was often up in Glasgow working as a hired gun on a freelance basis. Called in when all else failed locally. When dirty work needed to be exacted by a twisted psychopath with a hellacious chip on his shoulder.

Which was often in Glasgow.

Now Luciano was retired and wanted to go straight. The Screwdriver had had a good laugh. Owning a nightclub in Glasgow was not exactly going straight.

He took another drag.

Thought about the wee lass with the not so wee rack at The Penitentiary.

The start of a stonner.

Then the erection died a sudden death as cold gunmetal was pressed against the back of his neck. The Screwdriver blurted out to no one in particular, certainly no one who gave a rat's ass, 'Why the fuck didn't the pit bulls go ballistic?'

The Screwdriver let himself be frogmarched across the forecourt by two endomorphic apes. Allowed them to rifle through his pockets. A red Jeep Cherokee with tinted windows screeched up and he was shoved into the backseat. Ape on each side. Another upfront, driving. Balaclava city.

The Screwdriver was blindfolded and driven about twenty minutes away, he couldn't be sure. That could put him just about any place in Glasgow. Starts and stops. Potholes. Rush hour. More potholes. He tried to get a sense of the direction they were going. Listened for the sound of the river. The sounds of the city. The sound of his heart knocking out an 'I'm fucked' beat.

If he had to guess where he was being taken, he would have banked on the East End.

The motor finally jerked to a stop. He was roughly hauled out and hustled into the blackness of a building somewhere, which reeked of petrol. Christ! This must be the work of Tattoo McQueen. Tattoo was a fucking pyromaniac. They were going to kill him. Set him on fire. He was made to lay horizontal on a long board. Then he was strapped in place to restrain his arms and legs.

And he heard the first words of the entire trip.

'Brody?' A thick Glaswegian accent.

'Fuck ye!' he spat. He knew right then and there he wouldn't be killed. As long as he didn't give up the answer, he would live to see another day. He had never burst in his life, and he wasn't about to burst now. 'I'll rip yer faces off!'

'Brody?'

189

'I pumped yer maw in the arse!'

No more words were spoken. The board he was strapped to was tilted back. Blood flowed to his head. What the fuck were these cunts doing? Whatever it was, it wouldn't work. He wouldn't burst!

A smelly rag was laid over his mouth and nose as you would unfurl a napkin on your lap. Still not afraid. 'Fuck youse!'

And then the most effective interrogation technique on the planet was employed: Water was slowly poured over the rag.

And for the first time in his life, Denny the Screwdriver Sutherland thought he was going to die.

He was claustrophobic!

He was suffocating.

He was drowning.

And he passed out.

When he came to, he heard: 'Brody? Spain?'

'Please! No more! He's in Glesga! He's right here in fucking Glesga!'

'Where!'

'Brody doesnae say! Please! No more!'

But more water did come, and the Screwdriver drowned. Died. Took the express train straight to hell.

Or so he thought.

When he came around, he was still strapped to the board. And all was quiet. And Bible black. He struggled to free his hands. Finally succeeded. Undid his feet. Took off his blindfold. Looked around. Saw the red readout on a digital clock. Recognised that clock. The balaclava brigade had nabbed him, driven him round in circles and worked him over right in his own goddam fucking office.

But what the fuck was it that they did? He didn't know. The only thing he did know was that he didn't want to endure that kind of torture again. Ever.

Denny the Screwdriver Sutherland didn't know it at the time, but he had just become a curious statistic.

He was the first soul in Glasgow to be waterboarded.

# CHAPTER SIXTY

The AA meeting that evening was held at St Michael's church hall in Gallowgate, in the East End. It was the first meeting Sharkey had attended since falling off the wagon and almost falling off the edge of the earth. He had returned to the meetings because it was something Katie would have wanted. She was the one who got him to admit he had a problem in the first place. He had done it all for her.

For her alone.

Plus, he needed the alibi.

He sat in the front as opposed to his usual and less visible row in the back corner.

Those recovering alcoholics in attendance knew that Sharkey had relapsed, but said nothing. The flock always knew when one of its own had flown off course.

'My name is Ferris. I'm an alcoholic.'

* * *

There are two pubs in Govan that are best avoided. More so if you are the sort of person who can't handle yourself when the going gets less than cordial. When the clientele get frisky and belligerent.

Sharkey had already been to one. Now he was at the other. He lapped at his whisky and looked at all the other lost souls in there. Many of the crowd were second and third generation losers. Professional dolies. Never worked a day in their lives. Never even considered it, actually. They didn't have time for work. There were children to bear and children to raise and hell to raise and life to, well, bear.

This wasn't the first time Sharkey had attended an AA meeting and then fallen off the wagon immediately afterwards. He felt guilty and ashamed, but most of all he wished the barman would hurry with the whisky he had ordered. Once he took the first sip and the smoky fumes of the blended nectar swirled about his mouth and the malt whisky coursed through his veins, guilt would become a thing of the past. No good to feel guilty about taking a drink and not enjoy it. And then tomorrow, he would rationalise and say to himself that he had at least gone to the AA meeting and had made an attempt. And he would vow to never slip again. And he would be strong and resolute in his actions. And then it would happen all over again.

Katie had pushed her dad into AA. Of course he had fought her. Did the denial thing. Said he didn't have a problem. This would set off Katie and an argument would ensue. Katie's mum would join the fray. They would do a tag team against him, one having a go, then the other taking over. And it would always end the same way: Katie in tears, Mum in tears, and he would have had enough of unhappy families and escape down the pub.

Sharkey felt more at home in a pub than in his own house. The pub was always warm in the winter with the fireplace going and the company good and not judgmental. Plus there was something unique about a pub's ambience that he fancied: a roaring fire, the resident lurcher snoozing underfoot, Curry Night and Quiz Night and happy hour. Where everybody knew your name. And your game.

It was one big happy family.

One big happy family of drunks.

Back home, the cycle of domestic unrest had begun slowly and escalated as Katie pushed more and his wife continued to take Katie's side. Rightly so. Then one night, Sharkey stormed out, drank himself into the backside of oblivion in the Horse Shoe and afterwards decided to try to take the subway home, even though the subway didn't go within twenty miles of his postal code.

Sharkey left the pub on unsteady legs, descended into St Enoch station by the shopping centre and waited drunkenly on the platform for his train. When the next train approached, Sharkey stuck out his arm like we do when we're hailing a bus, waved his ticket in the air and stepped onto the train. But the train hadn't arrived yet and he fell to the tracks below, somehow avoiding the electrified rail. The train stopped in time, but Sharkey broke his wrist, a few ribs, chipped some teeth, and woke up in the Royal Infirmary. Katie came to visit. His wife didn't. It was the beginning of the end.

Katie gave her dad an ultimatum. If he was going to continue to drink, then she was going to start experimenting with drugs.

'Booze or me, Daddy,' Katie said, putting on an American accent. 'What's it gonna be? My sister may be dead, but you still have another daughter who needs you.'

Something had finally got Sharkey's attention. He chose Katie and he dried out. Joined AA. Was dry for nearly two years.

And now he'd chosen booze again.

Sharkey's mobile vibrated and ripped him from his wallow of self-pity. Christ, he was so leathered, he didn't know which pocket his mobile was in. Finally exhumed it.

'Sharkey?'

'It's me, DS Lyon-Jones.'

'Aye, I know it's you. No one else calls me this late.'

'Did I wake you?'

'What is it, Jones? When you ring at this hour, just give it to me straight and skinny.'

'Been a murder, guv…'

'For the love of God, Jones, you sound like you just stepped off the set of *TAGGART*.'

'Sorry, sir, just trying to sound…professional.'

'Well, it doesn't.'

'Sorry.'

'Where is the body?'

'At the city mortuary.'

'Already?'

'Not inside…outside.'

CHAPTER SIXTY-ONE

Lyon-Jones was already at the murder scene when Sharkey drove up, not so very concerned about the drink driving.

The pathologist had come and gone. SOCO were casing the *locus*, one with a high-definition video kit, another with a rather large digital camera, its flash blinding everyone within G1 5JU.

Sharkey parked the Polar Bear in front of the city mortuary. His mind shot back to when Katie had been lying there. Without shoes.

A private hire taxi rested at a wonky angle halfway up on the kerb in front of the mortuary. Glasgow's High Court formed the backdrop. Police tape surrounded the taxi. This was going to be the photo in tomorrow morning's newspapers.

Lyon-Jones approached and held the tape for her boss. Sharkey was struggling mightily trying to act sober.

'No need to go in, Jones.'

'Developing a conscience, sir?'

'Hope not. Talk to me.'

'Male. Dead less than an hour.'

'Witnesses?'

'No.'

'Who called it in?'

'He did.'

'Who did?'

Fiona pointed at the dead cabbie slumped over the steering wheel.

'Ye shittin' me?'

'No, sir.'

'Did he say anything else?'

'No, sir, just that he had been shot and his location.'

'Did you check with the taxi company's dispatch?'

'Aye, the fare was picked up in Govan and wanted to go to

Barlinnie prison. He told the cabbie to wait—'

'Who said it was a "he"?'

'No one, sir.'

'It might have been a woman, Jones.'

'Statistically, it's almost always a male, sir…88.8 percent of all homicides are committed by men to only 11.2 percent for women.'

'We don't rule out a woman. Carry on.'

'Right, he, I mean the fare told the cabbie to wait at Barlinnie, and…this is weird, sir…'

'Spill the beans, Jones. And what?'

'Then the fare wanted to be taken to the Glasgow City Mortuary.'

'Jesus.' Sharkey digested this for a moment.

'I've been on to Traffic, got uniforms scouring for a murder weapon…'

'Did you check the mortuary?'

'A uniform's in there right now, sir.'

'Let's take a closer look at the—'

'Sir, better have one of these, Procurator Fiscal's on his way.' Fiona interrupted, pulled out a pack of Fisherman's Friend. Shook out a lozenge for Fleet.

Sharkey took it, put it in his mouth. 'That obvious?'

'Yes, sir.'

'Thanks.'

Sharkey and Lyon-Jones inched closer to the *locus*. Lyon-Jones glanced back in the direction the taxi would have come.

'Look at the position of the taxi, Boss. He must have come to a complete halt in the street. Then here, under the back wheels. Tyre marks. He'd left the engine running, then suddenly stepped on the gas. That's when he was shot. The taxi ran up on the kerb, stalled and the perp fled. The cabbie called 999, then lost consciousness and bled out. Do you agree, sir?'

'Aye.'

'Besides this area, should I get CCTV footage from St Enoch subway station and Argyle Street Rail? If the perp went on foot, that might've been the route. Sir?'

'Oh, right.' Sharkey shook his head to clear it. 'And check with all the other taxi companies to see if anyone picked up a fare in this area within the past two hours. Male or female.'

A noise behind them, coming down the street: A Mobile Police Office slowing, pulling over to the kerb. Sharkey and Lyon-Jones watched the vehicle move into position.

Sharkey peered over the police tape. Tried to read the name of the taxi driver, but the corpse was slouched over, blocking it. 'Did you ask the taxi dispatch who the driver was?'

'Sorry, sir, didn't.' Lyon-Jones annoyed with herself.

'Better get on the horn then and find out.'

Lyon-Jones pulled out her mobile and punched in the numbers.

'You know the number by heart?'

'Of course, sir.'

The call was picked up on the other end and Lyon-Jones identified herself. It was the same woman working dispatch as before. Lyon-Jones re-identified herself and asked the name of the driver. Thanked dispatch. Rang off.

'Well?' Sharkey impatient.

'Donald McDonald.'

'Means nothing to me.'

'How about "Taxi Boy"?'

# CHAPTER SIXTY-TWO

It was nearly two in the morning when Sharkey's mobile vibrated in his pocket and he read the message.

He told Lyon-Jones that something urgent had just come up and he needed to go. When pressed for details, he ignored Lyon-Jones.

In reality, there had been no vibrating mobile. No urgent message.

But there *was* something Sharkey wanted to try. It had worked for him once before, and he wondered if it would work again.

Sharkey drove across the river and over to Govan. He parked just across the street from the Gaolkeeper as he had done when he'd spotted Decoy Brody with the Screwdriver after the football match. The pub was still doing a business. Sharkey just sat there. He knew Decoy Brody wouldn't put in an appearance, but he wanted to be 'near' where he had last seen him. This juxtaposing had activated his sixth sense a few years back. He had been the lead detective on a brutal slaying of a prostitute in the city centre. He had known the young lass when he had been in uniform and his beat had been the red-light district. As lead detective, he had gone to where the woman had been murdered. A shit-hole of a hotel just up from the river in the Saltmarket. He'd climbed the poorly lit stairs to the top floor and stepped over bin bags, broken plaster, rat poison and a junkie shooting up. Then he ducked under the police tape and entered the dingy room where the lass had been slain. There was dried blood all over the walls and the ceiling. He stood for a long time in front of the bed where she had been found dismembered.

And lay down.

It was after midnight, the same time as the prossie had been offed. Sharkey stayed there. Felt the presence of the killer.

Sensed the killer was somehow involved with the hotel. The next day he'd interviewed staff. The low-life manager. The ashen-faced night porter. A security guard who didn't speak English. Came up with nothing. Then he dug around and found out who owned the leasehold on the property. A Russian millionaire. Sharkey tried to track the man down, but he kept a low profile. Eventually Sharkey found him. A fireplug with a rodent's face. Sharkey said he wanted to interview him. The Russian millionaire was all attitude. Felt he was above the law. Balked. Sharkey pulled out a cotton swab and a plastic evidence bag. Said he was going to need a DNA sample. Said he was not leaving without it. Would welcome a refusal on the millionaire's part. The Russian millionaire said we would give Sharkey a hundred-thousand quid to disappear. Sharkey grabbed him by the balls and wouldn't let go. Gave him the full Rottweiler treatment and spoke a bit of German for effect. And the millionaire broke down right then and there. Knew he was buggered. And confessed. It had been a long shot in the dark, a goddamn long shot. But with a pinch of brio and a dash of machismo, he had the killer.

So here he sat, in front of the Gaolkeeper. Looking for a sign. Inspiration. Some sort of a signal. And then the signal came. He popped his boot, pulled out his laptop and booted it up.

Sharkey searched for any WIFI signals. Five appeared. All secure. He clicked on the Gaolkeeper's. It required a password. He remembered what Lyon-Jones had said: *Forty percent of passwords can be hacked within five minutes because the choice is simple-minded.* He tried BLUE NOSE. Then TENNENTS. Then simply GOALKEEPER, the pub's original name. And bingo again! He was in. Simple-minded, indeed.

Sharkey pulled up Google. Did a search for 'bait & tackle, Glasgow'. Eight came up. If Decoy Brody was a serious angler, he had to purchase his gear somewhere. Perhaps at one of these shops. A long, long shot in the dark.

In the morning, before work, he would pay a visit to each of these establishments. Show the photo of Decoy Brody.

See if he could get a bite.

* * *

198

Sharkey paid a visit to the bait & tackle shops on the south side of the river first.

No one recognized Decoy Body. Then he tried the shops north of the river of which there were three. No go at number one. Same at number two. The third shop he tried was located in Partick, across from McDonald's, and not far from the university. The proprietor of the tackle shop said he had never seen anyone who resembled the man in the photo.

And Sharkey knew he was lying.

Not only lying, but afraid.

Sharkey thanked the man for his help, exited the shop, jumped in the Polar Bear and nicked the WIFI from the McDonald's across the street. He was going to try Lyon-Jones' technique again. The bait & tackle shop was called HOOK, LINE & SINKER, so Sharkey started with fishing terms. Passwords may be basically simple-minded, but Sharkey struggled. Oddly wished Lyon-Jones was there to help him out. Then he struck gold. The password was simple-minded and a bit twisted: 'Master Baiter'.

And within minutes of hacking the files, he had a customer who went by the name of Brody.

And more importantly, Brody's address: 305 Broomloan Road, Govan.

Sharkey pulled his .38 out of the glovebox. Hid it under his scarf on the passenger seat. Cranked the key in the ignition. Sped as fast as he could to 305 Broomloan Road. As he approached the area, he spotted Ibrox Stadium where Glasgow Rangers called home. The address he had harvested for Decoy Brody was literally in the shadow of the prodigious stadium.

A litter-strewn empty lot.

# CHAPTER SIXTY-THREE

Sharkey arrived at the police station late and was immediately summoned to CI Squires' office to file his prelim on the previous night's murder.

He had had little sleep and was crawling out from under a life-sucking hangover, so he took Lyon-Jones along to fill in some of the blanks. More so to deflect the shite that was sure to fly his way.

CI Squires gestured. 'Have a seat.'

Lyon-Jones took a seat, Sharkey remained standing.

'Where were you last night, Inspector?'

'Home.'

'I rang you numerous times. You had your mobile turned off.'

'Charging it.'

'Mine will ring when it's charging.'

'Mine won't. I'm on a lower pay grade than you are.'

'Unacceptable.'

At the best of times, DCI Maggie Squires was one hard bitch, today she was one hard bitch in a foul mood. She was now getting serious pressure from above. Something she could do without. Something she went out of her way to avoid. Her game plan had been to keep her pretty, little nose to the grindstone, work hard, climb the ladder. She didn't have to be nice on the way up as she wasn't planning on coming back down. Superintendent was in reach. Perhaps even Chief Superintendent. She had no family. Didn't want one. She was married to the Force and it was a marriage made in heaven. At least from her side. The events that had transpired in the past week were wreaking havoc with her game plan. And she wasn't having it.

'Thoughts about last night's murder?'

Sharkey motioned for Lyon-Jones to go first.

'Taxi Boy was a Sutherland flunky. A part-time thug. Full-time brown-nose. The murder appears to be connected to the Pizza Face killing on Argyle. With Tattoo McQueen's release from prison imminent, he wants to level the playing field. He wants to let the Sutherland family know what's in store for them once he gets out.'

'Why use a knife for one murder and a gun for the next?'

'To keep the Sutherlands looking over their shoulder. Not knowing where the next hit will come from. Or how.'

Succinct, professional and well thought out. Squires was pleased with this assessment. DS Lyon-Jones was a rising star within the Force and that's just how CI Squires wanted it.

As long as Squires' star rose first.

'Sharkey?'

'There's no connection between the two murders. As I said previously, the Argyle killing was most likely done by Decoy Brody to silence the motor-mouth laddie. Last night's killing was about making a political statement. Barlinnie to the City Mortuary by way of the High Court. Someone is making mockery of the system.'

Squires smirking. 'Sounds like you.'

'What are you trying to say?'

No response from Squires.

'Look, Maggie, the McQueens don't kill with a single gunshot to the head. They kill to send a message. When they tried to take out the Screwdriver, they slashed his throat and stabbed him seventeen times...'

'Because the gun jammed...'

'After giving the eldest Sutherland son a Mozambique Drill in the body and *two* in the back of the head.'

'So who did it then?'

'My money's on Decoy Brody.'

'Brody! Didn't you pay attention at the briefing? He's on his way to Spain.'

'No, he's right here in Glasgow.'

'Says who?'

'One of my sources.'

Squires just shook her head at Sharkey in a condescending

way. 'One of your sources. Give me a break. If Decoy Brody was here, which he isn't, he wouldn't kill one of the Screwdriver's men?'

'That's exactly what he would do. The Screwdriver's orders. Make it look as if it's Tattoo McQueen's dirty work.'

'Why?'

'So when McQueen's released all eyes will be on him. The Screwdriver would kill his own mother if he'd thought it would keep him out from under the microscope.'

Squires regarded Sharkey for a long time. Two boxers at the weigh in. Puffing out their chests.

'We'll go with DS Lyon-Jones' finding and appraisal, just like last time. That's the line of enquiry we'll pursue.' She paused. 'Sharkey, I want you to go to Barlinnie in the morning and interview Tattoo McQueen about the killing of Taxi Boy.'

Sharkey was miffed. 'It's a waste of time.'

'And take DS Lyon-Jones with you. End of story.'

* * *

DI Sharkey slammed his locker shut, sat down, bent over, held his head with both hands. Was DCI Squires out to get him or was he starting to get paranoid? There was too much politics, backstabbing and inter-office rivalry within the Force.

But, soon none of it would matter.

'Pssst! Sir! Boss!'

Jesus Christ. Lyon-Jones' voice was like having a bad bout of tinnitus and Sharkey thought he was hearing things. He looked back towards the locker room door and Lyon-Jones had her head poking in.

'Is no place sacred to you, Jones?'

'Sorry, sir. Felt it was important.'

'Why didn't you just give me a bell?'

'You never answer…sir. Listen, you have a message. From a Mr Hat…H-A-T.'

'Did you answer my office phone again?'

'How did you know?'

'What did he want, Jones?'

'It doesn't make sense, sir.'

'Let's have it, Jones, we're not trying to crack the enigma code here.'

'It just says "Buckeroo 10". What does it mean, sir?'
'It means you and I are going out again tonight.'

# CHAPTER SIXTY-FOUR

Sharkey and his enervating shadow Lyon-Jones sat in the same back corner at the Grand Ole Opry. Both were nursing a fizzy water. Lyon-Jones was playing Sudoku on her iPhone.

Sharkey was looking in the direction of the line dancing, but not really seeing it, 'Cotton Eyed Joe' playing, not really hearing it. He consulted his watch. 'Ten twenty-five. Eddie the Hat's late.'

'Is Eddie the Hat always so reliable?'

'This is not like him. When he says he's going to do something, he does it.'

'But last time, he didn't even want to be seen with you. Why would he show now?'

Sharkey had no answer to this.

Lyon-Jones nosey again. 'Why the "Hat"?'

'Sorry?'

'Why is he called Eddie the *Hat*?'

'He was shot in the head about ten years ago. After a Rangers game. He has no forehead from the eyebrows up.'

'Jesus.'

'I used to work out at a gym in the city centre. Same gym that Eddie lifted at. I didn't know him very well, but I went to visit him in hospital. I was about the only visitor he had. Eddie's never forgot that.'

A saloon girl approached and Sharkey ordered another round of fizzy water. The saloon girl had given him a funny look when he'd said: 'Make mine a double.' Old habits die hard.

Just after eleven, Sharkey had had enough. He didn't know what he was going to do. Going home was still out of the question, so he decided to take Lyon-Jones back to the station, then he'd go to the District Pub on Paisley Road West, sit at the bar and try to regroup.

Besides, the whisky was cheap and, late at night, they over poured. He had had his fill of fizzy water for one evening.

'Big Hat, No Cattle' was now playing as Sharkey and Lyon-Jones stepped out of the Grand Ole Opry and were hit with a fierce wind. Sharkey looked around. There was litter swirling everywhere. He turned to Lyon-Jones, almost barked, 'Why do people need to litter? Why don't they take more pride in where they live? Don't they know how lucky they are to live in Glasgow? In Scotland? It's God's country.'

Lyon-Jones shrank a bit. 'Got to agree with you, sir.'

Sharkey and Lyon-Jones turned the collars up on their coats and crossed Govan Road, leaning into the wind, stepping over a pothole. Just past La Fiorentina, they turned left into the wee alley. The Polar Bear was on the right side, down by the bollards. Sharkey noticed that the street lamp was broken and had not been replaced. Not replaced on purpose by the council no doubt to prevent it from becoming a weekly frigging occurrence.

There was already a light frost on the windscreen, so Sharkey unlocked the driver's door, reached over to the glovebox and extracted his scraper. He moved to the passenger side first, lifted the windscreen wiper and scraped the frost away. He replaced the wiper in its original position, then stopped. There was noise behind them. Eddie the Hat? No. Coming down the alley from the direction of the 24/7 convenience store on Paisley Road West were five hooded figures wearing baggy clothing. They were boisterous and loud, and they scuffed their Nikes along the pavement and swapped swigs from a bottle of Strongbow. When they spotted Sharkey and Lyon-Jones, they stopped. Whispered among themselves.

Lyon-Jones felt her defenses kick in and her adrenaline shot through her body.

'Sir?'

Sharkey kept scraping. Tonight he would welcome trouble.

'Pssst. Sir?'

The hoodies moved closer; a pack of mongoose moving in on a cobra. The biggest of the lads sized up Sharkey and took the last swig from the bottle of Strongbow. He tossed the bottle on the ground at Sharkey's feet.

*Litter.*

Big Lad pulled out a blade.

'How 'boot ye gie us a tenner and ye wonnae get chibbed.'

Sharkey looked up at the hoodies. They were posturing and wiping their noses. He ignored them and went back to his scraping. Lyon-Jones couldn't believe it. Gave Sharkey a 'do-something look'.

'Ho! Fuck face!' Big Lad bellowed. 'Said "How 'boot ye gie us a tenner and ye wonnae get chibbed".'

The cobra looked up and smiled, and this greatly disarmed Big Lad and his hooded mongoose crew.

'How 'boot ye pick up yer boattle,' Sharkey said in heavy Glaswegian, pulling out his Smith & Wesson, 'and ye wonnae get shot.'

Big Lad held Sharkey's stare. He wasn't about to pick up the bottle and lose face.

So the cobra spat venom: he cocked his revolver.

Quickly, Big Lad bent down and picked up the bottle.

'Fucking A, no need tae get all bothered.'

Sharkey watched them scarper with their scrawny little tails tucked between their scrawny little trackie legs. Turned to Lyon-Jones, who was freaking out just a little bit, on many fronts.

'You carry a gun with you? Are you certifiable?'

'Would you rather I hadn't brought it tonight?'

Sharkey returned to scraping his windscreen. And that's when he saw it: Stuck under the windscreen wiper was a card of some sort. Sharkey extracted it. It was a beer coaster from the Grand Ole Opry. It had writing on it scribbled in a childish hand: 'Pilmuir Holdings, Fieldfare Farm. Mum'.

Eddie the Hat had just come through with the location of Decoy Brody's mother.

Sharkey handed the beer coaster to Lyon-Jones.

'High marks for the Germinator. Reliable as always.'

# CHAPTER SIXTY-FIVE

Sleep would not be a friend tonight for Sharkey.

Lyon-Jones recognised this and knew what Sharkey's plans were.

'I'll take you back to the station now...'

'You're going to go up there, aren't you, sir?'

'Not tonight.'

'Of course you are. I think I'll stay.'

'I need to be alone—'

'Sir—'

'I'm taking you back to the station, Sergeant. End of.'

And that's what Sharkey did, drove Lyon-Jones back to the station, then took the M77, climbed out of the Clyde basin, higher and higher, past the Silverburn Shopping Centre and left the motorway at the Newton Mearns exit. He swung on to Crookfur Road and ran into drifting snow as he motored up to the Ayr Road and turned right at the roundabout. Ever since the M77 had been expanded, the Ayr Road had become a quiet thoroughfare. Sharkey carried on past Parklands Country Club, The Avenue shopping mall and up to the Malletsheugh Pub and Restaurant. Just past the pub, Sharkey motored over a bridge which crossed back over the M77 and found the entrance to Pilmuir Road. The road would be muddy and wet in the summer. Now it was icy, rutted and treacherous. And there was deep snow at this higher elevation.

Sharkey brought the Polar Bear to a stop. The rolling hills in front of him were on the threshold of the Fenwick Moor. A Christmas card winter scene of sparkling white snow nearly a foot deep. If he went in there now, at this time of night, he might as well announce his arrival with blues and twos. The Polar Bear's headlamps would be visible for miles.

And that was asking for trouble.

Could he turn the headlamps off?

Absolutely, and with the snow that deep, that was asking for even more trouble.

# CHAPTER SIXTY-SIX

Five days until Christmas.

HM Prison Barlinnie is Scotland's largest prison. It has been overcrowded almost since the day it opened in 1882 and, partly owing to that, earned its place on the list of most infamous prisons along with Alcatraz, the Bangkok Hilton and the Scrubbs.

When the shocking squalor of slopping out was abolished in 2003, it lessened the powder-keg conditions, but the fuse was burning again with the increased population. Built to hold 1018 prisoners, the Big Hoose was now pushing towards 1786 and drug abuse and violence were high with a frightful mix of warders stabbed or slashed, cons assaulted, riots and dirty protests (defecating and urinating everywhere and anywhere).

Sharkey and DS Lyon-Jones arrived at Barlinnie and entered through the revolving front door just after seven in the morning, the hour when Barlinnie wakes up. Warders were checking each cell to see if anyone had escaped. Or if anyone had died. Sharkey and Lyon-Jones were ushered inside by a behemoth warder. A former rugby standout.

For Lyon-Jones' benefit, Sharkey had arranged a tour of sorts. The first stop was at the pharmacy where over 450 inmates were given their methadone, the largest number in the European Union, then Lyon-Jones was shown how a prisoner was processed, the infamous 'dog boxes' and then on to the weight room and the library.

Lyon-Jones was pleasantly surprised to see how clean Barlinnie was. And even more surprised to learn that the Barlinnie library had a massive section on Crime, much larger than any Waterstones. She asked the prison librarian if the library had *A Willing Victim* by bestselling crime writer Laura Wilson.

The librarian gave Lyon-Jones a wry smile. 'We have two copies. Both on loan. Haven't been returned...'

When it hit eight o'clock, Sharkey and Lyon-Jones repaired to the canteen for a coffee. Sharkey enlightened Lyon-Jones on what to expect from Tattoo McQueen.

'Tattoo McQueen is arrogant, defensive and aggressive. Strike the match too close to the open can of petrol and you just might get burned.'

'Geez, Louise, Boss, what kind of an analogy is that? I have had some experience in the interview room, you know.'

'Doing what? Grilling a bunch of Gordonstoun students on Easter Break who tipped a cow?'

Lyon-Jones swirled her coffee around in its cup. Wanted to throw the coffee in his face. Storm out of there. Perhaps that's what he wanted. And that's why she didn't. *You just wait, Boss, you just wait and see how I handle myself in the interview room.*

Sharkey and Lyon-Jones exited the canteen and went down to heavily guarded Interview Room A. Sharkey paused, this was the same interview room where he had once interviewed a relative of one of the defendants in the Ice Cream Wars. Now it was to meet with Tattoo McQueen. Ice cream to cold as ice.

Sharkey had had previous dealings with Tattoo, Lyon-Jones hadn't and she was taken aback when she stepped into the room and saw McQueen, in prison-issued jeans and a red sweatshirt, sitting behind a table. She was expecting the usual tattoos á la incarceration, but not every inch of the neck and face and ears, as well. Tattoo McQueen, a mass of purple swirls, said nothing just stared at Lyon-Jones. She stared back. Then her blood ran cold: his tattooed nose was not a nose, rather a thumb stitched where the nose should be.

Sharkey took the chair opposite McQueen, turned it round and put his arms on the backrest. Lyon-Jones stepped back and stood just out of McQueen's line of sight.

Sharkey turned on his tape recorder and gave the relevant date, time and who was present.

Tattoo turned to Lyon-Jones. 'A rich bitch, then. Nobody in Possil wit a name like that, hen.'

Lyon-Jones didn't respond. No need to be drawn into a pissing match with a male. Not yet.

210

Sharkey commenced. 'You ordered the killings of Pizza Face and Taxi Boy.'

'Did I?'

'Don't try to be funny.'

'Only jokers I see around here are ye lot.' His hands gripped the edge of the table.

'You're getting out. We think you're trying to level the playing field.'

'If I wis gonny level the playing field, I wouldnae start wit a piece o' shite sellin' chalk tae the recovering addicts at Hope House.' Tattoo snorted, looked over at Lyon-Jones. 'Cat got yer tongue, hen?'

Sharkey pushed. 'But that's the McQueen way, isn't it. Bully the small fry. Intimidate the weak. Afraid of the competition's brass.'

McQueen slammed his fist on the table.

'No!'

Easy to push his button. Quick to fly off the handle.

'If I had ordered it, the laddie an' the cabbie would've been missin' some bits.'

Lyon-Jones stepped forward. Broke in: 'What if we tell you they were. Bits and ballbags. Your MO, Mr McQueen.'

Sharkey looked at Lyon-Jones, impressed.

Lyon-Jones held Tattoo's stare, bored into his psyche. Tattoo was forced to look away.

Lyon-Jones ratcheted up the pressure. 'Would you like your solicitor, Mr McQueen?'

'This interview is over. I donnae need this shite from ye lot. I'll be out of here in a few days and ye cannae touch me.'

Sharkey put his finger on the tape recorder's OFF button. Pushed. Rose. Moved towards the door with Lyon-Jones.

Tattoo stopped them. 'How many cocks did ye have tae suck tae become DS, hen?'

Lyon-Jones spun back to Tattoo McQueen. 'Pent-up aggression, Mr McQueen? Are you missing your number-one son, then?'

With the thrust and commitment of Hannibal Lector, Tattoo McQueen lunged at Lyon-Jones but was jerked back in his chair by the two guards present.

Sharkey was taken aback.
Lyon-Jones hadn't even flinched.

## CHAPTER SIXTY-SEVEN

After returning to the station, Lyon-Jones took Sharkey aside: 'Tattoo McQueen's nose?'

'He had it sliced off with a samurai sword in a street fight when he was 16. Cosmetic surgery wasn't what it is today.'

Then Sharkey told Lyon-Jones to report to CI Squires. 'Give her all the grisly details. Tattoo's charm. His way with words. Leave nothing out.'

'Where are you going?'

'Dental appointment.'

'Really?'

'Aye, but I'll be the one pulling the teeth.'

# CHAPTER SIXTY-EIGHT

Over at HQ, Detective Chief Superintendent Danus Ferguson listened intently to every word Sharkey had to say.

'Was it one of your grasses gave you the address of Decoy Brody's mother?'

'Yes, sir.'

'And why haven't you gone to DCI Squires with the information first?'

'I've been warned off Brody, sir.'

'And you think by being approached by the informant does not constitute involvement?'

'That would be my position, sir, if I had to present my case. But to be honest with you, I'd bend it anyway I had to, to get results.'

DCS Ferguson regarded Sharkey for a long time. He liked his honesty. He like his moxie. Why hadn't his daughter married somebody like Sharkey instead of that arrogant schmuck she had. Sharkey had balls, his son-in-law, money. Ferguson would take balls over money any day. When he used to play rugby for Scotland back in the late 60s, he won fifteen caps. He had joined the Army so he didn't have to give up playing rugby. Army by day. Rugby by night. You had to have balls.

'You know I can't do it this way…'

'Jesus, sir…'

'But I just might get an anonymous tip. I have loads of old-school sources. What's that address then?'

'Fieldfare Farm in Pilmuir Holdings, sir.'

'I know Pilmuir Holdings. Friend gets his MOT done out there at Paterson's garage, every November. Leave it with me. I'll instruct surveillance, but I don't want you sticking your nose in there. Understood?'

'Loud and clear, sir.'

'And Fleet?'

'Yes, sir?'

'Keep below the radar. Squires wants heads to roll.'

CHAPTER SIXTY-NINE

The phone was ringing in Sharkey's office when he returned, but by the time he picked up the receiver there was no one there.

He dialled 1471. Then pressed 3. The number had come from Strathclyde Police station in Govan. That could only mean one person: Kojak. Sharkey's pulse jumped up a few notches. Did Kojak have some news regarding Decoy Brody?

Sharkey was about to dial back when his mobile vibrated. A text. From Kojak. It read: TALL CRANES 8 PM...LOSE YOUR SHADOW.

* * *

The Tall Cranes Bar in Craigton Road, Govan, was a dodgy wee boozer with a whiff of sectarianism.

There used to be a poster of a rat caught in a trap which had been signed by King Rat killer Crip McWilliams to celebrate the Maze murder. It had been dedicated to the 'staff and patrons of the Tall Cranes Bar, Govan'.

The police had the poster removed along with a small shrine to other IRA and INLA terror campaigns. The images included one of masked gunmen firing a volley of shots over a coffin, a tribute to the ten Irish Republican hunger strikers who died in the 1980s and there were paintings commemorating an IRA escape bid from the Maze.

The pub had made the news back in 2003 when police were called out to deal with a 'near riot' after a Celtic/Rangers football match. That did happen from time to time—with it being a Celtic pub located south of the river.

Sharkey pushed his way through the obligatory smokers sheltering on the entrance ramp and entered the dark confines of the lively pub and was struck by how smoky it still was inside. This was not where a person trying and failing to quit should do custom. He approached a surly barman with a shaven head and earrings in both ears: a recent graduate of Barlinnie prison, A-levels in antisocial behaviour and weightlifting.

'Pint of heavy, please.'

'Ye drank in here bifor?'

'Donnae think so.'

Then get yersel tae fuck!'

Sharkey held the barman's gaze. 'And a whisky. Grouse. Large.'

The barman ignored Sharkey and wiped down the transom with a scabby rag. But he was a bit dumbfounded. This didn't happen. Some bampot standing up to him. Who was this dick-flavoured arsehole? Didn't he realise the bar held the record for the most fatal stabbings in and around Glasgow? The barman glanced at Sharkey in the mirror. Sharkey was still staring at him. The barman didn't like the look of this cunt. There was a danger about him. An I-don't-mind-dying-in-the-process danger. And that was not something he felt like dealing with at eight in the evening. Perhaps later when he was good and oiled.

He pumped Sharkey's pint and poured his whisky. Placed them in front of this curious stranger. Studied him.

'Same for me.' Sharkey heard. He turned to see Kojak stroll in.

Sharkey watched the barman look back and forth between the two of them. Then the penny dropped. Perhaps he would just let these two sit here and drink and there would be no bother coming Sharkey's way later on.

Kojak lit up a fag.

'Aren't you going outside?'

'And if I donnae? What am I goin' tae dae, arrest mysel?'

Kojak proffered one to Sharkey. Sharkey shook his head 'No', then accepted it and lit up on Kojak's lighter.

'This doesn't strike me as your kind of place,' Sharkey said. 'What with your leanings.'

'Booze is colour blind.'

Kojak paid. His shout. They repaired to a table over in the corner where it was a bit more private and they could keep their backs against the wall and an eye on the front door.

'How ye holdin' up, Fleet?'

'I'm a guilt-ridden mess. Afraid to go to sleep. I have

nightmares about Katie. She's in jeopardy and I can't help. In the latest one, she's sinking in quicksand and yelling for me and I yell back that I don't have time right now. I'm busy. Maybe tomorrow…'

Sharkey took a long draw on his pint. Stared deep into space. Sucked on his fag.

'You got something on Decoy, Kojak?'

'No.'

'No? Thought that's why I'm here.'

Sharkey and Kojak watched as three new faces entered the pub. That's what cops did. He turned back to Sharkey. 'It's about yer DS.'

'Which one?'

'Miss double-barrelled.'

'Lyon-Jones? What about her?'

'Remember, ye asked me tae dig around and see if there was any connection between someone on the Force and Decoy Brody?'

Sharkey tensed. Moved to the edge of his seat.

'When Lyon-Jones was fifteen, she ran away from home. Came tae Glesga and got a job at the Bijou on Sauchiehall. She told everyone she was eighteen and looked it. Carried herself older. Had the body. She got heavy into drugs. Heroin. Started dating one of the pushers—a bouncer by the name of Denny the Screwdriver Sutherland.'

'You gotta be shittin' me.'

'Stayed nearly a year before a P.I. found her and dragged her kickin' and screamin' back tae her Da.'

'I don't believe any of this.'

'Donnae believe me. Go ask the manager of the Bijou. He worked the door back then.'

'So what are you saying to me?'

'I'm saying…Lyon-Jones is yer leak.'

'It just doesn't make sense, Kojak. Why would she come back to Glasgow?'

Kojak ripped the wrapper off a Wispa. Took a bite. Washed it down with his beer. Looked up at Sharkey. 'That I can't answer for you. I'm just tellin' ye what I'm tellin' ye.'

# CHAPTER SEVENTY

'I want Sharkey dead.'

The Screwdriver hadn't been the same since he'd been waterboarded. The past two nights he woke up screaming, thinking he was drowning, pushing the covers away from his face. Both times he'd scared the living shite out of his wife and made the weans cry. Then he couldn't go back to sleep. Was afraid to go back to sleep. So he lay there in the dark, thinking. And he'd finally come to the conclusion that Sharkey was behind the waterboarding. He knew that Sharkey had been a Marine in America. Sharkey would have learnt the technique over there. Fucking Americans were famous for using that creepy shite on people.

The Screwdriver and Decoy Brody were sitting in an empty car on the underground. Newspapers held in front of their faces. The Screwdriver repeated his request, 'Did ye hear me? I want Sharkey dead.'

'Heard ye the first time. It's goin' to cost ye...'

'I'll pay ye whatever ye want.'

'I want four kilos this time. Upfront.'

'Four! Are ye out of yer fucking mind?'

The Screwdriver actually put his newspaper down. Pulled Decoy's newspaper down.

Decoy just smiled back. 'Then do the job yersel.'

'Jaysus, Decoy. Customs have been cracking down. Our pipeline is clogged. I can't move that kind of product.'

'Then find a new way. Force your Da's hand and stop acting like a fiert wee shite, or you'll have more than just the Pouch and Sharkey to be frightened of.'

The Screwdriver looked into Decoy's eyes. Jaysus, he was like fuckin' Jekyll and Hyde. The Screwdriver's mind flashed back to his days at Bellahouston Primary in Govan. Decoy had been in the year below him. A docile runt. Two boys at school had bullied Brody for a good part of the school year, eventually pushing him in front of a lorry where he was knocked down and badly fractured his pelvis. When he came out of hospital, he had emerged with an evil side to his personality. And he had decided that he had had enough with being bullied. The next time the boys tried to bully him he was ready for them and he gave each of them such a beating with a baseball bat that one went to hospital and the other was off school for a month. He increased the terror on these two lads until one committed suicide by jumping off the Erskine Bridge. Feeling no guilt, and now enjoying the torture, he'd kept up the pressure on the remaining lad.

'I'll get the four kilos fer ye.'

'Don't ye disappoint me.'

# CHAPTER SEVENTY-ONE

She looked at him and smiled.

He did a double-take. Was she smiling at him? She was. How long had it been since a lassie gave him that sort of look? Forever, it seemed.

Only because it was.

She walked away, swinging her hips suggestively. And he followed. It was six in the evening and he had nothing better to do. He followed her along the high street and then down a wee lane. She stopped and looked back. Smiling that we're-having-a-moment smile of hers. Shite, he didn't know what to do now. It was obvious he had been following her. Oh, my God, she was coming his way. She approached and stopped directly in front of him.

'Are you following me?'

He didn't know what to say. And that accent was familiar? She was from somewhere, he knew that much.

'What's yer name?'

'Don't go by my Christian name,' he said. 'Just use my nickname.'

'What is your nickname then?'

'Fat Cheeks. Ye frae Glesga, hen?'

'Castlemilk.'

'What's yer name?'

'I go by my nickname, as well: Castle-Annie.'

Fat Cheeks couldn't believe his good fortune. Things like this just didn't happen to a fat fuck like him. He eyed the lassie. She didn't look like any gals he knew in Glasgow. She had platinum-blond hair, white, perfect teeth and a body to die for. Her boobies were spilling out of a colourful top that said: *aqui, se habla vino rioja*, and her legs were long, well-muscled and tanned. He thought she somehow looked familiar, but was too dim to realise that he couldn't place her simply because she had her clothes on.

Fuck, what did she see in him? Guess it was the way he carried himself. He was a big shot down here in Benidorm, working for the Pouch. Perhaps his new-found stature showed through in his persona, not that he knew what persona meant. The Pouch was paying him good money and he had become a right-hand man of sorts. Plus, the Pouch said he would drop a load of cash on him if he would make a run back to Glasgow. As a courier. Fucking A, he'd do whatever the Big Baron asked.

Castle-Annie smiled seductively. 'How 'bout I show you Benidorm and later you show me your hotel room?'

Fat Cheeks had moved into a high-rise hotel now. The same hotel where all the package holiday makers from First Choice stayed. The Pouch had put him up in there. Paid all the bills. In cash. Said he wanted Fat Cheeks to enjoy himself. Fat Cheeks liked the hotel, there was a full-English breakfast every morning, a bar that stayed open late and horny-flicks on the telly in his room. The Pouch said he could do whatever he wanted, except use the phone, of course. That was off-limits. He knew that because he had tried and it was blocked.

Castle-Annie smiled that smile at Fat Cheeks.

'Lead the way, ma princess,' was the only thing he could think of to say.

Castle-Annie began the tour in a part of Benidorm known as 'The Square'.

'The Brits call this area the "Square", but locals call it *La Zona Giri*. The "British Zone". Avoid it here, late. Everyone's drunk or looking to fight or spewing up.'

Fat Cheeks didn't see the problem.

They walked on and saw lots of down-market clubs and sticky pubs and greasy restaurants smelling of bacon fat. And it made Fat Cheeks miss home.

'The Square's the only area of Benidorm that have a police presence at night. To keep control of the lager louts. When it gets bad, the polis shoot their guns up in air.'

They strolled on. Fat Cheeks couldn't believe it, Christmas around the corner and he was walking around at night without his hoodie on. He felt fuckin' naked.

Castle-Annie pointed at something. On the opposite side of the street was a naughty little venue advertising two 'bosom-and-bottom' sisters who did a lesbian act, a club offering a Michael Jackson impersonator (oh, wow!) and a Dolly Parton impersonator (wow wow!), and another club featuring Sticky Vicky, a woman on the experienced side of sixty, who danced naked and shot Ping-Pong balls out of an anatomical crevice not usually associated with Ping-Pong.

And Fat Cheeks loved it here. He had never seen anything like this before in his life.

Even in Govan.

'Come on, I'll show you the Spanish side of Benidorm.'

Castle-Annie led Fat Cheeks down to the promenade along the Mediterranean. He couldn't take his eyes off all the high-rise hotels and apartment blocks. It reminded him of New York, not that he had ever been. They passed by a hotel with a huge Welsh flag hanging from a second-storey balcony and Fat Cheeks wondered what kind of a person would take a Welsh flag on holiday, especially with the poky limit on luggage.

Castle-Annie, took Fat Cheeks by the hand, which gave him an erection, and led him some circuitous route deep into the *Casco Antiguo* where they clambered up a long steep hill and all the way to the end of the Plaça del Castell. The plaza rested upon a rocky promontory and they gazed off at neighbouring and high-rise, twinkly Playa de Levante.

Just below the plaza was the lively artists' quarter and Castle-Annie suggested they stop and have a drink at an outdoor café with large overhead heating elements for when the temperature dropped. A waiter magically appeared and Fat Cheeks ungallantly ordered ahead of Castle-Annie, requesting a pint of Tennents, but they only had San Miguel in a bottle, so he settled for that. He wanted chips, as well, but he was becoming quite the man of the world and he knew the Spanish ate late. He would order the chips later and really impress the shite out of Castle-Annie. The drinks arrived, the pint for Fat Cheeks and a large glass of *rioja* for Castle-Annie. Castle-Annie made a toast to the two of them, Fat Cheeks clinked glasses, drank half the pint down without coming up for air and then burped. Mortified he looked over at Castle-Annie, but she just smiled back with a look of pure devotion in her eyes.

Fat Cheeks excused himself and went to the Gents. He didn't really need the loo, but he desperately wanted to pinch himself. He took out his mobile to give Pizza Face a bell, then remembered Pizza Face was dead.

With Fat Cheeks in the *servicios*, Castle-Annie could take her time reaching into her purse and extracting the wee green pill. It dissolved almost immediately, then she hauled out her mobile and knocked off a quick text.

Fat Cheeks returned and sat down. He was getting hypoglycaemic. Bugger it, he ordered a plate of chips. The chips arrived and he scarfed them down, not offering any to Castle-Annie. But Castle-Annie didn't seem to mind.

They finished their drinks and Castle-Annie suggested another place, so they slipped off deeper and deeper into the romantic warren that is the *Casco Antiguo* and eventually unearthed a little hole-in-the-wall of a bodega. Fat Cheeks couldn't believe how buckled he was on the one Spanish beer, but he ordered another one anyway. Sticking with the theme on her T-shirt, Castle-Annie ordered another large glass of *rioja*. And she ordered in Spanish. This would no doubt have greatly impressed Fat Cheeks, but he was pretty fucked up at the moment and just chose to stare glassy-eyed at Castle-Annie.

The hole-in-the-wall was on the Poniente Beach side of the *Casco Antiguo* and they could see the ocean and smell the salt in the air and Fat Cheeks felt as if he were lost well back in time, and he never wanted the night to end.

Fat Cheeks wasn't sure what time it was, probably after one in the morning, when Castle-Annie said, 'Let's go.'

'Where?'

'Your hotel.'

As they curled their way back down the hills of the Old Town and headed in the direction of Fat Cheeks' hotel located in package-holiday hell, he couldn't believe how many people were out walking.

And he couldn't believe how much trouble he was having walking.

And before he knew it, the two of them were in the lift, climbing slowly to the twenty-second floor. The lift shunted to a gentle stop on Fat Cheeks' floor and the doors hissed open. Fat Cheeks led Castle-Annie into a poorly lit hallway. He struggled to insert the plastic key into the door, so Castle-Annie did it for him. Then she turned the knob and ushered Fat Cheeks in and in the direction of the bed.

'Take your clothes off,' Castle-Annie commanded. And Fat Cheeks did as he was told. He lay there naked and pink. A beached manatee washed up on a foreign shore.

Castle-Annie took up a position in a chair that looked out at Benidorm below. And she enjoyed the view and she waited for Fat Cheeks to pass out.

And he did, with a hard-on.

Castle-Annie reached into her purse. Extracted a syringe. Injected 25 milligrams of potassium chloride in the dorsal artery at the base of his erect penis.

Seven minutes later, Fat Cheeks' heart stopped beating.

# CHAPTER SEVENTY-TWO

Four days until Christmas.

Sharkey opened the door to his office and stepped out. He scanned for Lyon-Jones, caught her eye and beckoned her over.

'There's something we need to talk about.'

Sharkey let Lyon-Jones in and closed the door behind her.

'What is it you wanted, sir?'

'You'd better sit down.'

Lyon-Jones sat. Sharkey sat. He studied her and it made her uncomfortable. It was as if he were defragmenting her hard drive.

'Listen, I'd prefer if you'd call me Fleet when it's just the two of us...'

Lyon-Jones didn't know where this was going. DI Sharkey had a way of disarming folk.

Sharkey continued: 'I think I owe you an apology. I've been so wrapped up in my personal problems, I never gave you the support you deserve. I'm sorry, Jones.'

Sharkey laughed out loud. Lyon-Jones had never heard her boss laugh.

'I mean...*Lyon*-Jones. So, there you have it. I apologise.'

'Apology accepted.' Gobsmacked.

'Fancy a cheeky pint after work?'

# CHAPTER SEVENTY-THREE

Alicante was once a major Mediterranean trading station known for its exporting of rice, wine, olive oil, oranges and wool. Now it was becoming more known as a centre for exporting drugs.

In the dank, fusty cellar of a private hospital near the harbour, Federico 'Freddy' Ibarrez, a forensic pathologist, commenced the post mortem on Fat Cheeks. Dr Freddy had always been fascinated by the human body and he lived for death.

Owing to the circumstances, Dr Freddy worked alone today and did not employ his usual *Diener*. Autopsy practice was largely developed in Germany and the German word for 'helper' had stuck.

He regarded the corpulent face of Fat Cheeks, smiled and cast his mind back to so many years ago when he was just getting started and how verification of death had not been so very sophisticated in Spain. The goal, of course, back then and now, was to make sure that the person in question was in fact very dead. Bad form to bury someone who was still alive —a very rare occurrence, although still not unheard of.

The verification tests of yesteryear consisted of placing a feather or mirror at the lips to check for breath and checking a finger or ear for a pulse. Other tests were to see if the body temperature was dropping, or purple and blue patches were forming as the blood pooled, or the muscles contracted as rigor mortis set in after a few hours, making the body stiff, though it later became limp again. Nowadays, and significantly more refined, people were checked for response to pain, light, inability to breathe without a machine, lack of muscle movement, lack of reflexes, involuntary actions such as blinking or swallowing, and presence or lack of brain waves as detected by EEGs or MEGs.

Dr Freddy snapped back to the present. Better get on with the job at hand. He began with a thorough examination of the exterior of the body, noting any and all distinguishable features or injuries. There were no visible injuries; however, Fat Cheeks did possess a frightfully inadequate penis. The pathologist decided against putting this in his report as time was of the essence. He was meant to have dinner with the judge who had released the body, and they were to split up the fat envelope of euros that Jimmy the Pouch had allotted for their services.

Usually the deceased's next-of-kin would have to agree to an autopsy being done, but the judge had contacted his golfing partner, the local coroner, and that step was simply bypassed.

The pathologist put down his tape recorder and donned his lead vest so he could take the X-rays. It wasn't customary to wear the lead vest, but he treasured every last squiggly spermatozoa and had never felt all that comfortable just slipping behind the lead shield and snapping away.

After the exterior of the body had been meticulously documented, and film taken, the pathologist used a razor-sharp scalpel and made a Y-shaped incision from both shoulders to mid-chest, down to the pubic region. There was little bleeding as the blood had already pooled. He then opened Fat Cheeks' rib cage with a Stryker saw. The Stryker was a specialized saw with a precision oscillating tip. It cut through bone, but did little damage to soft tissue.

In front of him, the pathologist gazed at the major solid organs of the body. Then he carefully freed up the large intestine and employed the standard Method of Virchow to remove, one by one: the heart, liver, lungs, and stomach, kidneys, spleen and adrenals. He weighed them on a basic grocer's scale and placed them in a heavy-duty binbag on the cement floor. He then removed a nearly full bladder and placed that in the bin liner, as well. Dr Freddy was surprised at the large size and orange colour of Fat Cheeks' liver and the streaky bacon appearance of his lungs. Such abuse for someone so young.

It had crossed his mind to harvest the few healthy organs and sell them on the black market, but Fat Cheeks had been dead for too long. Perhaps the next time he was pressed into service by the judge and *Señor* Sutherland.

Fat Cheeks was a large *chico* and the body cavity was enormous. This pleased the pathologist to no end as he was easily able to place the three kilos of cocaine (triple plastic bagged and heat sealed) inside and stitch the body cavity back up.

Since it is a pathologist's duty to examine anything that may have a bearing on the cause of death, he grabbed his scalpel and made a second incision, this time across the head, joining the bony prominences just below and behind the ears. The incision was then carried on down to the skull and the scalp peeled back. The skull vault was opened by using two saw cuts, one in front and another in back. These would not show through the scalp when it was sewn back together. The brain was then cut free from its attachments and removed. Another kilo of coke could be easily secreted here.

After the procedure was complete, Dr Freddy placed the plastic binbag in his backpack and glanced up at the sign on the wall above his stainless steel workbench. The sign was in Latin and it read: *Hic locus est ubi mors gaudet succurrere vitae* ('This is the place where death rejoices to help those who live').

Dr Freddy signed the death certificate. Fat Cheeks' cause of death was listed as 'Death by Misadventure', which usually meant that the deceased had choked on his/her own vomit. Dr Freddy knew this would not be flagged, as Death by Misadventure on the *costas* was nearly an every-other-day occurrence with these young Brit party animals.

Before dinner, he would ride his moped down to the harbour and toss the organs in the sea. The schools of voracious mullet that roamed the inner harbour would make short work of the body parts.

They particularly fancied the brain.

# CHAPTER SEVENTY-FOUR

So as not to raise any inter-office eyebrows, Sharkey suggested to Lyon-Jones they meet at a designated pub at the end of their shift. 'Meetcha the back a seven.'

He chose The Griffin, on Bath Street, located kitty corner from the King's Theatre and not far from the same Premier Inn that Decoy Brody had used as a crow's nest to kill the Rangers goalie.

The pub was warm and a few of the afternoon drinkers were still in, making life in Glasgow appear nearly normal. Sharkey and Lyon-Jones were seated by one of the large windows, looking out on to Bath Street. They'd had no trouble finding a seat by the window when they'd arrived. With a trigger-happy madman running amok, no one was keen to be featured in a fish bowl.

Sharkey was drinking Heavy. Lyon-Jones, espresso martinis. By the collection of empty glasses littering the table, they'd been there for quite some time.

Outside, Bath Street was already deserted, wet and wind-swept.

Lyon-Jones eyed Sharkey's pint. 'Don't know how you can drink that chemical rubbish.'

'Oh, excuse me Miss Morningside. We can't all drink those posh Edinburgh concoctions.' Sharkey held up his pint, toasted. 'To chemical rubbish. *Sláinte!*'

'*Sláinte Mhor.*'

Sharkey smiled at Lyon-Jones. She had changed clothes for their rendezvous. White blouse unbuttoned one too many. Hint of a black bra. Dark cardigan. Cashmere. Expensive. If his life weren't falling apart, and she the backstabbing, conniving traitor she was, he might have asked her out.

Lyon-Jones smiled at Sharkey over the top of her pint. The

smile of deceit? 'So why'd you come back from America?'

'Scottish by birth...Glaswegian by the gift of God.'

Lyon-Jones laughed. She had never seen this side of DI Sharkey. Any side, really, other than the pissed-off, surly and vengeful side. When she was young, she had always been attracted to bad boys. Sharkey was a bad boy, a seriously handsome bad boy with an endearing self-effacing sense of humour. A deadly combo. She'd better watch herself. Especially tonight. Rules had to prevail. She was blisteringly drunk. And wired.

Sharkey took a long pull on his pint. 'I missed it all, the way of life, the history, the different sense of humour, the beer. Big time on the beer...'

'I'll drink to that!' Lyon-Jones blurted out a bit too loudly and toasted Sharkey.

'...Guess I was homesick. I was trawling the Internet and saw the advert for the Strathclyde Police. Started in Shettleston. Went to Govan. Then to City Centre.'

Sharkey looked at Lyon-Jones and didn't see a young woman or a detective sergeant gazing back at him, he saw a shrink analyzing him. Studying him. A shrink with an agenda.

Lyon-Jones quaffed her drink. 'Why'd you really come back?'

Time for Sharkey to study Lyon-Jones. He had known all along she was intelligent and intuitive. But now he knew she was dangerous.

'That's for another day...'

'Sir...'

'Please, *Fleet*.'

'That won't be so easy, but here goes...*Fleet*, was it to settle a score?'

'What would make you think that?'

'Don't know. I read too many books.'

'You like books?'

'They are my raison d'être.'

Lyon-Jones seemed uncomfortable. She unconsciously scrunched up the sleeves on her cardie. Saw Sharkey looking at her scars. Self-consciously rolled the sleeves back down.

'Ever do drugs?'

'No...my father would have belted me purple. He believed

232

strongly in corporal punishment for his children.' Response suspect in its delay.

'Sure? No drugs?'

'Does nicotine count?' Lyon-Jones said, smiling that smile, changing the subject, rising from her seat.

'No.' Sharkey followed her out the front door. They huddled in the lee of the recessed doorway. Lit up. Smoked furiously.

Lyon-Jones removed a bit of tobacco from the tip of her tongue. Looked up at Sharkey. 'Cold?'

'Freezing my Baltics off.'

Sharkey studied Lyon-Jones from behind his cigarette. 'Didn't know you smoked.'

'Only when I'm nervous.'

'What's making you nervous?'

'You. You're being too nice.'

'I've getting in touch with my feminine side.'

'Is that why you're wearing Dior`?'

'It's a chick magnet…'

Lyon-Jones looked up at Sharkey. Into his eyes. Was uncomfortable again. She motioned with her head towards the door. They each had a last gasp of their ciggies. Lyon-Jones flipped her stub in the gutter and hurried back into the warm confines of the pub. Sharkey went and retrieved the stub. Stuck it in the little cigarette disposal receptacle at the side of the door. Did the same with his. Hurried in back inside. Joined Lyon-Jones at their booth in the fishbowl. Both were chilled now.

'Fancy a whisky, Fiona?'

'Had enough.'

'Live dangerously.

A long look at Sharkey. 'Just a wee swally.'

'You're becoming quite the Weegie.'

Lyon-Jones laughed again.

Sharkey went to the bar and returned with Island single malts. Toasted Fiona. 'Island malts. To Shetland.' Then: 'Did you get on with your father?'

'Until I was about five.'

'Any abuse?'

'Bags full. Physical and mental.'

Lyon-Jones looked for a reaction and saw that Sharkey wasn't listening and this infuriated her.

And once again it surprised her that he had an effect on her.

Then she saw why Sharkey was ignoring her: Sitting at the bar was a young father, holding court with the barman. On the young father's lap was his four-year-old daughter. Sharkey turned his attention back to Lyon-Jones.

'That was your father at the funeral?'

Sharkey nodded.

'What happened to him? The stoma?'

'You're nosey…' Said with regret. Had to remember why he was here. Not let the alcohol do the talking.

'Aye, very. So what happened?'

'He tried to break up a fight in a Shettleston pub. Got a broken bottle in the throat as thanks.'

Sharkey downed the remainder of his whisky. 'Ever spend any time in Glasgow before coming to City Centre?'

'Now *you're* being nosey.'

'And?'

'No.'

'What are you, the only person from Edinburgh who never visited Glasgow?'

'I've lived a sheltered life.'

'Yeah, right. So speak already.'

'Why the interest?'

'The city doesn't deserve what's happening. And it doesn't deserve the bad press it's getting. There are good folk here and this could be the greatest city in the world.' He paused. 'Can I ask you another question?'

'Shoot.'

'Are you a cutter?'

This stunned Lyon-Jones sober. Another chink in her impenetrable armour. She tugged on her sleeves. Avoided eye contact.

'Are you, Fiona?'

No response. Looking up. Trying to keep her eyes from spilling over.

'It's okay, Fiona. Talk to me.'

Lyon-Jones took a hanky out from her purse. Blew her nose.

Dabbed at the corners of her eyes. 'Went through a bad time. Depression.'

'What'd you use?'

'Rather not talk about it, sir.'

'Broken glass?'

'No.'

'Needles?'

'No.'

'What?'

'Please, sir.'

'What, Fiona? What did you use?'

Long pause. Lyon-Jones stared Sharkey down. Emotions swirling. Powerful resentment, first, then debilitating humiliation. Finally, she dipped her head. 'It's a secret.'

Trying to lighten the moment. 'Any other secrets?'

'Lots.'

'Like?'

'I have a discreet tattoo.' Lyon-Jones finished her whisky. 'Listen, I'd better go home and eat something.'

'Come to my place, I do a helluva ping-ping meal.'

'Ping-ping meal?'

'Microwave.'

'Tempting.' She knocked back the rest of her whisky. Slurred, 'I'll go to my place.'

'You can't drive.'

'I'll ring a taxi.' And she did.

The taxi arrived. They could see it out the window, motor running, waiting. Sharkey waved to the driver. Walked Lyon-Jones out. Had a good hard look at the cabbie. An elderly gent he had seen around. No worries here. He held the door and Lyon-Jones climbed in. Sharkey said he would see her in the morning.

The taxi started to drive off, then abruptly stopped. The back window powered down and Lyon-Jones whispered one word: 'Razor blades.'

The taxi drove off. Sharkey stood there watching it go, then he yanked his collar up against the cold, pulled on a pair of leather gloves and walked back to the City Centre station through light snow. At the station he opened his locker, took out

235

the Slim Jim he had brought back from America, went to the car park, checked the positioning of the CCTV—and broke into Lyon-Jones' red Mini.

Sharkey hauled a pocket torch out of his jacket, looked under the seat and in the side pouches. Nothing. He pulled on the glovebox handle. Locked. He jimmied the glovebox. The glovebox only contained two items: a small bottle of Daisy perfume…and a .38 calibre handgun with a two-inch barrel.

Loaded.

# CHAPTER SEVENTY-FIVE

Three days until Christmas.

Lyon-Jones nearly crawled into Sharkey's office the next morning wearing eyeglasses. Little rectangular lenses with no rims. Sharkey did a double take. Didn't say anything. Didn't need to.

'Don't ask, sir.'

'Wouldn't think of it.'

Lyon-Jones huffed. 'Contacts.'

'I wear contacts too!'

'Got home so inebriated last night I took out my contacts and put them in my spare contact case by mistake. This morning I woke up with veisalgia—'

'With what?'

'The mother of all hangovers.' Sigh. 'Put my contacts in. Unfortunately, I put two in each eye. Thought I had gone blind. Got any Resolve?'

Sharkey tried desperately to gain control of his twitching face muscles. Fought a losing battle. 'Know what you mean...'

Finally exploded.

Felt horribly guilty for experiencing mirth.

Lyon-Jones picked up on this conflict of emotions. Thought about consoling him. Changed her tack at the last minute. Let her agenda get the best of her education: 'Listen, Boss, I forgot to ask last night, but did anything ever come of that address that Eddie the Hat gave you for Decoy Brody's mum?'

'It's inaccessible this time of year, so that means he won't be there.'

'So where does that leave us with Decoy Brody?'

'It means we don't have a clue where he's holed up.'

## CHAPTER SEVENTY-SIX

It wasn't even midday yet and the three hoodies were up to no good. And why the fuck not? They could do whatever they liked and no fuckin' adult could tell them otherwise. And no one could lay a hand on them.

They had already been banned from the Braehead Shopping Centre for spitting down on the Christmas shoppers from the first level. Banned or not, they vowed to return the next day wearing different-colour hoodies to exact revenge. Their grand plan was to bring a dead cat in a shopping bag, throw it down into a crowd and video it with the iPhone they had pinched the previous week. The Christmas punters would freak and they would upload the video clip on YouTube and it would go viral.

Genius!

But wait. Hold on just a fuckin' sec. Where would they get a dead cat? Oh, aye…that would be the easiest part, same place they found 'em when they poured lighter fuel on the little bastards and torched 'em.

It thrilled the three teenaged miscreants that there was so much entertainment at a shopping mall. It was easy enough to steal handfuls of mixed candy from the candy barrow, as the Paki employee got flustered when they filled up three or four large bags of candy, let him weigh it all and then feigned horror at the cost and not pay. Then when he was running around like, well, a kitten that had been torched, agonizing over putting it all back in the proper compartments, they could easily nick as much as they wanted. If the lads were a wee bit peckish for something a bit more sensible, something that would stick to their ribs, they could always go into Sainsbury's, fill up a trolley with practical items, make as if they were shopping and eat their way around the store. Then there was the Gents. Two shredded toilet rolls would pretty much block the bog and flushing would create a very impressive flood all over the tiled floor, making it slippy as all fuck.

All that to do, but today's focus was on rogue trolleys from Sainsbury's car park. They were presently trying to set a new record of tossing trolleys in the Clyde.

Tossers, indeed.

The tossers' old record was three. It was a piece o' fuckin' cake to wheel them over to the boardwalk and dump them over the rail and into the river. They were about to dump the fourth trolley and set a new record when something off to their right, floating in the river, caught their eye. It was a football. And retrieving the football suddenly became much more interesting than destroying private property.

With the tide on its way out, the river was low and it was relatively easy for one of the hoodies to climb over the railing, drop down to the rocks below and pluck the football out of the river. And how his mates laughed when he started jumping up and down, acting like a monkey, as he shrieked for joy.

Or was it joy?

You see, that was no football he had grabbed hold of.

That was a head.

Loosely attached to what was left of a body.

* * *

The Police Marine Unit's zodiac boat cut through the waters of the Clyde and the three-man crew could see hundreds of rubber-neckers standing on Braehead's boardwalk pointing down towards the river.

Standing among the throngs were two of the hoodies, both fumbling nervously with roll-ups. The third hoodie was back in the mall, in the Gents, puking. He was sick from having touched a dead body and fuckin' livid that his new Lacoste trainers were soaked because some arsewipe had blocked up the toilets with bog rolls and the floor was flooded.

Using a boathook, one of the crew on the police boat was able to snag the rope tied around the feet of the victim. As he pulled, the crowd onshore gasped. In spite of all the divots that had been created by creatures feeding on the unclothed body, the corpse was clearly that of a young woman.

Nothing ever bothered the hoodies, but even they couldn't

stomach the sight of the nearly decapitated, bloated, greyish-blue corpse.

# CHAPTER SEVENTY-SEVEN

'Step right up, Amy Winehouse, how can I help?'

The skanky woman with the black, piled-high hair and the hideous tattoos was flagrantly insulted. 'Amy Winehouse is dead!'

In an attempt to amuse, the civilian employee working the bar at Strathclyde Police City Centre had made a poor choice of words. He was the only living soul in the free world who was unaware that the chanteuse had kicked the bucket. But not to worry, he had been working this job for over a decade and he knew how to put out a fire.

He called for reinforcements in the form of DC Wilson. By the grace of God, DC Wilson had been well rewarded in the looks department. He was tall and muscular and the only way to describe him was a Glaswegian Antonio Banderas. If that's even genetically possible. And he had charm. Oodles of it.

'Yer all bloody useless, ye are—' Amy was in mid-insult when she spied DC Wilson step out the door which led to the Interview Rooms.

'As ahm livin' an' breathin'...'

DC Wilson flashed a smile that could thaw a glacier. 'I'm Detective Constable Wilson. I'm here to help. I'm all yours.'

Amy actually began to purr like a cat. That was the closest she could come to formal speech. DC Wilson gallantly held the door for her, plopped her in the first Interview Room they came to and held the chair for her.

'Tea? Sugar? Milk?'

'Oh, aye,' Amy said, punching at her hair. She thought she was going to have an orgasm.

DC Wilson returned with Amy's tea. 'Made it myself...'

'Ah like a man who knows his way around the kitchen.'

DC Wilson smiled. Amy's fingers kneaded her thighs.

'Now what's on your mind, Mrs…?'

'It's Miss…ah huv a partner, but ah think he's buggerin' off.'

Amy noisily slurped her tea. Lapped it, actually.

'It's about ma lad. He's no' been home.'

'Where's home?'

'Govan.'

'Govan. Why are you on this side of the river and not at Govan PD?'

'Ma son works in the city centre.'

DC Wilson took out a notepad. 'Your name, ma'am?'

'Minnie MacDipple.'

'With two p's?'

'No, with double "n".'

'I mean MacDipple…'

'Oh, aye.'

'Your son?'

'Ma son, what?'

'Your son's name?'

'Micky.'

'MacDipple?'

Amy gave DC Wilson a curious look. 'Aye.'

'How long has he been gone?'

'Days. Cannae remember so well, what with, well, ye know.'

DC Wilson shook his head in a supportive fashion. He understood alright.

'How old is Mickey?'

'Fifteen. No, sixteen. No, fifteen…'

'And he lives at home?'

'Aye, he's got the wee room out back by the washing machine, which is really a blessing as it's next to the cludgy and he always needs the shitter in the middle of the night ever since he started playing all those video games and has had the bad nightmares—'

'Minnie?'

'Yes sir, officer?'

'Anything more specific?'

'Oh, aye, he's nitroglycerinic…'

'Ma'am?'

'I mean hypoglycerinic.'

'Hypoglycaemic?'

'That's what I said.'

'Right, did he leave a note of any kind?'

Amy shook her head 'no' and shifted in her seat as if she were laying an egg.

'Who is he employed with?'

'Same bloke.'

'Same bloke?'

'Aye, he was doin' car valet in Govan, but couldnae get up of a morning and was always late tae work.'

'Where did he work?'

'At the garage.'

'Which garage would that be then, ma'am?'

'Sutherland.'

'Sutherland Motors?'

'Aye.'

DC Wilson scribbled on his notepad.

Amy pulled a pack of cigarettes out of her coat pocket. 'Do ye mind?'

'We'll go outside in a minute.'

Amy took a cigarette out anyway and put it in her mouth.

'He gave him a job working nights in the city centre instead.'

'Mr Sutherland?'

'Aye.'

'Does Mickey have a bank account that I could check to see if he's been withdrawing money?'

'No.'

'Building society?'

'No.'

'Anything else you can tell me about Mickey, Minnie?'

'He often goes by his other name.'

'Other name?'

'Fat Cheeks.'

This time, DC Wilson didn't write this down, rather he picked up his mobile and hit speed dial. 'I need you. Interview Room one.' Almost immediately Sharkey opened the door and stepped in. And Amy's mouth dropped open. If all the officers in City Centre were as handsome as DC Wilson and this new bloke, it just might change her opinion of the polis.

243

Sharkey introduced himself. Took a seat right next to Amy. Sharkey on the left. DC Wilson on the right. Amy looked back and forth between these two hunks, repeatedly, as a fan follows an exciting tennis match at Wimbledon. The electricity generated by the two cops must have illuminated a light bulb within her wee head for she was able to construct an intelligible sentence.

'Wait!' Amy said, beaming brightly enough to create shadows. 'I jist remembered somethin', he said he wis going tae Spain…'

# CHAPTER SEVENTY-EIGHT

'A word. My office. Now!'

Sharkey looked up from his desk at Detective Chief Inspector Maggie Squires as she spun round and aimed for her office. For fuck's sake, she did that like a drive-by shooting.

'Ho!' Sharkey yelled after her, but Squires didn't stop. He couldn't believe she'd just done that. Treated him that way in front of all the other detectives out in the CID room. Embarrass him like that. He charged after her, but was stopped by a firm hand on his shoulder. Lyon-Jones' hand.

'She's baiting you. Wants you to explode so she can suspend you. Don't lose your rag.'

Of course telling Sharkey this was the same as telling a volcano not to erupt. Take your 8.0 on the Richter Scale and stuff a sock in it. No such luck. Not going to happen. The magma was boiling within the volcano, ready to be unleashed on the surrounding countryside and flow down to the sea.

By the time, Sharkey reached Maggie Squires' door he'd come to his senses and realised Lyon-Jones was right. He gently knocked on the door and waited for the command.

'Door's open!'

Sharkey turned the knob and entered. Could see CI Squires was itching to let the guillotine drop.

'You're looking bright-eyed and bushy-tailed this morning, ma'am.'

CI Squires was disarmed by Sharkey's colloquial charm and docile approach. She had expected a charging bull. 'Close the door, please. Have a seat.' Squires just knew that Sharkey would refuse to sit. He always refused. His childish way of rebelling.

Sharkey took a seat. Placed his hands in his lap. The perfect schoolboy.

'Did you get the report back from Traffic on the Argyle

murder?'

'Ah…not yet.'

She held up a computer printout. 'Well, *I* did. CCTV footage from the area around the Pizza Face murder. It shows the times of hundreds of vehicles moving near the scene of crime. Took unfathomable man hours to log them all, identify the registration numbers and look up the vehicles' owners on the computer…'

Squires paused for effect.

Sharkey crossed his legs. Waited patiently.

'Names have emerged from all the data, and one name stood out above the rest—*you*.'

'Me?'

'Bit odd don't you think?'

No response.

'It shows you in the area two hours before the murder, and then again just after. Can you explain yourself?'

Sharkey knew that any delay in responding would signal his guilt, and he was quick on his feet, so quick in fact, that he could form the beginning of a response while he was still working on the final verb.

'Aye, ma'am, I can explain myself. You see, I was there. In the area. Twice. I didn't want to say anything at the time, but now I will. I'll just come out with it.'

CI Squires was all ears.

'I met with a grass. That was the first visit to the area. I had approached him about Decoy Brody. I was out of my head. Clutching for straws. Later, I went to the Horse Shoe Bar just around the corner. Drowned my sorrows. You can check with the bartender, Quinn. And then you warned me off Decoy and that was that…'

Squires studied Sharkey. 'I will check with this bartender by the name of Quinn. Did the grass ever get back to you about Decoy Brody?'

'No, ma'am.'

'If he does, I want to be the first one to know, not the Chief Super. *Me*. Do you understand?'

'Aye, ma'am.'

'That'll be all.'

'Thank you, ma'am.'

Sharkey rose, turned and opened the door.

'Sharkey…'

'Yes, ma'am.'

'You're skating on thin ice.'

## CHAPTER SEVENTY-NINE

It had rained heavily off and on for most of the day. Coming in great torrents, then dissipating, then great torrents again. Then it somehow got worse. And it was unseasonably. Mild, that is, for Glasgow in winter. What little snow there was had become pockmarked, slushy and quickly disappeared. Would that be the case up on higher ground? Sharkey decided to see for himself.

He was going back to Pilmuir Holdings.

The western sky was a bruise of fading daylight as Sharkey drove away from the city centre and climbed up the M77. His arrival in Newton Mearns confirmed what he had suspected: No snow up here either. Sharkey guided the Polar Bear off the motorway and over to the Ayr Road and eventually pulled over in the car park of the Malletsheugh. Darkness now. The rain was taking a few minutes off. Probably to reload. Sharkey left the car running, pulled a navy-blue knit cap over his head and then aimed for Pilmuir Road.

He drove down the bumpy road through a vast rolling blackness devoid of houses and streetlights until the road started to swing back in a slow loop towards civilization, and stopped. Off to his right was a single-lane dirt road. No snow, but muddy as a pig poke. An old wooden sign hung at a wonky angle: FIELDFARE FARM .

Sharkey didn't enter, rather chose to drive forward a hundred metres and pull the Polar Bear over on the verge where it was less likely to be noticed. He killed the engine, removed two scopes from the glovebox, popped the bonnet and climbed out. He moved to the front of the car, raised the bonnet and made as if he were checking the oil. Then he fiddled with the cables. You never knew who could be watching. Finally he went to the boot, opened it and pulled out an empty five-gallon petrol can and a pair of Wellies. He sat on the rear bumper. Pulled the Wellies on.

grabbed the empty petrol can. Walked back a hundred metres and set off down the single-lane road leading to Fieldfare Farm. He had Google-earthed the farm and he knew it was set back nearly a mile.

If the surveillance team was on the lookout for Decoy Brody, then they would spot Sharkey, so he buried the petrol can under a pile of wet leaves and left the dirt road. He hiked over wet fields towards the east, stopping every minute to scan the area with his nightscope. Then he circled back to approach the farm from a dense wooded area. Sharkey positioned himself behind a tree, sat down on the ground and waited. Listened. Continued to pan the area with his nightscope. Then he did the same with his military thermal monocular. Only when he was satisfied that he hadn't been followed and that no one else was out there, did he make his final approach to the farm.

The farm was set between rolling hills in what the Americans would call a box canyon. A Glaswegian would call it idyllic. Sharkey used his thermal monocular to scan the hills surrounding the farm for any source of body heat. He spotted a field full of rabbits and one keen fox, but no surveillance team. Where was surveillance? Why weren't they here?

There was a secluded rise just to the east of the farmhouse. Sharkey climbed it. Steadied himself against a tree. Cased the area again with the thermal monocular. Then he put it away, took out his nightscope. Lights burned inside the farmhouse. He went window to window: the living room, a den with a fire burning in the fireplace, the kitchen. In the kitchen, he could easily make out two figures: an older woman and an elderly man. He waited and observed. He watched as the older couple sat down to dinner. His position was so unobstructed and the power of his scope so strong, he could easily make out the table was set for only two. He watched. Waited. There was no Decoy Brody here tonight. Sharkey worked his way back to his motor the same way he had come in. Same routine. Stopping. Casing the area again. He picked up the secreted petrol can on his way.

It was pitch black now. No sliver of light in the west. No stars. As he approached the road which led to Fieldfare Farm, he swept the area with his monocular. Nothing. Back on the dirt road, he made another sweep and finished at the Polar Bear. The thermal imaging showed a hooded figure hovering around the opened bonnet. Then a flare as a cigarette was lit. Before the hoodie could finish the fag, Sharkey had his S&W at the back of his head.

'Hands in the air and turn around slowly.'

Sharkey switched on his torch as the figure turned. Under the hoodie was a boyish face. A boyish face shiting himself. Sharkey hauled out his warrant card.

'For the love of Christ, Inspector! You scared the shite out of me. I'm DC Fife.'

'Let's see your ID.'

DC Fife reached into the pocket of his black parka and slowly extracted it.

Sharkey lowered his gun. Lowered his torch. Switched it off.

'Working surveillance?'

'Aye.'

'Just you?'

'Aye.'

'Just starting your shift?'

'No, sir. Finishing.'

'Who's in place now?'

'No one.' DC Fife took an I-nearly-shit-myself drag of his cigarette.

'How long were you there?'

'Twelve hours. I'm frozen solid. Suppose to be nine of us, but you know how it goes.'

'Budget?'

'Aye, sir.'

Sharkey regarded DC Fife's kit. He resembled a cross between a farm hand who lived out here, someone about to scale Everest and the Michelin Man: Down parka with hood, mittens the size of frying pans, baggy shells, Wellies.

'Any sign of the suspect?'

'No sir. Just an old couple. Man in his sixties, tall, hunched at the shoulders. Woman, same age, minus the hunched shoulders.'

DC Fife sucked on the fag, the end glowing like a fuse on a stick of dynamite.

'What are you doing out here, sir?'

'You didn't see me here, Detective...and you didn't allow

someone to sneak up behind you and put a gun to your head. Understood?'

'Understood, sir.'

Sharkey slammed the bonnet shut on the Polar Bear, threw the petrol can in the boot, changed out of his Wellies and jumped in.

DC Fife walked around to the driver's side of the Polar Bear and knocked politely on the window. Sharkey powered it down.

'Sir?'

'Aye.'

'Could I hitch a ride back to the Malletsheugh, sir? I walked in.'

On the way back to the pub, Sharkey grilled DC Fife again.

'So...couple never left. Suspect never approached?'

'Aye, sir.'

'Are you absolutely sure, Detective?'

'Yes, sir, absolutely one-hundred percent. Does that heater go any higher?'

'Only when it's of a mind.' Sharkey slapped the heater around, finally got it to respond. 'Nothing else, Detective. No movement whatsoever?'

'Just the Asda van, sir.'

# CHAPTER EIGHTY

Sharkey dropped a slowly thawing DC Fife in the car park of the Malletsheugh and headed back up the Ayr Road to The Avenue Shopping Centre.

He turned left in front of the shopping centre, then right again into the loading area of one of the mall's anchor stores— Asda. The loading area was the usual beehive of activity. This was where staff parked their cars and motorbikes. There were delivery bays to the left and a waste area to the right with skips spilling over with flattened boxes. Somehow a trolley from Marks & Spencer had found its way back here. It was being used to shift bags of grit and salt, and oddly kitty litter. Didn't look as if it would be returned any time soon. Sharkey wondered how many trolleys Mark & Sparks had that belonged to Asda. Would there be a prisoner swap at Christmas as a show of goodwill or would they all be held hostage until a later date?

The trolley wars.

Sharkey parked and was immediately set upon by an employee in a high-vis jacket with the welcoming warmth of a constipated Rottweiler. Sharkey flashed his warrant card. The warrant card froze the man in mid-bark.

'Want to speak to the van driver who does the home deliveries.'

High-Vis Jacket Man gestured for Sharkey to follow. He led him inside the building and over to a lad in the break room enjoying a steaming cup of tea and a sugary biqquie. Suddenly accommodating, High-Vis Jacket Man left Sharkey to do his job. It seemed to Sharkey that it was colder in the break room than outside.

Sharkey held up his ID to the van driver.

A warrant card can sometimes have the same effect as sodium pentothal.

'If yer here aboot ma partner, she's a lyin' hoor. Caught her

252

in bed wi ma flatmate and ah chucked the both of 'em oot, but ah dinnae touch the lyin' bitch.'

'I'm not here about you or your hen, mate,' Sharkey said, and held up a photo of Decoy Brody. Right off, the van driver's facial expressions showed that he recognized Decoy, then he remembered that he was supposed to keep his trap shut and rebooted the face.

'Ever seen him?'

'I don't know the bloke.'

'Didn't ask you that, I asked if you've ever seen him.'

'Never.'

Sharkey pulled a twenty pound note out of his pocket and thrust it at the driver.

'Let me ask you again, ever see him?'

'He pays me more than that...'

Sharkey pulled out another twenty. The driver reached out for it, nearly spilling his tea. Sharkey denied him.

'How many times have you taken him out there?'

The driver looked around. Didn't want this broadcast around. 'Jist the once.'

'When?'

A young female employee entered the break room. Glanced at Sharkey. Over to the driver. Back at Sharkey. Smiled. Grabbed the world's smallest yoghourt out of a fridge in the corner. Took her leave. Looked back at Sharkey. Gave him a come-hither move with her bum as she exited.

Sharkey turned his attention back to the driver. 'When did you take him out there?'

'Two days ago.'

'Did you bring him back?'

'Aye, after he dropped something off in a big duffel bag.' He held out his hand. 'C'n ah huv the other twenty?'

'Here's my card. You take him again, you give me a bell. Then you get the twenty.'

# CHAPTER EIGHTY-ONE

Two days until Christmas.

Willie Wallace stepped out of the front door of his basement flat and sent some sort of feral creature scurrying. He pulled on his gloves and climbed the stairs. He looked around. Up the street. Down the street. It was nearly eight in the morning and still dark.

God, he loved winter. Loved British Standard Time. It was cold out and he could see his breath. But no worries, he was kitted in a brown winter coat, with dark-brown scarf tied in the obligatory loop, practical, thick-soled brown shoes and a flat tweed cap. He loved hats. They kept him warm. Eighty-percent of a person's body heat could be lost if the head was exposed.

He had read that somewhere.

Willie checked his backpack to ensure he had brought along his hand sanitizer, extra Kleenex, germicidal wipes, disposable dental flossers and the special cloth for his spectacles.

He looked up at the sky. No stars. This brought a smile to his face. There was a thick cloud cover and it would remain dark longer. He turned right from his apartment building and limped up Orkney Street to Govan Road. Willie stopped here and gazed over at the fire station. He had great respect for the young lads as he was afraid of fire. He had never set a pan of chips on fire or anything like that, but somehow fire frightened him. He knew he had issues with fire, but there you go. Everyone had issues with something. That he knew.

He had read that somewhere.

Willie looked at his watch and hurried the best he could up to the Govan Subway Station. He didn't want to miss his train. He was going to the swimming baths over in the city. He loved his weekly swim. Kept him fit. Kept him a finely tuned machine. Just like a beaver or otter or snake, he was at home in the water.

And he could hold his breath longer than anybody else he knew.

Willie descended the steps into the over-heated Govan Subway Station and his glasses fogged. He took out the cloth for his spectacles. Wiped them. Waved at one of his colleagues working the booth, pushed through the barrier and descended further on down to the platform.

At last he could relax. He always felt better underground. Felt at home. Felt like he belonged to something grander than his mole-like existence. Another issue, perhaps. He glanced at his watch. His train would be arriving in one minute. He had it down to a science. Knew all the schedules. Knew all the coaches like friends. Each one had its own personality. Its own quirks. At least he wanted to believe that.

Willie was proud to be associated with the Glasgow subway as it was one of the few railways in the UK still remaining in public ownership and, more importantly, recognised as the world's third great underground railway after the London Underground and the Budapest Metro.

Willie had never been to Budapest and certainly never wanted to go. They had nasty bacteria in the swimming pools over there. And strange public commodes.

He hadn't read that somewhere, someone had told him.

Willie's train arrived, he greeted the driver with a little salute, then took his favourite seat all the way at the back, by a window, where he could keep an eye on the passengers and watch the punters standing on the platforms as the train came into each station. The SPT had a sterling safety record and Willie felt he was part of that success. That's why he sat at the back and made sure no one tried to get on or off the train when the doors were just closing. He may have been off-duty, but he believed in always being vigilant.

Willie was always careful to remain seated while the train was moving and, if he ever found himself in the unenviable situation of not having a seat, he would be sure to hold tightly to one of the handrails.

At rush hour and other busy times, employees were drafted to work down on the platforms. 'Regulators', they were called. To control the commuters. Willie enjoyed these moments a great deal as it afforded him the opportunity of being right there on the platform to aid passengers in any way he could. Many passengers didn't know about the phone located at the end of each platform to call staff if there was an emergency. Willie was always more than happy to point this out and it brought him great joy if a punter thanked him for being enlightened.

The only time Willie didn't relish working the subway was before, during and after football matches. Life was just too short to have to deal with substance-fuelled partisan and sectarian madness. But now he had gained a bit of seniority and usually he could get off for the matches.

Which he went to, religiously.

And ended up in the middle of substance-fuelled partisan and sectarian madness.

Somehow, it was different. Above ground.

The train pulled into the St Georges Cross station. Willie detrained. Waved at a colleague. Limped his way out of the subway. Perfect, it was still dark.

Willie fought a headwind all the way to Arlington Street and entered the Arlington Baths, one of Britain's last remaining Victorian bath houses.

Willie accessed the locker room and was thrilled to find his favourite cubicle available. Even though he wasn't modest by nature, he didn't feel comfortable changing in front of strangers. He removed all his clothes, being careful to keep his feet on the towel he had brought along so he didn't get athlete's foot or ringworm or God knows what. Wait a minute! Hadn't he read somewhere that athlete's foot and ringworm were one and the same?

Willie slipped into his cossie, tucked his parts in, put the swimming goggles around his head and exited the cubicle. What luck! His favourite locker over in the corner was also available. This way he wouldn't have to remember the locker number. Willie opened the door, put a pound coin in the slot and hung his clothes carefully so they wouldn't crease. He took an orange Sainsbury's bag out of his backpack and placed his shoes in it, then deposited the shoes on the bottom of the locker. He inserted his spectacles, keys and mobile into his shoes. He locked the locker. He didn't pin the locker key to his Speedos as he didn't want the puncture, so he carefully placed it in the little inner pocket provided just for these occasions. Then he had a pee. Showered in cold water. Tread through the foot bath and entered the 21-metre pool area.

After swimming his fifty laps, he practiced holding his breath by swimming a few laps underwater.

The first light of day could be seen streaming through the overhead skylights, so Willie took this as his cue. He climbed from the pool. Then procured a wrapping sheet from the attendant and entered the heated Turkish suite.

After baking for a half an hour, and power-napping for ten, Willie showered using his aloe vera shower gel, dressed and handed over his bathing costume for the complimentary cleaning, drying and storage.

It was light when Willie stepped back outside and that made him edgy. He hurried, moving with his head down, all the way over to Buchanan Street. Here he stopped when he saw two police officers arresting a transient for breaking into a public cigarette-stub disposal bin. The transient had been after the stubs. Sad, some people, trying to exist on the fringe of society.

Willie carried on to the Buchanan Galleries Shopping Centre's entrance, climbed the steps, slipped through the main doors and jumped in the queue at Costa Coffee. The queue moved along at the speed of lava and that made Willie anxious. He regarded the various punters in the queue. He had read somewhere that one-out-of-nine people had Chlamydia, so of course he wondered which one it was.

When he reached the top, he ordered a regular Americano and chocolate tiffin. He handed over the correct amount of money and his Costa Club card. Willie loved compiling the points. He had a Caffè Nero card, as well, but still needed the card stamped five more times to get the free coffee, so he had chosen Costa today. Perhaps the next time he was in the city centre, after the New Year, he would detrain at St Enoch and pay a visit to the Caffé Nero upstairs in the House of Fraser.

A young lad with tattoos on his neck working the till handed Willie his coffee and tiffin and his Costa Club card. Willie thanked him, then wiped the card clean of germs. It was as he was wiping the card that he saw it. Next to the till was a grainy photo of a young lassie by the name of Siobhan Wilde and a telephone number. Those grainy photos gave him chills. Looked like an obituary photo. What was that all about?

Willie finished his Americano, wiped his mouth with a napkin which had been provided, then took his tray, empty cup and saucer over to the work area next to the till and placed them on the counter. He didn't like to leave his debris behind so the next customer would have to shift it to another table. This always set off a chain reaction.

As he exited Costa Coffee and Buchanan Galleries Shopping Centre, he withdrew the hand sanitizer from his pocket and had a good squirt. He looked up Buchanan Street and then down Buchanan Street. There were CCTV cameras watching his every move. And it made him feel safe. He had read that the average citizen in the UK was caught on CCTV three-hundred times per day.

Willie began to whistle and strolled past a rough, glazed-eyed woman who looked as if she were hoping to work her way up to selling the *Big Issue*. She was handling out pamphlets about drug abuse. Could've written it, probably. Willie took one. When people on the street were handing out flyers or pamphlets, he always gladly took one. He somehow felt he was doing his part to help the little people. Those less fortunate.

Willie gave himself another squirt with his hand sanitizer and ambled down to W Regent Street and turned right. He read the pamphlet along the way: 'What You Should Know About Drugs'. Willie didn't know anything about drugs, other than they made people turn into lying, cheating, aggressive, irresponsible monsters. The pamphlet said that 25.3 percent of the population in England had tried drugs, 18.9 percent in Wales and 17 percent in Scotland. Somehow, Willie felt these statistics were skewed. There was many a day that almost everyone he came into contact with in Glasgow seemed to be on drugs.

A lass wearing sandwich boards walked his way. She was advertising a new café: 'The Mrs Bean'. Willie saw the establishment over the road. He watched as the young woman waddled across the street, opened the door to the café, turned sideways and got stuck going in. Willie rushed across the street. Helped the lassie gain access. Received a smile. Felt good for it.

He carried on down West Regent and watched a posh woman walking her Dalmatian. The woman could have been a doppelganger for Cruella De Vil. Cruella had a baggie attached to the lead so she could clean up after the pooch. The dog stopped, squatted, had a prolific dump. The posh woman cast furtive looks about, saw that no one was watching and walked quickly on. Willie wanted to confront the woman, but he didn't like confrontation. Tried to avoid it at all costs. He was annoyed. He saw things. Saw everything. Nothing got by him. It was a curse. Sometimes he wished he went through life with rose-coloured glasses on. Then he wouldn't see things. Wouldn't have seen the woman and the dog. Wouldn't feel the anger he was now feeling.

He curled left on Pitt Street and turned his attention back to the pamphlet on drugs. He read a testimonial of sorts: 'Ecstasy made me crazy. One day I tried to eat glass. I tried to bite it, just like you would bite into an apple. My mouth was full of glass. I nearly severed my tongue and almost bled to death.'

Crikey, Willie thought, this was giving him the heebie jeebies. He deposited the pamphlet in a rubbish bin. Had one last squirt and looked up. He had reached his destination.

In front of him was the imposing brick edifice of the headquarters for Strathclyde Police. And he entered.

The man at Reception was a civilian employee and originally from Malta. Willie had never heard anyone from Malta speak with a Glaswegian accent.

Willie looked up at the CCTV camera behind the man and then introduced himself. He wanted to speak to someone important. He was a tax-paying citizen, after all. He wanted to ask the questions that all of Glasgow wanted to ask: 'When is it all going to stop?' He was about to ask if he could indeed see someone important when he spotted a wanted poster. The poster was of a certain Derek 'Decoy' Brody. Above Brody's photo it read: HAVE YOU SEEN THIS MAN?

Willie stared at the poster. The fugitive's eyes seemed to be looking right back at him and it gave him, well, the willies. Frightened him so much, he fled out the front door of Strathclyde Police HQ without ever asking the question.

Forgot to have his squirt.

# CHAPTER EIGHTY-TWO

When Sharkey had been in a gang, his best skills had been leadership and recruitment. That, and kicking your arse to hell and back if you so much as snarled at one of his mates. Sharkey was exceedingly protective.

His gang was smaller than most. But they were fearless. And they were intelligent. All owing to Sharkey's recruitment. Just living in the same hood didn't guarantee you a place in Shettleston Aggro.

Most of the original gang eventually escaped the world of the street and made something of themselves: Sharkey for one, the Mayor, a pharmacist, two who became cops, one a fireman, and a diminutive ferret of a fellow called Scrounger (who had a talent for getting his hands on anything and everything when it was needed, like the character in *The Great Escape*). Scrounger was now an Immigration Officer. Sharkey had given him the heads-up on Fat Cheeks' peregrinations down to the Costa del Crime, and that heads-up was about to pay dividends.

# CHAPTER EIGHTY-THREE

Fat Cheeks' mum, now known as Amy Winehouse around the police station, waited outside in the cold at the back of Glasgow International Airport, out by Freight. It was noon, and she was never up this early. She lit up a fag and bit the end of her thumbnail. She took out a stick of gum. Threw the wrapper on the floor. Masticated. Chewing gum and smoking at the same time made her feel as if she were multi-tasking. Same as when she read a copy of *heat* while sitting on the cludgie.

Even though Amy was given five-thousand pounds by the Screwdriver to not get too gobby, she thought she still might cry when she saw her son's body. At least she hoped she would as she had been told Customs would be present and she needed to look sad.

What with the somber occasion, Amy had worn all black. She knew on account of the Baltic temperatures—and the occasion—that she was pushing it with the short skirt, the Perspex platform high heels, and open jacket with the mobile phone sticking out of her bra, but she hoped by looking just this side of slutty, she might catch the eye of the hot coppers if they turned up. She looked over at the imposing man standing next to her, posing as her partner. She didn't know much about him, other than everyone called him Helicopter. Perhaps that's why he'd accompanied her to the airport then? She reached out and grabbed his hand. She had been told that they must appear to be a couple.

'Not now for Christ sakes!' Helicopter hissed. 'When Customs get here.'

Even though they couldn't hear the dialogue, Sharkey and Scrounger observed this exchange from behind the tinted glass of an Immigration vehicle parked on the tarmac a short distance away. Sharkey noted: 'The bloke is one of the Screwdriver's thugs.'

Scrounger barked into a handset, 'Let them wait a while longer.' And he poured Sharkey another cup of steaming hot coffee from his tartan thermos.

After a long, cold hour, a Customs official stepped out a warehouse door and this caught the eye of the shivering Helicopter and Amy.

'Now!' Helicopter coached.

Amy clamped on as the coffin bearing Fat Cheeks' body arrived in the back of a lorry which had SEAFOOD painted on the side. The coffin was made of corrugated cardboard which confused Amy. She had hoped for a nice wood laminate. Or a flashy veneer.

Amy signed a few papers, taking longer to scratch out her illegible John Henry than it takes to write a chapter in a crime novel, then watched as the coffin was lifted out of the fish van with a forklift and loaded into the back of an old Volvo hearse with an expiring tax disc. Helicopter gallantly held the door for Amy and then climbed in before she could get her frozen limbs to move. Amy finally climbed in and then the tears came. Yes, the tears flowed, not because her only child was no longer among the living, she was crying crocodile tears because now she could afford those Ugg sheepskin boots and more importantly a month's supply of crystal meth. Amy had always wanted her very own pair of Ugg boots but was unable to save up enough dosh on account of needing it for beer and cigarettes. Those Uggs were so fashionable, plus she wanted to show the world how she could be the first person in Govan to be able to wear them without walking on the sides like everyone did with the counterfeit equivalents.

Sharkey and Scrounger followed the hearse as it stayed on surface streets all the way back into Govan. The hearse pulled into the drive of the Melville Brothers Funeral Home.

'Owned and operated by the Screwdriver's cousins,' Sharkey stated. 'I busted them twice when I worked out of Govan for trying to flog cadaver bones on the Internet.'

'The Screwdriver's cousins? Coincidence?' Scrounger asked.

'I think not.'

# CHAPTER EIGHTY-FOUR

In Govan, Fat Cheeks' mum, our Amy, was long back home from the airport. Her partner, who had just become her ex-partner, stood outside in the street picking up all his clothes and a few personal possessions that she'd dumped there: his rolling papers, a cracked bong, an unopened box of cherry-flavoured condoms and a sexual adjunct that had burnt out from excessive use. Amy had dumped all his junk there when he had gone down to the pub, for just one, and had stayed for hours (being bought rounds from mates and then scarpering when it was his shout). The ex-partner was feeling the effects of all the pints, plus he was coming down off three Preludin he had taken just that morning so he would be bright and perky when he went to pick up his benefit cheque. Presently he was cursing a blue streak and taking his frustration out on the knock-off brand clothing he had purchased at the Barras, the weekend flea market over in the Gallowgate in the East End. The ex-partner was screaming his head off at the front door of the block of flats even though the door wasn't locked and he could simply walk right on in: 'Where the fuck is all my underwear, ye bitch! Y'know, what ye bought fer me frae the bloke who had the sign: 'As Recently Featured on *Crimewatch*'.

Neighbours from the estate stood a not-so-respectful distance away, enjoying the meltdown from the cheap seats. Even old lady Brown was out there, sitting on a kitchen chair she had dragged out so she could observe the production from the front row. For this lot, a good domestic was decidedly more entertaining than being cooped up inside a dingy living room watching council telly.

When Amy was finished disenfranchising by dumping the counterfeit clothing and drug paraphernalia, she walked quickly back into the living room, sat on the couch, dusted her hands

263

and turned to the person sitting next to her, Helicopter.

Helicopter was glued to the box watching *Judge Judy*. Sucking on a can of Tesco lager. Inhaling a bag of Walkers prawn-cocktail crisps. Feeling as if he had known Amy for fuckin' ever.

Amy stared at the coal-effect fire, then the dimmest of light bulbs flickered and she smiled coquettishly at the whirlybird.

'Want to smoke a spliff?'

Helicopter turned and regarded Amy. 'Fuckin' A!'

Had he finally met Ms Right?

Amy mumbled something unintelligible, as unintelligible was her *lingua franca*, and began to undo Helicopter's bulging fly. She was going to do everything in her power to ensure her brand spanking new partner felt right at home.

# CHAPTER EIGHTY-FIVE

DS Fiona Lyon-Jones waited for Sharkey's white V-reg Rover to exit the car park behind the police station before reversing out of her parking space.

She tapped her sat/nav with an index finger, adjusted the heater, hit the rear-window defroster and set off, leaving the station pleased for the first time since she'd started. DI Sharkey had finally warmed to her. It had taken her longer than she had thought, but her determination, charm and guile had won out. She had him right where she wanted him.

The Polar Bear was hidden from sight in the fire station on the corner of Maitland and Milton as Lyon-Jones' red Mini shot by. The gal sure knew how to drive. Sharkey followed, but not in the Polar Bear, rather a fireman friend's black Passat. Sharkey was two cars behind as Fiona turned left on Port Dundas Road, then left again as she merged on to the A804. She was easy to spot with the duct tape he had stuck over one taillight just ten minutes earlier.

If Lyon-Jones was indeed the leak, what was she hoping to get out of it? Not many cops start out dirty, they have to grow into it. Having said that, crime families had been trying to infiltrate Strathclyde Police for donkeys. If Lyon-Jones had known the Screwdriver when she was a drugged-out tearaway, what purpose would it serve to maintain the contact? Was she positioned by the Sutherland crime family so they would have a mole on the inside? Whatever the reason, one thing was clear, she was bent on climbing the Force's ladder. Was it simply that she was so cold and calculating as to have little regard where she stepped on her way up? Sharkey had seen these types before. Status and power were the driving force and nothing came before it. Not relationships, not children, not family. And every means to an end was fair game.

All is fair in love and war…and working for the police force, many would tell you, was all about love and war.

Was Lyon-Jones a cold-hearted snake of the most venomous kind?

A clone of Detective Chief Inspector Maggie the Bitch?

Or something much more sinister?

Sharkey flipped on his indicators as he merged on to the M8. Lyon-Jones was speeding. Cops who speed. What was the hurry? If he shot out after her, and she was clever, which she was, she'd pick up the pursuit in her rearview mirror.

The Mini was ten cars in front as they crossed the Kingston Bridge and traffic was crisscrossing like fireworks at the finale of the Chinese New Year, jockeying to position for the bedroom communities of Renfrew, Erskine and Bishopton on the M8, or merging and lining up for the M77, direction Kilmarnock, Prestwick and Troon. By the time Sharkey had reached the turnoff for the M77 to Kilmarnock he didn't have a clue which way she had gone. He had to make a decision and quickly. Surely she was heading up the M77 towards home? Sharkey indicated, slipped into the inside lane and merged on to the M77. With luck the traffic would thin on the approach to the Silverburn Shopping Centre and he might be able to catch sight of the Mini as she climbed up and out of the basin.

Sharkey spotted the single taillight of the Mini just before exit #3, the exit for Giffnock and Lyon-Jones' flat. But she didn't exit, rather zoomed straight ahead and climbed higher and higher, finally leaving the motorway at exit #4 and Newton Mearns.

The Mini motored on, past the Osprey Restaurant and up to the Ayr Road by Parklands Country Club. The Mini turned right. Perhaps she was simply on her way to the Asda, he had visited the day before, to pick up something for dinner? But she didn't turn right to access Asda, she stayed on the Ayr Road and drove a mile more, finally turning into the car park for the Malletsheugh Inn and Pub. Sharkey motored on by and saw Lyon-Jones climb out of the Mini, carrying what looked like an overnight bag, and enter the inn. He swung the black Passat round and parked in the Malletsheugh's car park on the west end, well away from where she had parked. He killed the engine.

Climbed out. Walked across the half-filled car park to her Mini. Ripped the duct tape off. Stuck it in his pocket. Didn't want any evidence. Didn't want to litter.

The Malletsheugh had large windows. Easy for Sharkey to stay well back in the darkness of the car park and peer in. The interior was well-lit. Low cushioned settees. Too modern and institutional for Sharkey's tastes. Sharkey preferred the cosy warmth and ambience of the city centre pubs. Older buildings. Lots of wood. A whiff of debauchery. Dark to a fault. Loads of character. Lots of characters.

Sharkey spotted Lyon-Jones sitting deep in the back right corner pecking at her mobile. Had she come here for a drink? This bar was known for its well-heeled clientele. Was Lyon-Jones in the hunt? A punter approached. Lyon-Jones looked up. Smiled. From the body language, Sharkey could see the punter and Lyon-Jones were acquainted. The punter was a handsome man, tall, late twenties, early thirties. Dressed inappropriately for this bar. Too casual. Didn't seem to fit in with this crowd. Lyon-Jones and the handsome man turned and glanced towards the front window. Sharkey's blood boiled, then spilt over.

He recognised the man: Denny the fucking Screwdriver Sutherland.

Who said there was no such thing as a gruffalo?

# CHAPTER EIGHTY-SIX

Christmas Eve.

Glasgow woke up to powder snow on the streets and a crystal-clear blue sky overhead. With the promise of a white Christmas looming, some of the doom and gloom was lifted from the city. Glasgow is a gloriously beautiful city when it's bedecked with a few inches of fluffy white.

At City Centre, DI Sharkey strolled in with two Costa coffees and approached Lyon-Jones who was already at her computer.

'Logging in as Lyon-Jones or Al Pacino this morning?'

'Lyon-Jones. You changed your password.'

'Americano?'

'That's your new password?'

'No, Americano. Would you care for an Americano?'

Lyon-Jones' face lit up. 'You bought me a coffee?'

'Cream in the left pocket. Sugar in the right.'

Lyon-Jones laughed. 'Just one from the left this morning.'

'What happened to "three from the right"?'

'I'm being good.'

'Who's good at Christmas time?'

'Point taken.'

'It's Christmas Eve. Come on, Fiona, we'll drink them in the luxury of an eight-by-eight office with a view of the motorway.'

Lyon-Jones felt her cheeks warm. He had never called her 'Fiona'.

Always the gentleman, well almost always, Sharkey held the door for Lyon-Jones. Lyon-Jones pulled up a chair. Sharkey sat behind his desk. Looked out the window at a cerulean sky and streaming sun. With the bright sky, it was all the more apparent that the window was grimy. Sharkey did a playful toast. 'To working the holidays.'

'To working the holidays.' They both sipped their Americanos. Lyon-Jones glanced at her boss. Smiled, but was uncomfortable. Why did he make her feel so discombobulated!

'I'm going to say two words to you, Fiona. Want your feedback.'

'On you go.'

'Decoy Brody.'

Lyon-Jones didn't respond right off. Stared at her coffee Gripped it with both hands. Looked out the window. Noticed the grime. It reminded her of her first day in this office, when she got off on the wrong foot with her boss. 'Why do you ask?'

'You have a PhD in psychology...'

'No one's supposed to know that.'

'I Googled you. Plus, I'm your boss. I'm allowed to know. So what's your take on Brody?'

'I've had this theory from day one.'

'And why didn't you tell me this earlier?'

'Sensitive issue.'

'I'm a big boy. I can handle sensitive issues.'

'I'm not so sure.' Lyon-Jones sipped her Americano. Hid behind the *medio* container.

'Try me. I'm all ears.'

'Murder is sexual foreplay.'

Sharkey put his coffee down. 'Come again?'

'A murder in Kuwait, then a rape. A murder in Ireland, then a rape. The Kingston Pub. God knows how many we don't know about.'

'But murder as foreplay? A bit excessive.'

'Perhaps it began with handcuffs. Being tied up. Paddles.'

'Paddles?'

Lyon-Jones nodded. 'Shoving up against the wall. Ripping clothes off. Light choking Slapping. Whips. Crops.'

'Crops? Jesus, and this is something you learned at university?' Sharkey blew out his cheeks. Surprised by what he'd just heard, his heart hammered all over again thinking about his Katie.

\* \* \*

Sharkey spent the day trying to spin the Pizza Face case his way.

And watching Lyon-Jones' every move.

She was sending off curious signals, the same signals little children send off when they are sitting in a room where chocolate is present. And there is only one adult monitoring them. And the adult has to leave the room. And the children are told not to touch it. And they just smile innocently back.

* * *

Lyon-Jones waited in the car park. Adjusting her rearview mirror. Checking her lippy. Fiddling with the radio. Thumbing her mobile, but texting no one. Stalling. Waiting until Sharkey pulled the Polar Bear out of his spot and swung out on to Maitland Street.

Just like yesterday, as the red Mini hared past the fire station, Sharkey charged out and followed in the black Passat.

But traffic was unusually light and Sharkey had to keep well back in the inside lane. And he lost the Mini long before they had climbed out of the Clyde basin. He passed by Lyon-Jones' flat in Giffnock. Stopped. Observed. Peered up at her second-floor flat, but she wasn't at home. So he drove up to the Avenue Shopping Centre at the Cross and checked the car park at Asda and then Marks. With it being Newton Mearns, he found three red Minis. None belonged to Lyon-Jones.

A sickening feeling was churning Sharkey's insides as he motored up the Ayr Road to the Malletsheugh. Sitting in a corner of the car park was the red Mini. Sitting at the bar was Lyon-Jones, drinking, leaning close, chatting in an animated fashion.

With Denny the Screwdriver.

Sharkey watched from the confines of the Passat as his emotions blew through the roof. He reached for the glovebox, removed his Smith & Weston and placed it on the passenger seat. It was ice cold out. Ice cold in the Passat. And he was sweating. Shaking. He reached under the seat and extracted the quarter of whisky he'd brought along for emergencies. He drained it, pulled a knit hat on and grabbed the revolver off the seat. Then he opened the door and climbed out. A frigorific blast of wind out of the north slapped him viciously across the face as he walked toward the front door of the pub. He looked down at the .38 in his hands. What the sodding hell was he doing? He stopped. Walked back. Climbed back in the car. Fired up the Passat and slowly drove away.

Followed by the same car that had followed him all the way from the city centre.

# CHAPTER EIGHTY-SEVEN

Christmas Day.

In Troon, at his daughter's two-storey house on Kilmory Street, Detective Chief Superintendent Danus Ferguson was awakened at five in the morning by his two grandchildren, Louise, aged six, and Scott, aged five. He could hear them whispering with anticipation as they crawled past his bedroom door on the way to the stairs and their predawn goal: the Christmas tree.

DCS Ferguson smiled, slipped from the bed, being sure not to disturb his wife, tiptoed to the door and cracked it open. Both children froze when they heard the door go. Grandad stuck his head out, illuminated by a nightlight in the hall. Little Scott was afraid of the dark and every room of import needed a nightlight: the kitchen, the toilet, the hall.

Little Louise peered at her grandad through thick eyeglass lenses and smiled. Little Scott peered through sleepy slits. He hoped one day that he too could wear eyeglasses like his older sister.

Grandad put a single finger to his lips, whispered, 'Santa Claus hasn't arrived yet…'

'When's he coming, then, Grandad?' Whispered back.

'He only comes when the children are asleep.'

'Does he know we're not sleeping?'

'I believe he does.'

Both children remained on their hands and knees, letting this bit of unexpected and unwelcomed news sink in, then they quickly spun round: carpet crawlers scurrying back to their bedroom, keeping a low profile. For now.

Detective Chief Superintendent Ferguson never needed much sleep. He could get by on three or four hours if need be. Today just became a 'need be', so he slipped a robe round his pyjamas, did up the belt, pulled on his slippers and, careful not to awaken his wife of forty years, gently closed the door and headed downstairs.

He'd make a nice cup of Earl Grey, splash in some semi-skimmed 'moo juice' as the grandkids called it, check emails on his laptop, then turn on the Christmas tree lights, light the candles, build a fire and take a few bites out of the cookies the weans had left for Santa on the mantle above the fireplace.

* * *

In Whitecraigs, at five-thirty in the morning, Detective Chief Inspector Maggie Squires woke up, padded to the toilet, had a sip of water, then crawled back under her super-warm, 13.5 tog duvet. She stretched out on her king-size bed. Took the second pillow and put it between her legs. She was looking forward to the day and hoped like hell the new, noisy neighbours didn't act up again.

With the day off, she would have a lie in (a lie in to her meant seven a.m.), then she would get cracking in the kitchen, readying the Christmas bubblyjock, the ham and the cock-a-leekie soup, and wee bacon rolls, chipolata sausages, crispy roast potatoes, the oat-and-sage stuffing, and neeps, carrots, gravy and cranberry jelly. And mince pies. Can't forget the mince pies. She loved to cook, but only at Christmas. Didn't have time for it the rest of the year. Didn't have the patience. Didn't want anything to do with it, actually.

She was having family and close friends arriving mid-afternoon and wanted to show off her seven-foot-tall Christmas tree in the new conservatory that she had paid for out of the increase in salary by being named Detective Chief Inspector. The conservatory looked out on to Whitecraigs Golf Course, which she had just joined. She didn't play much golf, but it was the ideal place to schmooze and make contacts that could help her in the future. Plus, there was always the chance of a discreet one-night stand. Having said that, sex to Maggie was much like Christmas dinner, something she really only felt like partaking of once a year. There were more important things than sex. Plus sex, unless it was paid for, which she had considered, brought too many complications with it.

She rolled over and closed her eyes.

Then bolted stone-cold awake.

Shit! She wasn't going to let it ruin her Christmas, but tomorrow the axe was going to drop and heads would roll.

* * *

At five-forty-five, in Giffnock, Lyon-Jones' alarm rocked her from her sleep. She hated this alarm. All alarms, actually. They always scared the living you-know-what out of her and sent her blood pressure into the stratosphere. She sat up. Swung her feet out of bed and down on to the hardwood floor. She shivered through her entire body as she slipped into a tracksuit and a pair of trainers. She grabbed a purple woolly hat off a hat rack by the front door, scooped up her keys and the pepper spray off the mahogany table next to it and went for her morning jog. Funny she thought: She never once *wanted* to workout, but she always felt so good when she finished. So refreshed and alert. On fire to attack whatever (and whomever) the day held in store for her. Not once had she come back from jogging of an icy morning, or when it was chucking it down, and said 'I wish I hadn't done that'.

Lyon-Jones jogged over to Rouken Glen Park, back to the Ayr Road and up to Davieland Road. Then she did another lap and cooled down by walking back to her apartment, keys in the left hand, pepper spray in the right. Back home, she booted up her computer, tuned in Forth One radio station in Edinburgh and listened to some Christmas music. She preferred to listen to the radio stations back home in Edinburgh that she had grown up with, plus the accents of some of the local personalities in Glasgow put her off her high protein breakfast. Lyon-Jones listened to *Little Donkey Little Donkey*. Sang along, then did her Pilates and showered.

She stepped from the shower and towelled off. Then she applied Kanebo Sensai body cream and looked in the full-length mirror. Turned sideways. Checked her breasts. Didn't need the pencil test. Not even close. She checked her bum. Hot! Delectably hot.

But she wasn't about to use her body to advance her career. Why use her body when her mind was the sexiest part about her?

This was her first real Christmas in Glasgow—other than

when she was a whacked out runaway and couldn't remember anything—and she was really looking forward to it.

Everything was falling in place just as she had hoped.

* * *

At six-twenty, in Shettleston, DI Sharkey woke with a start in his dentist's chair by the window. A rug pulled up to his chin. He had fallen asleep in the chair and had overslept. With only one eye open, he looked around, disoriented. It could have been the 25$^{th}$ of December or it could have been the 25$^{th}$ of January for all he knew. He had forgotten to take his contact lenses out and his right eye was stuck shut. Plus he had a bad case of dry mouth and evil breath that would frighten predatory animals.

It was arctic in his flat. A couple spent containers of Pringles lay at his feet, alongside the murdered bottle of his precious Dalwhinnie. Ah, so that's why he had had the heartburn during the night and why the opened carton of skimmed milk was resting on the floor next to the dentist's chair. He rose, nearly kicked the milk carton, picked it up, smelt it, pulled a face, shuffled to the kitchen, dumped the milk out in the sink and threw two sachets of Resolve and some Guarana powder in the same glass he had used for the whisky. Then he squeaked on the tap. The old pipes moaned. Sounded like the Titanic going down. He added some water and glugged it before the fizz fizzled. The Guarana antidote was something he had picked up in the Marines. And it worked a miracle.

He did the walk-on-fire walk to the shower on cold lino and prayed the hot water would last for more than half a shower for once. His shower was one of those showers you couldn't turn on and let it run until the water got nice and hot, because that just might be all you were going to get.

Sharkey showered. Felt marginally better. Wait a minute, no he didn't, he felt marginally worse. Felt like shit, actually. The water klunked cold right on cue. He jumped out. Towelled off with a towel that felt like rough sandpaper. All his towels felt like rough sandpaper ever since the dryer packed up.

He peered in the mirror. Needed a scrape. Fuck it. The face of a patently troubled soul stared back. He dressed down, purposely. Bugger what anyone thought. Have 'em take it up with the powers that be who were home, still in the warm sack

275

or readying to sit in front of a roaring fire with family and friends.

He went into the kitchen, snagged a Snickers out of the larder and hurried out the front door.

* * *

At seven in the morning, in Govan, Amy and Helicopter were still awake. They had been up all night, sitting in front of the leaning tower of Christmas trees, strung out on methy. Twice they had tried to have sex, but Helicopter couldn't get it up. The joys of speed. Crank. Tweak. Ice. Call it what you want, but don't call it when you want a righteous boner.

Helicopter *told*, not asked, Amy to get him another beer out of the fridge. He was dehydrated from the meth. Amy's face was flushed and she was shaky. Christ, what did they cut that glass with? She opened the fridge. She'd bought the Tesco *Import* lager to impress her new partner. And a turkey. But who the fuck could think of food when you're wired like the national grid? She'd roast it later or perhaps they would eat it on Boxing Day if Helicopter didn't have to work. He said his boss had something he needed done and he didn't want to talk about it, but fuck it, she didn't care what he did as long as it brought in some money. Big money. But they'd have to be careful. Bad form to flash the boudo and still collect the benefits. She knew all about benefit fraud. She had her head screwed on the right way. Oh, yes she did. She smiled. Reckoned Helicopter was just as much attracted to her brains as he was to her body. That's probably what he found sexy about her. That and her predilection for doing it doggie-style.

Not that he could get it up.

* * *

At seven fifteen, in leafy, upmarket Whitecraigs, Denny the Screwdriver and Jade were just wrapping up the first Christmas Eve in their new two-storey detached. They stood in the drive, waving goodbye to all their close friends: owners of nightclubs, owners of taxi companies, owners of tanning salons, owners of agencies which supplied bouncers, owners of those salons where you stick your feet in a fish tank and the little scaly blighters eat and suck all the dead skin off. Important people. The Screwdriver and his wife were pleasantly surprised how many

276

'friends' had come for the all-nighter, but then again, when you're offering unlimited booze and pharmaceutical blow, friends are easy to come by.

So big fuckin' deal if they woke up a few of the new neighbours with the noise. Who really gave a royal shite when it came down to it? They had more money than the neighbours, and if the neighbours didn't like late, noisy parties, they could call the polis. The Screwdriver knew how to deal with the polis, just bully them hard and heavy. They were all a bunch of wee fannies when it came down to it. Oh, sure, they'd come round once to appease the neighbours, then when he was through with them, they'd never come again. He'd shape these neighbours up. This was his neighbourhood now and the sooner they understood that, the better.

Fucking bunch of old poncey geezers.

And that one hottie single woman who lived alone. The one with the new conservatory. He might just have to go over there and introduce himself.

Find out what she did for a living.

* * *

At seven thirty, in Riddrie, a north eastern district of Glasgow, Tattoo McQueen strutted out of Barlinnie prison a free man.

Christmas morning or not, a veritable gaggle of TV reporters, newspaper journalists, family and even paparazzi were stomping their feet in the cold, waiting for him as he stepped out in all his glory—or perhaps lack of it—for the moment he spotted the assembled media, he gave them the two-fingered salute and yelled, 'Fuck the Sutherlands! Tattoo McQueen is back! To celebrate, I'm going doon to one of the offies at the bottom of the road!'

So many flashbulbs went off at the same time, it took a moment for the assembled to notice Tattoo's left eye explode and pinkish-grey brain matter blow out the back of his head. The force of the hit carried such velocity, Tattoo was propelled right back through the door of Barlinnie where he should have stayed, not come out on the streets of Glasgow where it was becoming less and less safe for criminals. There was so much confusion and chaos around McQueen's lifeless corpse, nobody noticed a red motor parked a thousand yards away, slowly driving off.

## CHAPTER EIGHTY-EIGHT

Not many relish the thought of working on Christmas Day, but at City Centre, the cops were making the best of it. DC Wilson had dressed up as Santa Claus and handed Sharkey, his mentor, a Christmas present. Sharkey held the gift in both hands. Shook it. Clearly a bottle. He ripped at the corner of the Chrissie paper. Peeked in: a bottle of 151 Rum! About as strong a spirit as you're going to find that's not bootlegged or made in an illegal still in the mountains of North Carolina.

'Careful with that, sir, lethal stuff. Almost as lethal as that moonshine you used to drink.' DC Wilson was smiling so much it looked as if he would swallow his ears.

Lyon-Jones had brought in Christmas cookies, shortbread and scones her Aunt Ella had baked especially for the officers. Sharkey had arrived with an entire Christmas cake Mrs Gladstone had whipped up just for the occasion. He had taken some stick for being so late to work, but when the officers saw him holding the Christmas cake, all was forgiven.

DC Wilson was feeling the Christmas spirit and decided to hang mistletoe, so he delegated the coffee making to a uniform, and this brought great joy to the world.

But the joy was not to last. Word of Tattoo McQueen's demise swept through the city like a runaway freight train. When DC Wilson suggested, 'Let's not let it ruin the festivities, he will still be dead tomorrow!' he was met with groans and guffaws. In reality, the police didn't know how to react. No one was saddened by the offing of the drug lord McQueen, only chagrinned by the timing. Kill the bloody bastards was the general unspoken consensus, just don't do it on my watch.

Lyon-Jones wanted to find out what DI Sharkey's thoughts were and she found him alone in his office. At the computer. Door open. For once, Lyon-Jones knocked.

'Jesus, Boss, I don't know what to think.'

'Only one person could have made that shot: Decoy Brody. Christ, no one even knew which direction it came from.' Then: 'Best way to kill a snake is to cut off its head. The Sutherlands want the whole pie to themselves.'

'Lots of clichés, Boss, but if you're right, and it was Decoy, it will be all hands on deck again. Squires will have to let you back onboard.'

Sharkey shrugged, turned to his screen, closed a file, smiled. 'Lots of clichés yourself.'

Lyon-Jones returned the smile. 'Listen, while I'm here, just wanted to say thank you.'

'For what?'

'Taking me under you wing and guiding me. And putting up with my pushy ways.' Lyon-Jones handed Sharkey a printout.

'What's this?'

'From the Blog Hog.'

Sharkey perused the irreverent Glaswegian blog put out by some well-connected, mysterious soul. It read: TATTOO McQUEEN IS NO MORE! Good riddance, say I. One less piece of shite roaming the streets, force feeding skag to our children. Our world is a better place. We can only be happy someone has come along to rid Glesga of the scum. It's time we took back our city from the drug families. Time we took back the streets. Time the crims paid, not the victims. May God bless the vigilante!

'What's your take, Boss?'

Sharkey looked up at Lyon-Jones. 'No vigilante, Fiona, just Decoy Brody doing what he does best.'

\* \* \*

Later that afternoon and evening, as Glaswegians sat down to Christmas dinner, along with the festivities came a gnawing undercurrent of increased anxiety. Would there be a power vacuum in the city with the Sutherland clan seizing coveted McQueen family turf, or were there still enough McQueen lieutenants and flunkies remaining to mount an attack and start World War III?

It made for indigestion.

\* \* \*

In Troon, Detective Chief Superintendant Danus Ferguson sat on the newly installed hardwood floor and became air traffic control for the circling weans.

Little Scott was alternating between a remote controlled Ferrari, an electric keyboard—and the Cadburys. Little Louise was screaming back and forth between a 'crocodile seesaw', a doll's house—and the Cadburys.

DCS Ferguson was romancing a Christmas brandy, enjoying the unbridled chaos of children at Christmas. Retirement wasn't that far off and he would be able to spend a lot more time down in Troon. A lot more time with the grandchildren. Tomorrow was Boxing Day, he had the day off as well, and he was taking Louise and Scott to their first panto, *Aladdin*, at the King's. It had been donkeys since he'd been at a panto, and he was really looking forward to going, seeing the wonder that only children seem to possess and escaping for a few hours from a dark world outside into the magic that is theatre.

\* \* \*

In Whitecraigs, DCI Maggie Squires was serving pud to her guests.

The dinner had gone down a bomb, everyone had raved about the new conservatory and the conversation had been riveting. The topic had surrounded Edinburgh, of course, what with all of Squires' guests being from Edinburgh. It had been good to catch up with the goings on back home: the state of the tram, for example. One guest had seen Michael McIntyre's *Comedy Roadshow* when it came to Edinburgh. And McIntyre had summed up the tram fiasco, succinctly: 'Leith to the airport? Leith to the airport? People in Leith donnae bloody go on holiday.'

Someone else had despaired of the zealous tactics of the Blue Meanies. The Blue Nazis someone else had called them. 'Trying to convince us they've gone green with the implementation of the electric scooters, when all it does is allow them to cover more territory and hand out more parking tickets, even at 2AM!'

Maggie Squires turned to the guest next to her and whispered, 'Glad you could make it…'

'Sorry I was late,' DS Lyon-Jones said.

\* \* \*

In Govan, Amy and Helicopter were having a hard time coming off the crystal meth and there was trouble in paradise: They were arguing.

There was strife because Amy wanted to go score some more meth. Helicopter wanted to go for some Nembutal. One wanted up, the other wanted down. And neither one had eaten since the previous day.

Since it was Amy's money that was to be used, Amy made an executive decision: They would go down to the Gaolkeeper, score on *both* the drugs they so coveted, it was Christmas after all, and chill. What better place to spend Christmas than in a bar with wasted folk of similar ilk?

* * *

In Whitecraigs, Denny the Screwdriver was just leaving the new homestead. He told his wife Jade that he had some urgent business to take care of. He'd be back in an hour or two, in time for a late Christmas dinner. Jade had a face on her like a sad panto dame and wanted to protest, but then the Screwdriver always flew off the handle and smacked her. She didn't want to get hit in front of the children, like the last time, so she kept her cakehole shut. Bit her tongue. Actually bit her tongue.

The Screwdriver had planned to take the Audi with the soft-top, but on account of the McQueen hit, chose the armour-plated BMW. He was over the moon that Tattoo had been taken out, but he hadn't ordered it and wondered who the hell had pulled the trigger. Now the sodding polis would be all over him like a cheap suit, interviewing him, pointing their fingers, talking down to him, but fuckin' let 'em. He had his alibis lined up like ducks on a fuckin' pond.

He drove down the Ayr Road into Giffnock. That's where he was meeting his mistress. He would give her that bracelet from Tiffany's that she had been going on about. Christmas was all about giving and not receiving, so then he would give it to her good and hard, as well. Shower so his wife couldn't smell another woman on him. And go back home to finish celebrating with the weans.

* * *

In Shettleston, Fleet Sharkey was preparing a Christmas ping-ping meal.

They made them, you know, roast turkey and gravy and potatoes and carrots and stuffing and cranberries. The works.

Without thinking, Sharkey put a Christmas CD on, Country and Western artists singing their favourite Christmas songs. Then had to turn it off.

He went to the fridge, took out a can of Carling. Put the beer back. Went to the larder, grabbed a bottle of Shiraz off the shelf and screwed off the top. He was going to let it breathe, but: 1) he wouldn't know the difference if he did, and 2) wasn't it somehow heresy to let wine breathe that came out of a bottle with a screw top?

Sharkey pulled a TV tray out of the cupboard and set it in front of his dentist's chair by the window, then he grabbed a clean plate, a paper towel for a napkin and a fork and 'set the table'.

He looked out the window. The Cottage Bar was doing a business. Those who had no one, had each other. Sharkey was desperately lonely. Hurting. Aching. He had hoped to have Christmas dinner with his dad, but his dad had been having more bad days than good days of late, and it just wasn't to be.

Then he came up with an idea. He crossed to the front door, unlocked the first Yale lock, then the second Yale lock, then the mortice.

'Ho, Donny! Are ye doon therr?'

'Aye, Mr Sharkey. Jist tryin' tae keep warm?'

'Are ye feelin' peckish?'

'Sorry?'

'Ye fancy a wee nosh? A real Christmas sit-doon dinner?'

Sharkey listened. No verbal response. Just shuffling. Rustling. Footsteps clopping up the stairway. Fast.

# CHAPTER EIGHTY-NINE

Denny the Screwdriver Sutherland went to his office after porking his mistress and sat there in the dark.

He'd being doing that a lot lately -- sitting in the dark, so no one would know he was in there. So no one could do a drive-by and empty a machine gun in his well-lit face. He drummed his fingers on the top of his desk and tried to keep his leg from jitterbugging up and down.

He wondered if Decoy Brody had gone rogue and blown Tattoo McQueen's brains out the back of his head. Decoy had a certain predilection for blood lust, which seemed to have skyrocketed over the past year. Thank Christ Fat Cheeks and the three kilos of coke had arrived. He would give it to Decoy tomorrow, then Decoy could take his blood lust out on Inspector Sharkey. That would be one less person he would have to worry about.

The Screwdriver rose. Went to the window. Split the blinds with thumb and index finger. Peered out. It was pitch black on the forecourt. No movement on the streets. Not a living soul. Tomorrow the polis would come round all high-and-mighty and pound on his door, be condescending to his boys and want to interrogate him about the McQueen hit. That had not concerned him. What did concern him was that Fat Cheeks' three kilos of cocaine were on the premises. He had thought about moving it elsewhere, but running around Glasgow with three kilos of coke in the boot of your Beemer wasn't so very clever. Sure, he could entrust the deed to an underling, but he'd had his fill of these teenage fuckups for a while. Number one, they were unreliable, number two, they had shite for brains, number three, they were just as likely to do a runner as a delivery.

The Screwdriver had a Burton wall safe with an electronic lock in his office. Including installation, it had set him back nearly a thousand fuckin' quid, but it was just for show. He used it as a red heron or whatever the fuck the expression was. He had Decoy's coke (and a few ounces he'd skimmed off the top for himself) stashed in a place no one would ever think to look, right out in the open. Sealed in alu foil and heat-sealed baggies, wrapped up as prezzies under the Christmas tree. He would have to move his personal stash by the 6th of January. Or was it the 7th?

No big deal though. Piece of fuckin' Christmas cake.

Shite! The Screwdriver slammed the desk with his fist. What the fuck was he thinking? He had ordered *four* kilos of nose-candy. And here he had been talking just the three. Where was the other fuckin' kilo? With all the palaver of getting the coke here and with the holidays and the polis and the killing of Tattoo McQueen, he'd fucking spaced out the maths. He slammed the desk again. How could he be so fucking brain dead? He'd been a swot with maths at school before he dropped out. Alright. Alright. Alright. He didn't drop out. He got expelled, okay? Just for selling to the primary schoolers. What was the big fucking deal? It wasn't like he was some big-time dealer. He'd needed the money to buy new trainers.

The Screwdriver pulled out his mobile and called his cousin who ran the Melville Brothers Funeral Home. It was picked up on the first ring.

'Shugsy, it's me. Got a big problem here. I'm counting three, not four, ye sure that's the lot?'

'Sure as shite, I dug it all out.'

'What aboot the fucking heid? Did ye check the fucking heid?'

There was protracted silence on the other end.

'Shugsy, talk tae me!'

'Cannae say I checked the heid.'

'Where is he?'

'Southern Necropolis. Six feet under…'

Now there was a long silence on the Screwdriver's end.

'I want it, and I want it tonight.'

'Jesus, I'm at the panto wit the family.'

'Tonight! I need it for tomorrow!'

'Right, I'll jist waltz into the Southern Necropolis in the

middle o' the night, dig up a body, ask the fucking guard to hold the torch while I unscrew the top of the heid!'

'Tonight, Shugsy, or ye'll be the one six foot under.'

The Screwdriver slammed the phone down. 'Shit!' The Screwdriver yelled it out so loudly, the pit bulls started barking. Reluctantly, he picked up the phone. Dialled the Pouch down in Benidorm. After a few rings it was answered on the other end with: 'Now what the fuck do ye want?'

'It's me, Da, we got a big problem up here...'

# CHAPTER NINETY

It was now eight in the evening in Benidorm, balmy, and with it being Christmas, Swifty Dugan had been celebrating all day. And he was enjoying Spain immensely. He had never been to Spain before. Never been in an aeroplane, actually. No, it wasn't a fear of flying, but Swifty was a weightlifter and had abused anabolic steroids. The steroids had buggered his prostrate and he never flew anywhere since he'd heard airlines were beginning to charge to use the toilets.

Misinformed or not, Swifty didn't want to waste good beer money.

Swifty was from Glasgow and was presently in a bar that had the sign out front: FOR GLASGOW RANGERS FANS ONLY. Music played in the background: Pink's 'Let's Get This Party Started'.

Swifty had begun Christmas morning with a liquid breakfast and was now quaffing his twentieth San Miguel. What a buzz he had going, but he was antsy. Antsy as hell. His testosterone was squawking at him and he was in serious need of female companionship. That and the toilet. His prostate was giving him conniptions.

He had spent the last hour listening to some rabbiting old dobber by the name of Jimmy go on and on about how he'd moved from Glasgow down to Spain and how he was shagging every bird who came within a toss of his postal code. When Jimmy left, saying he had to drive back up to the village of Finestrat, Swifty had been greatly relieved. Checked to make sure he still had an ear after having the bleedin' thing talked off.

With his faculties not hitting on all cylinders, Swifty wasn't able to separate fact from fantasy. Fact: He was tall, burly, built like a rugger and ugly as feral sin. Fantasy: He was presently being chatted up by a gorgeous young lassie who had seized

Jimmy's barstool so quickly it had still been warm. Something clearly didn't compute, but the motherboard was way past caring. And then there were the testes.

Swifty gazed at the young lassie with the platinum-blond hair and the scanty, skanky dress, and she gazed back at him with a look in her eyes of just wanting to please.

'So, yer big. Are ye a bouncer?' She shunted her stool closer.

'Front door manager. Where ye frae?'

'Glasgow.'

'Well shit on me. Me, too, hen. What part of Glesga?'

'Castlemilk. When do you go back?'

'Too soon.'

'I'll show you Benidorm. Then you show me your hotel room.'

'Why donnae we jist cut tae the chase and go tae my hotel room now?'

'Oh, yer naughty, but I like ye. Finish yer drink.'

'Ahm going fer a slash first.'

Castle-Annie watched Swifty rise, rub his bum back to life, then she plonked her infamous wee green pill into his San Miguel.

But Swifty had been working in many of the hottest/seediest clubs in Glasgow, and one thing he had learnt over the years was to not trust anybody. And don't leave anything unsupervised, such as a drink. Or a date. That's why—twenty-San-Miguel-sheets to the wind, or not—he had stopped on the way to the *servicios* and waited to see what the gal with the platinum-blond hair was going to do, if anything, and sure enough, there it was.

When Swifty returned, Castle-Annie ran a hand up his thigh.

'Drink up, then we'll go to yer hotel.'

'Sounds good, but first this.'

And Swifty pressed a small dram vial into her hand.

'Perhaps ye should go powder yer nose.'

Castle-Annie's eyes lit up and she scooted off her stool. Couldn't get to the toilets fast enough. Swifty watched, made sure she entered, then poured the remains of his beer on the Cruzas Beer towel covering the bar in front of him.

* * *

Swifty was staying at the Princessa Hotel on Boulevard

287

Mediterraneo. The Princessa was twenty-storeys high and afforded a view out over Playa de Levante and the *Casco Antiguo*, the Old Town. It had two swimming pools, seven bars, a crèche, a face painter and clothing-optional karaoke.

Something for everyone.

Up on the nineteenth floor, Castle-Annie stood at the window, staring at the vista below, wondering why the drug wasn't working its black magic. Swifty was an enormous lad, precisely why he was chosen, but perhaps that was the reason he wasn't flopping over like Fat Cheeks had. It better happen soon, she hoped, she wasn't about to have sex with this beast. Those were the thoughts coursing through the little mind she possessed when Swifty grabbed her from behind, spun her around, held her arms above her head and ripped her dress off with one swift motion. Castle-Annie pushed him away and slapped him hard across the face. But it didn't even rock Swifty. Swifty slapped her back so hard, she flew backwards on to the bed. She scrambled to get away, but Swifty's big meathooks grabbed her by the ankles. He pulled her back into the middle of the bed, split her thighs as if he were making a wish with a wishbone and thrust himself deep inside.

Castle-Annie screamed, startled by Swifty's size. He was hung like a donkey. Then, just like that, he climaxed and it was all over.

Swifty.

Afraid that he would kill her, Castle-Annie bolted for the door, but Swifty had her by those platinum locks and he jerked her back and slugged her so hard across the temple, she was unconscious before she hit the floor. Swifty, grabbed her again by the hair, opened the door with the other hand and dragged the completely naked girl out into the hallway. There he lifted her up with no effort and dumped her in a maid's bed-linen trolley, covered her with a sheet, wheeled her to the lift and pressed the button. The lift doors hissed open, Swifty hit the button for the lobby and the doors hissed closed.

Of course what Swifty couldn't know was that a gaggle of five pissed-to-the-gills lads from Scunthorpe were waiting for the lift to arrive down in the lobby. When the doors hissed open, they dragged a semi-comatosed mate in. One lad punched '8', another lad lifted the sheet to piss in the trolley and saw the naked lass curled up in there.

'Jesus H Christ!'

'Is she dead?'

'Don't think so. Just fucked-up. Let's stick her in the room with Simon. That'll shock the shit out him when he wakes up.'

# CHAPTER NINETY-ONE

The trip from Troon into Glasgow can be a sincerely gorgeous drive. On a clear day you can see the Craigs of Ayr off to the right, enjoy the moody expanse of the Fenwick Moor and then spot snow on the Campsies behind Glasgow as you descend towards the city centre and a view that was once used as the opening shot of *TAGGART*.

But today, Boxing Day, it was six in the morning, deathly dark and DCS Ferguson couldn't see shite. Today was supposed to be a day off. Spend it with the daughter and the grandkids, take them to the matinee panto. But here he was, driving to the station to deal with a festering sore that had now become endemic.

And he was livid.

There would be hell to pay and he wasn't planning on taking any prisoners.

* * *

Everyone at City Centre knew something was up. It was in the air. The air was acidic and poisonous.

Everyone was afraid to breathe lest they bring attention to themselves.

Those who had arrived early had seen the rare sight of Detective Chief Superintendent Ferguson in their building. He had stormed in, bulled his way through CID and upstairs, so incensed, so powerful, he could still take the field for Scotland. Everyone immediately scurried for cover and dug deep into their work, banged away on keyboards, avoided eye contact, praying it had nothing to do with them. Male officers were afraid to go to the toilets lest they run into their Chief Super and were putting their bladders through overtime. Little coffee was consumed.

DI Sharkey walked in sporting a three-day-old beard. He was late. Had overslept again. He was greeted with furtive glances and Lyon-Jones who looked as if she'd seen a ghost having a bad day. In reality, she had seen Ferguson blow in and that was much more frightening than seeing an apparition.

Sharkey sensed the toxic atmosphere and held open both hands, palms up.

Lyon-Jones pointed to the ceiling. Upstairs, toward DCI Maggie Squires' office.

'Who?'

She pointed at Sharkey. 'The Chief Super wants to see you.'

'Me?'

'Now.'

Sharkey took his coat off and threw it in his office, turned and headed towards the stairs. Looked back at Lyon-Jones as he went.

Sharkey knocked on Chief Inspector Maggie Squires' door. Waited for the bark. The bark came. He opened the door and went in.

'Looking for me, sir?'

'Have a seat, Inspector,' Ferguson said.

Oh, oh, Sharkey thought, he always calls me 'Fleet'. Sharkey looked round, saw CI Squires seated in a corner. For some reason, she looked happy. But his Chief Super didn't look happy.

'Listen, sir,' Sharkey began, 'I was late this morning because…'

Ferguson slammed a meaty fist on his desk. 'Quiet! You will not speak until you are spoken to. Is that clear, Inspector?'

'Yes sir…'

Sharkey glanced over at Squires. She was gloating. Enjoying each and every second. She had waited a long time for this.

Ferguson reached out a hand towards CI Squires. She handed over a large manila envelope. Ferguson took out four photos. Blow ups. Threw them across his desk in the direction of Sharkey.

Sharkey picked up the photos. Glanced at each one. They were night shots. Photo #1 was of him sitting in the black Passat, casing Fiona's flat. Photo #2 was at the Malletsheugh, wearing a knit cap, climbing out of the Passat. Photo #3 was of him, approaching the front door of the Malletsheugh, holding something in his hand. Photo #4 was an enlargement of what he was holding: his Smith & Wesson .38 calibre handgun.

'Explain yourself, Inspector.'

Sharkey's face drained of colour. He looked back and forth between his Chief Super and Maggie Squires. 'Where did you get these?'

'I shot them,' Squires answered.

'You followed me?'

'I left work and my mobile rang. I pulled over near the fire station. I saw you pull in and change cars. Then DS Lyon-Jones shot by and you pulled out after her…'

Sharkey looked from CI Squires over to DCS Ferguson, then back again. A drowning man looking for that elusive straw.

'Listen, I can explain everything.' Sharkey shifted in his chair. 'DS Lyon-Jones is tight with the Sutherlands. She ran away when she was a teenager and worked in the same club on Sauchiehall as the Screwdriver. I followed her to the Malletsheugh because she was meeting the Screwdriver. It was the second time they met. She's a mole…'

Sharkey knew they would understand, come round to his side.

'That wasn't the Screwdriver,' CI Squires began. 'That was DC Fife. He's working surveillance at the Brody farm.'

'But I saw the Screwdriver…'

CI Squires was smug. 'You saw what you wanted to see.'

Sharkey was flummoxed. Denny the Screwdriver Sutherland. DC Fife. They both had short dark hair. Boyish faces. Shit. He was losing it. Losing it big time.

DCS Ferguson was outraged, but he was hurting, as well. 'Where'd you get the gun?'

'I brought it over from America.'

'How'd you get it in the country?'

Silence.

'I want to see the paperwork. Today. You don't have the paperwork, you're looking at jail time, Inspector.'

CI Squires felt compelled to do a tag-team. 'If the Press gets wind of this, there'll be hell to pay.'

Ferguson kept the pressure on. 'You followed DS Lyon-Jones. You keep the gun in your car. Your car is downstairs. Go get it. I want the gun. *Now.*'

Squires threw one more poisoned dart. 'You seem to think you can make up your own rules.'

Sharkey ignored Maggie Squires. Rose. 'Right back, sir.' He went to the door, opened it, then closed it respectfully. To get to the carpark, he had to pass through the CID office. Sharkey could feel the eyes following him as he slipped through. Lyon-Jones approached, then backed quickly away when she saw the explosive state Sharkey was in.

Outside, the rain was drilling the ground. Sharkey ran, pointed his zapper at his car, threw open the door, jumped inside and ran his hand through his wet hair.

He sat there collecting his thoughts. Couldn't believe this was happening. That he'd been so stupid. Let that cow follow him. Let his guard down. His career was hanging by a thread. No, check that. His career was over. Just like that. Just like Katie's life was snuffed out. Now what? His life had already been in the toilet and now someone had flushed. Swirling. Spiraling. Down and down and down.

He popped the glovebox, pulled out the Smith & Wesson. Rested it on his lap. Put both hands on the steering wheel and rested his forehead on his hands. The rain came down in torrents. He lifted his head, watched the rain scud across the windscreen, masking his view to the outside world. A world that he no longer belonged in. Believed in. Wanted to be in.

That fast, the rain eased. He glanced in his rearview mirror. Then his wing mirror. Looked for the spider that lived in the casing. Sheltering now. Every morning the spider built a new web. Every day, it was destroyed. Destroyed like Sharkey's life. Should he be inspired as Robert the Bruce had?

He fingered the pistol. He could see through the windscreen again. Could see the police station. The backdoor leading in. The world that awaited him. He would go inside. Hand over his weapon to a man he aspired to be like. A man who had now lost faith in him. He had brought the gun into the country illegally and he didn't have a permit for it. He would go to jail. And that would be that. He would go to jail for trying to uphold justice.

And CI Maggie Squires would rejoice.

The spider would prevail. Sharkey would not. He had woven a tangled web. He knew what he had to do. What he needed to do. He threw his door open, climbed out and checked to make sure the gun was loaded. Then he crossed the carpark and moved quickly towards the backdoor of the station.

# CHAPTER NINETY-TWO

Down in Benidorm the early morning sun was just lighting up the peaks of the Puig Campana.

The temperature already a very agreeable seventeen degrees Celsius. Wind out of the southwest at eight. An offshore breeze. The sea aquamarine. A few fishermen were plying the waters in their small skiffs, casting nets for bait fish.

In the Old Town, café owners were hauling the tables and chairs out from the stacks inside and lining them up on their respective pitches, wiping them down, readying for the early birds, the same clients they had been serving for the past thirty years.

Just down the road on Boulevard Mediterraneo, eight floors above, Simon Bartholomew of Scunthorpe awoke, desperate for the loo. He thought his bladder was going to burst. He swung his legs over the side of the bed and sat up. And then it hit him: Fucking Christ, what a bloody headache. He thought his eyes were going to bleed. Enough, already. He made a bogus vow right then and there to never drink that much again. He looked over at the other bed. His mate was crashed out, snoring like an OAP with sleep apnea. Someone had drawn a penis on his mate's forehead with a black marker pen.

Simon stood up. Buck-arse naked. Almost fell back down. He shuffled into the toilet and forgot to lift the seat. He started to pee. What a fucking relief! For the love of God, how much had he had? Had he mixed the grape and the grain? He remembered he'd started with the San Miguels just after breakfast at an Irish pub in the Square. Then he'd moved to Spanish coffee with some shit sugary liqueur just after lunch. Not that he ever ate lunch. One of his mates had said it was what locals drank. Found out it was what locals avoided. Then he and the mates had drunk a metre of beer each at a sports bar and had watched Championship highlights. His team, Scunthorpe United, was featured in the Championship lowlights.

The lads wanted to meet some members of the fairer sex, so they had repaired to a foo-foo glass-and-brass wine bar run by an aging, colourful queen who reminded him of Robin Williams in *The Birdcage*. Everyone had tasted different wines to impress the ladies, only to discover the ladies weren't impressed at all, but the lads still had to pay. By then, he knew he was well-crocked, so he'd downed some Red Bull, but that had made him nothing more than a really wired drunk. And that was it. Other than taking a quick kip at an English pub near the prom, he couldn't really remember anything else. Not even how he got back to his hotel room. He blew out his cheeks. Fucking hell, that was the longest pee he had ever had and much of it ended up in the pan. He shook his dick off.

Christ he could pee for England.

Scunthorpe, anyway.

Simon turned towards the mirror and screamed! Someone had drawn a penis and ball sack on his face, as well, the nose being used to great effect and to give a three-dimensional effect. He tried washing it off, but it was indelible ink and it wouldn't come off. When he labelled his gym kit with the marker pens back home, it always washed off too soon, but down here in Spain, fuck if he could even get it to smudge.

He was padding back to bed, being careful not to awaken his mate, not that a satellite plunging to earth and crashing into the building would wake him, when he saw her. A girl with platinum-blond hair on the other side of his bed, asleep under the sheets. Tucked up all nice and cosy. Fucking Christ! Had he pulled? Unlikely, as he had a worse record than his football team. A lot worse. He inched closer to the girl, lifted up a corner of the sheet. Naked! He quickly put the sheet back down. Lifted it slowly back up. Inched closer. She had a killer body. He always had the worst luck with girls, and here was this goddess asleep under his sheets.

He let the corner of the sheet down. Then lifted it back up again. He felt like a voyeur and that aroused him. The lass was lying on her stomach, arse protruding in an inviting, just-do-me sort of way. Oh, oh, hold on, now he was getting a serious erection. An erection like he had never had before.

He touched his throbbing wiener and began to stroke it, then he spat on his hand and lubricated the end. He slipped up close to the edge of the bed. Knelt on it. And entered the platinum-blond girl. He thrust deep inside and pumped away as he had seen in some films a mate had back in Scunthorpe. And he was surprised how quickly he was brought to orgasm, and as he spewed his seed deep within her, he screamed. That would surely wake her and she would turn, look back at him with pouting lips and doe eyes and ask him to do it all over again. And do you know what? He'd reload and be ready to shoot. Fuck yes!

But she didn't wake up. And he couldn't fathom why, so he screamed again like the nerd extraordinaire that he was, but this time it wasn't a scream of divine sexual ecstasy, this was a scream of unfathomable horror.

He had just become a necrophiliac.

## CHAPTER NINETY-THREE

Sharkey reached the backdoor of the police station and stopped. He heard a noise behind him. An unmarked car was pulling into the carpark. It was DC Wilson. Sharkey quickly tucked his gun in the back of his jeans, reversed directions and headed back to the Polar Bear. DC Wilson gave him a wave and a smile. Sharkey climbed in the Polar Bear, fired her up and screeched out of the car park, heading through the city centre toward the river.

Sharkey crossed the Clyde on the Albert Bridge and parked near the Citizens Theatre in the Gorbals. Then he just sat there and wrestled with how the hell he was going to find Decoy Brody before the police found him. His mobile vibrated twice while he sat there, but he had ignored it. He knew who it was.

After an hour, the rain started again and Sharkey crossed back over to the north side of the river and headed into the East End and his flat. In front of his apartment block, he pulled over on the right side of the street as he always did. Then pulled back out. Drove down two streets. Parked there. Walked back. Cautiously cased the area. Got soaked.

He inserted the key into the entrance door to his block and stepped into the darkened close. Still no lights.

From under the staircase. 'Someone been here lookin' fer ye.'

'Donny?'

'Aye, Mr Sharkey. Ah wis shelterin' across at the church. Saw him come.'

'What'd he look like?'

'Yer age.'

'Police?'

'Cannae say.'

'How ye know he wis lookin' fer me?'

'He leaned on the buzzer till the rainbow girls upstairs opened a windae an' told him tae fuck off. He asked if they'd seen ye.'

'What did Patty and Tinski say?'

'They told him to fuck off again.'

'Good. We've always looked after one another.' Sharkey paused for a moment, still staring into the darkness. 'Have ye eaten, Donny?'

'Cannae say that I huv.'

'Here's a fiver fer ye.'

'Ta, Mr Sharkey, ye always been good tae me.'

Sharkey slipped back out the front door, ensured it was closed securely and made his way back to the Polar Bear.

Lashed by a ferocious wind and icy rain.

# CHAPTER NINETY-FOUR

In Benidorm, the Garda Civil had erected a crime scene and were crawling all over the hotel room of Simon Bartholomew from Scunthorpe. Forensics were in there as well, dusting and taking DNA samples. There was plenty of DNA.

Simon Bartholomew was being led away in handcuffs. Our Simon was protesting vociferously, but it's hard to be taken seriously when you have an anatomically correct penis painted on your face.

Watching Simon as he was unceremoniously removed were three men: The Coroner, a Forensic Pathologist by the name of Freddy, and Jimmy the Pouch Sutherland.

'Such a pity. I've known her a long time,' the Pouch said.

'We'll need to do an autopsy,' the Coroner said.

'I'll do it today,' Dr Freddy said.

All three men appeared quite solemn. As one would. And should.

Then the Pouch added. 'I'll make arrangements for the body to be flown back to Glasgow. I'll cover *all* expenses.' And then in a whisper: 'Are ye up for a round of golf later?'

# CHAPTER NINETY-FIVE

There's a street in Glasgow's East End called 'Gallowgate'. The name comes from the medieval 'Gallowgaite'…'gaite' meaning 'Road to'…Road to the gallows.

And the Delmont Hotel was on Gallowgate. The Delmont was a hostel for the homeless, a dumping ground for the destitute and desperate.

It had been described as the worst in Scotland. The conditions were appalling and unsanitary. Electricity and running water were more the exception than the rule. It was literally the proverbial roof over your head. Nothing more. There was no care package. Addictions were not addressed.

The Delmont boasted 100 residents, losers who had been abandoned by the statutory services, health, housing, and they were left there, unsupervised, totally excluded from society.

If you scraped the bottom of the barrel, this is where you scraped.

As one former resident noted: 'I've been in Cheapside Street. Bell Street. Auldhouse. Great Eastern. The worst hostel I'll tell you, without a doubt, was the Delmont. People are better off on the streets.'

It was growing dark when Sharkey approached the poorly lit entrance to the hotel. A group of hardened residents stood outside in a misting, leeching drizzle. Smoking their brains out. Spitting. One bloke suddenly started to make regurgitating motions like a cat does when it's coughing up a fur ball. He pulled out a bloody cotton wool bud. Spat blood. Stuck the bud back in his mouth. Sucked his roll-up halfway down. Cotton Wool Bud Guy eyed Sharkey suspiciously. Saw something in his eyes he didn't like. And stepped aside. The others followed suit.

Sharkey pushed on a ratty old door, entered the building and was hit square in the face by the stench of squalid living. A single bulb snaked down from a long cord. The entryway was a threadbare carpet, littered with needles. A druggie was propped up over in a corner, flying solo, on final approach to la la land. An elderly man with no front teeth sat in a wheelchair in a dark corner. He had diarrhoea and was complaining to deaf ears that there were no facilities for those confined to a wheelchair. His chair was caked in faeces. Commotion in the form of a drunken argument seeped out of the TV room where drunks lay asleep on the floor. The halls stank of vomit and reeked of rage, despair and hopelessness.

Sharkey took creaky stairs to the top floor, to his single room, unlocked a padlock which secured the door, and entered. He closed the door behind him and slipped the snib. The room was the size of a prison cell. One greasy window faced Gallowgate. The road to the Gallows. He heard a siren go by. Would be hearing a lot of that. His room had a stained sink with hairs. A cracked mirror splattered with someone's DNA above the sink. Sharkey needed the toilet. The closest toilet was down a flight. Sharkey slipped back the snib. Creaked open the door. Listened. Heard crying down the hall somewhere. Plaintive wails. Christ. He stepped out. Fixed the padlock in place. Went down a flight. Opened the door to the lavvy. There was blood on the pan from someone shooting up.

He went back to his room and did the 'open door lock door routine'. Pissed in the sink. Turned on the tap. Sluiced the sink. Pulled his gun out from the back of his jeans. He too reeked of rage, despair and hopelessness.

Sharkey lay down on a single bed covered with just a soiled sheet and rested the gun on his stomach. Nobody would ever find him here. Even the police in Shettleston avoided the Delmont.

The Delmont, close to local amenities: Barlinnie prison, Ally's beer and wine shop, the Glasgow Royal Infirmary.

The Delmont, formerly owned by Tattoo McQueen. Now owned by his heirs. His thrilled heirs, as the dump brought in five-hundred thousand quid a year in Housing Benefit.

It had never crossed Sharkey's mind to seek safe harbour at his father's. Didn't want to drag the old man into the shite. But he needed a change of clothes. And he needed a few more 'toys'.

He would head over there when darkness fell.

A knock at the door startled Sharkey. He had fallen asleep. His eyes snapped open. He stopped breathing. Another knock. No spy hole. Another knock. Louder. Longer. Then: 'Fleet! It's me!'

Sharkey sat up. Realised the tap was still running. Turned it off. Went to the door. S&W at the ready. Cocked. Opened the door.

'Fuck me!'

Standing there was Sharkey's mate, the Mayor.

'How'd you know I was here?'

'Someone blows their nose in the Gallowgate, I know about it. Here.' The Mayor handed Sharkey his favourite takeaway: vindaloo. 'Decommission the Polar Bear, laddie. Everybody knows the Polar Bear.' The Mayor turned to go. Stopped. 'You know you don't need to ask...*whatever* it is.'

With a heavily overcast sky and a fog hugging the river, darkness came quickly, so Sharkey slipped out of the Delmont and drove the Polar Bear out of the East End under cloak of crap weather and out to his dad's place in Dunlop via a back road.

Sharkey had phoned ahead and his father was waiting for him at the front door. His father hadn't slept well the night before, so he told Fleet that he was going to leave him to it, then he wheeled himself back in front of the fire and nodded right off. Sharkey went to the fridge and extracted the key to the garage out back. He opened the garage door, found the key for the red Mustang, jumped in and turned the ignition. The Mustang spluttered a few times then roared to life. He backed it out. Engine rumbling. The beast waiting to be unleashed. Then he swung the Polar Bear into the garage and removed the cables from the battery terminals. She could hibernate for a while.

Sharkey accessed the safe room at the back of the garage and gathered the clothes he needed. He opened the boot of the Mustang and loaded it with a few of his favourite weapons from his private arsenal.

Quietly, Sharkey sneaked back into the farmhouse and went to check on his father. His father was still in front of the fire, chin on chest, snoozing happily away. Sharkey put another log on the fire, then stuck the key back in the box of bicarbonate of soda in the fridge, went back out, fired up the Mustang, exited the farm by the same back road he had come in on, drove over the Fenwick Moor, which was socked-in with low-lying cloud, and back into greater Glasgow.

# CHAPTER NINETY-SIX

At City Centre, DCS Ferguson was livid. He'd missed the panto and had received word that the weans were presently crying their eyes out. Angered or not, about to blow his top or not, he was still wrestling with what to do with Sharkey. He had had such hope for him. Believed in him. Went to the wall for him. Loved him like a son. But now…

Ferguson picked up the phone, hit speed dial, got DCI Maggie Squires on the horn. 'I want everyone in the incident room.'

Ten minutes later, down in the incident room, DCS Ferguson addressed his troops.

'By now you have all been briefed about the situation with DI Sharkey. He has failed to return or report in. Messages to his mobile have gone unanswered. All attempts to communicate with him or make contact have failed. We have an officer outside his flat in case he turns up there…'

DCS Ferguson couldn't believe he had to say what he was about to say. He cleared his throat.

'I've sent out a Circulation on DI Sharkey. He's not to be approached. He is to be considered armed and dangerous.'

# CHAPTER NINETY-SEVEN

Within the hour, the Blog Hog posted just two words: 'SAVE FERRIS!'

# CHAPTER NINETY-EIGHT

Denny the Screwdriver Sutherland sat in the dark in his office again.

He had just got off the phone with the Pouch. There had been a hiccup down in Spain, with the 'mule', but an alternate courier had been found. As much as he hated his father, he had to admit the old sod took care of business. Everything would turn out okay. The coke would arrive. He'd pay off Decoy. Sharkey would be killed. And he'd have the bloody thorn out of his side.

Forever.

The Screwdriver decided to celebrate. He would pay a visit to his mistress. Fuck her every which way, but loose. Then he'd stuff some of his fortune up his nose. Go down the pub. Hang with the lads.

The Screwdriver locked his office door, walked into the work bay, opened the door to the forecourt and stepped out. He locked the door behind him. Rattled it. Turned. Looked up at the sky. It was a clear night. No rain. But cold. A good night to spend it under the covers with a hot hard-body. He laughed to himself. He hauled his mobile out of his pocket and texted his mistress. Then he took out his pack of fags. Lit a match. When the match flared, it lit up the Screwdriver's face.

And the face of the person standing directly in front of him.

Denny the Screwdriver faltered back, his eyes went wide, mouth open to let go with a primordial scream, but the baseball bat was already crushing all the bones in his face.

The assassin stood over the Screwdriver. Pulled a home-made chib out of a pocket. Yanked open the Screwdriver's trousers. Cut off his penis. Castrated him. Took the end of the baseball bat and stuffed the Screwdriver's privates up his anal passage as you would stuff a Christmas turkey.

Denny the Screwdriver Sutherland had been wrong about his cousin Shugsy.

The Screwdriver was going to be the one six-feet under.

# CHAPTER NINETY-NINE

Just before eight o'clock in the morning.

Dark as hell this time of the year. This far north.

Sharkey pulled the red Mustang up in front of Sutherland Motors. Swept the forecourt with his headlamps. Clocked the Screwdriver's body. Left the motor running. Climbed out. Saw the pit bulls watching expectantly from behind the chain-linked fence. Not so much as a growl. It was freezing out here. He took shallow breaths. The cold bit his lungs. He could see his breath in the glow from his headlamps.

Sharkey moved quickly to the Screwdriver's corpse. Rifled through his pockets. Took out the Screwdriver's mobile, returned to the Mustang and sped off.

Now, at last, he knew how to find Decoy Brody.

It was simple.

It was genius.

Decoy Brody was now going to find him.

* * *

The mechanic with all the tattoos on his arms found his boss lying in a pool of coagulated black blood when he arrived at work at 8 o'clock sharp.

In actuality, he hadn't 'found' the body, rather tripped over it and fell spread-eagle on top of it. He had been yammering away on his mobile to his landlord about mould in the bath, cockroaches in the kitchen and rats in the loft, and hadn't been paying attention where he was walking. He didn't ring the police until he had finished reaming his landlord's arse. Told him off well and good. Would hold back the rent until the situation was resolved. And if he didn't like the rent being withheld, he could take it up with his solicitors: Mr Chib and Mr Baseball Bat.

# CHAPTER ONE-HUNDRED

Detective Sergeant Kojak was already managing the murder scene.

Christ, he had never seen so much blood. He kept his mouth closed, better able to keep the bile from spilling from his throat. He was getting too old for this shite. He was glad he had brought a flask of coffee laced with Irish whisky.

News travelled fast. DS Lyon-Jones pulled up in her red Mini, climbed out and hurried over to coffee-sipping Kojak, turning heads as she went.

She showed Kojak her ID. 'Have you heard from Inspector Sharkey?'

'What's it to ye?'

'We're all concerned, that's all.' Lyon-Jones pointed at the corpse. 'What can you tell me?'

'I can tell ye that yer on the wrong side of the river.'

Lyon-Jones ignored Kojak. Looked around the scene. SOCO was present. Already photographing the body and videoing the scene. Uniforms were spreading out from the *locus*, searching for clues. Kojak had the entire scene tightly controlled.

Lyon-Jones fixed her eyes on Kojak. 'Who is it?'

'You tell me.' Loads of subtext.

DS Kojak led DS Lyon-Jones over to where they could view the body without contaminating the scene. He knew she would squirm when she saw a pool of blood the size of a horse emanating from a dickless corpse. Knew she would be emotional when she saw who it was. He was taken aback when neither happened.

Lyon-Jones knelt and studied the body's position. Studied the lacerations where the Screwdriver's privates had been severed. Saw the bloodied baseball bat protruding out of the anal cavity. Knew what it meant.

If Lyon-Jones recognised the deceased, she didn't let on.

DS Kojak smirked. 'Any thoughts, *Detective?*'

'Just one. If you're going to jack that coffee with whisky, quit using the rubbish you're using.'

Lyon-Jones left a fuming DS Kojak gnawing on a handful of Smarties and mumbling to himself. She jumped in her Mini and drove off.

Convinced that this was Sharkey's doing.

Shortly after she departed, DS Kojak got another surprise visitor: The Screwdriver's wife, Jade Sutherland. She pulled up in the soft-top Audi with the children strapped in the back. She saw all the uniforms, wondered if they had found the stash, then saw her husband's corpse on the ground.

And she didn't seem too surprised.

She knew it would come to this one day. It only had been a matter of 'when' not 'if'.

Jade spotted DS Kojak coming her way, just as the Press were arriving. And she burst into tears. Not for the loss of her once beloved husband. Not for the benefit of the polis. Not even for the flashbulbs and cameras. She was bawling like a wee babe because that's when she remembered the Screwdriver had changed the will and his younger brother was to inherit everything—including the new villa in Whitecraigs.

The Screwdriver's wife pulled out her mobile. Hit speed-dial.

* * *

Just above Benidorm, in the foothills of the Puig Campana, all was quiet at Villa Nariz-Azul.

The table of young crumpet were present. Some disported, topless, in the heart-shaped pool, others floated on Li-los, while yet others, completely naked, soaked up the rays, sunny-side up or over easy. It was an idyllic setting until the phone shattered the peace and a few moments later Jimmy the Pouch Sutherland staggered out, brandishing a handgun, firing it wildly like the madman he was, up into the air, at the distant mountains, then in the direction of the azure Mediterranean below. The young lassies scrambled from the pool and dived for cover. When the last round was spent, the Pouch opened his mouth and the most primal wail emanated.

And he collapsed on to the floor.

# CHAPTER ONE-HUNDRED AND ONE

Lyon-Jones finished her shift, changed into jeans, sweater and a leather jacket, exited the backdoor into perishing cold and crossed to her Mini.

The Mini was parked where it was well-lit and within clear view of the nearest CCTV camera. She unlocked the door, checked the backseat, then climbed in and quickly re-locked the doors. She unlocked the glovebox, withdrew her .38 and placed it on the passenger seat.

She turned left out of the carpark, turned again on Maitland, then pulled over in the forecourt of the fire station. Waited. Watched. No one was following her. She swung out and headed towards the M8. Traffic was unusually heavy, even for this time of night. She crawled along at the approach to the Kingston Bridge. As she crossed the bridge and slipped over into the inside lane, she noticed a motor, three cars back, mimicking her every move. She sped up and transitioned to the M77 and the car followed. Then the car was next to her, in the outside lane. A T-reg black Golf. Not washed since the last Millennium.

Lyon-Jones shot a glance over. Two hoodies. One blew her a kiss, the other took a fist and pumped it in front of his mouth. As she began the climb towards Silverburn, she held her position in the inside lane. The two hoodies moved in right behind her and tailgated. Just ahead was the exit for Silverburn. Lyon-Jones sped up. The Golf charged. Right on her arse. Lyon-Jones waited until the last second, then flipped on her windscreen wipers, front and rear, and the spray blew back on to the windscreen of the filthy Golf covering its windscreen in an opaque mask. By the time the two hoodies got the wipers working, the windscreen was a smeared miasma of months of neglect.

And the red Mini with the hot lassie was nowhere to be seen.

Lyon-Jones arrived at her flat and drove right on by, then did a U-turn in the middle of the street and pulled over. If anyone had been following her, she would have had him dead to right. She waited, then pulled into her drive, stuck the .38 in her coat pocket and grabbed her bag off the passenger seat floorboards.

As she climbed out of her car, her mobile jangled.

It was CI Squires.

'Yes, ma'am?'

'That body of the young woman that was found in the Clyde...'

'Aye?'

'Same MO as the inspector's daughter.'

'DNA?'

'They match each other, but no one in our database. Forensics reckon she'd been in the river at least a week. They couldn't narrow it down any more than that. The body was badly decomposed and feasted on.' CI Squires rang off.

Lyon-Jones was troubled. An alarm bell was going off. She cast her mind back to what she had said to Sharkey about murder being sexual foreplay. She had run across cases in graduate school of taking a life for sexual pleasure. If Decoy Brody had had a sexual urge after the Kingston Pub and made Katie Sharkey his victim, who had he killed before having sex with the Irish lassie found in the Clyde?

Lyon-Jones inserted her key in the communal front door of her apartment block, then suddenly she had trouble breathing. A hand covered her mouth so she couldn't scream. Another hand restrained her arm, so she couldn't go for her gun. She lashed out with a leg, backwards and upwards, aiming for her assailant's twins, but he had been ready for that and blocked her kick. She went to an old trick she had seen working the club in Glasgow as a teenager, she flopped to the ground, using all her deadweight. The hoodie wasn't ready for this and he lost his balance and toppled over on top of her. Lyon-Jones rolled to get away, but he had her by the hair. He pulled her head back and thrust a gun barrel into the area of her carotid artery.

The hoodie pulled her up, kept her in front of him, frisked her, found the gun, pushed her towards the door, growled: 'Open it!'

Lyon-Jones' mind raced as she opened the front door to her block of apartments. The hoodie pushed her forward, the gun barrel at the base of her skull now.

'Someone will see you!'

'Go!'

The hoodie frogmarched her down the hall to her apartment. Forced her to open her door. Pushed her inside. Dragged her to the windows and closed the curtains at the large bay window which looked out on the Ayr Road. The hoodie switched on the lights and only then did he release her and let her turn around.

And Lyon-Jones was not just shocked by the hoodie's rough appearance: unshaven, unkempt, smelling of booze, she was shocked when she realised she knew this man.

'I know you're the leak.'

'Jesus, Boss, what the hell are you doing?'

'Shut the fuck up!'

'I'm not the leak!'

'SHUT THE FUCK UP!'

Sharkey grabbed Lyon-Jones' bag. Rifled through it. Took out her mobile. Jammed it in his jeans.

'I'm not the leak, Fleet.'

'Where's your bedroom?' Motioned with his gun.

'No.'

Gun in her face. 'Where's your fucking bedroom?'

'No!'

'Move!'

Lyon-Jones was freaking out as Sharkey forced her down the hall and into her bedroom. He turned on a light next to the bed.

'Get on the bed!

'No!'

'GET...ON...THE...FUCKING...BED!'

Frightened out of her skull, Lyon-Jones slipped onto the bed. Sat up.

Sharkey pulled a pair of handcuffs out of a back pocket. 'Put these on.'

'No, please...'

'Put the fucking handcuffs on!'

Lyon-Jones complied.

'Lie down!'

'No!'

Sharkey cocked the gun. 'DO IT!'

Lyon-Jones relented and did as she was told. Sharkey lay down next to her. Held the gun in his left hand. Put his right arm under her neck.

'Need to sleep. Need to think…'

Lyon-Jones looked at Sharkey's feet—*cowboy boots*.

'Pizza Face. Taxi Boy. Tattoo McQueen. The Screwdriver. That was you wasn't it? You've taken the law into your own hands.'

But Lyon-Jones didn't get an answer from Sharkey. He was already asleep.

CHAPTER ONE-HUNDRED AND TWO

At an outdoor kiosk the next morning, newspapers were selling like steak pie at New Year, and the headlines were electric.

The *Sun* reported: SCREWDRIVER SLAIN.

The *Herald* read: McQUEEN/SUTHERLAND GANG WAR ERUPTS.

The Daily Record quoted: RIVER CLYDE: MAGINOT LINE NO MORE.

Meanwhile on BBC Scotland a morose newsreader stared back at us with baleful eyes. 'Major portions of rival drug gangs have been wiped out…others who are still alive, are too afraid to venture out of doors. Low-level members of both gangs are committing petty crimes and then allowing themselves to get caught so they will be put in jail where it's safe…'

And the Blog Hog: LONG LIVE THE VIGILANTE, AT THIS RATE THERE WILL BE PEACE IN GLASGOW!

# CHAPTER ONE-HUNDRED AND THREE

Sharkey was fast asleep.

Lying on the bed next to him, Lyon-Jones was wide awake and owl-eyed. She hadn't slept a wink. She had been cold the whole night. Could have snuggled up to Sharkey to keep warm, but that had never been an option. And she desperately needed to pee.

A mobile chirruped. Sharkey awoke. Pulled it out of his jeans' pocket. Read the screen. It was Lyon-Jones' mobile.

'It's Squires. Ask her about my whereabouts. Do it!'

Sharkey handed Lyon-Jones the mobile. She sat up, answered. 'Morning, ma'am.

'Have you heard from Inspector Sharkey yet?'

'No, ma'am. Anything your end?'

'We think he'll go to his father's farm. We have it under twenty-four hour surveillance.'

'Understood.'

'Let me know if you hear anything.'

'Will do. See you at the station.' Lyon-Jones rang off.

'What did she say?'

'They think you'll return to your flat in Shettleston. They have it under twenty-four hour surveillance.'

'Try again!'

'That's verbatim…'

Sharkey pointed his gun at Fiona. 'WHAT DID SHE REALLY SAY?'

'They think you'll go to your father's farm…'

Sharkey rose. 'Let's go!'

'Where?'

'Move it!'

'I need to go change my contacts…'

'So do I… MOVE!'

'I need the toilet.'

'Make it quick.'

Lyon-Jones made for the toilet.

'Let's have it back.'

'Sorry?'

'Give it to me.'

'What?'

'Your mobile.'

Lyon-Jones exhaled heavily. Took her mobile out of her pocket. Handed it over.

Lyon-Jones held up her hands with the handcuffs. 'Could you remove them so I can go?'

'No.'

Lyon-Jones entered the loo and started to shut the door.

'Leave it open.'

'I need privacy.'

'Keep dreaming.'

'Can't you at least turn your head?'

'No. Mind over bladder, Jones.'

'Can't wait.'

'Do it now or do it in your knickers later.'

When Lyon-Jones was finished, Sharkey moved her towards the front window.

'I'm no leak…'

'Of course you are.'

Sharkey peeled back the curtain and checked the street. Looking for something that didn't fit. Something askew to his street-smart senses.

At the door, Sharkey peered through the spyhole.

'We meet anybody in the hall, you keep your trap shut. You open it, I *will* kill you. Believe me when I say it.'

Lyon-Jones held her hands in front of Sharkey. 'The handcuffs?'

'We leave them on.'

'Somebody will see.'

He grabbed a purple woolly hat off a hat rack to the side of the front door.

'Hold this.'

Sharkey cracked the front door. Opened it wide. Guided Lyon-Jones by her elbow. Gun down the back of his jeans. They moved quickly to the front door. Suddenly in front of them, the cleaning lady, a hunched crone, the poster child for osteoporosis. The old babe stopped. Looked at Lyon-Jones. Looked at Sharkey. Looked back at Lyon-Jones. Ach, these young lassies and their powerful sex drives. She had it once herself. No, not a long time ago. Just the once. She smiled at Lyon-Jones.

'He's a handsome devil, this one.' An east coast lilt.

Lyon-Jones forced a smile. Wanted to blurt out *Call the goddamn police*. Caught Sharkey's eye. All of this happening in a split second in real time, but taking a lifetime in her distressed mind. The biddy started to move off. Sharkey blew out his cheeks. Then the old woman stopped. Turned. Just like Colombo.

'Say, where did you get that woolly hat?'

'Marks.'

The crone smiled. 'Up at the Cross?'

'Aye.'

The crone smiled again. 'Can I see it on?'

An awkward moment.

A life-saving moment?

Sharkey gripped Lyon-Jones' elbow hard. Tugged. 'Next time, perhaps, love. We're late. Dental appointment. Scrape and clean.'

The crone understood, but she wasn't through with them. 'Ach, I cannae say I fancy goin' tae dentist. But then again, these teeth, ye see, they aren't real. Used tae huv my own, but they were all pulled oot of my heid when I wis a wee lass. Donnae ken why they did it. Nowt wrong wit 'em...but, I'll tell youse somethin' about dentists...' The crone kept rabbiting on, unaware that Sharkey and Lyon-Jones were no longer there.

Sharkey hustled Lyon-Jones along the street to where his Mustang was parked. Opened the passenger door, got her installed, seatbelt secured. He closed the passenger door. Moved to the driver's side. Removed his S&W. Jumped in. Cranked up the car.

'Mid-life crisis?' Said with an agenda to open a dialogue.

'Brought it back from America.'

319

'For the love of God, Fleet, this isn't the Wild West where you can clean up the streets with a gun.'

Sharkey ignored her, threw the stick into first and started to let out the clutch. Then pushed the clutch back in. Two uniforms had crossed the street and were motioning to Lyon-Jones. 'Roll it down!'

Lyon-Jones struggled to roll down her window. Stared at her salvation just inches away. Saw her breath in the cold air pouring in. Felt the gun in her side as Sharkey leaned across her to speak to the police and covered her handcuffs with the hat.

'Gentlemen?'

Both uniforms were young. Could've passed for Laurel and Hardy when they were starting out. 'Sorry, sir. Ma'am. We noticed the left-hand steering. Wondered what year it was.'

Sharkey replied in a perfect North Carolina drawl. 'It's an eighty-seven, officer. Only has sixty-seven thou on the clock.'

Constable Laurel, scratched his head. Looked at the Mustang in awe. 'Is it like the one in *Starsky and Hutch*?'

'No, sir, officer. That would be your Ford Gran Torino. A real mo-fo, kick-your ass muscle car.'

Both officers regarded Sharkey for a moment, not sure what he'd just said, then PC Hardy. 'Oh, right. Bye the nu.'

'All y'all be careful out there,' Sharkey said.

Sharkey nudged Lyon-Jones with the barrel of his gun and she rolled the window back up. He slipped the Mustang into first and pulled away from the kerb.

And Lyon-Jones was trapped between fear and anger.

Sharkey drove up the Ayr Road past the Malletsheugh. Past the turnoff for Pilmuir Holdings and on past the recycling centre. About a mile later, he turned off the main road and headed down a dirt strip.

'Where're we going?'

Silence.

Starting to get light. Lyon-Jones, frightened out of her skull. Road leading to the backside of hell. This was not where she wanted to spend any time.

Sharkey eventually pulled the Mustang over by a small lake. A thick ground fog hugged the ice. Thin ice.

'Get out!'

'Where're we going?'

Sharkey pointed his gun at Lyon-Jones.

'GET OUT.'

She climbed out. Laboured breathing. Heavy condensation with each breath. Wondered if it would be her last.

Sharkey made Lyon-Jones walk to the edge of the lake and out on to the thin ice.

'Don't do this, Fleet. Katie wouldn't want you to end this way.'

'Cut the shrink shit! How much were you being paid?'

'I wasn't the leak!'

'Walk!'

'No!'

Sharkey cocked his gun. Lyon-Jones walked. The ice cracked all round her.

'Get down on your knees.' Said in a whisper.

'NO!'

'DOWN!'

'I wasn't the fucking leak!'

'You lied! You fucking lied!'

'No!'

'Did you know him!'

'Who?'

Sharkey fired a round into the ice next to Fiona. The ice spider webbed. Lyon-Jones screamed.

Sharkey bellowed, 'Did—you—know—him!!!'

'WHO THE FUCK ARE YOU TALKING ABOUT!'

'Sutherland...'

Lyon-Jones sobbed uncontrollably. 'He raped me! Okay? He raped me when I was passed out!' Lyon-Jones dropped to her knees. 'Not Denny the Screwdriver...the father. When I was a teenager I hated my parents. I ran away to Glasgow and ended up working in a club the Screwdriver's father owned.'

Sharkey lowered his gun. Walked out on to the ice. Helped Lyon-Jones up to her feet.

'Jimmy the Pouch?'

Lyon-Jones couldn't stop crying. Couldn't stop shivering. Had trouble getting the words out: 'He gave me a drink at the club. Right off I felt funny—'

'Don't believe you.'

'HE DRUGGED ME!'

'Rohypnol?'

'No, Scopolamine.'

'Scopolamine?'

'It comes from Bogotá. Works similar to Rohypnol. He asked me if I wanted to lie down. I said I did, then he took me into his office. I couldn't even lift my arms.'

'Victims of these drugs don't usually remember the rape.'

Difficult for her: 'I— remembered—every—last—detail.'

'Did you call the police?'

'He said he'd kill my father if I did. I said "Be my guest". Then he said he'd kill me.'

'So why didn't you tell me this?'

'I had an abortion. I was fifteen. Didn't want the whole fucking Force to know.'

Sharkey stood there regarding Lyon-Jones. She was shivering and sobbing. She was telling the truth. He tried to hold her. She pushed him away. He reached out. She pushed him again. Hit him viciously with both hands, still cuffed. Beat him. On the chest and in the face. Laid into him. Sharkey stood there. Took it. Let her get a life's worth of bad taste out of her mouth.

He unlocked the cuffs, took her in his arms, held her and wouldn't let her go. Tears welled up in his eyes. 'I'm so sorry. I'm so goddamn sorry.'

'That's why I cut myself. Why I joined the Force. I want them dead. I want them all dead.'

Sharkey turned to guide Fiona back to the Mustang when CRACK! they both plunged into the icy waters.

# CHAPTER ONE-HUNDRED AND FOUR

In the foothills above Benidorm, Jimmy the Pouch lay in the middle of his king-sized bed. The curtains were closed. The room draped in black. Two pit bulls, Bruno and Bruiser, lay asleep on the bed with him.

Conundrum: He was mourning for his number-one son, yet burning with the fever of revenge. What to do?

Then his upbringing won out.

He was going to personally find the scum who had killed his lad, and he was going to make him suffer. First he would inject him with cocaine to heighten his senses, then he would kill—in front of him—that person he held most dear.

If it was a woman, she would be gang raped.

If it was a man, he would be gang raped.

Then he'd kill that loved one by injecting his veins with a cruelly vicious substance—helium. When the convulsions and the vomiting stopped, he would turn to the killer of his boy and he would peel his skin off with a Stanley knife and pliers. Then he would douse him in saline solution and let Bruno and Bruiser finish him off.

A phone rang at the side of his bed. The Pouch reached for his mobile. Glanced at the readout.

'How the fuck did ye get this number?'

'Listen carefully,' the voice began. 'I'm only going to say this once. This is Detective Inspector Sharkey of City Centre, Glasgow. I killed Denny. I killed your boy. I cut his baws off and took pleasure from it.' A pause. 'And now I'm on my way to Decoy Brody's farm to slit his ma's throat and give her a send-off.'

Sharkey threw the mobile out on to the ice of the lake. It skidded along, bounced and fell through the hole that he and Lyon-Jones had just climbed out of.

Down in Benidorm, the Pouch was still holding the phone in his hand. And his hand was shaking. Partly from rage. More so because he could tell from the tone in Sharkey's voice that Sharkey had been smiling during the proclamation. And that greatly unnerved him.

Soaking wet, clothes freezing solid like boards, Sharkey and Lyon-Jones hurried to the warmth of the Mustang and jumped in. Sharkey fired up the car and fumbled with the heater.

'Thought the farm was inaccessible.' Teeth chattering.

'Snow's melted. There's a towel behind my seat.'

'You were smiling when you told the Pouch that you killed his son...' Lyon-Jones grabbed the towel.

'An old trick I learnt when I was a gang member.' Sharkey banged the heater with the palm of his hand. 'Smile when you are threatening someone. It can be more intimidating than pulling out a weapon.'

'Who'd you learn it from?' Vigorously drying her hair.

'The leader of our gang. He was only sixteen, but he knew how things worked on the street.' Sharkey hit the heater again and it started to blow hot air. Finally.

'Did he turn his life around?' Hands held in front of heater.

'He became a City Councilor. I call him the "Mayor". He's like a big brother to me. Where's that towel?'

'Here. Did you really kill the Screwdriver?'

'No. Went by the next morning to pump him for information and found him dead. I nicked his mobile.'

'Does the heater go any higher?'

'It's cranked.'

'Taxi Boy?'

'No, I was at an AA meeting.'

Lyon-Jones was surprised by this admission. 'Pizza Face?'

'No.'

'Forensics found a footprint of a cowboy boot. You weren't there?'

'I *was* there, but after the fact. Went there to rough him up and found the body.'

'Tattoo McQueen?'

'No. No, I didn't kill him. Did you?'

A mobile in Sharkey's pocket vibrated. He took it out. It was

Lyon-Jones' mobile. He read the incoming call.

'Squires.'

He handed it to Fiona. Reached into his coat pocket. Returned her gun.

Lyon-Jones looked at her gun. Regarded Sharkey. Arresting him would do wonders for her career. But that wasn't what she was about. 'Morning, ma'am.'

On the other end, CI Squires: 'One of the Screwdriver's lieutenants was killed early this morning.'

'Who was it?'

'A goon who goes by the name of Bluetooth. He was shot in the back of the head in the middle of sexual accommodation.'

'Sexual accommodation?'

'A blow job.'

Jesus. Lyon-Jones wasn't used to this kind of language coming out the mouth of her CI.'

'How could've he been shot in the back of the head during a blow job?'

'He was giving it.'

Lyon-Jones gave Sharkey a look of *you won't believe this*.

'Did the recipient see anything?

'No, he said he had his eyes closed.'

'How's he taking it? Excuse the expression…ma'am.'

'Not well. He's a politician. Bullet barely missed his—'

'I get the picture, ma'am. Where'd it happen?'

'The gay red-light district. St Vincent Street toilets. I'll need you to go over there.'

'Understood, ma'am.'

'You sound like your teeth are chattering.'

'Just a bad connection.' Lyon-Jones rang off. Told Sharkey what she'd just heard. Spared no detail. Wondered out loud: 'McQueen family?'

'No. There's no one left to sanction the hits.'

'Who then?'

# CHAPTER ONE-HUNDRED AND FIVE

At the Brody farm, the weather was deteriorating as fog crept in from the Fenwick Moor.

Decoy observed his mother's farm through a pair of Steiner military binoculars. Then he turned to the person next to him. 'I'm getting bad vibes—Wait!'

Down below at the farmhouse there was movement. Decoy's maw, walking with a cane, a head-scarf and long-length waxed jacket against the elements, emerged from the side door to take the washing off the line.

Decoy pulled out his mobile and punched in a number. At the other end, his maw's partner picked up.

'It's me.'

'Where are ye?'

'Close by?'

'I'll huv yer maw put the kettle on.'

Decoy watched as his mother's partner, dressed in hunting gear, came out and helped take the clothes off the line. The person next to Decoy moaned. 'Cannae hack this anymore. Freezin' ma baws. How long?'

'Until I say it's time, ye eejit. Shut yer fuckin' gob.'

Decoy watched until they had collected nearly all the laundry. 'I'm goin' doon. Cover me and donnae make a bollocks of it like ye usually dae.'

Decoy Brody slipped down the hill effortlessly and quietly. Like a sniper should. Like the boy who spent summers in these hills growing up. Playing sniper with rabbit and grouse. In fact, Decoy was so quiet, his mother didn't even know he was behind her until he reached out and touched her on the shoulder and turned her round, and you would have thought she would have been startled. But she wasn't. Decoy was. It wasn't his maw wearing a scarf on her head and a ratty-old wax jacket.

It was Lyon-Jones.

Decoy looked to his maw's partner for an answer, saw Sharkey kitted in the hunting gear. Sharkey with his gun drawn charging him with the fury borne of vengeance.

Lyon-Jones yelled. 'Don't!'

But it was too late. Three shots rang out, but Decoy Brody didn't fall to the floor mortally wounded, Sharkey did.

Lyon-Jones took off running for the woods behind the farm, just as Decoy's mate hurried up pointing the murder weapon.

'Get the fucking bitch!' Decoy Brody hissed.

As she dived into the woods, Lyon-Jones shot a look back. Saw Sharkey on the ground. Decoy bursting into the farmhouse to check on his mother. Decoy's mate coming after her. Lyon-Jones knew she could outrun Decoy's mate.

Detective Sergeant Kojak was grossly overweight and frightfully out of shape.

Should have cut down on the Smarties.

Inside the farmhouse, Decoy found his maw and her partner tied up. He untied them both, ran into the kitchen, grabbed a butcher knife and burst back outside to give a send-off to Sharkey's corpse.

But the corpse was no longer there.

## CHAPTER ONE-HUNDRED AND SIX

Sharkey grimaced in pain, side stinging like hell, as he drove past the turnoff which led to his father's farm.

An unmarked police car was parked at the mouth. Two detectives, bored to tears, sat inside. Neither one even glanced at the red Mustang as it motored by. Piss-poor surveillance. Yet *two* to look for him, a cop, while only *one* to look for Brody, a murderer.

Sharkey shot a quick look over. The driver was sipping from a Styrofoam cup. The passenger had pen poised to a newspaper: Soduko. What was it with Soduko?

Sharkey carried on and came around his dad's farm from the backside. There was an unused lane back here. Always good to have an escape route or, as in this case, a clandestine way in. The Mustang bounced along the dirt road, killing his wound, and eventually came to a stop behind the garage.

Sharkey's dad opened the front door and Sharkey, soaked in blood, collapsed into his father's arms.

'Two cops at the bottom…'

Terror on the father's face seeing his son this way. He jerked up from his wheelchair, grabbed his cane and with surprising strength guided his son into a back bedroom. Swiftly and professionally, he went to work, pulling off the hunting kit, looking for wounds. Fleet had been shot three times: twice in the chest and once in the side. The left love handle. Fleet's dad smiled, his son was wearing Dragon Skin Body Armour, a bullet-proof vest so sophisticated it could withstand a grenade blast. He peeled the body armour off. Fleet had two nasty welts on his chest which would turn into impressive bruises. The senior Sharkey checked for broken ribs. Damage to the sternum. There was none. The wound in Fleet's side had been caused in reality by an errant shot. The shooter had been way off target. He had been aiming for the heart, but a bullet had slipped below the body armour. Fleet's dad could see that the bullet was still in his son. He made the gesture of using a syringe.

Sharkey waved a hand. 'No sedation.'

The senior Sharkey understood. Sedation meant a loss of control. It was foolhardy to be in the back-of-beyond of consciousness when the polis came knocking at the front door asking for a cuppa.

Sharkey's dad hobbled to the kitchen. Banged around in there. Brought back the necessary implements to remove the bullet and close the wound: surgical forceps, Celox blood coagulant, an antiseptic cotton tampon to insert in the wound, isopropyl alcohol, 0-grade nylon to suture the wound, suture scissors, a canoe needle and a bottle of Jack Daniels.

He was a man well-prepared.

He was a man who had been here before.

The senior Sharkey sterilized the forceps with rubbing alcohol and cleaned the wound with Dettol. Fleet knocked back some whisky. The whisky burned on the way down. Forceps did the same as they were inserted into the wound. As his father probed for the bullet, Fleet cried out in pain and asked for something to bite down on. His father gave him the nearest thing at hand: a copy of the latest paperback book from bestselling author Karen Campbell.

It didn't take long to extract the slug. Perhaps Sharkey would not have agreed. His dad held the glistening slug up for his son to see. He mouthed 'Polis?'

Sharkey nodded.

His dad sprinkled a healthy amount of the coag-powder into the wound, cut the antiseptic tampon in half and inserted it into the wound, a technique used in the field in Afghanistan. Then he threaded the canoe needle and made the first puncture. Sharkey bit down to chapter eight. It took fifteen stitches to close the wound. When it was over Sharkey felt as if he'd given birth. In reality, knew it couldn't compare. Didn't come close. Had even greater respect for women.

He needed to sleep, but knew he couldn't.

'Fiona…'

Sharkey tried to sit up, but nearly retched with the pain.

'Give me an hour's sleep. Then wake me.'

The senior Sharkey patted his son on the shoulder and smiled. And Sharkey drifted off.

It was dark when he awoke.

With murder in his eyes.

# CHAPTER ONE-HUNDRED AND SEVEN

On the third storey of an abandoned warehouse, Decoy Brody made up a bed.

The bed was a four-poster bed, dripping in wisps of sheer chiffon. It rested in the middle of a room lit with only a candle. The room had a high ceiling, beams, long windows. Meticulously, Decoy arranged a plastic sheet over the mattress and tucked it in. Placed a jar of KY jelly on a beautifully finished bedside table. Then a serrated, razor-sharp fishing knife. Carefully, almost lovingly, he peeled back the plastic wrapper on a 1cc insulin syringe, pierced the seal on a bottle which read KETAMINE, drew the golden liquid in, pointed the syringe in the air and let go with the obligatory squirt.

Then he licked his lips and crossed to a figure tied up to a chair next to the four-poster bed. The figure squirmed, tried to call out, but the gag...

And then he plunged the needle into Lyon-Jones' arm.

Lyon-Jones fought against her restraints and there was fire in her eyes. Decoy challenged her with his eyes. Bore into hers. Then he blinked. She held his gaze. And he was somehow unnerved. There was no fear in the detective sergeant's eyes. Only defiance and a chilling hate. What was this woman made of? What had this woman gone through in her life? Decoy looked away, then looked back and deep within her eyes. Now the defiance and the bone-chilling hate were fading. Then there was nothing. Nothing at all as her eyes rolled into the back of her head.

Decoy leaned close. Brushed her cheeks with his lips. Licked her. 'Induces amnesia. Not that amnesia will matter where yer goin, hen.'

Decoy regarded Lyon-Jones and he actually salivated. He would have to take his time with her once the ataxia set in.

Savour each thrust. Each incision. Carve her up a bit while she was still alive. Let her hold on to some sort of hope. Then he would pull the carpet out. A blood-red carpet by then. This one was different. The others didn't know they were going to die. This one had to. He had to dominate her. Let her know he was in charge. It might take some convincing.

He had all night.

'Please! Please save some for me...' A voice out of a darkened corner.

Decoy looked in the direction of the voice. A filthy mattress and a load of candy wrappers lay on the floor below one of those long windows. With the syringe dripping Lyon-Jones' blood in his hand, Decoy crossed to the dirty mattress and held up the glistening syringe for the strung-out Detective Sergeant Kojak to see. Kojak was unshaven, sweating and absolutely gagging for the drug.

'Yer some hoor,' Decoy whispered, and he injected Kojak.

# CHAPTER ONE-HUNDRED AND EIGHT

Sharkey blinked his eyes and fought fierce pain.

And then his mobile vibrated. He read the caller ID: 'Kojak'. Flipped it open.

'Cunt!'

But it wasn't Kojak on the other end, it was Lyon-Jones. Barely audible. Clearly drugged.

'He's going to kill me. Sutherland Motors. Hurry!'

Back at the warehouse, Decoy Brody had a gun to Fiona's head.

This plea, just a ploy.

\* \* \*

Sharkey pulled the Mustang over to the kerb. Killed the engine. Turned off the headlamps. Held his side as he struggled to get out. Popped the boot. Felt the area of his wound. It was seeping. He reached inside his USMC bag, removed a sachet of Quick-Clot. Lifted his shirt. Applied the powder to his seeping wound. Grimaced. Then he took out a syringe. Ripped off the wrapper. Pulled out a vial of adrenaline. Withdrew three CCs. Squirted out any air. And injected himself in the muscle on the side of his right thigh. The adrenaline took effect as it coursed through his veins.

Sharkey felt his strength coming back. His resolve. His vengeance. He went back into the boot of the Mustang and rifled round a veritable arsenal, pulled out what he needed. Started the approach to Sutherland Motors on foot.

Out in front of Sutherland Motors, it was darker than the road to hell. Deathly cold.

And eerily green.

Sharkey adjusted his night-vision goggles. He scanned the garage area. The forecourt. The fenced-in area. Where were the pit bulls? Perhaps removed when the police shut down the scene of crime? Decoy Brody wanted to draw him into a trap, not have him scared off.

Sharkey lowered the night-vision goggles and switched to a thermal-imaging monocular to case the area.

No heat sources. Wait! Around the far corner. Beady eyes. A large form. Pit bull! No. Just an urban fox doing his rounds.

Sharkey traded the thermal scope for the night-vision goggles again and scanned the abandoned warehouse. There were three floors above the garage. Lyon-Jones was being held up there. But Brody would be watching. There would be eyes behind those long windows. He couldn't risk coming any closer.

Then he got an idea. He pulled out his mobile and dialled.

\* \* \*

From his position on the third floor, Decoy Brody saw flashing blue lights moving fast down the street. The police. He stepped back from the window. Watched the patrol car shoot by to points unknown. Something else caught his eye. More blue lights. Decoy stepped to the side of the window. Squinted. The blue lights weren't flashing. He watched the vehicle approach. Just a Domino Pizza delivery. Through the scope on his rile, Decoy could see the pizza lad trying to read the address above the office door of the garage, then checking his sat/nav. Wrong address. The van motored off. No delivery here tonight.

Or was there?

Sharkey, wearing a rucksack, was pressed flat against the warehouse wall. He pulled the night-vision goggles back on and silently snaked along the perimeter. A noise. He froze. Just a sewer rat with a weight problem. The rat scurried off. Sharp little toenails scratching frozen tarmac. Fleet held his position. Took in a deep breath. Winced. Then spotted it: Just above, on the corner of the warehouse, a CCTV camera. Sharkey rummaged in his rucksack, pulled out a paint-ball gun and SPLAT the CCTV camera lens was covered in a rich cadmium red.

Sharkey slipped under the CCTV, around the corner of the building and came to a window. He tried the window. No go. Nailed shut. He took off his rucksack again. Rooted in it. Pulled out a stethoscope. Blew warm, moist air on the diaphragm and stuck it against the window. Listened. Nothing. Wait! What was that? Moaning. Faint moaning coming from somewhere upstairs, high above.

Sharkey jammed the stethoscope back in his rucksack and moved along the wall until he came to a down spout. The pipe was freezing cold. Fleet blew on his hands and, knowing he was going to tear his side apart, scaled. First floor. Second floor. Pain ripped through his wound. He paused. Tried to breathe without pain. Couldn't do so. Climbed higher. Third floor and up and over on to the roof. And he collapsed. Held his side. Writhed in bloody-God-awful pain. Up here the moaning was more pronounced. Sharkey limped silently in the direction of a warm glow. A skylight.

He reached the skylight and looked down. He was shocked by the depraved scene below. DS Kojak lying on a dirty mattress in a corner. A four-poster bed in the middle of an empty room. Fiona, naked, tied to the four posts. But she wasn't lying spread-eagle on her back, rather she had been rolled over on to her stomach and had her knees drawn up, tied into position, as were her hands and feet.

Moaning.

Sharkey whipped out his mobile. Went to his address book. Scrolled until he came to DS Kojak's name. Texted a quick message.

* * *

His mobile vibrated, then chimed. A drugged-out Kojak endeavoured to read the text. He sat up, didn't hear the window open behind him, didn't realize Sharkey was there until he felt the cold gun barrel against the back of his neck.

'Turn around. Slowly.'

Kojak turned. Fought to focus on Sharkey.

'Where's Brody?'

'Donnae know.'

Sharkey forgot about his pain. Bolted to Lyon-Jones' side. Began untying her. Lyon-Jones was doped-up and groggy, and shivering uncontrollably. He threw a blanket around her shoulders and grabbed her clothes lying on the floor.

Across the room, Kojak blubbered, 'I had tae do it, Fleet. Oh, Jaysus God, I'm so fuckin' drugged up, but I had tae do it.

Donnae ye see? Always had tae do what he told me. Ever since we were in primary together...'

Sharkey froze. 'Primary?'

'Bellahouston Primary. He bullied me and a mate until the lad jumped off the Erskine Bridge. Then he concentrated on me!' Kojak began to whimper. 'Is he still alive? Is Decoy still fuckin' alive?'

'Aye.'

Sharkey looked into DS Kojak's eyes and saw the life seeping from them. Before he could react, Kojak stood up. Burst into tears.

And threw himself out the open window.

A split second later, the sound of a sack of potatoes hitting the tarmac and the splintering of bone.

Sharkey recoiled back, then recovered. He had Lyon-Jones firmly in his arms and moved as fast as physics allowed towards a rickety service lift. Was Decoy nearby? Was he toying with them? Were they pawns in his big game?

Part of his foreplay?

They would be sitting ducks in the lift, advertising their whereabouts. Sharkey threw open the metal gate, nearly retched from the pain, then slammed the gate closed without getting in. He reached in through the gate, pressed the button for the ground floor, quickly removed his arm. The empty lift juddered violently, jerked and started a slow descent down into the pitch-black warehouse. Sharkey pulled on his night-vision goggles and held Lyon-Jones close. His breathing was laboured as they made for a stairwell in the far corner. He used the moaning of the lift to mask their movement. Moved step-by-painful-step downward, leading with his S&W. Fiona was dead weight, but she was fighting the drug. She had been there before and knew enough to keep quiet. He could hear the lift creaking its way down floor by floor. Then the lift shuddered and stopped dead. They froze in the stairwell. Sharkey illuminated the dial on his watch. He could feel Fiona's warmth against his body. Could feel her trembling. Somehow it gave him strength. He whispered, 'I won't let anything happen to you.' She touched his arm. Gave it a weak squeeze. He helped Lyon-Jones to the floor. Sat down next to her. Helped her to get into her clothes. Quiet as children on Christmas morn. Wrapped the blanket around.

And they waited.

The strength of a sniper is his patience. His cunning. The ability to sit, frozen, like a hare, not moving a muscle. For an eternity. Sharkey let his pulse settle down. Regulated his breath. Exorcised the pain. Lyon-Jones sensed Sharkey's intent and mimicked.

As a sniper, Sharkey knew it was extremely difficult on the eyes to use a spotting scope for more than twenty minutes and that's what Decoy was doing. Positioned on one of the floors. Watching and waiting. The hunted were going to wait out the hunter.

And they waited.

The cold settled in.

His wound began to bleed again.

And they waited.

Would he lose consciousness from lack of blood?

Sharkey heard a noise. He opened his mouth to allow for more acute hearing. Another noise, barely audible. And coming from above. How could that be? Had Decoy been up there all along or did he go back up?

A loud sound. Lyon-Jones jolted but didn't cry out.

The lift was moving. Going back up. Was someone in it or was it going to fetch someone?

A slurred whisper from Lyon-Jones. 'Dish...virgin...'

Sharkey didn't understand. Put his mouth to Lyon-Jones' ear. 'Say again.'

'Di...virgin...Diversion...'

Decoy had set the lift in motion to create a diversion. A noise diversion. He wasn't using it to convey. He was using it as background noise just as they had done.

And they waited.

Struggling to keep warm. A losing battle.

Decoy Brody knew the cold would be taking its toll on Lyon-Jones.

Sharkey shifted his weight and put his hand in something sticky on the floor. Then his mobile vibrated. He read the caller ID. The caller was Kojak. Decoy Brody had gone back up to the top floor to retrieve Kojak's mobile.

Sharkey hit a button. A text came up: COME OUT, COME OUT WHEREVER YOU ARE:(

Half an hour later, another text: I WILL KILL YOU AND THEN I WILL DO TO LYON-JONES WHAT I DID TO YOUR DAUGHTER:)

And they waited.

There was no logical way out. Sharkey was going to have to ring the police. He wanted Decoy Brody dead, but he was not about to risk endangering Lyon-Jones any longer. His own life meant nothing to him, but he couldn't jeopardize hers. She had a future. She had a career. She deserved to live, not become collateral in some fierce vendetta. He would get Maggie Squires on the line, tell her to get the ARU down there AS-fucking-AP. Decoy Brody wasn't careless. He would see them coming. Make his escape. And he would be long gone from Glasgow by the time Sharkey was released from jail.

Long gone.

Sharkey flipped his mobile open. Thumbed in Squires' number. He could hear it ring at the other end. Felt Lyon-Jones stir next to him. Saw her try to focus on the readout.

'No!' she whispered. 'Fire brigade...Fire brigade...'

Confused, Sharkey killed the call to Squires and dialled 999.

The call was picked up by the operator. 'What's the nature of your emergency?'

In that moment, Sharkey knew what Lyon-Jones was trying to tell him. In her state of demented drug-dom, with her brain fried like a pan of chips, she was still more switched on than he was.

'What's the nature of your emergency?' Repeated, with a hint of attitude.

'Fire,' Sharkey whispered. 'Fire at Sutherland Motors on Broomloan Road.'

The closest fire station was in Govan, just down the road from the Govan Subway Station. Within minutes, they heard the sirens off in the distance. Approaching. Sharkey knew that Decoy Brody would think it was the police on the way and that he would scarper. Sharkey pulled his thermal image scope out of his rucksack, handed it to Lyon-Jones. He helped her to her feet and, now helping each other, they made their way down the inky staircase to the second floor. The first floor. The ground floor.

The sirens were loud. Engines roaring down the street. Sharkey guided Lyon-Jones to the front door. Padlocked and chained from the inside! He tried windows. Nailed shut! He moved Lyon-Jones to a side door, hit it with his shoulder, screamed in silent pain, cracked it open and slipped out to safety.

The night air was piercing, but welcoming. Scrambling for their lives, Sharkey led a rubber-legged Lyon-Jones around the corner of the warehouse and they hit a patch of ice. Crashed to the ground and slid into a berm. Only it wasn't ice and it wasn't a berm. It was blood. And the lifeless corpse of DS Kojak.

Covered in blood, freaked-fucking-out, Sharkey and Lyon-Jones struggled to their feet as the fire brigade lit up the surrounding buildings with shards of blue. Lyon-Jones sucked air hard, trying to will the drug out of her system. They both turned their heads to look at the arriving fire trucks. Turned back round and ran smack into strong arms, hanging on, not letting go. Just a smelly old drunk staggering down the street to see what all the excitement was about. Sharkey pushed the drunk away. Kept moving. Pushing forward.

And then they were at the Mustang. Sharkey opened the passenger door, helped Lyon-Jones in, jumped in the driver's side.

'Kiss me!'

'What?'

'Kiss me!'

# CHAPTER ONE-HUNDRED AND NINE

Sharkey grabbed Lyon-Jones and kissed her full on the lips, just as a patrol car cruised by, slowed, officers looked over, carried on down the road toward where there had been a report of a fire.

They stopped kissing. Lyon-Jones felt wetness. Held up her hand. It was covered in blood.

'Christ, let's get you to the Southern General.'

'No, he's still here. Nearby. You don't have to be part of this…'

'Bit late for that.'

Sharkey's mobile erupted.

'Just wanted you to know…with your daughter Katie. When I was fucking her in the arse…I didn't cum 'til I felt the warmth of her blood ooze from her throat…' And Decoy rang off.

Sharkey dropped the mobile out of his hand. Sat there. Shocked senseless. Wringing the life out of the steering wheel. Then he looked over at Lyon-Jones with eyes dilating like hell.

'I heard a sound in the background. I know that sound but I can't place it. I think he's on the river.'

'The river? Yesterday morning. I got a call from Squires. She told me that they found a teenage girl's body floating in the Clyde. Throat slashed. Same MO as—'

'He's got a boat. The sound I heard was of a boat's engine. Let's go!'

The first hint of dawn streaked the sky, as Sharkey eased the Mustang on to the approach to the Erskine Bridge, seven miles downriver from Glasgow. He motored into the middle of the lofty expanse, pulled the Mustang over and flipped on the emergency flashers. They were 38 metres above the Clyde.

Sharkey and Lyon-Jones climbed out of the Mustang. Moved to the east railing. Saw a flower memorial to the latest suicide victims: two teenage girls who hadn't even started life, but thought they had already had enough.

They peered through the mist at the river below.

Nothing.

'He's got to come this way. He'll want to lay low for a while in the archipelago.'

They waited. And waited. The sun was just starting to hit the tops of the bridge's girders. Lyon-Jones scanned the river below. Nothing but an eerie silence and an eerie fog. Sun above, fog below. When the odd irate motorist blared his horn, Sharkey gave him a two-finger reminder of Agincourt.

They heard the sound of the boat before they saw it. The same chugging sound Sharkey had heard on his mobile. And then Decoy Brody's fishing boat pierced the mist. And a shot rang out. A bullet whizzing by their heads.

'He knew we'd be here!'

Sharkey and Lyon-Jones took cover and kept back from the rail. When Brody was within range, Sharkey opened fire and emptied his handgun.

'We're fucked!' Lyon-Jones yelled.

'No, it's just beginning. Give me your knickers!'

'What!'

'We don't have time!' On that, Sharkey thrust his hand down Lyon-Jones' jeans and ripped her underwear right off. 'Hold these!'

Speechless, for once, Lyon-Jones watched as Sharkey limped to the Mustang. Threw open the boot and extracted a Christmas present.

'What the hell're you doing?'

'Going to re-gift this!'

Sharkey ripped off the Chrissie paper and held up the bottle of 151 Rum that DC Wilson had given him. Then he took Lyon-Jones' underwear, soaked them in rum and sealed the soaked knickers back in the top of the bottle.

'Come on!'

Sharkey limped across to the other side of the bridge, followed by Lyon-Jones. He handed her his cigarette lighter. 'Light your underwear!' Lyon-Jones did. Sharkey held the bottle of rum in his hand until the knickers were bursting with flames.

Peered over the side of the bridge. Saw the bow of Decoy's boat just coming out the west side.

And he let the bottle drop.

'Bon voyage, motherfucker!'

The Molotov cocktail landed on the afterdeck, right behind the open wheelhouse and burst into a fireball which rolled forward and aft.

And even at this height, they could hear Decoy Brody's scream. And then he appeared, clothes on fire, a twitching, kicking figure burning in hell.

And he plunged into the dark, swirling, unforgiving Clyde.

'*Sláinte*, Decoy.'

# CHAPTER ONE-HUNDRED AND TEN

Lyon-Jones let the hot water rush over her body. Washed away the warehouse's grime. Couldn't wash away what could have been.

They had arrived at his dad's farm the back way. Sharkey's dad had made them tea and breakfast. Checked his son's wound. Dressed it again. Warned them surveillance was still down at the entrance to the farm.

In the garage out back, Sharkey stowed his US Marine Corps bag of tricks. He unlocked the door leading to his arsenal. Smelled cordite. Someone had fired the Glock and the sniper rifle.

Sharkey went back inside the house and confronted his father.

'Having trouble with the rabbits?'

The elder Sharkey regarded his son. Wheeled himself to his writing table. Scribbled two words on a piece of paper.

Held it up: NOT ANYMORE.

\* \* \*

Detective Chief Superintendent Danus Ferguson was addressing a group of officers in the Incident Room when Lyon-Jones and Sharkey walked in.

DCI Maggie Squires was present.

Sharkey had his S&W in his hand. Seriously tense for a moment. He limped past a rattled Squires and handed the gun over to his Super. Ferguson took the gun from him. Gave his charge a look of disappointment and frustration, then softened to one of concern: 'You're bleeding.'

Lyon-Jones added: 'He needs the hospital.'

She went to Sharkey's side. 'He saved my life…'

# CHAPTER ONE-HUNDRED AND ELEVEN

He felt his groin stir.

He'd been observing the three young women holding sway at the bar for the past hour. He was a sucker for gorgeous blondes: eastern European blondes. This was a dancing venue along the promenade in Benidorm, but the three weren't dancing. Hookers? Unlikely, just drinking, teasing and refusing all who dared ask for a dance. Well, they sure as hell weren't going to tease or refuse him. Not once they saw what he had to offer.

Jimmy the Pouch Sutherland was grieving for his son, Denny, and he would never get over the loss, but the best way to forget about his loss was a good fucking session. Shite, he might just do all three at once.

He rose, arrogantly strode across the packed dance floor and sidled up to the three sirens. Ach, all in tight, sexy dresses: white, blue and red. Like the flag of bloody Russia.

'Can I buy ye three lovely lassies a bevvy?'

The three young women just stared back. Didn't have a clue what had just been said. Didn't even know which language he had used. For sure, it wasn't English.

The Pouch laughed. 'No speakee the lingo?'

The women continued to stare. Unamused. The Pouch decided to use the international language known by all in the free world. He reached into his pocket. Pulled out a gram of coke. The three lassies immediately perked up.

The Pouch leaned close. Brushed his groin against the knee of the one in the blue dress. She didn't seem to mind. 'You come to my house, no?'

'No,' said Blue Dress.

'We stay,' said White Dress.

He handed the smoky-brown vial to Red Dress. She quickly slipped from her barstool and made for the *Damas*. The Pouch

344

flashed a wad of euros. Told the barman in his flawless Spanish to pour them a round. The barman poured: one JD and Coke, one Spanish Cava and one Flirtini.

Red Dress returned. Had a sip of her Flirtini. Handed the coke over to Blue Dress, bypassing the Pouch. Blue Dress made a beeline for the toilets.

The Pouch smiled at Red Dress. She smiled back. Christ, he was getting a hard-on. He wanted to do her right there and then. '*Bailar*? Dance?'

'No.'

The Pouch couldn't believe it. 'Ye'll snort my coke, but ye donnae want tae dance?'

Red dress didn't have a clue what he was saying. Just continued to smile back.

Blue Dress returned with the cocaine. Handed it to White Dress. White Dress didn't even bother to go to the toilets, she tooted up right there at the bar, then handed it back to the Pouch. The Pouch was gobsmacked. The three lassies laughed. The bar was so dark no one had a clue.

The Pouch liked White Dress' spunk. He made a dancing movement with his body. Smiled. All charm. 'Dance?'

White Dress nodded. The music began. The Pouch led her to the dance floor. '"Lady" by Kenny Rogers,' he whispered. He prided himself on knowing the names of all the songs. They danced. He ground into her pelvis. Had his hands all over her arse. The two other girls watched from the bar. Giggled. Tittered. Whispered behind hands over mouths.

When 'Lady' was over, the Pouch and White Dress walked back to the bar. White Dress reached deep into the Pouch's pocket, rooted around for the vial of coke, lingered. Fondled.

The Pouch smiled as the letch he was. 'Red card! Red card!'

White Dress laughed, she understood that, then squeezed his joint. She took the vial from his pocket and she and Blue Dress slipped away to the toilets.

And failed to return.

Red Dress kept looking back towards the toilets, waiting for her friends to return.

The Pouch leaned next to Red Dress. 'Ye been dumped. They've done a runner with the Charlie.'

Red Dress was clearly pissed. Now she didn't have a way home. And she was stuck alone in this seaside club with a randy seventy-year-old hormonal freak.

'Dance?'

Red Dress looked once more over her shoulder towards the toilets.

'Dance?' All charm. All panto.

'No.'

The Pouch reached into a different pocket and pulled out another vial of coke. 'Dance?'

Red Dress took the vial. Placed it in her cleavage. 'Yes.'

The Pouch couldn't believe his good fortune. The lassies, they always came around when you offered nose candy. He took her to the dance floor and they danced. 'Lionel Ritchie. "My Love",' he whispered. When the dance was over, Red Dress motioned that she wanted to pay a visit to the toilets. The Pouch nodded okay. He knew she would be back. When the young girls saw that he had what appeared to be a limitless supply of cocaine, they never strayed very far. It was as if he had them tethered to one of those dog leads that lets the dog run off for a bit, but can always be reeled back in. This girl would be no different than the hundreds of others he had seduced in his life. By the end of the night, he would have her in his bed and be doing things that she never knew existed. Then tomorrow, she would want it all over again.

Red Dress returned from the loo as expected and she took the Pouch's hand and led him out on the dance floor. Oh, how quickly the tides turn. Another slow dance. The Pouch recognised the tune, but couldn't place the name. Roberta Flack, but what was the fucking name of the song?

He placed his hand on her back. Her back was bare. He ran his hand down to the curvature at the top of her bum. A delicious rump. He would spend some time back there later in the evening.

He knew she didn't speak a word of English, so he whispered in her ear. 'I'm going tae use beads and stuff them up yer pussy, then I'm goin' tae fuck ye in the arse with my big cock and slowly remove the beads until it takes yer breath away. Then

I'll stick the beads up yer arse and fuck ye with yer legs over yer heid.'

As the song climaxed the two moved rhythmically. With the room so dark, the Pouch took his chances and put a hand down her bum crack. This seemed to excite Red Dress and she snuggled into the curve of the Pouch's neck.

A smile of deep satisfaction came to her lips.

Then a razor blade to her teeth.

And the cut was so swift, the Pouch didn't even know what had happened until he heard the raspy exhalation of his own breath. Already dying, he clutched wildly at his throat, slumped to his knees and then fell face first on to the hardwood dance floor. Deep crimson blood spurted from his carotid and seeped slowly away from his convulsing body.

And only then did the screams come from the other revellers.

Outside of the nightclub, Red Dress emerged and put her arm through the arm of a passing man in a tuxedo and they strolled casually along the busy beach promenade, *Paseo Marítimo*, on a mild night for this late in December.

'You'd look good as a blonde,' Sharkey said.

Lyon-Jones just smiled. 'We make a good team.' Then she burst into tears as the closure to all those wasted years hit her.

They cut down a narrow passageway. Lyon-Jones removed the blond wig. Stuffed it in the *basura* at the back of a restaurant. Removed the vial of coke from her bra and flung it as far as she could. Sharkey took off his jacket. Covered her shoulders. Covered her red dress.

And Sharkey and Lyon-Jones disappeared into the dark Costa Blanca night.

'Killing Me Softly' still playing back at the club.

# CHAPTER ONE-HUNDRED AND TWELVE

The alarm went off at 6.30 a.m., awakening Willie Wallace.

Willie hit the alarm, sat up and swung his feet off the edge of the bed. Willie wore flannel pyjamas and woolly socks. He reached for his glasses on the bedside table and double checked the time on the alarm clock. Took the glass of water he kept by his bedside and drank it down.

Willie switched on the radio. The DJ on Clyde Radio Two was talking about New Year's resolutions. Willie listened to the New Year's resolutions that no one would keep.

He would keep his.

Always did what he set his mind on.

Willie had breakfast. Showered. Towelled off. Put his glasses on. Wiped the mist off the mirror. Frowned. He opened the bathroom cabinet and took out his antibiotic ointment. He placed a dollop about the size of a tuppence in the palm of his left hand and slowly and carefully rubbed it around his eyes, forehead and ears. He would leave it on until he got to work at the subway, then he would slip into the Gents and remove it before anyone noticed.

Willie combed his hair, applied underarm deodorant and repaired to his living room/bedroom. He stepped into his boxers. Always the left leg first. Pulled on his socks. Always the left one first. In the wardrobe to the right of his one window, Willie removed his SPT uniform. He put it on. Put on his black shoes that he had polished the night before. Always the left one first. He returned to the mirror and had a good look at the figure staring back at him in the mirror. Frowned.

He looked over at that photo of Jimmy Reid he had hanging over his bed. Crossed to it. Adjusted the right side, up a fraction.

Then he practiced his limp.

Finally he was ready.

And he was nervous.

It was his first day back at work.

He hoped that people wouldn't stare too much.

He hoped that no one would ask him what had happened. But if they did, he would simply tell them.

It had been a chip pan fire.

## EPILOGUE

Detective Inspector Fleet Sharkey was suspended.

As was Detective Sergeant Fiona Lyon-Jones.

Sharkey and Lyon-Jones went back to The Griffin to toast their suspensions. Lyon-Jones drank red wine. Sharkey, soda with a lime. Lyon-Jones offered the upbeat: 'Statistically, sir, 70 percent of suspended officers get reinstated.'

Sharkey shook Lyon-Jones by telling her he was going to return to America. Back to the Appalachian Mountains in North Carolina. There was nothing for him in Glasgow any longer.

Lyon-Jones countered, suggested—if they weren't reinstated—that perhaps they should start up their own private investigation firm.

Sharkey briefly hesitated, then said he needed to get away from Glasgow.

'But you love Glasgow!'

'It hurts too much to stay now.'

'Thought we made a good team...'

Sharkey didn't know how to respond. Didn't know anything anymore.

* * *

Gangland activity was at an all-time low, thanks to the culling of the Screwdriver, Taxi Boy and Tattoo McQueen by the vigilante.

The senior Sharkey slept better at night thinking the Glasgow he loved and had grown up in, had become a safer place.

Maggie Squires was promoted to Detective Superintendent. Portrayed as a saviour by all the newspapers. Portrayed as a schmuck by the Blog Hog.

Detective Chief Superintendent Ferguson took the weans to a later panto. The show was dedicated to Gerard Kelly and there wasn't a dry eye in the house.

DC Wilson considered telling Sharkey that he was the mysterious soul behind the Blog Hog. Then decided against it.

Councillor Cal Bridges, the 'Mayor', looked to be reelected. Again. No one dared run against him. On account of his popularity. Allegedly.

* * *

Despite all that had transpired over this holiday season, Glaswegians were looking to the future with renewed energy and hope. They had resolve. They were hearty. They were as tough as anyone on the planet. Life could only get better for them.

But it was not to be.

The Chinese triads sensed the vacuum and moved on to Sutherland turf on the south side of the river while keeping a stronghold in the West End.

The fifteen-year-old-leader of the Riddrie Hole-in-the-Wall posted a hit list on Facebook. The hit list consisted of all members, lieutenants and enforcers loyal to the McQueen clan. He was seizing power and taking over the drug trade on the north side of the river. He had two younger brothers and a sister in a posse of over one hundred, many of whom delivered drugs on those little aluminum street scooters. The youngest being eight. There was much chatter on Bebo. Even though his weapon of choice was a handmade triple-bladed chib (so the facial wound couldn't be stitched), no one took him seriously: the police, the remaining McQueen gang, the Triads. Then he killed Tattoo McQueen's partner by drilling holes in her head with a power drill. Forensics reckoned she had been alive when the first drill pushed through her skull.

Everyone was taking him seriously now.

At the University of St Andrews, a young student by the name of Wiggy was on course to be named summa cum laude for his graduating class and postgraduate studies in the School of Economics. Wiggy was the black sheep in the family. No one else had even finished school, let alone gone on to university or postgraduate studies. Wiggy was a black sheep because he was ethical.

And honest.

And now, what was Wiggy Sutherland to do? He had just inherited an empire, albeit, a dirty empire.

Would the son sit on this empire?

Lyon-Jones' younger sister graduated from the College and was assigned to Strathclyde Police, City Centre.

The Chrissie prezzies that had been under the Christmas tree at Sutherland Motors were confiscated by the police and donated to the Delmont hostel for the homeless. The residents had a belated white Christmas.

Willie Wallace's New Year's resolution was to kill DI Sharkey.

Oh, aye, he would keep his bespectacled guise with the subway. It gave him access to his domain: the subterranean network of used and disused train tunnels, and freight and mine shafts which snaked beneath Glasgow. There were miles of them. And he knew every inch of the underworld. He could easily slither about beneath the city and like a cobra pop up when he needed to inject venom.

Willie Wallace and the tunnels of Glasgow.

A marriage made in hell.

He would let Decoy Brody remain at the bottom of the Clyde.

He'd create a new persona for the Hyde side of his personality. Re-invent something equally sick.

And a new name.

Jack Tripper, perhaps.

He'd keep the sex angle. That went without saying. But he needed a new hook, something twisted and sinister to frighten the police, the public and the Press.

He'd use various means to kill, to keep the polis on their polished toes and so they couldn't develop a profile.

Then he'd devour part of the body.

He'd start with Ferris 'Fleet' Sharkey.

And then he'd have Fiona Lyon-Jones for dessert.

Just deserts.

# GLOSSARY

**Alex Ferguson** – Born in Glasgow, Sir Alex managed perennial football powerhouse Manchester United for about a thousand years. If you ask someone from the UK who their favourite team is, they will respond with unbridled enthusiasm. If you ask the same person who their second favourite team is, the answer will come in the form of a snarl: 'Whoever's playing Man Utd.'

**all ballied up** – using a balaclava as an accessory

***aqui, se habla vino rioja*** – (Spanish) – red wine spoken here

**Armadillo** – affectionate name given to Glasgow's iconic Clyde Auditorium, as it resembles, well, an Armadillo. Must be seen to be believed (and appreciated). Comparisons have been made with the Sydney Opera House. This, however, was not the intention of the architects, rather that the building appear to be an interlocking series of ships' hulls, to honour Glasgow's shipbuilding heritage.

**Asda** – supermarket found all over the UK, now owned by, yes, Wal-Mart

**ARU** – Armed Response Unit (police)

**Ashton Lane** – quirky cobbled lane in Glasgow's West End. Haunt of university students and other discerning folk. Noted for quaint watering holes, and the licensed Grosvenor Cinema, which sports couches. One cool venue.

**bahookie** – one's derriere

**Baltic** – colder than a witch's t*t

**banjoed, bottle, malkies** – 1) kicked sb in the nuts, 2) thrust a bottle (preferably broken) into sb's face or throat, 3) a head-butt (s)

*barranca* – (Spanish) – a ravine

**barras** – the barras, or Barrows Market, is a funky flea-market of sorts in Glasgow's East End. Almost anything can be found here, much of it legal.

*basura* – (Spanish) - trash, garbage

**baws** – colloquial for balls, testicles

**boabie** – a male appendage

**boaked** – vomited

**bog** – the toilet

**bollocks** – bullshit, testicles, can also be a retort of exasperation

**boudo** – cash

**Boxing Day** – the day after Christmas. A holiday, just when you need it the most.

**Buckfast** – a fortified red, highly caffeinated, almost black wine, made by Benedictine monks at Buckfast Abbey down in the county of Devon. Popular in Scotland among neds**, who are drawn to its fine taste and heroin-like buzz.

**Buckfast commandos** – connoisseurs of Buckfast wine, traditionally intoxicated, aggressive and fearless

**Buckfast Triangle** – The area of Coatbridge, Airdrie and Bellshill where there are markedly high sales of the strong, caffeine-high tonic wine. Offences involving alcohol last year, were one every two hours, costing almost £250,000 a day. The constituency has the highest rate of alcohol-related deaths in the UK, with a death every nine days due to alcohol consumption.

**buddie** – A supporter of the football club St. Mirren

**bugger** – expletive, Oh, darn! Schucks! Nowadays used instead of 'fuck', except around those old enough to understand its origin

**buggered** – screwed

**buggerin' off** – taking one's leave

**buggery** – I don't really need to explain this, do I?

**bumped** – robbed and possibly have the shit beaten out of you

**buttie** – heaven on earth, bread slapped with mounds of butter, adorned with chips or bacon. To die for.

**bye the nu** – by for now

**caps** – a coveted appearance with, say, your national team

**charred on cider-piss** – intoxicated on cheap cider

**chib** – a knife, a blade, a homemade killing machine made from razors, could even be a pool cue used in a bar fight

**chibbed** – to get stuck with above said instrument of pain

**chippy** – a chip shop, a fast food outlet offering fish & chips, a good reason to move into a neighbourhood

**Christmas cake** – only the best thing on this earth to consume at Christmas, other than all the alcohol

**CID** – acronym for Criminal Investigation Department (detectives)

**circulation** – APB, all-points bulletin

**Clockwork Orange** – affectionate slang for the SPT, the crack Glasgow subway system

**cludgie** – the Gents, toilet, loo, bog, shitter, need I go on?

**cock up** – screwed up, fucked up, messed up. Possibly stemming from archery where, if the 'cock' feather was uppermost, the arrow would not fly straight... or ... When wine or beer is ready to be run-off for bottling, a stop-cock is driven into the barrel and a sample is tasted to check for quality. If the beer or wine has turned sour, the cock is twisted upside down showing that the batch is unfit for consumption.

**Cornish Scrumpy** – A potent rough cider, popular amongst young people due to its low cost, made in Cornwall, the south-western county of England. May be drunk in large volumes if not planning to use one's legs

**cossie** – bathing suit

**Costa del Crime** – Costa Blanca, Spain, holiday, second-home and Mecca to felons

**crèche** – a day-care centre

**crims** – criminals

**cuppa** – a cup of tea

**curry** – de rigeur meal of Strathclyde Police Force, Indian sub-continent fayre to die for

**Doc Martens** – footwear apparel of cops, serial killers and Goths

**dobber** – (Glaswegian) – a penis

**doddle** – easy as pie

**dog boxes** – infamous claustrophobic holding cubicles at HM Barlinnie prison in Glasgow

**doin' ma edgy** – I was just acting in the capacity of a lookout

**doley** – an unmotivated slug who has chosen to drink beer and live off the state rather than seek gainful employment and drink beer

**doley-arse** – lazy ass

**'doon tae offy'** – 'Went down to the off-license' (Visiting your local liquor store)

**'Don't lose your rag'** – don't lose your temper

**double-barrelled** – an individual with a hyphen between surnames, e.g., Lyon-Jones. These individuals usually feel they are somehow superior to the rest of us.

**double-yellow** – a no-parking zone

**dosh** – money

**DVLA** – Driver and Vehicle Licensing Agency, located in Swansea, Wales

**edgy** – a lookout

**Edinburgh** – The greatest city in Scotland. Also the capital city

**eejit** – an idiot

**faggots** – in this case the reference is to sausages, a succulent ball of minced lard, gristle, fat, liver, intestine, and occasionally pork meat…not to die for

**fiert** – slang term for scared

**filth** – slang term for the police, used mostly south of the border. Glaswegians tend to prefer employing the term 'polis'

**First Choice** – UK based travel company, sometimes used as a last choice

**fitba** – football match, in Glasgow parlance

**fleeto** – Scottish word used to describe a gang of neds**

**full fry-up** – A common British breakfast dish – can be served at any time of day. Not recommended for those watching their caloric intake.

**Gerard Kelly** – the undisputed king of panto** at Glasgow's King's Theatre (he headlined the show for 20 years). Raised in Glasgow's East End, he died suddenly on 28 October 2010 after collapsing with a brain aneurysm. 'Bye-ya, Pals!'

**get a leg up** – engage in coitus

**Gibraltar monkey** – Barbary macaques, the world's biggest pest, other than that neighbour from hell of yours

**glaikit** – Scottish word meaning ugly, ineffectual, stupid, foolish, dim

**Glasgow** – The greatest city in Scotland. Wishes it was the capital city, having said that, it is the largest city in Scotland.

**Glasgow send-off** – jamming a shotgun up your nemesis' anal cavity and pulling the trigger. This technique can also be used with a knife, meat hook or samurai sword.

**Glasgow smile** – torture method used by gang members. Typically, two small incisions are made at the corners of the victim's mouth. Then, further pain is inflicted by various creative means until the victim screams, which rips the incisions further toward the ears. The end result is a hideous scar/smile almost clown-like in appearance.

**Glesga** – Glasgow in the Scots language

**Gob** – one's mouth

**gobsmacked** – awestruck

**Gordonstoun** – a boarding school for the rich and privileged, in Moray Scotland. Many of Prince Charles's recurring nightmares stem from his years here. Gordonstoun also has a notable fictional alumna, Lara Croft, the heroine of *Tomb Raider*.

**grass** – a snitch

**grass me up** – report me

**gruffalo** – character in a children's book: a 'monster-like hybrid that's half grizzly bear and half buffalo'. The gruffalo is purported to be fictional, then at the end of the book turns out to be… You'll have to go and read it yourself, be sure to include a 5 year old.

**guffy** – a lesser creature, oft described by Scots as someone originating from south of the border

**Hadrian's Wall** – a miniature version of the Great Wall of China, stretching some 73 miles across the north of England. Begun in AD 122, during the rule of the Roman Emperor Hadrian, to mark the northern limit of Roman Britain – and to keep out 'barbarians to the north'.

**Health and Safety** – what you say when you need an excuse to tell someone that they can't do something they want to do right then and there

***heat*** – UK equivalent of *People* magazine

**heavy** – A grade of Scottish beer. Exceedingly satisfying.

**heavy stunner** – hot chick

**heid** – a 'head' in Scottish slang

**hen** – a Scottish term for a female

**hen party** – bachelorette party, reason to get fall-down drunk, experiment with drugs and have sex with total strangers – and wake up the next morning, if not with a clear head, then at least a clear conscience

**Hogmanay** – the Scottish equivalent of New Year's Eve. The partying generally lasts through New Year's Day – and even into the 2nd of January, also a holiday in Scotland. A reason to move to Scotland.

**House of Fraser** – five-star department store

**Ibrox** – A stadium where the best football in the world is played

**Ice Cream Wars** – In Glasgow's East End, in the 1980s, conflicts erupted between the owners and employees (henchmen) of rival ice cream vans. This was not about a swirl or a Cornetto, rather drugs being doled out of the vans and encroachment on one another's territory. The conflicts involved daily violence and intimidation, and led to the deaths by arson of six members of the family of one ice cream van driver and a court case that lasted for 20 years.

**INLA** – Irish National Liberation Army is an Irish republican socialist paramilitary group that was formed on 8 December 1974. Its goal is to remove Northern Ireland from the United Kingdom and create a socialist united Ireland. The United Kingdom views the INLA as a terrorist group. The Republic of Ireland views it as an illegal organisation.

**Irn-Bru** – elixir of the gods, a caffeine rich, sugar-laden, fruit-flavoured soda very popular in Scotland

**Ivy** – The Ivy is an insufferably posh and expensive restaurant in London which caters to right poseurs and hangers-on. Valet parking is only £15, a glass of burgundy £12.50.

**jellies** – downers

**Johnny** – a condom

**Kelvinside** – upmarket area of Glasgow

**kit** – a person's attire

**lager louts** – imbeciles made that much richer by alcohol abuse

**lavvy** – a toilet

**leathered** – drunk like a skunk

**Leith** – a section of Edinburgh, known for its proximity to the

Firth of Forth, and high percentage of unemployed wastrels

**Loch Lomond** – paradise within reach of the Glasgow city centre

*locus* – a crime scene

**Magnums** – shoes/boots that cops wear

**malkie** – a head-butt, Glaswegian style

**Manumission** – a bacchanal venue in Ibiza, where drugs can be purchased from many of the staff who are supposed to be making sure no drugs are bought or sold

**Maryhill** – a downmarket area of Glasgow which borders posh Kelvinside. *Taggart,* a famous Glaswegian detective television drama was set and filmed in Maryhill, at the Maryhill Police Station. Singer/songwriter Donovan was from Maryhill, as was actor Robert Carlyle (*The Full Monty*). Part of the 1996 movie (also starring Robert Carlyle) *Trainspotting* was filmed in Maryhill. There, now you know more about Maryhill than most.

**Maze murder** – took place at the notorious Maze Prison in Northern Ireland

**Merchant City** – vibrant, hip residential, shopping and leisure area, mirroring London's Covent Garden. Originally, the residences and warehouses of the wealthy merchant tobacco lords who prospered in, among other things, tobacco and shipping.

**moonlight flit** – hightailing it in the middle of the night with the whole family and all your worldly possessions, so as to avoid rent owed on your shit accommodation

**Morningside** – an affluent area of Edinburgh

**MoT** – acronym for Ministry of Transport, but refers to the yearly, forced full physical examination of your motor, so it may live to drive again

**Mozambique drill** – a close-quarter shooting technique in which the shooter fires twice into the torso (a double tap), then plants a shot to the head. The aim (no pun) of the third shot is to destroy the brain or sever the brain stem.

**mucker** – a term, originating in West Belfast, for friend or companion

**ned** – is a non-educated (sic) delinquent. A connoisseur of fast food and Buckfast wine, someone who wears tracksuits/shellsuits and lives in government housing. This bottom-of-the-barrel creature is likely to sport chunky fake gold chains, sovvy** rings and a bad attitude.

**nick** – jail

**nicked** – arrested, stolen

**Noddy suits** – Glasgow slang for forensic suits, drawn from comic characters who don similar kit

**OAP** – old-aged pensioner

**Old Firm match** – a local football derby, read: life or death struggle (see Celtic and Rangers)

***Open All Hours*** – a jaunty former BBC TV sitcom with a carnivorous till (cash register) that would snap at the proprietor like an underfed moray eel

**Paki chippy** – A fast-food outlet whose owner often hails from Pakistan. Even if you come from Bangladesh your business will still be coined with this racial slur.

**panto** – beloved Christmas theatre fayre, the pantomime, where kids and adults alike join in and *Boo!* the bad guys, and yell: *'Oh, not it's not!'* as a response to the antagonist's *'Oh, yes it is!'* Simply a must over the holidays. Sneak a bag or tin of Cadbury's chocolate in with you, and life cannot be better.

**Parkhead or Celtic** – a stadium where the best football in the world is played

**parliamo Glasgow** – in the 1970s, Glasgow-born comedian Stanley Baxter parodied the Glasgow slang (patter) on his television sketch show, *Parliamo Glasgow*

**petrol costing $1.16 a gallon** – a distant memory

**pinched** – stolen

**pish** – piss

**poke of chips** – food container, usually a bag, containing a portion of chips

**polis** – Glasgow slang for police

**poncey** – pompous

**porkies** – lies (Cockney rhyming slang) – pork pies

**poteen** – industrial strength, bootlegged Irish moonshine, one of the strongest alcoholic beverages in the world, and for centuries was illegal in Ireland, historically drunk by members of the clergy

**pothole** – a regular feature of many streets in and around greater Glasgow

**pre-2006** – before the smoking ban was instituted in pubs in Scotland

**procurator fiscal** – is a public prosecutor in Scotland. They investigate all sudden and suspicious deaths, similar to a coroner in other legal systems, conduct fatal accident inquiries (a form of inquest unique to the Scottish legal system) and handle criminal complaints against the police.

**puds** – desert

**pull** – to pick sb up, with designs on swapping body fluids

**Raoul Moat** – a serial killer from down in England. A massive manhunt, the largest in modern British history, was launched and he was eventually cornered. After six hours of negotiation, while holding a sawn-off shotgun to his head, a shot was fired, and he died right in front of police officers who were positioned no more than 20 feet away.

**Red card! Red card!** – a penalty in football of the worst kind

**Resolve** – a sachet of powder which will save your life (and dignity) if you wake up with the mother of all hangovers

*rioja* – a type of Spanish red wine, pronounced *ree-oak-a* in the UK, *ree-o-ha* in Spain

**rubbery gub** – a big mouth, you know who I'm talking about

**Saltire** – flag of Scotland, purported to be the oldest national flag in Europe

**scobe** – a low-life slug, traditionally stemming from Dublin, Limerick or Cork

**Scotch eggs** – Cockney rhyming slang for legs

**scouser** – someone originating from Liverpool

**scrape** – shave

**senga** – a female ned

**sgian-dubh** – the small, singled-edged *knife* (Gaelic *sgian*) used by Scottish Highlanders. Part of the dress code for those sporting a kilt. Can be found tucked into the top of the kilt hose (or the stomach of an English football supporter).

**shaggers hair** – the way my hair looks like when I wake up in the morning. And yours doesn't?

**shite** – shit

**shout** – if it's my *shout*, it's my turn to buy a round of drinks in the pub

*sláinte* – a toast, cheers!

**sláinte mhor** – the response to that toast, from your drunken companion. Now go buy another drink, it's your shout.

**slash** – urinate

**Smarties** – the finest chocolate you can find for 20p out of one of those little machines on the wall at the pub, next to the toilets

**snib** – the bolt or fastening on a door or window (Scottish)

**sod** – a fool, idiot, bastard, that neighbour of yours just down the street

**sodding** – softer way of saying 'fucking'

**sooky** – felatio

**sovvy ring** – bling of choice for neds. A *sovereign* ring which typically has a gold sovereign as a primary decorative feature. Being authentic is not a requirement.

**stickmen** – henchmen

**stonner** – (Glaswegian) an erection

**STV** – Major Scottish Television station

**swot** – a student, one who is clever and/or gets good grades…and sometimes gets bullied for it

***Taggart*** – Popular Scottish T.V. police show

**tardis** – a time-travelling machine, which is much bigger on the inside than the outside – featured in a popular British TV series

**tea** – 'No tea for ye tonight!' – dinner, supper

**tiffin** – in this reference, a petite-afternoon chocolate tea cake, Death by Chocolate

**tip** – a garbage dump

**TomTom** – a Sat/Nav

**toss** – to masturbate

**tosser** – a dickhead, jerkoff, prick, idiot ... In the UK, used around your mother instead of 'c*nt', so as to avoid having your ears boxed

**within a toss** – within a short distance, you can figure out the rest

**trams** – the headache, pain-in-the-behind reason it is now physically impossible to get from one place in Edinburgh to another in under about a month. The streets are all ripped up and track is being laid for the trams. Scheduled to open May 2014. Allegedly.

**two-doc PM** – two doctors, working at the same, time performing a post-mortem

**up the spout** – pregnant

**Villa *Nariz-Azul*** – Villa *Blue-Nose*

**V-reg Rover** – a fine motor car of 1999 vintage

**WAG** – acronym stands for Wives And Girlfriends (of football players), not to be confused with young women who have ethics and ambition

**wank** – to service oneself

**wanker** – a jerk-off

**wankstain** – do I need to explain this?

**wean** – (Scottish slang) young child, a 'wee one'

**Weegie** – derogatory slang for someone residing in Glasgow, usually hurled by someone from Edinburgh. Glaswegians may hurl something other than an insult back.

**wee shite** – little shit

**wee swally** – just a tipple, a small sip

**Weegies and Edinbuggers** – colloquial for Glaswegians and Edinburghers

**Wellies** – God's gift to dry feet

**White Lightning, Lanlic and El Dorado** – adult beverages of the low-rent kind

**Yeoman Warders** – known by most of us as the 'Beefeaters', they are ceremonial guardians of the Tower of London. They are responsible for looking after prisoners in the Tower and safeguarding the British crown jewels. They are a tourist attraction in their own right. The origin of the name Beefeater is often considered to be from the Warders' right to eat as much beef as they wanted from the King's table.

**yonks** – years, e.g., 'I haven't eaten beef in yonks.'

If you've enjoyed **DEATH BY GLASGOW**, check out lighter, more whimsical fayre in Jon Breakfield's travel memoirs, available as eBook or paperback:

**NAKED EUROPE**: Searching for a Soul Mate in Paris, Amsterdam, Venice, Austria, Sweden, the Basque Country, the Canary Islands, Iceland, Hamburg, Gibraltar, and a bunch more

And its sequel **KEY WEST**: **Tequila, a Pinch of Salt and a Quirky Slice of America.** What would you do if you were on holiday and your better half said 'Let's not go back'?
Would you stay?
Would you stay if staying meant giving up everything back home in the UK to live on the backwater island of Key West, Florida?

And **LIVERPOOL... Texas, LONDON, Arkansas**
a short story available as an eBook.

Watch out for the sequel to **KEY WEST** coming soon to a flat screen near you.